THEIR LOST
SOULS

BOOKS BY ROGER STELLJES

AGENT TORI HUNTER

Silenced Girls

The Winter Girls

The Hidden Girl

Missing Angel

The Snow Graves

ROGER STELLJES

THEIR LOST SOULS

bookouture

Published by Bookouture in 2023

An imprint of Storyfire Ltd.
Carmelite House
50 Victoria Embankment
London EC4Y 0DZ

www.bookouture.com

ISBN: 978-1-83525-261-1
eBook ISBN: 978-1-83525-260-4

As some of you may or may not know, in addition to being an author, I'm also an attorney with an active and thriving law practice. That practice thrives because of my law partners: Scott Crossman, Amy Court and Christy Lawrie, and Their Lost Souls is dedicated to them.

I have worked with Scott and Amy for twenty years and Christy for thirteen. The four of us are much more than business partners. There are few events in any of our lives upon which we don't discuss and consult with one another. This past year has been one of significant change for our group, leaving the comfort of our old law firm for the unknowns of the new. The four of us took the leap of faith together and I am excited for what the future brings. I truly appreciate their friendship, counsel, tolerance of my writing career, and, on occasion, allowing me to surreptitiously steal little character and story ideas and tidbits at coffee or cocktails.

Here's to our new beginning.

The next round is on me.

Cheers.

ONE

"DOUBLE NOT GOOD."

Luke Bryan's 'That's My Kind of Night' thundered from the radio as the gravel road ahead narrowed when it entered a slender shoot of pine trees. Once through the shoot, they emerged into a small flattish area of lake cabins as the road made a sharp ninety-degree turn to the right.

"Which one is it?" Reed asked, leaning forward, peering at the modest row of mismatched cabins.

"The end one," Ally answered. She'd spent the weekend there with her friend Julie two weeks ago, which was when Julie planted the seed that Ally could use it with Reed when he visited. She parked her car in the small cutout in the woods on the far side of the road and then looked over to the two-story white clapboard-sided cabin.

"You're sure her parents won't, you know, mind?" Reed asked, reaching behind his seat for their small cooler.

"Oh, I'm quite sure they'd mind," Ally replied with a smile so bright and excited it was enough to light up the night. "But that's the fun of it, isn't it?" she said mischievously.

Reed was smart, chiseled, and to her, devastatingly gorgeous. But he came from strict parents who had engrained in him a certain reserve that checked his spontaneity, even when they were a hundred miles away. She'd learned, however, that with a little seducing, a loose button here, a seductive look or lingering kiss there, he would go for it, eventually. And what girl didn't want a little challenge? She leaned in and held his chin seductively with her index finger, moving in slowly, nuzzling his nose with hers a little before kissing him softly, letting her soft lips dance tantalizingly over his, feeling his excited reaction to her.

"They'll never know," she whispered. "Nobody will. We'll be gone by sunup."

Reed exhaled a breath and smiled. "Let's go then."

She led her boyfriend around the backside of the two-story cabin, across the dark yard leading down to the lake and to the back door of the old-school boat house perched on the edge of the shoreline. With the flashlight app on her phone, she found the key hidden under one of the bricks framing the small flowerbed, just where Julie told her it would be. She unlocked the door, and they slipped inside.

"It's just this one room then," Reed said, taking a quick look at the three beds aligned on the walls and the round table and chairs situated in the middle.

"Yes. This is the bunkhouse. An extra place for people to sleep, or in our case—"

"Play," he replied as he picked her slender body up, pulling her legs tightly around his waist.

As he slowly walked her to the bed in the corner, she made a show of crossing her arms and pulling her skintight tank top up and over her firm braless breasts, twirling the tank in her finger before flinging it away.

"I so love when you do that."

"Ha, ha, ha," she giggled, leaning back to let him kiss them. "I can tell."

He set her down on the bed and she instantly pushed up

onto her knees and slid her hand under his T-shirt, shoving it up.

"I love these abs," she said, her fingers lightly caressing his chiseled stomach and then upper chest, looking up with her eyes while she kissed his body.

Reed leaned down to kiss her while she undid his shorts and pushed them and his boxer briefs to the floor, making him fully naked.

"That's not fair," he said as he slowly laid her down onto her back and undid the button on her shorts, "you still have some clothes on."

Reed took a long drink of beer, closing his eyes as he swallowed, the cold liquid flowing satisfyingly down. The sheets and blankets lay on the floor around the bed, the two of them lying naked, uncovered, a light breeze rippling the window curtains, the air sultry, matching the woman to his right.

He looked down to Ally, her head resting on the soft pillow, her long hair messily arranged around her face, her naked summer-tanned body stretched out lazily beneath him.

She was gorgeous. Pretty, smart, funny, and oh yeah, her family was crazy rich which he didn't know until several months after he'd met her. He still didn't know how it was he'd lucked into her but he had no intention of letting the luck run out.

He leaned down and kissed her one more time, a long, slow, lingering, loving kiss.

"Hmm," Ally purred. "I could... do that again."

"You mean again, again?"

"Yes," she said, smiling, cupping his chin in the fingers of her right hand. "You know what I really wish we had?"

"Edibles."

"You know me so well."

"I'm learning. I guess you'll just have to settle for some ice-cold beer."

She took the beer from his hand and took a long drink. "Yes, this will have to do."

"Hmmm," he replied as he let his left hand wander gently around her right breast and then slowly down and around her hip and then behind, gently raising her right leg and pulling her to him, kissing her softly, a kiss she eagerly returned. She felt so good, her naked body pulled to his.

Ally flicked the hair away from his eyes and let her right hand wander along his muscled chest and then further down, feeling the corded muscles of his abdomen before reaching lower.

"Ooh. Ahh," Reed said, recoiling just a bit.

Ally cackled. "I thought you were, you know, ready. You don't quite feel ready."

"Ha! I will be." Reed smiled and pecked her on the lips and pushed away, standing up, hunting around the floor for his shorts. "I need to do something first."

"Ah, nature calls," she replied, before pulling him back down. "You're not going out au naturale?"

"No."

"Why not? It's not like there is anyone around here."

"Still," he said, pulling on his shorts. "Some modesty is in order, even for the ducks."

"Well, Mr. Modesty, I'd hurry back if I were you."

"I'll make great haste."

He stepped out of the cabin and around the back to the side opposite the bunkhouse, exhaled a long sigh and did his business, breathing in the damp night air. As he finished, he heard rustling behind him, the scraping of footsteps along wood, the sloshing of water, the murmur of voices.

"You good?"

"Yeah. I'll see you at the boat launch."

He spun around and looked out to the dock. A man was in the boat under the neighbor's boat lift canopy.

It was the middle of the night, what were they doing?

He glanced to the neighbor's cabin and there were no lights on. There were no lights on in any cabin along this stretch of the lake. He took a couple of tentative steps toward the dock.

What the heck?

There were actually two men at the boat lift. One of them started walking along the dock in his direction. And then the man saw him and started running, his feet pounding heavily on the dock. He must be fleeing.

Or not.

When the man reached the end of the dock he turned and ran straight at Reed.

"Oh shit," Reed murmured as he took one step back, then another.

The man was massive, a big dude, moving like a black bear.

"Oh, oh." He turned to run and slipped in the grass still moist from the earlier rainstorm, face-planting to the ground. He started pushing himself up and slipped again. "Ally, dial 911! Dial 911!"

"What!" her voice called from inside.

"Call for help!" Reed yelled as he stood up. "Oof."

The massive man tackled him from behind, landing on top of him, his forearm pressed against the back of his neck, driving his head into the turf.

"Get... off!" Reed growled as he wrestled and thrashed to push himself up.

The back door to the boathouse flew open and Ally came rushing out in a T-shirt, holding her cell phone. Her eyes went wide. "Oh my God! Help me! Help! No! No! Stay away!"

"Yo!" the man on top of him grunted. "Get her!"

Reed squirmed, trying to break free but the man was a

monster. For a second he felt the man's right arm pull away from him and he tried rolling to his left side to throw him off.

"Ahrg." He seized up at the searing pain in his back, shooting up under his ribs. "Ohhh."

Reed felt the knife come out from his back. He tried one more time to roll the man off, but he couldn't push up. His body wasn't responding.

The knife plunged in again.

"Ahhh!"

The man's hand was hard against his back, the knife probing in deeper, twisting, paralyzing him. He felt his arms giving out, his body giving way.

He opened his eyes to see another man, knife out, charge into the cabin after Ally.

Ally yelled: "No! No! Get back! N— Oh... ah..."

"Al—"

The knife plunged in again.

Oh God.

* * *

Backed up to the warmth of Braddock's body, Tori lay in the softness of her two pillows under the light linen sheet, the comforter, and his long-left arm at her waist, the cool yet humid summer night air drifting in with the light breeze through the opened windows. It was perfect sleeping weather. If only she were sleeping.

Her mind wouldn't stop racing. It was doing that a lot lately.

Ring! Ring! Ring!

Her eyes creased open to see the digital numbers of 3:30 a.m. on the nightstand clock.

Ring! Ring! Ring!

"Oh, oh," she murmured.

"Yeah," Braddock moaned. "Nothing good ever happens at three thirty in the morning."

Ring! Ring! Ring!

He rolled over to reach for his phone. "And it's Boe."

"Double not good."

"It must be bad," he said sleepily, putting the phone on speaker. "Braddock."

"Will, it's a double," Sheriff Boe said without preamble. "I'm on my way and I need you, both of you, right now."

"Aren't Nolan and Reese on tonight?"

"They are. And they're on their way too but you *and* Tori have to get out there as well."

"You want me?" Tori asked, sitting up. "Why?"

"One of the victims is Ally Mannion."

Tori looked to Braddock. "Oh God, no!"

TWO

"THEY DIDN'T HESITATE TO ESCALATE."

Tori stared blankly out the passenger window into the darkness of the night, the flashing police lights of Braddock's Tahoe illuminating the skinny stem trunks of the Norway pines. Her thoughts were of Kyle.

Kyle Mannion was the man who from extremely humble beginnings built a multi-billion-dollar corporation from the ground up in Minnesota's vacationland. Starting with a small family restaurant on the lake and then a drone business, he had steadily over the past twenty years built Mannion Companies into a financial empire, making him one of the wealthiest men in the state. He owned dozens of local businesses under the Mannion Companies umbrella and had funded programs at Central Minnesota State University to continue feeding employees into his ever-expanding corporate campus just northeast of town. His business success and acumen were almost single-handedly responsible for Manchester Bay doubling in size in the last decade, becoming known for something besides the lakes and a college town—it was now also the home of Mannion Companies.

It was almost two years ago when Kyle, of all people,

someone she barely knew at the time, risked his life to save hers. While Braddock had drawn away fire, it was Kyle who had come down the narrow stairs into the secret bunker under that shed, shotgun in hand. It was Kyle that sliced through her restraints and then right alongside her charged back into the fire to help her save Braddock and shoot the man who'd taken her sister's life twenty years before.

It was the shared bond of that night, that event, and what it meant to each of them, that had brought them together. Since that day, Kyle Mannion had been her and Braddock's good friend. It was Kyle who always said to her, "If you ever need, or want a job, I'll have one for you." They'd gone to dinner with Kyle and his wife Brianna many times. The Mannions entertained often, whether at their restaurant or at their vast compound on Northern Pine Lake. Christmas, New Year's, Halloween, the Fourth of July—she and Braddock were invited and never missed. And in that process, she and Braddock had come to know the whole Mannion family, including their only daughter, Allison, a beautiful, kind, fun, outgoing girl.

Even now, after all the therapy, the moving on from the deaths of her sister and father, it was still the rare day that went by that Tori didn't think of that night two years ago. The memory of it could be triggered simply by looking at a sharp knife, a bottle of wine, a pair of nylon handcuffs, a security monitor, or even something as simple as a set of steep narrow steps going up. And every time she saw Kyle the two of them shared a little look and nod in acknowledgment of those frantic moments that would bind them to each other for the rest of their lives.

As they came around a bend in the road, flashing police lights came into view. Deputy Frewer greeted them somberly at the end of the gravel road, leaning in as Braddock pulled to a stop.

"Take the road all the way to the end and the last cabin on the left. It's... God, it's just awful."

"Boe?" Braddock said.

"She got here a few minutes ago. Reese and Nolan are already here. The medical examiner and BCA jumped right on it with Boe's calls and are here too. It's all fresh."

"Witnesses?"

"None so far that I'm aware of. Canvass is underway."

Braddock drove down the narrow gravel road while Tori pulled on her baseball cap, filtering her ever longer ponytail through the back.

"We know for certain it's Ally?" Braddock said to Boe as he exited his Tahoe.

She waved for them to follow. "Deputy Renee Collins was the first on scene."

"The rookie?" Braddock said.

"Yes. She was a couple of years ahead of Ally in school but knew her. She looked inside the boathouse and recognized her immediately. She... went in and checked for a pulse but she was gone. You'll see why. She immediately called it in and started a search of the grounds." Boe pointed across the gravel road. "Collins found a car parked over in that cleared out notch. She ran the plate and it's registered to Kyle Mannion."

Boe walked them between a dark-red one-story cabin to their left and a two-story white one to the right. A portable light had been set up and the medical examiner, Dr. Renfrow, was examining a body lying in the grass, while a forensic officer took pictures. Reese was crouched, observing, taking notes. He saw Braddock and Tori and stood up, holding a wallet in a plastic evidence bag. "Reed Schafer, aged twenty-one. Driver's license lists an address in Grand Rapids. There was also a University of Minnesota ID in the wallet, so he goes to school there."

"As does Ally," Tori murmured. "As... did Ally."

"Cause of death is the four stab wounds on the right side," Dr. Renfrow said, gesturing to the large pool of blood. "I'll know more when I get him back to examine them but even in this light you can see that the wounds are deep and wide, just under the rib cage."

Braddock glanced to his right and saw Reese open the door to the boathouse and wave them over. Tori stepped just inside behind Braddock. Ten feet away, Ally was lying on the floor, her head wedged against the left wall, turned such that they could see the left side of her face. She had a pool of blood all around her head, and her arms were at her sides. There were lines of blood spatter on the wall and then a wide vertical streak that started two feet below the spatter lines. The killer had sliced her neck from behind and then she'd fallen to the floor against the wall.

"Oh... Ally," Tori said quietly, choking up, her eyes moist. "She's twenty-one, Will. Just a kid," she said, wiping away a tear.

"Yeah," Braddock murmured softly. He turned to her, and said quietly, "You want a minute?"

"No." Tori shifted her eyes to him, a flash of anger. "I want to find who did this to her."

Braddock nodded, drawing in a long breath. "Let's go to work."

Drawing in a breath of her own, Tori closed her eyes for a moment and then went into work mode. Keeping back from the body, she examined the blood spatter lines across the wall. "Her neck was sliced left to right." And the slice was deep given the bloody streak down the wall and the broad blood pool her head lay in. "It looks like her head was damn near sliced off her neck."

"There's a vicious purposefulness to it," Braddock said as he carefully walked to the bed, noticing the clothes on the floor, the small cooler, beer bottles on the nightstand, the sheets and blankets strewn about. "These two are out here all alone. Or were they?"

"Spurned lover?" Reese offered.

Braddock shrugged. "Possibly." He gazed around. "Do the Mannion's own this property? Or is it Schafer's?"

"Neither actually," Reese reported. "The cabin and boathouse belong to Gregory Taylor. He also has an address in Minneapolis. He has a daughter, Julie, aged twenty-one so possibly a friend of these two. We have not contacted him yet. If I had to guess, one of these two knows the Taylors, knew this boathouse was here and snuck out for a little romantic rendezvous. There are two empty condoms in the garbage can."

"And maybe it wasn't over. She's barely dressed," Tori said. "No underwear. And—" she tilted her head "—dirt, soil, and grass on her feet. And on the floor here. Might get a shoe or boot tread."

"Let's step out of here then," Braddock said. "Let forensics do their thing."

Back outside, Braddock asked Boe, "There was a 911 call, right?"

"Yes. It was from Allison's phone. The 911 operator didn't get much out of her beyond loud panicked screams for help. No address or anything. But sound travels clearly across water. A distant neighbor at the far end of the bay called a few minutes later. He was out walking his dog and heard someone yelling frantically for help. He wasn't sure if it was someone on the lake itself, so search and rescue was deployed, and deputies began checking the area. Collins found all this and called it in."

Braddock took another look at the man's body. He was in nothing but a pair of shorts.

"What are you seeing here?" Boe said. "Crime of passion?"

"Maybe," Braddock said, hands on hips, peering around. "I

think our man here comes outside. Maybe to relieve himself or maybe he heard something."

Tori nodded. "He's attacked first. Ally had dirt on the bottom of her feet. She hears noise outside, comes out and finds her boyfriend being attacked and manages to call 911, but isn't able to give them a location. Do we have the recording of the 911 call?"

"I just got it," Nolan said, walking up. She pulled it up on her phone and hit play.

"911, what's your emergency?" the operator answered.

"Oh my God! Help me! Help! No! No! Stay away!"

"Ma'am? Hello? Ma'am!" the operator called calmly, talking over Ally Mannion.

"No! No! Get back! N— Oh... ah..."

There was a thud, the phone dropping to the floor.

"Ma'am? Ma'am?"

Click.

"Pretty gruesome," Nolan commented. "You hear the last gasp of her... voice. That's when the knife—"

"Goes across her throat, ending the 911 call," Tori said. "It didn't hang on?"

"No. It was ended," Reese said. "Her phone is bagged inside. If there's a print, hopefully forensics can lift it."

"Play the call back again," Tori said.

Ally Mannion's voice started again. *"Oh my God! Help me! Help! No! No! Stay away!"*

"Stop a second. Take it back about five seconds, right after she says 'Help' the second time."

Nolan played it back and they all listened closely. "In the background. The voice. I can just hear it. It's low."

She replayed the section again. *"Help! No! No! Stay away!"*

"I hear it too," Nolan said.

"One more time," Tori said. "There's the 'Help! No! No! Stay away!' and then something else, very faint."

Nolan played it again. "I hear it too, Tori. It's a different voice: Get... something." She replayed it again. "Get..."

"Her!" Tori said and looked at Braddock. "Get her?"

Braddock nodded. "One more time."

They replayed it and confirmed the man's voice had said, *"Get her."*

"He's saying 'Get her,'" Tori said. "Partner?"

"Hmpf," Braddock said. "Two men then. Maybe not a spurned lover."

"If not that, then what?" Tori said as she stepped back from the group and away from the boathouse, hands on hips, scanning the area, trying for a wider view to get a sense of what had happened.

Two men at least. *Here for what reason? It has to be that they knew Ally and Reed were out here. Otherwise, why would this happen? For what reason?*

There were five cabins along the road. And they were *cabins*, modest somewhat rustic summer places on what looked to be a small weedy bay, if the thick cattails along the entirety of the shoreline were any indication.

"Will, Tori, check this out," Renfrow called to them.

"What?" Braddock said, walking over.

Renfrow had lifted the right side of Reed Schafer's body and pointed to a small black remote under his right hip. "What do you make of that? Is it a key fob?"

"Not for a car," Braddock said, crouching. "That's a remote for a... boat lift," he said, recognizing the small black square rubber device. "I have one of those."

Tori immediately looked to the dock running out from the boathouse. The Taylors had two boat lifts, but both the pontoon and speedboat were up out of the water and covered. She looked to the left, to the neighbor's dock and boat lift.

"Huh."

"Huh, what?" Braddock said, having noticed her looking about.

"Come with me," she said as she walked over to the neighbor's dock and then out to the end and the boat lift, flashlight in hand, focusing the beam on the boat. "Does that look odd to you?"

Under the lift canopy was a Malibu surf boat, a newer model like many she'd seen on their lake. The boat lift was lowered into the water and the boat was cockeyed, floating at an angle. Tori scanned it with the beam of her flashlight, walking front to back. The far corner of the rear swim platform was wedged against the boat lift's back canopy post.

"This is what, a hundred-thousand-dollar boat?" Tori said.

"One-hundred-fifty brand new, and this looks like new," Braddock said. "The lift is down, it's wedged in here, the cover is off in a rolled-up ball in the bow. If the corner of the rear swim platform didn't catch the rear post, this boat could have floated out to the middle of the bay."

"No way someone leaves it like this after the weekend, right?" she asked as she braced herself with her left hand on the canopy frame and peered inside the boat. "Quinn has been begging you to buy one like this, hasn't he?"

"I expanded the house instead."

"Boats like this though, they have a touch screen start, right?" She leaned out further. "You tap in the code, hit start and away you go."

"Yes."

"Then what do you make of that?" She focused her light beam on the emergency key ignition to the right side of the dashboard, behind the throttle.

"Oh boy." Braddock's eyes bulged. "Come with me," he said, and he started walking quickly back toward the one-story cabin next door to the crime scene. "Reese!"

"Yeah?"

"Over here." He waved to the neighbor's house. Boe saw them and joined as Braddock led them around to the back of the house and tried the door with his gloved hand. It opened right in.

"What is it?" Reese said.

"Tori noticed the boat for this cabin floating in the water. It's a new Malibu wakesurfing boat. A really nice one. The emergency key in the ignition."

"Ah shit," Reese said, throwing his head back in anger. "You've got to be kidding me."

"What?" Boe asked, not following.

"We've had a recent rash of boat thefts," Braddock said.

"I saw a memo on that. What's the story on them?"

"There have been five boats so far that we know of," he replied as he aimed the beam of his flashlight inside the cabin. "Tonight, might be an attempt at number six."

"Three surf boats like the one out there, a high-end pontoon, and two weeks ago a Boston Whaler," Reese recited.

"What do we know about the thieves?" Boe said.

"We think at least a two-man team. They break into the cabin, grab the keys, or in this case, the emergency key, and steal the boat. They pull it out of the lake, most likely at the public boat launch. I figure one man in the boat, one with a truck and trailer. All stolen from cabins like this one on smaller lakes filled with weekend cabins, not year-around houses."

Tori saw where he was going. "Homes have security systems, people living there. This is a cabin. It's filled with hand-me-down beds, couches, televisions, plates, décor, the basics for a weekend. No jewelry or art. Places like this don't have anything of real value inside—"

"Except for the keys, or in this case, the emergency key for a $150,000 boat," Braddock finished. "Pick the lock, lift the keys and away you go in the dark of the night. Drive the boat across the water to the launch and pull it out onto a trailer. At worst, it's the morning before anyone notices that it is gone, and if lucky, it's days."

"But not tonight," Boe said. "I'll get forensics to expand their work to this cabin and the boat." The sheriff walked off, phone to her ear.

"Will?" Reese said, looking despondent. "I... I..."

"Don't worry about it," Braddock said.

"But—"

"Focus on this. We'll deal with all that later."

"Deal with what?" Tori said after Reese walked away.

"The boat thefts are his case. He's worked it but he's on other cases too, and since this was more a property theft situation, he wasn't working it like the others."

"I see."

"Then again, I haven't pressed him on it either because until tonight, nothing like this had happened."

"I get it," Tori murmured. "If that's what this is, you can see how it all went down."

Braddock walked around to the front of the cabin. "Ally and her boyfriend sneak out here for the night. They park in the woods on the other side of the road so nobody sees the car, just in case someone did come along. They sneak into the boathouse for a little private time."

"In the meantime, our thieves show up next door and break-in and grab the boat keys. They get out to the boat, lower it, get the cover off. They're getting ready to pull out of here when—"

"Reed pops outside," Braddock speculated. "And he either sees them, or they see him."

"They had a decision to make," Tori said. "Fight or flight. They didn't hesitate to escalate. They went from stealing a boat to murdering two kids like that." She shook her head. "There hasn't been anything like this on the other thefts, have there?"

"No," Braddock replied, shaking his head. He walked back out on the dock. "Why leave the boat though?"

"Neighbors heard a call for help. There was a 911 call. If the police show up and this boat is gone, or if all of a sudden a boat is racing away from where the calls for help are coming from, and that gets reported, you're stuck on the lake. You're separated because one guy is driving the boat, the other the truck and trailer."

Braddock nodded. "So they cut their losses and got out of here." He took a moment and shook his head. "Until now this was not a big priority."

"Boats are insured. The victims get their boats replaced and the only damage is that their insurance premiums go up. Move on."

"Basically." He shook his head in disgust. "It wasn't the highest priority for us, but it is now." He let out a sigh. "Tori, we need to—"

"I know. Go see Kyle and Brianna."

They made a stop a mile short of Kyle Mannion's home, to pick up his younger brother Eddie. Kyle and Eddie had both been abused by their father as children, though Eddie took the major brunt of it. For years Kyle looked after Eddie in the sense that he made sure he had a job and money but, in many ways, had enabled a carefree lifestyle that nearly landed his brother with a life sentence in prison for crimes it looked like he committed, but didn't. It was all related to Tori's sister's disappearance, as well as the disappearance of many other women. After Kyle saved Tori that night two years ago, he did what he should have done long before and got his brother the help he needed. Eddie was two years sober, engaged, thriving. It had brought him and Kyle closer together.

"He's going to need you, Eddie," Tori said when she told him about Ally.

Braddock drove them to the house, the sun just starting to

peek above the treetops. Braddock rang the doorbell and the three of them waited on the front stoop.

Kyle opened the door, saw the three of them and went white. "What is it? What happened?"

Brianna came down the hallway, seeing everyone on the steps. "Oh God."

Eddie stepped forward. "Kyle, Bree, something terrible has happened."

"I'm so sorry," Tori said, her eyes moist, her lip trembling. "I'm so sorry. It's Ally."

Kyle sat on the living room couch in an almost trance-like state, his face a frozen blankness, his eyes distant. His left arm was wrapped around Bree, who buried her head in his shoulder. Eddie sat to his right, leaning forward, his elbows resting on his thighs, quiet. Tori had pulled an armchair up to them and waited for them to be ready.

"It's Ally *and* Reed?" Kyle said quietly.

"Yes," Tori replied softly.

"How? Why?"

Tori and Braddock first asked a few questions. Was there a jealous ex-boyfriend or girlfriend that either Ally or Reed had? Anyone who would have any reason to want to harm either of them?

"I understand these questions," Kyle said. "Reed is a good kid. I liked him. He had plans to go to law school. He was good for her, a mature, steadying influence. Ally was always a bit of a wild child. She often pushed the boundaries, but she was ruminating on law school too. I think Reed corralled her and she loosened him up a bit. The two of them had dated for several months. I never heard a word about anyone else being a problem."

"Bree?" Tori asked.

"No problems and I talked to Ally every day, even when she was down at the U in Minneapolis. Why are you asking these questions?"

"We're just covering our bases. Ultimately, we don't think what happened to them had anything to do with either of them."

"Then what happened to them, Tori?" Bree asked angrily. "Who killed my child? What aren't you telling us?"

Tori sighed. "We think they were just in the wrong place at the wrong time. Here's what we found." She walked everyone through the crime scene, avoiding the grizzliest of details.

"Julie Taylor is one of Ally's sorority sisters at the U," Bree explained while dabbing at her eyes. "That cabin was her family's place. Ally's been over there several times the last couple of years so it wouldn't surprise me that that's where she and Reed might go."

"Where did you think she was last night?" Braddock asked.

"She said she was going to another friend's house to stay overnight. I kind of wondered if she was up to something else. You know, a mother's intuition."

"Obviously she was," Kyle said, closing his eyes. "So, what you're telling me is they interrupted a burglary. These men were stealing a boat. A surf boat, just like the one we have down at the lake. Reed saw them and they killed him... and my daughter. Over a goddamn boat."

"Yes," Tori whispered.

"Will, hasn't there been a recent spate of boat thefts?" Eddie asked.

Braddock nodded. "We've been investigating."

"Is this related to that?"

"It could be," Tori replied. "Until last night—"

"It wasn't a priority?" Kyle snorted.

Will sighed in regret. "I'm so sorry, Kyle. Bree. Nothing like this had happened before last night. We should have—"

"No, Will," Kyle said, shaking his head. "I'm not blaming anybody other than the men responsible. My question is what are you going to do now?"

"Find them," Tori replied directly.

Kyle looked her in the eye. "See that you do."

THREE

"THE USUAL SUSPECTS."

Vee buttoned her cream blouse and stuffed it into her skinny black jeans, then pulled on a light-blue thin blazer. It was a salesy look, although she wished she had a little jewelry to enhance it. At least she still had most of her clothes. The debt collectors hadn't taken those yet at least, just everything else.

Dressed, she took the steps up out of the basement and went to her daughter's bedroom and opened the door. "Hey, sweetie."

"Hi, Mom," Sarah whimpered, lying in bed, both her legs in casts, along with her right wrist.

"How are you feeling?"

"I'm a little sore." She'd been in the leg casts for two months. The wrist cast was likely to come off this week. The legs would take another month or so.

"How about some ibuprofen then." She helped Sarah sit up and then handed her a capsule and her glass of water from the nightstand. Sarah took her medicine and drink of water and handed the glass back. "Do you want to rest some more? Or do you want to get up?"

"Rest," Sarah said as she slid back down so she could lie on her back. "I'm tired. I didn't sleep very well."

"That's okay, sweetheart," her mom replied, lightly brushing her hair behind her ear before leaning in and kissing her on the forehead. "I have to go to work."

"Bye, Mom."

She closed the door and walked into the kitchen. Her mom, Mona, was making some scrambled eggs, while Dan was at the kitchen table, a cup of coffee in front of him, on his old laptop freshening up his LinkedIn page. He was job searching. However, despite his years of experience owning a business, running a kitchen, restaurant, and gift shop, he'd found no takers. He'd gotten close on a couple of occasions but was certain the financial background check had ended the process.

"We got another collection notice." He handed her an envelope stamped with a red *Final Notice.*

"Let them send it to collection," she replied bitterly. "With all the others. There's no blood left in the turnip."

"I made you a sandwich," her mother said. "It's in the refrigerator. I tossed in a couple of apples. I have bananas here too if you want to grab one."

She retrieved the sack lunch out of the refrigerator, along with two cans of Diet Coke. "Thanks, Mom." To Dan: "I'll be late. I said I'd take an extra shift so I'm working tonight too."

"So basically, from open to close?"

"As long as they need me."

"Okay," he said, looking up wearily from the aged laptop. "How was Sarah?"

"Tired, sore. She just took an ibuprofen." She took a sip of coffee out of Dan's cup. "What's on the television?" A reporter was standing with flashing police lights in the background. The chyron read: Double Homicide—Shepard County. "Is that... here? Where?"

Dan nodded. "Rabbit Lake."

"Who?"

"They haven't said yet beyond two younger adults, whatever that might mean."

"Home invasion?"

"No. Boat theft according to the police," Dan replied. "They're possibly looking for two men. Apparently there has been a series of boat thefts recently."

"Boat theft?"

"You've seen some of the boats around here. They can be worth hundreds of thousands of dollars so I can see it, I guess. Apparently this one went awry somehow."

"Murdering someone? Over a boat?" Vee said. "Who does that?"

The fact of the matter was, they did know people who had once done something like that but that was long ago.

Dan observed his wife and her holding a sandwich bag. "When you eat your lunch. I'll come and sit with you for a bit."

"Okay," she replied and kissed him on the head.

The ten-year old white Mazda 6 was parked at the end of the narrow driveway, still with its faded Florida license plates. She would have to get those changed soon now that they were back in Minnesota. That would cost more money, unless at some point the creditors decided to take the car away as well.

Ten minutes later she clocked into work and stored her lunch in the little refrigerator in the upstairs lunchroom and pinned on her name tag that read Veronica. She'd been called Vee since she was ten years old, when she was a gymnast and another girl at the gymnastics club was also named Veronica. The coach called that girl Veronica and her Vee. The nickname stuck.

She gave herself a quick look in the mirror. She was thirty-nine, and these days felt a lot older than that. It hadn't always been the case. As recently as last August, she thought she looked younger than her age, particularly with her then stylish, short pixie hairdo. Now, her brown hair looked tired in body and color and was growing out, by necessity. There currently wasn't the money to do much of anything else with it.

She stepped out into the front of the store at 9:00 a.m. sharp and two minutes later the front doorbell clanged, signaling their first customer.

"Good morning," Vee greeted. "Welcome to Fashion by Julia. Can I help you?"

"Yes. I'm looking for a summer dress, something floral."

"Terrific. We can help with that. Let me show you what we have. What is your name?"

"Debbie."

"I'm Veronica, but everyone just calls me Vee."

* * *

Braddock, Reese, and Nolan sought refuge in Braddock's office. Steak and Eggleston were in as well. A case like this, at least initially, was all hands-on deck for the Shepard County Investigations Unit.

Sheriff Boe joined them, still in plain clothes, slowly folding her tall body tiredly down into a visitor's chair. Pulling out her hair tie, she freed her short blonde ponytail, letting her hair fall to her shoulders. She closed her eyes for a moment, wiping her face and temples with her hands, groaning.

Braddock knew the look. "Who has called so far?"

She looked up with a wan smile. "The usual suspects. County commissioners, business leaders and the mayor, of course. The voicemail light is still red, so I'm sure there are others."

"I'm sure they're all *very* supportive."

"They were. Told me whatever I need, just ask."

"Oh, I just bet they did," Tori said as she came into the

office. "What they're all really doing is wetting the bed," she added cynically, skeptical of most politicians, even local ones.

Boe snorted a laugh. "Both things can be true, I suppose. This does entail a double homicide with one of the victims being the daughter of our most prominent citizen and one of the state's wealthiest men. They would help any way they can, and, yes, they are afraid of the longer-term ramifications. Events like this aren't good for local business you know."

"Jeanette, are you sure you want to become one of the jackals?" Braddock said with raised eyebrows. Boe had hardly concealed her aspirations for higher political office. A case such as the one they were now confronted with could aid in that pursuit, if resolved, or kill one's career, if not.

"If I do one day actually seek and reach higher elected office than that of sheriff, I promise I'll try not to be what Tori calls a bed wetter," Boe replied and then looked to the sack Tori was holding. "What did you bring?"

"Food and fuel." Tori handed out coffees and breakfast sandwiches to everyone. They'd all been up half the night.

"Reese was about to fill us in on this boat theft ring," Braddock said.

"I'm sorry to say," Reese started, "that I haven't really made much progress. And, Sheriff, I've worked it but honestly, not that—"

"Hard," Boe said. "They were boats. They're insured. They get replaced... by newer boats. That's on Braddock and me, don't worry about it."

"Ally Mannion can't be replaced. If I had—"

"No, Detective, we're not going to play that game. And I won't let the other... bed wetter's do it either. It was but one of many things on your pile of things to be working. Until now, they hadn't done anything violent. Now they have and now we have a reason to throw everything at this, and so we will. I couldn't care less about the boats other than they're a tool we can use to catch two murderers. This is now exclusively about Ally Mannion and Reed Schafer. We're not looking for just thieves, but killers, and it will be investigated and resourced as such."

Reese nodded. "On that, Sheriff, I spoke with Greg Taylor. He had no idea Ally Mannion and Reed Schafer would be using their boathouse."

"Yet they were there."

"That's due to his daughter, Julie, who is on a study trip abroad in Chile. She fessed up to her father that she told Ally she could go there, where she would find a key and that nobody would ever know. Neither the Mannions nor Schafer's parents were aware of anyone either of their kids were having trouble with, such as jealous ex-boyfriends or ex-girlfriends. They were good students, good kids, no record of any real trouble whatsoever. Those kids were just in the wrong place at the wrong time."

"Let's talk to Julie," Braddock said, looking to Nolan. "Confirm her story."

"On it," Nolan said.

"Who owned the boat floating in the lift?" Tori said.

Reese answered, "Neal Wallace. He and his family own that cabin. I just spoke with him. He said that his family was up there for the weekend. They left around six thirty last night to drive back to their home down in the Twin Cities."

"Tell me more about these thieves," Boe directed. "Scratch that. Killers."

"They started in mid-April when they stole a pontoon."

"Were all thefts like last night?" Braddock asked Reese.

"Yeah, pretty much, other than, you know, the two murders."

"We got the basics last night. Tell us more."

"There is a distinct pattern to it, Boss. Take the pontoon theft in late April. The boat was a new Bennington Tritoon, bought last fall. Top end, thirty-footer, two or three hundred horsepower motors, fully loaded with all the bells and whistles. Luxury on the water. The cabin owners came up from Minneapolis for the weekend, used the boat, covered it up and went home. They got a call from a neighbor on the Tuesday to report their boat was gone."

"And the break-in?" Boe asked.

"Picked the lock on the back door. Grabbed the boat keys and remote for the lift. The boat lift was still down in the water when I got there. The cabin was nice but nothing special, just a nice weekend place. No security system."

"And was that the first weekend they'd had the boat this year?"

"The second. It was stolen sometime on Sunday or Monday night. Pretty similar story for the other boats. Last night would have been the fourth surf boat."

"Tell me about the boats," Boe inquired.

"Pontoon. Boston Whaler. Three high-end newer wakesurfing boats, two Malibus and one Master Craft. The pontoon was a $100,000 boat, the whaler was $70,000 and had all the fishing tech you could possibly imagine, and the surf boats were all in the $125-$150,000 range. Now, you can steal them, re-sell them, and walk away with a nice pile of cash. I've spoken with a few of the boat dealers out along the H-4. They all said that there is a shortage of wakesurfing boats, new and used. Limited inventory but a lot of demand."

"Someone is responding to that demand and moving stolen boats," Braddock said. "Were the trailers stolen too?"

"What do you mean?" Boe said.

"The boats were stolen, were their trailers as well?"

"No," Reese replied. "Why?"

"You have to be able to get the boat out of the lake. Pontoons, whalers, wakesurf boats all require different kinds of trailers to tow them, especially if you don't steal the trailer too. Who would have all those trailers?"

"Marinas," Tori replied. "Places where they sell or store boats."

"Or anyone who also owns such boats," Braddock added. "Not sure about the whaler, but plenty of people own both wakesurfing boats and pontoons. You have to have the right trailer for these boats and they're big trailers too." Braddock looked from Reese to Steak to Tori. "On the pontoon, how did they identify it if the owners only had it out of storage for a week? Where was it stored?"

"Umm… Deerwood Storage," Reese said, flipping through his notes. "You know the place I'm talking about?"

"I do," Steak said. "That place has four or five mass storage buildings. They store everything there, RVs, boats, cars, whatever."

"That's the place."

"Where were the others stored?" Eggleston asked.

Reese grimaced. "You know, I don't know that I asked. Didn't seem relevant at the time but I can follow-up on it. Do you think they're identified by where they're stored?"

"Possibly," Braddock said. "There are literally thousands and thousands of boats just in our county on the hundreds of lakes we have. So how do they pick *these* boats? We know they've been stolen from summer weekend type places where the folks are gone during the week, but again, there are thousands upon thousands of those places. And that's just in this county. We should see if there have been other thefts of a similar nature in nearby counties. Check that."

"On it," Reese said.

"They're not only identifying the boats," Tori said. "You don't just show up and steal them. They were successful five times that we know of, they must scout these places, watch and move in when it's all quiet."

"If they did all that, wouldn't they have seen Ally and Reed last night?" Reese asked.

"Depends," Tori replied. "When did the Wallace's leave their cabin?"

Reese flipped a page in his notes. "Six thirty p.m. or so. They spent the day on the lake until about three thirty, returned before the storm rolled through, cleaned up and left."

"They left at six thirty and it's still light at this time of year until nearly ten p.m.," Tori replied. "If these guys were watching from somewhere, they'd know that the Wallaces had already left. In fact, they probably knew that everyone along that row was gone.

"Ally left home just after eight p.m. The 911 call was around two thirty a.m., which leaves a window of several hours. They weren't there the whole time. There is only one road leading back to those cabins so they couldn't be there or the Wallaces would have seen them, they had to be somewhere else." She looked to Braddock. "We could go back and give that a look."

"Ally and Reed no doubt slipped in after dark as well," Boe said. "Plus, Ally parked in the woods. Had these guys seen her parked, say in the driveway of the Taylor place, they might have waited another day."

"Maybe, maybe not," Tori said. "Once these guys saw Ally and Reed, they didn't hesitate, they didn't just flee. They rock'n rolled right then and there."

"What are you saying?" Reese said.

Tori paused for a moment. "There is a lot more to these guys than just stealing boats. They've done this before. Stabbing someone, slicing their neck, that's up close and personal. And this was done in a no-nonsense, efficient, kill them quick way." Tori looked to Nolan. "They might be thieves first, but they're killers too. Do we still have the 911 call?"

Nolan nodded and pulled it up on a laptop computer. She

replayed the call. Tori had her limit it to the part where the one man said, "Get her."

"You notice how he says that?" Tori said. "He says 'Get her,' in a very low, calm voice. He was most likely engaged with Reed, but he wasn't panicked, it was... business. It was: You know what to do."

"He was flat line," Boe said, nodding.

"If these two were just simple boat thieves, if they saw someone or sensed any danger of being detected, they'd have run. It's dark, who could really see you. Flee and hope you get away. If you got caught, you might get a little prison time and that would be it. But these guys?" Tori snapped her fingers. "They killed just like that. These guys are not just starting out, they've been doing it for some time. Their mindset was to leave no witnesses. Eliminate all risk. They've killed before."

Braddock nodded in agreement. "We're adding that to the hopper."

"So, what's the plan?" Boe asked.

"Assignments," Braddock said. "Much to be done."

When they left the Wallace cabin the first time to go see Kyle and Bree, it was still dark, the sunlight a tiny ribbon along the eastern horizon. Upon their return to the Wallaces' cabin in the full light of the day, they found the forensics team examining the back door. The homeowner, Neal Wallace, had arrived and was watching them work.

"We were here yesterday until six thirty or so," Wallace explained. "We just got off the lake ahead of that thunderstorm that rolled through. I got the boat in and raised the lift and was literally running into the cabin to beat the big raindrops. We packed to go home and the last thing I did was secure the cover on the boat. We never leave it uncovered when we're not here."

"Of all the cabins in the row here, was everyone up this weekend?"

"Yeah," Wallace said with a nod, "they were, now that you mention it, but that's pretty normal on the weekends. Other than the Taylors, everyone else has bought their cabin in the last few years so they're all up here a lot. The newness factor."

Wallace hadn't noticed anyone unusual hanging around the cabin. "It's just the five cabins here at the end of road, it's a dead end, so if someone drives down here, they likely would be noticed."

"Are you up here every weekend?" Tori asked.

"Pretty much," Wallace said. "My wife and I both work but we have Wi-Fi here, so we often come up Thursday nights to get an extra day out of it."

"And you've owned the boat how long? It looked new or newish."

"It's brand new this year. We ordered it last year, but it didn't come until late April. There's a big backlog on orders. Then when we got it, we still couldn't put it in the water until the new boat lift arrived. That was another two weeks. Supply chain issues all around I guess."

"And your old boat?" Braddock asked.

"Traded it in for the new one at Bay Marine."

"You've had the new one a few months then?"

"Yes."

"And your boat keys, where do you store those?"

"Up until last night, on the hook just inside the back door. If you looked in the window for the back door, you'd see them just hanging there. Pretty stupid when you think of it. From now on, they'll be hidden and locked up."

Tori and Braddock walked around to the front of the cabin and out to the end of the Wallaces' dock. A forensic officer was examining the boat.

"Anything?" Tori inquired.

"No prints or hairs that I've found. There is a small clump or two of mud in here. That thunderstorm yesterday left the ground soft and wet. I don't know that that will tell us much. Lots of prints on the wheel, dash, and emergency key so we'll see what turns up, but I suspect the prints will all belong to Wallace family members or friends. Plus, I'd be surprised if your killers weren't wearing gloves."

Tori and Braddock stepped to the end of the dock. The five cabins were located in a row along the northeast corner of a small oblong bay framed by a vast reed patch to the south that had a narrow channel sliced through it into the lake proper.

"In a way you understand why they bought such an expensive boat," Braddock noted, peering around the dock. "No real place to swim with all the lily pads and reeds and—" he looked down into the water "—muck. Jump in the boat and cruise out the channel to the main body of the lake and let the fun begin."

Tori was shading her eyes, gazing across the bay to the far side.

"What are you looking at?"

"Wallace says he saw nobody unusual hanging around and it would be hard for anyone to hide back on that road."

"Aye."

"Assuming these guys were watching, where would you watch from?"

"This bay is pretty small, so I don't think they were on the water," Braddock said, scanning about.

Tori had the map app open on her phone. "There is a road on the other side of the bay that we should check out."

Ten minutes later Braddock had navigated them on a series of gravel roads to the northwest corner of the bay. The road looped around a tight corner that overlooked the bay before leading to a series of cabins on the main body of Rabbit Lake. The corner of the loop provided a clear view of the five cabins across the lake. There was a narrow jut of longish grass just off the road and the grass was trampled down in two thin rows, about the width of a truck's tires.

"Looks like someone went in there and parked," Tori murmured.

She and Braddock got out of the Tahoe and carefully walked the grass strip out to the edge.

"You're looking right over there from here," Braddock murmured. "With binoculars you'd be looking right at them."

"And maybe they were," Tori observed, crouched. "Sun-flower seeds. Lots of them. And tire impressions, in this small mud patch. And—" she gestured with her pen "—something we've seen before."

"Tobacco pouches." Braddock reached for his radio.

FOUR

"TIME TO GO SEE MIGHTY MOUSE."

"Hi, Dan."

"Hello, Ruth Ann."

Vee came down the steps with her lunch bag. "Ready?"

Dan was quiet as the two of them took a short half-block walk down the bustling main street of Manchester Bay, the blue waters of the lake and the broad sandy public beach two blocks ahead. There was a fair amount of hustle and bustle for a summer Monday, not unlike the buzz they'd been accustomed to for many years in Florida.

They grabbed an open park bench under a shade tree on the opposite side of the street from the row of food truck vendors that had set up shop to cater to both the beachgoers and those working the energetic business and shopping district.

Vee took a bite of her sandwich and her shoulders slumped at the pain of doing so. Eating a paper sack lunch wasn't in and of itself demoralizing, nor was it that the chicken in the sandwich was the bland out of the sealed package kind from the supermarket. For Vee, it was the fact that at the age of thirty-nine she and Dan were back in Minnesota, living in her mother's basement, and it was her mom who had paid for and made the sandwich. It was that total overall scenario that made her angry.

Despite Mona's best efforts, it wasn't a delicious Vee's Beach Grill sandwich, found on the white sandy beach of Fort Myers Beach, Florida, or at least it once was. Every day for years she could pick an item off her own grill menu, sit out on the expansive deck, and gaze at the waves of the Gulf of Mexico all while her skin was kissed by the warm sun. Later at night, sometimes she would go back outside with a piece of key lime pie and watch the sunset. They worked hard, but it was a pleasant life.

They'd had the bar and restaurant, and then later added a small, attached gift shop. She spent her days catering to the locals and vacationers to southwest Florida, filling their stomachs and selling beach towels, hats, sunglasses, shot glasses, drink glasses, T-shirts, and local trinkets. They had Sarah, and a comfortable modest one-story house with a small swimming pool five minutes away in Fort Myers. They'd taken a dangerous one-time risk fourteen years ago that paid off handsomely and used the proceeds to build a life. She'd had a feeling of contentment and control and security.

Mother Nature ruined everything.

Five years ago was the first hurricane, Irma. The once in a hundred-year storm. At first, they thought they'd dodged the worst of it as the storm veered ashore to the south of Fort Myers Beach at the last minute. Instead of sending in a massive storm surge as expected, the winds pulled the water out to sea. However, as the storm moved northeast, the winds came around the backside of the hurricane and there was a later, unexpected surge of water. The grill and gift shop rested on a lower stretch of beach. The building itself largely survived the storm surge intact but the insides were flooded with seawater, destroying everything, especially the grill's kitchen.

When they made their insurance claim, their business property insurance wasn't as comprehensive as they'd thought. The insurance company said the policy didn't cover the flood damage, only wind damage. They battled the insurance company, the State of Florida, and the federal government for two years and gave considerable thought to walking away from the business, tearing the building down, selling the lot and cutting their losses. But they loved their life, owning a business, being their own bosses. Vee wanted her daily beach view back. They took what little they could get from the government and insurance company, withdrew their remaining life savings, cut expenses everywhere they could, and rebuilt. It was a once in a hundred-year storm. It couldn't happen again.

Just when they were back up and running, Covid-19 hit. Even with Florida's defiant anti-shutdown stance, it still took another two years of work, promoting, advertising, until they started to see light at the end of the financial tunnel. As of a year ago, she felt like they were on a sustainable path. They just needed one more good year.

Then came Hurricane Ian. The second once in a hundred-year storm in five years.

Irma had been bad.

Ian was catastrophic.

The grill and gift shop were destroyed, nothing left but a pile of rubble. Their house suffered the same fate, totaled under the massive storm surge.

They lost everything.

They hadn't paid the bills off from the first rebuild and while their insurance on the business was a bit better this time, like many of their neighbors, they'd been unable to get flood insurance for their house. More debt piled upon the mountain of debt they already were trying to dig out from, and they had nothing left to draw on.

The house was gone. The business was gone. Their life savings which they'd re-invested to get the business going again, were gone. They couldn't even find an apartment in the Fort Myers area that would rent to them, given their financial condition. They were completely wiped out.

Vee's mom offered them the option to live with her. "Come back home. Get away from all the troubles. Make a fresh start."

Exhausted, bankrupt, hounded by creditors, and with no other viable option, four months ago they'd packed what few personal belongings they still had into their two cars and drove home to Minnesota.

The fresh start was short-lived.

Home two months, Dan took Sarah out to get ice cream on a Friday night. Just a little treat for their girl. On their way home, they had to swerve to avoid a deer in the middle of the road and careened into a massive tree. Both were injured, Dan with a broken wrist and a bad concussion. Sarah took the brunt of it with internal injuries, two shattered lower legs and a broken right arm.

With their business failure in Florida, they had lost their health insurance and had not replaced it. The unpaid medical bills piled up and a new set of bill collectors were now hounding them anew.

"Anything on the job search today?" she asked Dan between bites.

Dan shook his head. "No. Just more rejections." He had gotten his real estate license to expand his options. There were openings at the local agencies, but he wasn't getting hired.

"What about the agency in Crosslake?"

"Rejected this morning. I might have to broaden what I'm willing to do, Vee. I saw a restaurant manager opening out by the shopping mall for one of the chain restaurants. They should hire me on the spot for that."

"Yeah?" Vee said hopefully.

Dan sighed. "You know what'll happen. They'll like me, but

then they'll run that financial background check and poof. So long opportunity."

"It'll get better," she said more hopefully than she really felt.

Dan shrugged and took a drink of his Diet Coke. "I don't see how. I just don't."

It had been good fortune that she was able to get the job she had, having suffered the same string of rejections when she first ventured out to job hunt. She and Dan had both been reluctant to talk about what had happened to them in Florida. It was embarrassing. The store's manager, Ruth Ann, was a gymnast a few years behind Vee in high school when Vee had been the captain. She was ready to hire Vee on the spot, but then called her about the background check. Vee told her the whole story. "I really need this, Ruth Ann," Vee had said, breaking down. "I don't know what else to do. I need a job. I'll do whatever you need, whenever you need it."

"Okay," Ruth Ann replied. "You've got the job."

They at least had that.

She took the last bite of her sandwich and finished her Diet Coke. The two of them started walking back.

"Even if I find something, what is it really going to accomplish?" Dan muttered. "The hole is so deep. Whatever we make, *they* take. They're taking a third of your paycheck. Anything we earn where there is a W-2, they take. They take, they take, they take!"

The only real answer was to let the bankruptcy process in Florida and now Minnesota, play out. It was their only option but for two prideful people who had operated a small but successful business, it was a personal stain. They had nothing now. Would they ever again?

"Someday we'll get it all behind us," Vee said.

Dan exhaled a long breath. "Man, that seems so far away. I'm going to be forty and not have a pot to piss in."

Vee leaned up and kissed him on the cheek. "Remember, I still love you. So, you still got that."

"And that's not nothing."

Dan watched as his wife walked back inside the store. He walked along the street, hands in his pockets, gazing around at the thriving businesses along Lake Drive, shaking his head. All he needed was one person to give him a break. Just one.

As he walked along the street, he glanced to his left, glimpsing a white repair van pulling away from the other side of the street. There was a familiar face driving it.

"Huh."

* * *

Braddock and Tori grabbed a late lunch at a restaurant in Deerwood and were finishing up when Reese called.

"The pontoon and the surf boat stolen the Tuesday after Memorial Day were stored in Deerwood. The whaler and one surf boat were stored with Garvin's Repair and Service in Manchester Bay. The Malibu wakesurfing boat stolen two weeks ago was stored at... Garrison Boat Works."

Braddock smiled. "Ah, my guy."

"Your guy?" Reese asked.

"I stow my speedboat there in the winter." He took a moment. "Tori and I are making our way back from Deerwood, we'll divert to Garrison and go see Red Moody."

"And just so you know, Will," Reese added. "That's also where Kyle Mannion stores his boats."

The drive to Garrison took fifteen minutes.

"I don't know if this is lost on you or not, but it always

amazes me how Mille Lacs looks like the ocean," Braddock said as they reached the intersection of Highways 18 and 169 in Garrison.

Lake Mille Lacs was one of the largest lakes in Minnesota. A massive semi-roundish body of water, it was fifteen miles across east to west and a bit more north to south. Even on a perfectly clear late afternoon, the sun bright at their back, the distant horizon was a merging of light-blue sky and deeper-blue water, not a speck of land visible in the distance, just blue.

"Get out there when it's windy and it's just like the ocean, the way the boat will rock," Tori said. "I went on a fishing charter from Garrison Boat Works once. It was windy. The boat, she was a rockin'."

"Did you get seasick?"

Tori snorted a laugh. "No, although Jessie did. Puked her guts out over the side."

"Something I'm sure you never let her live down."

"Well, duh."

Braddock veered right and drove a half-mile south of the town to Garrison Boat Works located just to the west of Highway 169 as it hugged the western shore of the lake. The boat works building sat to the west of the highway while the marina was on the east, flowing into the lake. A bridge just to the south covered a channel that also gave the repair shop lake access.

Braddock had called ahead, and Red Moody was waiting for them out front when they pulled up. "Will, how are you?" he said, extending a hand. Braddock introduced Tori. "Now, tell me, are you the one who was Big Jim's daughter?"

Tori smiled. "I am."

"It is an honor to meet you. I was quite fond of your dad. He and I did some business back in the day."

"Fishing business I assume," Tori said. "I went out on one of your charters once."

"I seem to have a vague recollection of that, Big Jim showing up with little twin girls in ponytails and life jackets. Did we go to lunch over at The Goose after?"

"We did," Tori said, smiling. "It's a good memory."

"Your father and I talked fishing often, but we also kibitzed on matters of the law and crime too."

Tori picked up his drift and shared a look with Braddock.

"To that point," Red continued, as he led them into his back office to sitting chairs, "I can't believe this about Kyle's daughter. Do you both know Kyle?"

"Yes," Braddock replied. "He and Brianna are quite good friends of ours."

"God, it's just awful. Kyle is a good man. I love having his business and the business he refers. And you wanted to see me about those murders last night?" He stopped and looked warily at them. "How can I help with that?"

"With insight, Red." Braddock laid out the murders, the boats stolen, where they were stored and if there was some connection in all of that to the killers they were looking for. "They could pick the boats out randomly, but that doesn't feel right. We think they're targeted and scouted. We're trying to figure out *how* they identify the boats. If they do, and we could figure that out, we could dial in on who the killers are. The big three storage facilities have all stored at least one of the boats stolen in the last few months. Would there be any commonality between you, Deerwood and Garvin's Repair and Storage?"

Red sat back in his chair for a moment and shook his head. "Not that I can think of. From what you describe, yes, these guys are after very valuable boats, but stolen from more modest lake places relatively speaking. Deerwood is strictly storage, and they store just about anything: RVs, campers, trailers, cars, not just boats. Garv is an old friend of mine. He does terrific service and repair, but his storage capacity is small compared to me and the boys in Deerwood. None of my guys also work at those places. Now, we'd have the trailers for sure because some folks with boats don't have them, so we launch and deliver their boats. Same for Garv. At Deerwood you have to have a trailer, or they won't store your boat."

"You run background checks on your employees?" Tori asked.

"You bet," Red replied. "Boats are valuable items. I can't have someone running one out the back door with the keys and stealing one. I can't speak for Charlie and Eric up in Deerwood, but I think they have mostly family working for them. I know Garv is careful about that too."

There was a brief knock on the door behind them, a thick muscular man in a green T-shirt and jeans with a fishing hat on, stepped in and handed a sheet to Moody. "I just inventoried the boat. That's a list of what it will need for tomorrow's charter."

"Okay," Red said as he quickly reviewed the list. "Thanks, Heath. Close the door, will you? I'll see you in the morning."

"Yes, sir."

"Back to your situation," Red said, looking up from the list. "Two of those boats were stored with me it looks like."

"How many do you store?" Tori asked.

"We have capacity for a couple of thousand boats in our storage barns, plus another couple thousand at least outside that we shrink wrap," Moody said as he examined the list, evaluating the boats stolen. "I see surf boats, pontoons, and even a whaler were stolen. You'd need the trailers," he said. "I can see why you'd check on a place like mine. I have ones for all three kinds plus a few more."

"You do work on the surf boats?"

"Oh sure," Moody said. "We can fix them easily enough. We're just not the first place people think of for that, being that we're on Mille Lacs. It's not a lake for those kinds of boats. Too wavy most of the time. Garv is more known for that. How do you figure these fellers found these boats to pilfer?"

"That, Red, is why we're here. Any thoughts?" Tori asked.

Red scratched the back of his head and thought for a moment. "As I think about my operation here, if an employee got on the computer, looked up a boat and address he could learn a thing or two. Look at the satellite map and see that it's more a cabin than a house, but that's not real easy to tell that way, I don't think."

"You'd have to go out and take a look," Tori suggested.

"Yes." Red turned to his computer. "Let's test the theory. I'm looking at the two boats I store that were stolen." He made several mouse clicks before finally shaking his head. "Unless I can't trust my son-in-law who I'm grooming to take over the operation, and my daughter, his wife, they're the only ones who've looked at those accounts, in the past year anyway. My daughter on the surf boat, my son on the whaler, both entries related to storage. Does that mean someone else working for me couldn't have put two and two together?" He pursed his lips. "It's possible, I suppose."

"Hey, Red, I'm not here to accuse you of anything," Braddock said. "That's not why we're here. And to your point, I tend to agree given how the boats are dispersed amongst storage facilities, they were identified another way. Still, we think there is some commonality between all the boats and the owners. Some connection."

"That's what I'd think too," Red said. "Someone is spotting them somehow."

"You mentioned you did business with my dad. You do it with Cal as well?" Tori said.

"Oh sure. Cal and I were very friendly. I haven't met Sheriff Boe yet. She hasn't stopped in."

"She's not much into fishing, I don't think," Braddock said.

"That might explain it then."

"What did that business with my father, with Cal, entail?" Tori asked.

"Oh, you know, if I heard of something, I might place a call to your father or Cal. They'd stop by, have a cup of coffee, we'd talk fishing and I'd share. It would be little stuff usually. You know, you run charters, you hear things. Poaching. I heard what I thought was for sure a guy describing how he was embezzling from his company. I called your pops over, told him what I heard. A few weeks later, a man was arrested for that very thing."

"Let's circle back to our issue. Do you know anything about stolen boats?" Braddock asked.

"Like what?"

"Who trades in them? Who operates a boat like chop shop?"

"I don't, but..." Red sat still for a moment, leaning his head back. "When was that?"

"When was what?" Braddock said.

Red held up a finger and picked up his phone and hit a button. "Can you step into my office for a second?"

A moment later there was a knock on the door and a woman stepped inside.

"Detectives, this is my daughter, Eve." He introduced Tori and Braddock, explaining why they were there. "Eve, who was it a few years ago that told you they heard about a stolen boat for sale, or someone who could hook that up?"

Eve looked to Tori and Braddock and grinned. "You must know Jones?"

Braddock smiled. "Do you mean Eff'n Jones?"

"That's him. Ethan and I know him well enough. We were over at The Outskirts one night a few years back having burgers and beers and he was at our booth, giving us grief."

"Shocking," Tori said.

"I know, right. Anyway, we're in the boat business so he was laughing and telling us about a guy who lost a chunk of money on a boat because it was hot. The police showed up, confiscated the boat, and he was out like eighty grand. Jones claimed he told the guy not to buy it, but the guy didn't listen."

"And you took from that?"

"Jones knew the guy selling the boat and knew it couldn't have been legit. I don't remember the name of the buyer or seller in all that, but I guarantee you Jones will."

Braddock turned to Tori. "Time to go see Mighty Mouse."

The highway turned hard to the left as they drove west from Garrison back to Manchester Bay, and the glare of the sun hit them.

"Man is that bright," Braddock said as he flipped down the sunshade to assist his sunglasses in shielding his eyes. "Blazing."

Tori sat quietly in the passenger seat. Even with her aviator sunglasses on he could tell that her look was distant, one she had when deep in thought.

"What are you thinking about?" he asked.

"Red Moody had two of the boats. Only his daughter and son-in-law accessed the records, at least according to Moody and I don't question that."

"Nor do I. So?"

"I was thinking of a twist on something he said."

"Which is?"

"He said it would be hard to put the boat and cabin together through his shop."

"Yeah. They could be just out driving around and identifying them," Braddock suggested. "You could do that. Heck, you could do it from the lake. See the boat, evaluate the cabin, and go from there."

"True," she replied. "And if they are, then all the investigating in the world won't matter. But that's not a terribly efficient way to find targets. Takes a lot of time. I'm betting that's not what they did. But we've been thinking of this from just a boat perspective. Maybe we ought to broaden it to also look at it from the perspective of the cabin. Maybe there is something in common there. Is there someone who would be able to put the boat and cabin together? Who would know about the boat out on the lift, and that the cabin would be easy enough to get into? I mean that's the first step, isn't it? You have to get inside the cabin."

"That's something to ponder."

The diminutive Ryan Eff'n Jones owned The Outskirts, a bar just west of Manchester Bay. The Outskirts owned a somewhat notorious reputation, catering to the working-class locals and those who many would consider rougher around the edges. Braddock thought the reputation was overwrought. Was the crowd a little rougher? Sure, but so what. He liked the place, and it was growing on Tori. They played in a sand volleyball league there on Thursday nights in the summer with hockey parent friends. The place had character, a dive of the first order with a highly underrated kitchen that stuck to what it knew. Burgers, sandwiches, and pizza.

Jones was also a helpful source on occasion. In addition to being a bar owner, he was also a bookie. Braddock often wondered which paid more, the bar or bookmaking, and suspected it depended on the week or time of year. However, Jones's dual operations did foster something of an "anything goes" environment and mentality. And Jones himself was unconflicted if his bartenders, cooks, and servers occasionally provided a drink or burger to a drug dealer, thief, or con artist. Their money was the same color as everyone else's. As he'd said more than once to Braddock and Steak, "I don't conduct background checks on my customers. That's *your* job."

As a result of his sometimes-unsavory clientele, he would, from time to time, overhear certain pieces of interesting information that he would file away and share with Steak and/or Braddock, especially if he was in need of the sheriff's department to look the other way on some minor infraction committed by one of his patrons, or if said crime were committed at The Outskirts.

Braddock called ahead and Jones met him and Tori in a small back office behind his kitchen. The first order of business upon their arrival was ordering cheeseburgers and fries to go.

"Okay, order sent. Now, what the fuck do you two want?" Jones asked good-naturedly, once again confirming why everyone called him Eff'n Jones. "I ain't done nothing fucking wrong—lately."

"Lately," Tori said skeptically, eye to eye with him.

"Come on, Tori, I keep it clean most of the time," Jones said while he let his eyes take a walk all over her. He fancied himself a ladies' man, regardless of whether the ladies fancied him.

His lingering gaze did not go unnoticed by Braddock.

"Okay, you little leering lech, focus for a second," Braddock ordered. "A patron of yours some time back bought a boat that turned out to be stolen. Do you recall?"

Jones chortled with a big smile. "Ted McFadden. What a fucking pigeon."

"How so?"

"He was talking about this sweet, fully loaded surf boat he was going to buy for a song from Wade Chew."

"Chew?" Braddock said, eyes raised.

"And Wade Chew is?" Tori said.

"A fence," Braddock said quickly. "He was busted, what? A couple of years ago?"

"At least four now, I think," Jones said, folding his arms. "I told Teddy boy then: You know why the deal is so sweet for that boat? Because the boat is fucking hot. Sure, as shit, it was. I tried warning him off, I did, but he didn't listen. I mean if I'm warning you off, you gotta listen, right? What a fucking dumbass."

"You knew Chew?"

Jones nodded. "He'd been to the bar a few times before then. He was in the book. My only surprise was that he was dealing a boat and that's what got him pinched and sent to the clink. That wasn't what he usually trafficked in, at least from what I understood."

"What was his preferred product?"

"Jewelry, electronics, art, cars, and trucks, given his auto repair shop and used auto-lot. Boats usually weren't his jam. I was a little surprised by that but a guy like Chew, if he could make a buck, he'd do it."

"Do you know of anyone who does deal in stolen boats these days?" Tori asked.

Jones thought for a moment. "Not that I've heard of. You know me, I don't ask about things, I just—"

"Listen," Braddock finished. "Yeah, yeah, whatever."

"What the fuck? Why are you busting my balls?"

"The double homicide last night. There's a... team out there, probably two men, stealing high-end boats from cabins. Those two kids stumbled onto such a theft last night."

"Ah fuck," Jones said, shaking his head. "Ally Mannion?"

"Yeah."

Jones shook his head in disgust. "I don't know Kyle Mannion, but I've known Eddie for years, he used to come in before he cleaned himself up. I have customers who work at his company. What can I do to help?"

"You hear something, call me, immediately," Braddock said. "Don't wait until you need to make some sort of trade. You follow?"

"I do," Jones replied with a headshake and there was a knock on the door. It was the cook with their burger bags.

. . .

As Braddock transferred their dinner from the big white sacks to plates, Tori powered up her laptop computer and then retrieved her Beats earphones from her office.

"What are you working there?"

"Nolan texted that she emailed me a copy of the 911 call. I was listening to it on my phone, but I want to listen with better earphones."

Braddock set her plate down in front of her, along with a beer. He took his seat and dug into his double bacon cheese-burger and took a drink of his beer as he observed Tori. She listened and then hit replay again, closing her eyes and putting her hands to her ears, pressing the headphones tight to her head.

He took another bite and saw her lean forward just a bit and then her eyes got wide.

"What is it?"

"Shh!" she replied and replayed the call again, closing her eyes, nodding along.

"What?"

"Shh. One more time." She replayed the call, listening intently again.

She had his attention. "Tori, you're killing me here."

"Listen to the call." She handed him the headphones and spun around her laptop and scooted her chair next to his. "Listen very carefully after the second yell for help."

He slid on the headphones, and she hit play.

"911, what's your emergency?" the 911 operator answered.

"Oh my God! Help me! Help! No! No! Stay away!"

"Ma'am? Hello? Ma'am!" the 911 operator called.

"No! No! Get back! N— Oh... ah..."

"Ma'am? Ma'am?"

Click.

"Did you hear it?"

"Play it again."

Tori hit play.

Ally Mannion's voice started again. "Oh my God! Help me! Help!... it... er..."

He looked at Tori. "In the background. The voice. I can barely hear it. It's really low."

She had isolated the section of the call. She replayed it again. "Help me! Help!"

"Stop," Braddock said. "There's the 'Help me! Help!' and then something else, it's really faint."

Tori played it again.

Braddock's lips moved with the tape. Help me! Help! "Get... her." He looked to Tori. "I just hear the 'Get her' we heard before."

"There's a bit more." She replayed it. "Listen."

Braddock leaned forward. His lips moved again. Help me! Help! "Yo." He looked to Tori: "Does he say: Yo?"

"I think so. He says: Yo. Get her!"

"Like it was a conversation."

"Exactly. I mean when people say something like 'Yo' it's almost casual. He says: 'Yo, get her.' That's like saying: 'Yo, give me a hand with this. Yo, what's up?'"

"Where does that get us?" Braddock said.

"Voice match, maybe," Tori said. "Maybe there's more here. Nolan said forensics will see if they can get more out of it. I bet we could isolate the voice better."

"That's another avenue for exploration. How the boats are identified is an avenue and now, Wade Chew is also an avenue. Not a bad day's work."

* * *

"Vee, go ahead and clock out. You've been here all day. It's nearly eight, we're slow. Go home, get a bit of rest and I'll see you tomorrow," Ruth Ann, the store's manager said.

Vee nodded. She was exhausted and her feet were killing her. "Thanks, Ruth Ann."

"Can I ask you a question before you go?"

"Sure."

"I saw where there was a Help A Friend page set up for Sarah's medical bills."

"Yeah." Vee sighed sheepishly, shaking her head. "My mom did that."

"I'd like to help, I mean more than just donating, which I just did. I'd like to promote it."

"You don't have to do that."

"I want to. Can I put a sign up by the checkout area for it? Would that be okay with you?"

The last thing Vee wanted to do was advertise her and Dan's financial struggles. But pride was one thing, absolute need was another and they were in absolute need right now. Embarrassed as she was, if it got them a few more dollars, she couldn't turn it down.

"I don't want you to feel like you have to."

"No, I want to. It's not much I know but if I can help even a little more, I'd like too. That's what good people do. They help."

"Well... thank you. Have a good night."

Vee slipped out of her dress shoes and put on her old running shoes and her feet felt instantly better, as did her lower back. Pulling a double in heels, even for someone as small and still relatively limber as she was for nearing forty, was taxing. She walked out of the back of the store and to her car, glancing to her right at the flow of people going in and out of the jewelry store next door. Some of the sale traffic had managed to find its way into Fashion by Julia throughout the day.

Why not. She could use a little distraction.

She strolled through the store's back door and perused the cases: the bracelets, earrings, brooches, necklaces, rings, sparkling diamonds, and other gemstones. It was surprising to her the sheer volume of merchandise packed into the tight confines of the building.

"Can I help you?"

Vee turned around to see a woman named Carole, or at least that's what her name tag said. "Hi. No, I'm just looking around. I work next door."

"I thought you looked kind of familiar."

"I wanted to see what all the hubbub was about. You have quite a bit on sale."

"We do. And if you do see something you like or there is something that you're looking for that isn't on display, we do have more items in the back that I could also check, so just let me know."

"Thank you. I will."

Vee watched as Carole slipped behind one of the display cases and down the back hallway and through a door on the right. She saw her emerge a minute later with several jewelry cases from which she proceeded to take out bracelets that she placed inside the display case.

She spent another five minutes just absentmindedly walking around, looking at all the items she could have once afforded, but now couldn't. Based upon the traffic inside the store and how busy the checkout area was, there were plenty of people about who could. It had amazed her in the months she'd been back at how the town and area had changed, had taken on a certain air of wealth. When she was a kid, the moneyed folks were all from the cities, not the locals. Now, that wasn't so much the case. Sure, there were plenty of people from the Twin Cities who still came up but with Mannion Companies it seemed a lot more of the locals had money and were spending it, whether here in the jewelry store, or at Fashion by Julia, or at any of the other shops along Lake Drive. And as she walked around passively checking out the display cases, she couldn't help but think that a year or two ago, she would have been one of those people, able to walk along the street and maybe not buy anything she wanted but certainly could have bought the occasional thing. She could have walked into the jewelry store and bought a pair of earrings or necklace given the sale prices. She'd had some nice jewelry before the last hurricane, but it was all gone now. What the storm hadn't taken the debts had.

Ten minutes later she arrived home and looked in on Sarah who was lying in bed, her eyes closed, a movie playing. She crept in and turned the television off, pulled the blanket up and kissed her on the head. Her mother appeared to be out, and Dan was sitting out on the small back deck, drinking a beer. She pulled one from the refrigerator and joined him.

"Tired?"

Vee nodded, taking a sip of her beer and then closing her eyes. "Long day."

"Lots of those lately," he said and put the beer to his lips. "Do you think we can ever get it all back?" he said. "Be honest. Can we?"

She shook her head. "I don't see how."

"Me neither. Not... legitimately anyway."

She shot him a quick side eye at the use of "legitimate". "What are you saying?"

"Oh nothing. Just that I caught a glimpse of someone from our past today."

FIVE

"THAT JOB IS A PIPE DREAM."

Druk sat on the front porch, drinking a beer, the sun setting behind him as he looked out across Highway 169 to Lake Mille Lacs. This late in the day, the water along the shoreline was almost glass-like, what breeze there was only affecting the water much further out from this area of sheltered shoreline. As he took a drink of his beer, Heath's Dodge pickup truck passed in front of the house and signaled his turn into the driveway. A minute later he came out the front door although oddly without a beer in his hand.

"What's up?" Druk asked, noting Heath's look of concern.

"I got the call from Kellin. He's—"

"Nervous?"

"Shitting a brick more like. He doesn't have a boat to deliver. He wants to meet up. And then there's one more thing."

"Which is?"

"Detectives showed up to talk to Red. It was Braddock and the woman, Hunter. I've seen their pictures before. On the news. They took down those Mob guys a few months back up in Cullen Crossing."

"Why were they talking to Red?"

"I heard one of them say something about insight on the boat industry. Whatever that meant."

"It means," Druk replied, "they're trying to figure out how we identified those boats. Kellin is right. We do need to talk."

Kellin was waiting for them in a secluded back booth. He was hunched over his shot of whiskey and tap beer on the table in front of him, his cell phone to the right, his baseball hat turned around, still in his work boots and jeans. A short man was chatting with him. The little man saw them approach.

"Are you sure you want to sit with him? He smells like fucking shit!"

"Yo, you do smell like shit," Heath affirmed as he slid into the opposite side of the booth, followed by Druk.

"Hah! Hah!" The little man laughed and then left.

The server arrived taking their drink order. She was back with the beers in two minutes.

"What's up?" Druk asked casually after carefully sipping his full beer mug.

"Seriously?" Kellin snapped.

"Yeah, what are you up in arms about? The money?"

"I didn't sign up for this shit."

Druk smirked, leaning forward, his voice low. "You think what we've been doing comes without risk? That your money came without risk attached? Come on, Denny."

"No, but—"

"That's the nature of the beast, my friend. You should know that after all these years."

"This ain't nothing we haven't dealt with before," Heath added flatly.

"This?" Kellin's eyes went wide. "Before?"

Heath and Druk both stared blankly back at him.

"Oh, Christ. You've—?"

"Keep your head," Heath growled lowly.

"Denny," Druk started, taking a small sip of his beer, always the lighter touch of the two, "have you ever been arrested or done time?"

"Uh... I was arrested for that bar fight. You two dodged it, but I spent the night in jail and ended up with a drunk and disorderly charge I didn't deserve. That guy started the fight, the fucker."

"We dodged it because we prevented you from getting killed."

"Yeah, I suppose. Glad somebody killed that fucker a few months later."

Heath chuckled at that.

"What's so funny."

"Nothing."

"Denny, anything else?" Druk asked.

"I was busted for pot like fifteen years ago."

"That's it?"

"Yeah."

"Well, that ain't much, dude," Druk said breezily. "No reason to be under any suspicion. And look, he and I?" He gestured to Heath. "We've never been arrested or spent a day in jail and we're not going to now. In the unlikely event the police come around, just listen to the questions, and answer carefully, but respectfully."

"Okay."

"And whatever you do, don't try to be their buddy or their pal because they are not your friend. You don't know nothin' about nothin'. Right?"

Kellin exhaled a breath and nodded.

"But if they do come around, you'll let us know, right?" Heath said.

"Yeah, yeah. For sure. And you'll do the same?"

"Exactly," Druk replied.

"Eh," Heath waved dismissively. "It'll be fine."

"Denny, just keep your head down," Druk said before he

took a drink of his beer. "The boat gig is done for now."

Kellin nodded and took a long drink of his beer. "It sure was nice getting the extra cash."

"You didn't put that cash in the bank, did you?"

"No. It's not in a bank account. And do I look like I've been out flashing cash? I know better than that. And for sure I ain't doing that now." He took a drink of his beer. "You two got anything else going I could get in on?"

Druk shrugged. "We'll let you know."

Kellin understood the response for what it was. "You've got something, don't you?"

"Maybe. I'm not sure it's up your alley."

"Yeah, why not?"

"You're too fucking big," Druk said.

"Well, if you need my... services, you know how to find me."

"Yo, Denny, you just sit there smelling like shit, and you'll be fine," Heath needled. "Smelling and looking like that, nobody will ever suspect you of jack shit."

"Fuck off."

Druk laughed. "Let's get one more round of beers."

An hour later, they were driving back to Garrison, the sun setting behind them.

"That went fine, don't you think?" Druk mused.

"He's nervy," Heath replied. "But, then again, so am I."

"Yeah?"

"Seeing the detectives with Red today. I mean I stopped in the office, and they were right there. It just kind of shocked me, you know."

"Understandable. You weren't expecting it."

"Got that right."

"They pay you any mind?"

"Nah," Heath replied.

"Maybe it's time for another move for a bit?"

"You think?"

"We've done it before when things have gotten a little... worrisome. Get out of sight, out of mind. Lay low and let the dust settle."

"To where?"

"I don't know, maybe someplace south again. We could go back down to Florida for a few years for a change of pace. Lots of fishing guides bailed after the hurricane. There's a need. We could fill it. And if we get the itch, plenty of options down there to address that. Hit a place out on Sanibel or Captiva again, or scope Naples. We'd find something."

"Maybe," Heath said, working his teeth with a toothpick. "The change of weather would be good. Are you thinking we stick out the season here at least?"

"Yeah, for now. If we up and leave, with both our schedules pretty full through Labor Day weekend, that raises eyebrows too. Those cops show up to see Red and then we bail on him? Plus—"

"Plus, what?"

"Well, if we find the right sort, we could take the store. We have everything we need to do it but the key to unlock it. And then on the charter today, did you hear those two guys talking. It was like they were competing to see who had more—"

"Money."

"One of them is local. I looked him up."

"I don't know," Heath replied with raised eyebrows. "Wouldn't that be pressing our luck?"

Druk shrugged. "We're not pressing it unless we do it. And we're not on the spot yet. I'm just saying, I overhead enough today that it's all at least worth a look-see. I'm sensing there could be seven figures there. Take forty percent of that and if we go away for a few years, that would be some good walking away cash." They approached an exit for Manchester Bay. He hit the turn signal.

"Where are you going?"

"Just a little drive-by to look at all the pretty jewels."

"Pfft," Heath blurted. "That job is a pipe dream."

"It could be huge."

"Sure, if we can get in, which we can't."

Druk motored his way through town to Lake Drive and made a left turn and pulled up along the curb on the right side. The street was quiet, late on a Monday night, just a few folks out still shopping at the stores.

The two-story building had recently been rehabilitated. It was a hundred-year-old brownstone taken down to the studs and recently remodeled before two businesses moved in. The one on the right was Lakes Jewelers.

An acquaintance worked for the subcontractor who built out the electrical for the jewelry store space. He noted how certain interior systems, once installed, were vulnerable. "You just need to figure out how to get to them. If you do, you can take them all down at once. Do that, you could walk in and take all the time you wanted."

But there was only one way in to get around the security system.

It required someone very small.

SIX

"LET'S GET IT ON."

Tori caught the feel of a light breeze on her bare toes coming in the open bedroom window. Her eyes flitted open and the curtains were billowing lightly with the breeze, the sun lighting up the green of the tree leaves she could see out the window. Her eyes open, she let them wander about their newly renovated master bedroom.

Tori had moved fully into the house last summer and it had quickly become apparent that her presence made the house feel small, particularly when it came to having enough closet space to hold her wardrobe. And Quinn was twelve and only growing. He would be tall and lanky like his six-foot-four father. He needed room to roam.

Braddock was comfortable financially between what he'd inherited from his parents upon their deaths, life insurance for Meghan's passing plus the sale of her business, and upon moving to Manchester Bay, Roger had given him the keys to the house. Braddock just had to pay the property taxes.

Given how idyllic the spot was on the lake, he had no interest in moving to a bigger house. That left making the one he owned more spacious. He hired a contractor friend, and the remodel was on, expanding the house back and over the detached garage, tying it all together in one big structure. It doubled the size of the master bedroom and Quinn's bedroom, left an office for Braddock and then added a game room space for Quinn to use with his friends out over the garage. And there was some left over to remodel the family area of the basement to make it more open and useful, particularly in the summer. It was, as Tori's friend Tracy had said to her a few months ago, "A forever house."

Tori was starting to think of things in that way.

Rarely one to linger in bed once awake, she slipped out to let Braddock sleep and quietly stepped into her favorite part of the remodel, their newly expanded walk-in closet. For Braddock his favorite parts were the expanded bedroom, the fireplace and flat-screen mounted over it, and the long dual-headed walk-in steam shower. For Tori, it was the closet, a bit of a silly dream realized. One night when she and Braddock had stumbled along a show where thieves were raiding Kim Kardashian's closet, Tori had said, "What I wouldn't give for a closet like that."

Braddock had filed that little remark away and, as a surprise, had provided her the space for one, albeit on a much smaller scale. "You design it," he'd said. "Whatever you want, within reason, of course."

She liked just walking around, considering what she wanted to wear for the day. Long and wide just off the bedroom and master bath, it had built in floor-to-ceiling shelving and racks all around and a built-in dresser in the middle with a granite top, like the center island for a kitchen, one side with pullout clothing drawers and the other lighted shoe racks.

She had a little smile as she ran her hand across the granite top, thinking of last Friday night. She had gone out with some of her old high school girlfriends for dinner and wine. Braddock had been off with his friends golfing, and had just taken a shower and was fresh and clean when she found him in the closet in a bright white terrycloth towel wrapped around his waist, and nothing else. His back was to her, running his right hand gently along the section where her many coats and blazers hung.

"What are you doing?"

"Simply staring in amazement at the sheer expanse of your wardrobe," he said, smiling, his damp black hair swept sexily back, smelling freshly of body wash and shampoo. He looked so good.

"Well," she said, locking her eyes on his, "I do like nice clothes." She stepped out of her open-toed platform wedges and then slowly walked toward him, taking off one hoop earring and then another, setting them near her jewelry box. "And... I like how they make me look," she said as she casually raised her hands up to gently push away the spaghetti straps for her red floral summer mini dress, letting it slowly drift down the curves of her body to the floor.

"I do... too."

"I like how they make me feel," she added, looking up to him as she slowly slid down her skimpy red lace underwear, stepping out of them and leaving her toned and tanned body fully exposed to him. "And I very much like how they make you look at me," she added in a whisper as she loosened his towel, letting it fall to the floor to leave his long, lean, body fully exposed to her.

As she breathed him in, she had let her hands slowly work their way up from his waist, through his torso, feeling the contours of his chest, sensing his growing hunger for her. She let the tips of her thin fingers feel the corded muscle of his triceps and then shoulders as he let his hands wander down the soft skin of her back to her buttocks and then lift her lithe body up to him, pulling her legs around his waist.

She wrapped her arms around his neck, bringing herself in

close, "And you," she said breathily, kissing him, her tongue tantalizingly brushing his, "really like how they look on me."

"Yes, I do."

Braddock started to slowly walk them out to the bedroom.

"No," Tori whispered. She let her eyes seductively drift left to the granite top of the dresser and then back to his eyes.

"There?"

"Uh huh," she said, kissing him again. "That's what I want."

Now, she couldn't help but giggle at the vision of the two of them on top of it. Later, in bed that night, she was lying on him, her chin resting on her clasped hands, her legs dangling lazily behind her, naked, relaxed, happy, their sexcapades long since complete, and they'd laughed about it.

"I can't believe we did that," he'd said, brushing her messed hair from her face. "On the dresser in there. That was... wow."

Tori giggled, still bawdy. "Braddock, I thought about doing that the first time I saw it in there."

"You did?"

"Oh yeah," she said, pecking him on the lips, nuzzling his nose. "There is no way, at some point, as a reward for it, I wasn't having sex with you in that closet. I came in there tonight, saw you in nothing but that towel and said—"

"Let's get it on."

"Yes!" she replied, laughing. "That is exactly what I was thinking. It was the perfect moment."

He smiled. "You know, if we're talking fantasies of the sexual kind."

"Oh, I think that is the topic of the moment."

"I kind of had thoughts about the new shower, all the space in there, what I'd like to do were you willing."

"Well—" she smiled, leaning in, nuzzling his nose again, her lips brushing his "—there's always the morning."

They'd been together two years now.

Braddock was a widower. His first wife Meghan had died

eight years ago when they lived in New York City. Meghan was from Manchester Bay and was an aspiring clothing designer at the Parsons School of Design when she met Braddock, a native Long Islander, then at college at Long Island University. They married a few years after graduation, an odd couple of sorts, he a New York City cop and she a fashion designer, and later they had Quinn.

Meghan had created her own clothing line and was starting to get noticed and make some money when the headaches started. She was diagnosed with glioblastoma. The brain cancer took her two years later. Braddock, an only child with no remaining family of his own, and now a single father to a five-year-old boy, was drowning emotionally, physically, and professionally when his in-laws threw him a lifeline. He moved to Manchester Bay to raise Quinn with the help of Meghan's parents and sibling.

Braddock took a job as the chief detective for Shepard County and settled into his life on the lake with Quinn. Roger and Mary were a half-mile down the road, his brother-in-law Drew and his wife Andrea and their children, another half-mile down the same road, on the same bay of the lake. He had a family, a good job, and a settled life.

That's where Tori found him two years ago.

Tori had no such intentions of re-settling in Manchester Bay when she came back for the first time in nearly twenty years. Her return was not a happy one. A highly decorated agent with the FBI specializing in the disappearances of children, she returned to investigate the disappearance of a local woman who vanished on the twentieth anniversary of Tori's twin sister Jessie's disappearance. The manner of disappearance had been nearly identical. And just in case Tori wasn't inclined to return to pursue it, the killer made sure Tori saw what had happened.

Braddock, as the county's chief detective, was leading the

investigation.

The two of them butted heads immediately.

Used to being in charge, Tori didn't like riding in the back seat, her investigative desires subject to the approval of someone she didn't view as an equal. And Braddock, a former first-grade NYPD detective, had a city cop's aversion to the arrogance of the Bureau and to him, Tori thoroughly embodied it.

Then, over the course of the investigation, the two began to respect one another, and then warmed to one another personally, and then came the need for each other. However, as relationships go, the entry was far from smooth.

Tori didn't stay in Manchester Bay after the investigation was finished, running away back to New York City. The trauma of losing her sister, and her father, who'd been the sheriff, to a heart attack, all before she turned twenty, had not only driven her away from Manchester Bay but had left her so closed off and emotionally unavailable that she never let anyone get close to her. Yet when she went back to New York City and her job with the FBI, it wasn't the same. Something was missing. The job wasn't enough anymore. She realized she wanted more out of life, and that more was Braddock.

But if it was going to work, her head space had to be right. A few months of intense therapy put her on the right path. She came back to Manchester Bay to find Braddock waiting for her. They'd been together ever since.

She gazed at the framed photo on the small shelf above her jewelry box, an 8 ½ x 11 of the two of them, his arms wrapped around her, standing on a bluff overlooking the Pacific Ocean in Costa Rica as the sun set a few months back. She scoffed a laugh, often amazed at how life had changed for her.

"Hey," Braddock said, bursting into the closet. "It's warm early and not a breath of wind out there. Quick swim?"

"Yeah."

They started the coffee maker, slipped on their swimsuits and bright yellow swim caps, and went for a morning swim in the lake. The cool water was awakening as they swam the equivalent of a mile, from their dock to Roger and Mary's a half-mile south and then back. Braddock was waiting, floating on his back by their dock when she finished.

"Took you long enough," he quipped.

"Whatever, Michael Phelps, your arms are like windmills. It takes me three strokes to your one," Tori retorted. "Just for that, you make breakfast."

"Fair enough."

Forty-five minutes later, just before 7:00 a.m. the two of them entered the government center. Reese and Nolan arrived at the same time. Braddock and Tori reviewed what they had learned.

To Nolan, Braddock said, "Sunday night is connected to the other five. What connects the six beyond owning boats purchased in the last year? We think it's something. How are the boats identified? Are there any commonalities amongst the homeowners?"

"Like what?"

"We know the boats weren't bought at the same places nor serviced or stored at the same facilities, so scratch those. Is there a common friend? Bank? Infraction? What connects them? We need to go back and re-interview all the cabin owners."

"Who has been to their cabins in the last year?" Tori suggested. "Where have they gone or who have they talked to in the last year or so about their lake places. Is there a common friend or visitor? Maybe there is a service provider in common."

"I'm tracking." Nolan nodded. "I've already started. I'll keep going."

"Eggs will help on that too." Braddock turned to Reese. "Track down the investigation that led to the prosecution of a guy named Wade Chew."

"And he is who?"

"A fence." Braddock gave him the details they learned from Red Moody and a confidential source that would remain nameless but that everyone knew was Jones. "Get a copy of the investigative file. He went to prison. Where? How long? Maybe we go see him."

"The guy is in prison. What do you expect to learn there?"

"A fence is only as good as those bringing him items to fence. Who were those people?"

"Plus," Tori added, "we don't think this is the first time these guys have killed nor the first time they've robbed somebody. There is a history there we need to tap into."

"Pretty vague," Reese replied.

"We'll build it out," Braddock said. "As we learn more, it may direct that search. Steak will help on that as well."

"Copy that. And you two?"

"We're pushing on the murders," Braddock replied, checking his phone. He looked to Tori. "Looks like our next stop is the medical examiner."

Tori pulled up short of the door to the medical examiner's office. She exhaled a breath and closed her eyes, her jaw clenched.

"Ally?" Braddock said.

"Yeah," Tori said, shaking her head.

"I can handle it if you want to do something else."

"No. No, no, no," Tori said, shaking her head. "Just... you know."

"I get it."

"Doesn't it... get to you?"

"I'm dreading this," Braddock said.

"You're hiding it well."

"I'm using it for motivation. I want to get these fuckers, Tor. And... I don't necessarily want to catch them."

She knew what that implied. "I needed to hear that."

He opened the door. She exhaled a breath and walked through.

"You have something for us?" Braddock asked as he saw Dr. Renfrow.

"I might. Come with me," he said, waving for them to follow him into the examination room and to the refrigerator units. He pulled out the tray that had Reed Schafer's body on it and pulled the sheet back to reveal the back of his torso. "You see the stab wounds here? There are four in total all under his left rib cage."

They both nodded.

"He was found face down. I found grass and mud in his mouth, his nose, the wells of his eyes. Your killer jumped on top of him, pushed him face first to the ground and stabbed him from behind." He gestured to the wound pattern. "You can see the bruising, in part from the killer driving in the hilt of the knife. At the bottom of the wounds, the entry is clean but the top of the wound, you can see this slight ripping."

"Serrated edge?" Braddock asked.

Renfrow nodded and opened a folder. "Your killer stabbed with a powerful thrust in and up, pulled it out and did it again and again."

"The thrusts up are purposeful," Tori said.

"They were."

"I assume he hit vital organs with that thrust."

"Not as much as I would have initially thought." Renfrow nodded. "The thrusts didn't strike that deep. Deep enough certainly that the liver and kidney were struck. They were fatal in that he bled out quickly, but the strikes, while effective, weren't *that* deep. I was able to get a good tomographic image of two of the wounds and get you an idea of the knife." He took out a stapled series of photographs. "You're looking for a four to five-inch blade with a serrated edge along the top. I'm leaning towards a—"

"A what?"

"Fishing knife," Renfrow said.

"That doesn't look like the wound of a filet knife, Doc," Tori said.

"No, it's not. Think tackle box."

Braddock nodded. "Utility knife?"

"Yes. The reason I lean towards that sort of knife is this here." He gestured to the wounds again. "See this tearing here right on the top edge of the wound? I don't think that's just the serrated edge. Something was catching and tearing there. I think it could be a cut hook."

"To cut fishing wire," Braddock said, nodding. "I have a knife kind of like this in my tackle box." He flipped through the photos on his cell phone. "Here's mine. You've seen this one," he said to Tori.

"The yellow handled one."

"Right. This sharp rounded notch near the hilt, deeper, sharp, hooked. I cut fishing line with that." He looked at the images again. "I see what you're seeing, Doc."

Renfrow re-covered Reed Schafer and pushed his body back inside the refrigerated case.

"Now let me show you something else." He opened another door and pulled out Ally Mannion's body and pulled the sheet down to her shoulders.

Now cleaned up, Tori saw it immediately. "She was sliced twice across the throat."

"Yes. And I think with the same kind of knife. The first cut was with the serrated edge, the raggedness of the slice and it was a left to right slice and at the end, I see similar tearing as if the—"

"Cut hook caught," Braddock said.

"Right. Tori, can I demonstrate on you?"

"Sure, Doc."

He moved behind her, reaching his left arm around her front, just above her chest and held a knife in his right hand. "You okay with me like this?"

"Do your thing, Doc."

"I think it was like this with Ms. Mannion," Renfrow said as he mimed the killer's movements, holding the knife just in front of Tori's throat.

"Be careful, Doc. You're not a surgeon. You only cut when they can't complain."

"Funny, Tori." He pulled his hand left to right. "The cut was with the right hand. He pulls his knife, I'm thinking maybe from a sheath on his belt, and pulls it across but realizes—"

"It's backwards," Tori said, seeing how Renfrow was holding the blade.

"The serrated edge slice might not be enough. He has to either flip the knife or roll or pronate his wrist to pull the straight edge across," Braddock said. "And that's the second cut. To make damn sure she died."

"I think so," Renfrow said, miming the cut across her throat before releasing Tori. "Now, I was there Sunday night and saw you guys working through this. You think it's two men, correct?"

"Pretty sure," Tori said.

"Well, if one took Reed and the other Ally, I think they're both perhaps using the same kind of knife. So that's something to look for. I also found some particles in her wounds that seemed odd. I sent them over to Ann Jennison at the BCA for analysis." He showed them a photo.

"What do you think those are?" Tori asked Renfrow.

"Fish scales."

"We're looking for a couple of fishermen," Braddock said. "That carry the same fishing knife."

"Terrific," Tori replied, caustically.

"Hey, it's something."

"It's Minnesota. That only narrows it down to about two million people."

SEVEN

"SHE COULD BE THE UNICORN."

Druk parked briefly on a narrow road on the opposite side of a small bay from the house out on the point.

"It's an awfully big house," Heath remarked, scanning with his binoculars. "Not the typical northern Minnesota log cabin look either. And you said you heard what about this place?"

"The owner, this is their primary home. He talked about his little corporate jet he had hangered at the Manchester Bay Airport, and their winter home down in Naples, Florida, and that he sold his business and made out like a bandit and his wife went on an art buying spree, blah, blah, blah. All I heard was money, money, money, ka-ching, ka-ching, ka-ching. I mean look, what's that parked in the garage?"

Heath zeroed in with his binoculars. "Aston Martin. That tells me he has a nice car. Doesn't tell me—yet, that there is a lot inside the house."

"I'm pretty sure there is."

"You want to bank on a pretty sure?"

Druk handed over his phone. "That's them two years ago at a charity fundraiser down in Minneapolis. Look at the jewels she's sporting."

Heath examined the photo. The woman was wearing a large diamond necklace, along with earrings and then he noticed her bracelet. "Very nice."

"That is several hundred thousand dollars just around her neck and wrist plus what she has on her ears and, based on what I heard yesterday, I have a pretty good idea when she'll be wearing that all next."

"It's not in the house?"

"It may be or it may be stored in a safe deposit box at the bank. It's only worth it if she's wearing all that. We have to hit them on a night when she is and there is one coming up. And if he was to be believed, there is art in there. We have the guy in California who will take that. And you just know, you just know, guys like this always have cash in a safe. We do it right, it could be a big hit."

"And a security system for the house. That probably means going in hard. You sure you want to do that?"

"That part makes me pause a bit, but only from a logistical standpoint. That's why an extra body or two might be helpful."

"Kellin offered."

"I don't think so. You saw his reaction when you alluded to having done something like Sunday night before. He's too nervy for this," Druk said. "We need to find someone else."

* * *

"Hey," Dan greeted Vee as she affixed the hanger clips to a skirt and hung it on the rack, the box before her now empty. "You want to go get some lunch."

"I packed one."

"Well, I found a twenty-dollar bill in an old pair of jeans. It's burning a hole in my pocket. Let's go down the street and blow it."

"Go," Ruth Ann said with a wave. "We're good. Have lunch."

"Okay," Vee said with a sigh and walked out the front door with Dan, putting on her sunglasses and hooking her arm through his as they walked west toward the lake and food truck row.

"Burger, sandwich, or barbeque?" Dan asked.

"Barbeque."

They stopped at the Pig Machine truck and bought pulled pork sandwiches that came with slaw and found a park bench under a shade tree.

They ate quietly, soaking in the pleasant warmth of the day. It reminded Vee of the days in Florida, sitting on the deck of the restaurant, the warm waters of the Gulf a hundred yards away. Today, it was warm, a clear blue sky with the city's sandy beach two-thirds full on a Tuesday afternoon.

"How was Sarah?" Vee said. "She was still asleep when I left."

"Tired, confined... sad. It's summer. She's twelve and can't do a damn thing and is worried about school and that... we're living with Grandma and you're working all the time. And that you and I seem so... down. She's noticing, Vee. She knows things aren't good."

Vee nodded; her eyes closed behind her sunglasses. "It's hard to be up, you know. I mean, I think I saw another second-notice bill on the counter as I was walking out early this morn-ing. I could hardly bring myself to look at it, let alone open it. And I'm making fifteen dollars an hour selling retail. We paid our employees more than that. My mom resorted to posting a Help a Friend page to help pay Sarah's medical bills." She tossed her head back. "I should have listened to you, Danny. We should have walked away after that first hurricane. But no, I had to—"

"Don't do it. Don't do it to yourself—"

"I should have listened. If I had—"

"Just stop. Just... stop," Dan said, putting his right arm around her, pulling her close, not wanting to rehash a conversation it felt like they'd had a thousand times in the last several months. Their regrets were many. The decisions were made. They couldn't take them back. "If I'd have truly not wanted to do it, we wouldn't have done it. I wanted it all back too. We can't do a damn thing about any of that, now. It's happened. Heck, if I hadn't taken Sarah out for ice cream, she wouldn't be in the shape she's in. I wouldn't still have these headaches."

"Still?" Vee asked, turning to him. "I thought—"

"I don't want you to worry. Yes, I still have them. They're not as bad as they were. I am getting better. Just not as fast as I would like. I still have trouble concentrating for long periods of time."

"Reading?"

"Yeah, I can't stay focused for too long it seems."

Vee nodded and kissed him on the forehead.

"Look, about what I mentioned last night, who I saw. I shouldn't have brought that up. I know you said you never wanted to do something like that ever again. That we did it once and that was enough. I was frustrated about... things. I won't bring it up ag—"

"No," Vee said, patting him on the hand. "I heard what you were saying. Things are bad. And I don't know that I see another way either."

"Yeah?"

"Yeah. Go find them."

"I think I know where to look."

* * *

Tori and Braddock walked down the street, just past 8:oo p.m., calling it a day, heading to The Bourbon Room for dinner.

"Long day," Braddock said as Tori leaned into him, letting him wrap his arm around her.

"Any news from Quinn?"

Quinn and his cousin were invited to a hockey camp for top players their age. "He's loving this select camp. He said there are lots of good players there from down in the cities and he says he's right there with them play wise, so he's excited. He says the coaching is intense and I think he's digging that."

Tori smiled. "He's tall. Big for his age. And he'll probably end up taller than you."

"Most likely," Braddock agreed. "He's only going into seventh grade but I'm starting to see that he's a pretty good player. Even being tall and gangly, he skates so well, smoothly. If he keeps progressing—"

"It could be something?"

"Maybe," Braddock said with a shrug. "He loves it. The challenge will be not getting consumed by it."

"Him *and* you."

"Exactly. Some of these hockey parents are batshit crazy about their kids. You know who Tyler Lewis is, right?"

"Yeah, he was on Quinn's team last year. Little guy, but fast. Parents are a little out there."

"They're on Pluto, Tor. His dad, Blayne, was telling me he thinks they need to hire him an advisor."

"An advisor?"

"Yes."

"For what?"

"Positioning him for college scholarships. Making sure he gets exposure."

"For a twelve-year-old?"

"Yeah, although Blayne says he'll be thirteen and the scouts start watching and they need to be ready," Braddock said, bewildered. "I'm not objective, but he's nowhere near the player Quinn is and I am not hiring an advisor."

"Some of these people are just nuts."

Braddock stopped and turned to her. "Don't let me become one of those. If I start behaving like that, I grant you unfettered permission to absolutely unload on me with everything you got."

"Hah!" Tori laughed out loud.

"I'm serious. Don't let it happen."

Tori smiled. "You won't," she replied unworriedly. "You're far too level-headed for something like that." In fact, most of the parents they knew were, but she'd seen the Lewises in action. Valium before hockey games would help them both.

They passed by the front of Fashion by Julia.

"Oh, I love this place," said Tori.

"The closet is nearly full already."

"The operative word in that statement being 'nearly.'"

Braddock scoffed a laugh. When it came to clothes, it was pointless to try and stop her. "Go on in if you want. I'll walk on ahead to the restaurant. If all they have is bar seating, does that work?"

"Of course."

Tori entered the store and was immediately greeted by Ruth Ann. "Tori, how are you? It's been months since I last saw you. I was beginning to get worried."

"I've been busy, of course."

"The other night?"

Tori nodded sadly.

"So terrible," Ruth Ann said. "What brings you in tonight?"

"I just wanted to look quick at the summer dresses. Braddock and I have a wedding we're going to in a month. I don't know, I just *miiiiiight* need something for it."

"Let's go to the back and have a look." Ruth Ann started to walk to the back when an employee came up to her seeking assistance.

"Ruth Ann, it's okay," Tori said. "I know where to look." She made her way to a circular rack and started perusing the selections. She found a navy-blue dress with a nice floral print and a neckline that she liked. Moving to the mirror she held it up to her body. It was close to the right size. She went into the changing room and quickly slipped into it, coming out to look in the mirror. *I like it.*

"Tori? Tori Hunter?"

Tori spun around and saw the small woman with dresses on hangers draped over her arm. *No way.* "Veronica? Veronica Creen. Vee!"

"Yes." Vee smiled back at her as Tori approached for a hug. "It's Akton now," she said, taking in the embrace.

"Akton? As in Dan Akton? You married Danny?"

"Yes. You remember?"

"How could I forget. How many years did we play soccer together?"

"Oh God, too many to count," Vee said, smiling. "Those were the days. We had fun. The out-of-town tournaments."

"Were the best," Tori replied, smiling. "I'd heard somewhere that you were back here. I haven't seen you in, my gosh, it has to be since—"

"High school," Vee finished. "I'd heard you were back here too. Or at least I remember seeing something on the news about that... drive-by shooting last March. Crazy stuff."

Tori sighed. "Yeah, it was. You know, I shop here from time to time. I didn't know you worked here."

"It's only been a month or so," Vee replied. "Dan and I moved back from Florida in the spring."

"What brought you back?"

"Oh, we lived in Fort Myers Beach."

"Was it the hurricane?"

Vee nodded. "Yeah. Wiped us out. We're kind of starting over."

"Oh, Vee. I'm so sorry to hear that you and Dan are dealing with all that. If there is anything I could do? Anything at all. Any call I could make."

"It's fine. We'll be fine. Now, I see you're looking at a dress here. Let's take a look."

"Oh, yes." Tori turned to the mirror. "I really like it although it might be a touch too long. It fits nicely otherwise. What do you think?"

"Hmm, I like it on you," Vee said, reaching for a measuring tape and tailor's chalk. "Will you be in heels?"

"With something like this, three-inch beige or blue wedges maybe. It's for an outdoor wedding."

"How are we doing?" Ruth Ann asked, coming back to check on them.

"Good," Tori said. "Vee and I were just catching up."

"You two know each other?"

"Sure. Tori and I played soccer together," Vee replied. "For years and years, probably since we were what? Five or six."

"I suppose you two were in the same grade. Makes sense."

"It was just soccer for me though. Not gymnastics like you two," Tori said with a laugh. "I could never do all that tumbling and somersaulting you two did. You guys were amazing at that."

"She sure was," Ruth Ann said of Vee.

Vee smiled at the memory of those better days. "If I did a tumbling run now, I'd probably break something. As for this dress, Tori. You might want to take it up two inches, like this," she said, folding two inches under. "Just a little above the knee but showing plenty of those nice, toned legs. We can have the alterations made."

"Then I think we should," Tori said, knowing Vee would

make a little commission. That, and she really did like and want the dress. "I'll take it."

"Excellent," Vee said.

"You can finish up those dresses, Vee. I'll ring Tori up," Ruth Ann said.

"Oh my God, it was so good to see you," Tori said, reaching for Vee's hand. "We should get together when we have some more time."

"I'd like that."

"Say hi to Dan for me."

"I will."

"Say, did you know those from our graduating class are gathering in a few weeks at the Steamboat Bay Tap Room down the street? I mean Lizzy, Corinne, Mickey, Steak, that whole crew generally go. Everyone would love to see you and Dan."

"Oh, I don't know."

"I didn't either when I got back here," Tori said. "Now, I never miss it. A lot of people would be thrilled to see you guys. Just think about it."

"I will. Now, don't be a stranger."

Tori laughed. "Braddock would laugh because he knows I won't."

Tori walked to the checkout counter and when she reached it, Ruth Ann gestured to the flyer she had slipped under the glass top. It read: "Help for Sarah" on top, with a photo of a young girl in a wheelchair with two broken legs and a cast on her wrist.

"That's Vee's daughter," Ruth Ann whispered. "She was in a terrible car accident just after they moved back here. They didn't have health insurance at the time. She has a lot of medical expenses."

"Oh man," Tori said, sneaking a peek to the back of the store. Vee was hanging up dresses. She read the flyer. There was a web address for donations. Tori took a quick picture of it.

"If you could maybe make a donation?" Ruth Ann murmured hopefully. "I know it would help."

"Consider it done," Tori said. "And I'll spread the word."

"We'll have the dress back in about ten days or so."

"Sounds good."

Five minutes later she found Braddock sitting at the bar, a Whisky Old-Fashioned in front of him and a fresh one waiting for her.

"Ah, nectar of the Gods," she said, savoring the taste before leaning in to softly peck Braddock on the lips. "Hmm."

"Took you long enough," he said.

"Oh, I just ran into an old friend at the store. She's working there now. Which reminds me," she said, pulling out her phone. "I need to make a donation."

"Donation? For what?"

"That old high school friend I just mentioned." Tori explained who Vee and Dan were and what had happened to them and their daughter. "I played soccer with her for years. We started in kindergarten I think."

"She was a friend?"

"Oh yeah, a really good friend of me and Jessie. She was part of our big friendship group. Vee played soccer, but that was because we all did. What she was really great at was gymnastics. And her husband Dan was a state tournament wrestler. So, they were jocks and hung out with those of us who were in sports."

"You said they're back here now?"

"It sounds like they're in some financial distress. They had to move back here after Hurricane Ian. I didn't ask for details, but based on the tone of Ruth Ann's plea, it sounds like things are not good for them. And their daughter's accident. I just feel so bad for them."

"That's brutal," Braddock said as Tori tapped in her credit card number. "Two hundred dollars? That's pretty generous."

"You should have seen the photo of the little girl. She looked so... sad and she's Quinn's age. I thought about him, imagined him in that situation and I'd do damn near anything to help him. Anything. And so would you."

He reached for his phone. "I'll make a contribution too."

"Nah, you got the home expansion, I'll cover this," she said with a smile. "But I'm going to up it."

"Your generosity knows no bounds," he retorted as she changed the $200 to $500 and hit submit. Her donation went through.

"Feel better?"

"You know, I do feel a little better." She kept tapping at her phone. "And I'll feel even better after I send this text to my high school friend group text string." Tori's fingers flew over her phone screen. "There. Now about sixty more people know about it. That Help a Friend page is about to draw a big financial surge, I think. And I'll have Quinn look Sarah up at school in the fall."

"You're a good egg, Hunter."

"I try."

"Are you done now?"

"Yes."

"Good. How about you look at the menu. I'm starving."

Dan parked the Mazda and looked at The Goose, the bar and restaurant for the town of Garrison. Despite its prime location on Lake Mille Lacs and being located at a key state highway junction, the town itself only had a population of just over two hundred residents. Thus, The Goose was the only restaurant and bar in town, serving Garrison and everyone else along the west side of the massive lake.

It had been fourteen years since he'd last set foot inside. The last time he'd been here was intended to be a celebration. Instead, it had been an awful night no matter what he and Vee had ended up with. They left for Florida not long after.

He stood inside the vestibule and peered around. The place was about two-thirds full. All the seats along the bar were filled, along with others standing about. The tables and booths were scattered with diners and drinkers, going on past 9:00 p.m. on a weeknight. He made his way to the bar and ordered a tap beer. He took another look about when he saw them come strolling through the front door in fishing hats, T-shirts and blue jeans and make their way to a booth, sliding in and taking off their hats. After they'd been served their beers, he made his way over to the table.

Druk glanced in his direction as he approached, his eyes raising. "Dan Akton, as I live and breathe."

"Druk. Heath. Mind if I join you guys?"

"My first question," Druk said, "is what are you doing here?"

"It's a long story," Dan said, before taking a drink of his beer. "Hurricane Ian wiped us out." He went on to explain the last several months. "I'm looking a long way up just to get to zero. Honestly, I don't see how we'll ever get there. It'll take a very long time."

"That's a tough deal, man," Heath said. "We were only there the one time, but I really liked your place there right on the Gulf. Good food. Great view. Sorry to hear about all that."

"Yeah, so... we had to come back. No choice. We're trying to start over and now, get our daughter healthy."

"When you say we and us, I assume Vee?" Druk said. "You two are still together?"

"Yes," Dan said.

"What is she up to?"

"Tonight, she was working. She works at a clothing store in Manchester Bay, Fashion by Julia."

Heath turned to Druk; his eyes raised. "Fashion by Julia? Is that?"

"Right next door. What do you think?" Druk said.

"What?" Dan asked. "What are you two talking about?"

"She could be the unicorn. Do you think she could fit?" Heath said to Druk.

"Fit what? What are you two talking about?" Dan pressed.

Druk turned to Dan. "Is Vee in good shape physically? Still small, almost tiny, gymnast like? She seemed that way when we saw you two in Florida but that was, what? Six or seven years ago?"

"Uh, yeah, I suppose," Dan said. "She hasn't changed much. Same size, you know, Vee is tiny. Always has been. Why?"

"Look, Dan. You and Vee, Heath and I, I wouldn't say we're exactly friends, right?"

"We're not enemies," Dan replied.

"No, that's true and we've all kept our mouths shut for fourteen years. But now, you're suddenly here and you're in a financial hole."

Dan nodded.

"Are you here because you're looking for a way to start climbing out?"

Dan's eyebrows raised. "It sounds like you have something in mind."

"You saw them?" Vee asked.

"Yes."

"Where?"

"At The Goose."

"Not much has changed I see."

"Yeah, I know, but they weren't at the house so that seemed like the most likely place I would find them."

"And?"

"They have something for us."

"What?"

"They need you to do another Duluth."

EIGHT

"WE'RE NOT NOWHERE BUT WE'RE NOT CLOSE."

Tori rustled in the bed, flopping onto her back, breathing hard, the call, the conversation again. The same dream she'd been having for the past few weeks.

"That's a big ask."

"Is it?" Maggie replied.

"Why would I do that for you? After all you've—"

"Done. After all the people I killed. Tori, I'm not asking you to do it for me. I'm asking you to do it for Rob. He's a victim in all this. He did nothing wrong other than foolishly pursue me, fall in love with me, years ago."

"I don't know—"

"You and I are a lot alike, you know, Tori."

"Now hold on a second—"

"We're similar age. We both suffered loss of those we loved the most as teens to murder. One of us lost our sister and our sheriff father when they were a teenager and went on to become one of the most highly decorated women special agents in the history of the FBI. The other lost her father at nineteen to a Mafia hit and became a professional killer because she wanted revenge. An eye for an eye. Tori, you had your influences in your life. Cal Lund, good friends, Boston College, the FBI. I had mine. Angie DeEsposito. Tell me. Did you not want vengeance on the man who killed your sister?"

Tori burst awake and sat up, breathing hard, her body sweaty.

"Same dream?" Braddock asked sleepily.

She turned to see him looking up at her.

"The Maggie Duncan phone call dream again?"

She nodded. Maggie had stunned her with a phone call a few weeks ago from halfway across the world and said some things that resonated with Tori. The call had been tormenting her since.

"I suspected," he said calmly. "The way you were... sleep talking... your face was anguished. Was it the: 'You and I are a lot alike' part again?"

Tori nodded; her face buried in her hands.

He reached under her nightshirt and lightly scratched her back. "You're not, you know."

"Aren't we?" Tori replied. It was the very thought that they weren't that much different that gnawed at her, that was causing the repeated nightmares. "I can't help but think I could have been her. I was that angry. I was."

"But you didn't."

"But—"

"You are not Maggie Duncan. You weren't a Mob hitwoman who murdered more than twenty people. You didn't kill an FBI agent, even if you want to believe she did it in error. You didn't seduce and lie to Rob Duncan and his kids for a decade about who you were. And yeah, her father was murdered when she was a teenager and you lost Jessie when you were seventeen and your dad at nineteen. But those events don't make you alike."

"Doesn't it? Aren't we similar?"

"Only your experiences. You didn't turn out how you did

because you had people like Cal, and friends, and a support network around you. Hell, you ran from all that. You left it all behind to go to Boston College. You didn't come back here for twenty years, right?"

"Yes."

"You turned out how you did because of who you are, in there and there," Braddock said, patting her heart and then her head. He wrapped his long right arm around her, gently kissing her on the forehead. "You could have never been her. Not possible."

Tori fell into Braddock, in need of the embrace. Yet, while she appreciated his reassuring words, Maggie Duncan had asked a "what if" question she couldn't get loose of.

He kissed her head again. "It's almost six. Let's just get up." He stood and walked to the window and peered outside. "It's cloudy and looks a little cool and windy."

"Well, I'm not going out and swimming in that," Tori said. "It's Friday. It's been a long week. If we're exercising, we're running."

"Sounds fair."

The two of them put on their running clothes and ran a three-mile loop, first south along the shoulder of the county road and then back north on the road that took them back to the house. When they arrived home, they found a black Cadillac Escalade idling in the driveway.

Kyle Mannion.

When he saw them he stepped down from the SUV. "I'm sorry to barge in like—"

"You're not barging, Kyle," Tori said. "No, no, no, not at all."

"Come on inside," Braddock added.

Tori sat down with him at the kitchen table while Braddock poured them all cups of coffee. It had been five days since Kyle's daughter had been murdered. He clearly hadn't slept much given the bags under his eyes, the slowness of his gait and the weariness in his posture. She'd seen it before, the blank faraway look days after the tragedy. The hope that it was all just a bad dream from which they would awake. She'd seen it so many times over the years and knew the feeling all too well.

Boe had called or stopped by his house every day. Braddock and Tori had stopped by two days ago as well but had wanted to give him time and space. That and they didn't want to disappoint him and knew right now, they would.

Braddock set a cup of coffee down on the table. "You look hungry, Kyle. Let me make some breakfast."

Kyle didn't argue, he simply nodded. Tori led Kyle outside onto the deck, the two of them sipping their coffee, peering out to the water churning in the wind, white caps as far as the eye could see. For Tori, she always found the rhythm of the waves, the crash of the water into the shore to be soothing.

"Have you been up awhile?" she asked.

Kyle nodded, setting his cup on the deck railing. "I couldn't sleep. I left the house at two a.m. and just started driving."

"Where?"

He blew out a sigh. "You know... I'm not even sure. I just needed to get out of the house, get away, but you don't get away." He took a small sip of his coffee. "It's so..."

"I know," Tori said, reaching for his hand, clasping it gently.

"I've just been driving for hours. Nowhere in particular, just... driving." He glanced to Tori. "When you... God, I'm sorry, Tori. I didn't mean to—"

"It's okay."

"Didn't you ever just want to do that? To just try and escape it."

Kyle was transporting her back to the days after Jessie disappeared. He was trapped at home where every inch of the house was a reminder of Ally.

It had been the same for her. She was stuck in the house, trapped with all the photos of her family and just her sister's empty bedroom was asphyxiating, all hope lost, knowing Jessie was dead and gone, even though nobody could say it officially without a body. Friends were at the house in constant support, but in smothering her with support and love, no matter their good intentions, she was suffocating in it all. Their constant presence, the sympathetic looks, the hushed tones, their own sadness, only served to remind her of what had happened to bring them all there to begin with. And with Jessie not being found, there was no ability to plan a funeral, to lay her to rest, to get any measure of closure. It just went on and on.

The need to escape built. She just wanted to be off somewhere else, away from it all. It was, in a way, a foreshadowing of what her next twenty years were to be.

One day, a week after the disappearance, she did exactly what Kyle had. She took her father's pickup truck and drove west of town. She wasn't sure how far or for how long. At some point she turned off the highway onto a random gravel road. She had no idea what road it was. Even now, all she remembered about it was that the gravel road divided two endless soybean fields. Maybe a mile or two along she found a little area to pull off by a swampy pond. She parked, sat, eyes closed listening to nothing but the occasional bird calls, the croak of a frog from the soupy pond, the light gust of wind through the truck cab. In the distance, when she opened her eyes, she recalled watching the massive waterspouts from the crane like sprinklers in the farm field watering the soybeans. It was mindless and soothing to watch the cadence of it, one after another, the water cascading high in the air and then falling in a mist to the lush green field. She sat there for what seemed like hours until the sun began to fade. It was a respite, however brief, from all that had happened. It was what Kyle had been searching for in his drive.

"I do know how you feel," she said softly.

"I know you do," he said to her. "So, you also know why I found my way here."

Braddock stuck his head out. "Breakfast is ready."

He had made quick scrambled eggs, toast, and fruit, three plates on the table and a fresh pot of coffee. The three of them ate in silence, the only sound that of the forks scraping the ceramic of the plates, until Kyle spoke.

"You haven't come to see me. The reason is you're nowhere in the investigation on who killed Allison."

It wasn't an accusation. It was a cool, knowing assertion of the truth. They both imagined this was probably what it was like to work for Kyle. No superfluous verbiage. Right to the point.

Taking Kyle's cue, Tori didn't duck it. "We're not nowhere but we're not close."

"What do you know?"

"The only thing we think we know for sure is that the killers are these boat thieves we told you about. That's where we're focusing our investigation, those five prior thefts and on Sunday night."

"And you're where on that?"

"We're digging," Braddock said, before taking a quick drink of coffee.

"And there are some... threads to pull on there," Tori added.

"Like what?"

Tori looked to Braddock. Typically, they would leave it there but this was Kyle. Braddock nodded for her to continue.

"Two men. One killed Reed, one killed Ally. They didn't hesitate when they saw them at the boathouse. They didn't try to get away until after they—" she shook her head at the coldness of it even now "—until after they made sure there were no living witnesses. Now, that suggests to us that this was not the first time they've killed someone. They have a history of some kind. We're looking into that."

"We're looking at the boats, the cabins they were stolen from, the owners to see if there is a commonality of some kind.

"Today we're going down to the state prison in Oak Park Heights to press an inmate who can maybe plug us into who is moving the stolen boats," Braddock added. "Now, I don't care about the boats, Kyle. I only care about them in that they can lead us to the killers."

"There is all that and we have an idea of the kind of knives used," Tori noted.

"Which was what?"

"Fishing knives," Braddock said. "Four-to-five-inch blade with a serrated edge. Same or very similar knives were used on both. It looks like the blade for the knife I have in my tackle box."

"Do you think you'd ever find those knives? Be able to link them?"

"Highly unlikely," Tori said. "You can wipe them down, but blood residue lingers. But given how they killed those two kids, I can't imagine them holding on to the murder weapons."

"And it's probably a common or brand-name type of knife," Braddock noted, "but it paints a picture. It's someone who carries such a knife with them, probably with a holder on their belt. In fact, two someones."

"You're looking for two fishermen? Around here that doesn't really narrow it down," Kyle asserted.

"I said the same thing. Nevertheless, it's a piece," Tori said.

"That ain't much," Kyle said, shaking his head.

"No," Tori agreed. "But sometimes little pieces that seem like nothing, become something because of one more little piece. That's what Will and I are... holding on to. That, like in other cases we've worked and identified the killer or killers, we'll find that piece that breaks it. You have to hold on to that too."

"And trust that your friends..." Braddock's voice drifted away, his eyes closing, steadying himself. "Trust that your friends will do whatever it takes to find those responsible. I'm giving you my word on that."

"You can't promise me anything though."

"No," Tori said. "I've been in your shoes and what you need is the truth and that's what we've given and will give you."

Kyle nodded. "Is there anything I can do? Anything you need that I can get? Any call I can make? A marker I can call in? A lot of people owe me. I mean, I have to... do something with—"

"All that you have," Tori finished the thought.

"What good is all of it if..." His voice trailed away, his eyes moist. "If I couldn't protect her. If I can't..."

"Don't," Tori said, reaching for his hand. "None of this is your fault, or Ally's fault, or Reed's. It's the killers."

Kyle closed his eyes and nodded. "Are you going to find these guys?"

"The only promise Tori and I can make is that we'll do whatever we can to hunt these guys down."

With Kyle's visit, they didn't make it into the government center for their morning investigation check-in until 10:00 a.m.

"Where are we at on the cabin owners?" Braddock asked.

"Reese and I, as well as Steak and Eggleston, have reworked all the old scenes," Nolan replied. "I have assembled what we have by way of records, forensic reports, witness statements in the file here."

"Anything you are still waiting on?" Tori asked.

"I have search warrants here that need to be served on some service providers to get their service records. I don't anticipate any issues, but the business owners wanted the protection of the warrant before they turned the records over. Reese and I will be going around and picking them up today."

"What are we talking here?"

"Electrician records, dock and boatlift installation, plumbing, septic service, remodeling contractors as three of the cabins were remodeled in some fashion in the last year or so, four of the five have lawn services so they don't have to come up and spend time cutting the grass. We're still collecting some insurance records, banking, and mortgage information, and we're pulling records of anyone who serviced anything at the cabins, on the boats, from this year and last."

"Anyone consistent on all six?"

"Not yet," Nolan said.

"How about anything in re-interviewing the cabin owners. Anything you've gleaned from that?"

"Not that Eggs and I have been able to discern," Steak said. "Reese had the first go around. We thought Eggs and I should take the second run at it, a new perspective. We've shared notes with Reese. No discrepancies or changes in accounts thus far."

"We've heard nothing that has made us think we found anything new to work," Eggleston said. "It's all kind of the same. The boats were stolen not long after the weekend, late at night, following a break-in of the cabin. I don't know if it matters, but not only are the boats stolen from what we all would consider more weekend cabin type places, but they're also located amongst cabins that are weekend places."

"That means there is nobody around when the theft takes place," Steak said. "In the middle of summer, windows are open. A boat starting might draw some attention. These surf boats don't sound like a fishing boat or pontoon when they're started. They wanted nobody around. And nobody was supposed to be around last Sunday night."

"And forensics?"

"Nothing new," Reese said, handing Braddock a report on the fishing knife. "Other than confirmation that the detritus that Renfrow found in the wounds, what he thought were fish scales, were in fact that, scales for a walleye. I'm not sure that gets you anywhere other than your killers used the knives on fish recently. The images of the possible knife blade are included."

Reese then handed a file to Braddock. "This is the Wade Chew file. Warden Sills has you two set up at three p.m. to see this guy."

"CliffsNotes," Braddock said.

"He was prosecuted by Itasca County. He's in year four of a twelve-year prison stretch. He'll get supervised release at eight years, so basically four to go."

Braddock nodded and handed the file to Tori. "We're going down to see this guy. Keep pushing on the prior thefts. There has to be something in all of that." He glanced at his phone. "I need to check in with Boe."

"You know, this could all just be random," Steak said, sitting back in his chair. "I know nobody wants to hear that, but it just might be. Kyle Mannion's kid was in the wrong place at the wrong time. We might just have two douchebags driving around in a pickup truck looking for nice boats at cabins that they can get into quick, snap up the keys, and take the boat. You can take all week driving around to identify one and in the middle of the night, with absolutely nobody around, break in, take it and flip it for fifty, sixty grand cash and then start all over again finding a new one. And then when you're not thieving, you're out fishing for walleyes, hence the scales on the knife."

"It could be that," Braddock said. "You just want to conclude that now? You want to go tell Kyle Mannion that?"

"Well—"

"Hey, Kyle, sorry about your daughter, but it's just two random assholes and we can't find them."

"I'm not saying—"

"And if it is just two douchebags then the six of us ought to be able to find them or we're not very good at our fucking jobs!"

"Whoa, I know Kyle is a friend—"

"Goddamned right he is," Braddock charged. "So, I'm not

going to him with 'it's two random dudes with knives' after five days. Get your ass out there and fucking work it, Detective. Find me something. All of you."

Braddock stormed out of the room, leaving everyone speechless. Tori had never seen him go off on anyone like that. He was normally the calm one in the storm and it was Tori who was prone to outbursts. The room was quiet as she picked up the file from Reese and headed out. Steak chased her down.

"What the hell was all that?" Steak asked.

"You kind of stepped in it there, didn't you?"

"All I did was point out a reality."

"And your timing, as usual, was impeccable."

"Wha—"

"Kyle came to see us this morning at the house."

"Ah shit."

"You can imagine how that went. He was there for a couple of hours, and we didn't have any answers for him."

Steak sighed and nodded. "That's what you mean by... stepping in it. You know, one of you could have told me."

Tori sighed. "That might have been fairer. Look, I've been on your end of it from my bosses when I was with the Bureau. He's sending a message. You're his top investigator. His best friend even. If he'll come down on you like that—"

"He'll come down on anybody."

"And will," Tori said. "Look, I see the logic of your point, but I don't think we're dealing with just two random guys driving around, and come on, neither do you. These guys have a history. They are pros of a kind, the way they just up and killed those kids like that," she said, snapping her fingers. "Now, if they have done it before, when and where? Who? There's a record of it somewhere. A detective of means such as yourself might get his *fucking ass* out there and start working that angle."

Steak nodded. "What would parameters of that search look

like? Two guys, knives, that's awfully general, I'll end up with the phone book."

"Unsolved murders tied to burglaries. Two men unafraid of violence with knives as the weapon of choice, though probably not the only kind they'd use. They're operating in a prominent vacation area here, maybe that's a filter. They used a fishing knife here, maybe that fits somehow. They were stealing boats, maybe around here wasn't the first time. We have to start somewhere and sift."

"I'll get my fucking ass on it." He turned to walk back.

"Hey."

"Yeah?"

"You know he didn't mean anything by it."

Steak smiled and nodded. "It's nothing we won't work out over a few beers, that *he* buys."

NINE

"YOU DON'T HAVE THAT KIND OF JUICE."

"What did Boe want?" Tori asked as she snapped her seat belt.

"Same thing Kyle wanted. Same thing Reed Schafer's family wants. The same thing the mayor, the county commissioners, reporters, and everyone else leaving me and Boe messages wants. To know who was responsible for Ally and Reed's murders," Braddock muttered bitterly before turning on the radio to the Power Loon for some classic rock and jacking up the volume.

This was going to be one of *those* rides.

She knew it was best to leave him in his own thoughts for a while.

Tori took out the file on Wade Chew and spent an hour quietly digesting the investigation and then prosecution of his case. Finishing that and seeing that even behind his sunglasses Braddock had that faraway look, she took another hour and read through the case file. Most of it she had seen already but Reese and Nolan had updated it based on their follow-up work with the other victims of the boat thefts.

When they were driving through the midday traffic of the

Twin Cities, fifteen minutes from the prison, Braddock finally
piped up. "What's our plan here?"

"He speaks."

"Sorry, sorry," he said, shaking his head.

"You gave it to Steak pretty good."

He sighed. "I'll have to... rectify that and will—later. In the
meantime, you've had two hours of relative silence to digest the
file, Special Agent Hunter. Tell me what we know about this
Chew guy."

"Wade Chew is this guy." She held up a mugshot photo of
him with his thick black hair and bushy mustache. "He operated an auto repair service station and used car lot in Grand
Rapids. For several years local law enforcement suspected he
trafficked in stolen goods."

"I knew that much by name and reputation, after the fact.
How is it they came to that conclusion?"

"Initially, as far back as ten to twelve years, it was based
mostly on whispers and rumors. Chew was careful, at least
early on. The service station and used auto-lot were legitimate
and successful businesses. They're still operating, albeit under
new ownership. A cousin took it over."

"The cousin wasn't implicated?"

"Apparently not. He moved back here from Green Bay to
take it over. Best I can tell, Chew kept his fencing operation
from his family and employees. At least none were implicated."

"Itasca County and the Feds bought that?"

Tori nodded. "I can see how. Chew didn't necessarily do
anything to draw attention to himself. He lived a low-key lifestyle. He operated his legitimate businesses. Lived in a modest
house on a small lake. Never married. No children. No real
flash to his life."

"Yet there were rumors he was dirty. Eff'n Jones knew it."

"He's the kind of person someone like Jones would know,"

Tori replied. "In part because Jones took bets from him. We both know that Jones, for all his bluster, is careful about who he does business with and what he says about them. I don't think he takes money from people without knowing who and what they are and what they're mixed-up in."

"I would agree with that assessment."

"And what do you bet, someone came into The Outskirts and whispered to Jones, I have something I came across that I need to sell. Do you know anybody? And what do you bet that Chew on occasion made his way through The Outskirts, either for business or to place bets. Connection made."

Braddock smiled. "If it was someone Jones knew and trusted. He'd send him to someone he knew and—"

"Trusted," Tori finished. "That's why you and Steak talk to him. As for Chew, at first, he was moving small things. Jewelry, for example, electronics, some art. He was careful not to get out over his skis. He kept things small and only dealt with people he knew because it wasn't like he didn't know he might be under observation. From time to time, city and county investigators would show up, look around, sweat him some but there was never enough for a search warrant. Chew was always cooperative. Didn't otherwise cause any trouble. No history of violence or anything like that. And like I said, lived a generally quiet life. But you always see it."

"The money?"

"Yeah. You get a taste of that money, that tax-free easy money and you want more. It's like a narcotic. To get more you get a little bolder and bolder because if you do, the reward is greater and greater. And as it turns out, he had built himself a network to basically become a mover of a lot of stolen goods. And not just small stuff but bigger items. Merchandise from hijacking, for example."

"How?"

"His auto repair operation was of a good enough size that he had deliveries coming every day. Delivery vans, trucks and semi-tractor trailers were stopping all the time. Again, all for mostly legit business. But within one of those delivery chains was a semi that delivered auto parts that regularly crossed—"

"The Canadian border."

"Yes, going up to Winnipeg," Tori said. "The semi came across one day up in Pembina at the North Dakota/Canadian Border crossing when they had drug sniffing dogs and lo and behold the dogs caught a scent of something inside the trailer."

"Drugs. But Chew wasn't moving drugs, was he?"

"No. But this guy was someone who on occasion had moved stolen items for Chew across the border into Canada and then delivered payment."

"Courier for a fee."

"On the drugs, he wasn't hauling for Chew that trip. Nevertheless, he dropped Chew's name, and several others while being interrogated. Word of that was passed along to the Itasca County Sheriff's Department and with what they got from the Feds, they started a real investigation on him."

"And then what happened?"

"Turns out they had been looking in the wrong place. They discovered Chew also owned a chunk of land near Blackberry."

"Blackberry? Where is that?"

"Southeast of Grand Rapids. An unincorporated town. The acreage was way out in the woods. He'd bought it five years before the sheriff's department started paying him any attention. It was hunting land and it was used for that purpose, but covered from view deep in the woods was a house and a good-sized pole barn."

"And in the barn?"

"Stolen cars, trucks, and a few boats. And in the house, there was a safe that netted some previously stolen jewelry and small art pieces. And about a hundred thousand dollars in cash."

"Quite the operation."

"Chew started dropping names as well. But even with that, he ended up with twelve years."

"So maybe he'll deal. But you said boats? Not just the one Jones told us about?" Braddock said as he pulled into the parking lot at Minnesota State Prison – Stillwater.

"Indeed. There were two found inside, a fully-loaded Larsen fishing boat and then another newer wakesurfing boat, in addition to the one Jones mentioned to us," she added. "The circumstances of the theft of that boat were kind of interesting, and the other two boats found in his possession as well."

"Interesting?"

"The thefts are not dissimilar to ours. But there is something else here that seems to be... missing."

"Missing?"

Tori nodded. "Yeah. Where did the boats come from?"

"Hmpf. Let me have a look at that."

Kellin parked his truck and stepped inside the office, dropping off the paperwork for his morning stops and picked up his afternoon repair schedule. He went into the small lunchroom and took out his sack lunch and cracked open his Coke and started going through his afternoon services calls.

The bell for the front door rattled.

"Can I help you?" the owner's wife Joyce asked.

"Yes," a woman replied. "I'm from the sheriff's department."

He looked up and leaned a little to his right to see a woman in plain clothes, a bulge on her left hip for her gun, holding up a badge. "I'm Detective Nolan. We spoke earlier. I'm here to pick up the records we requested."

"Do you have the warrant?"

"Yes, ma'am."

The detective handed over the sheet to Joyce, who slipped on her reading glasses.

"Looks in order." Joyce reached under the reception counter. "Here are the copies. Now let me explain these bills and such. They cover a few years for these properties. Are these the only people affected?"

"No. I'm on my way to Ewald's as well."

Kellin stuffed his lunch back in his bag, grabbed his afternoon service slips and ducked out the back door and to his truck. There would need to be a detour in his afternoon route.

* * *

"Nice to see you two again, although I certainly wish it were under different circumstances," Prison Warden Earl Sills said as he greeted them. Sills had been helpful on a prior investigation, a murder spree involving two men and how the killings related to a dying prisoner.

"What can you tell us about Wade Chew?"

"Prisoner Chew has a twelve-year sentence for trafficking in stolen goods. He has done a hair over four and with good behavior, has a little under four years to go before he's out on supervised release for the last four."

"Any issues inside?"

"No more than any other prisoner," Sills said, handing over a file to Braddock. "He had a few run-ins early. Tests. There was an altercation, he got beat some."

"Who was his combatant?"

"He never said. Not a word. He hasn't had any issues of that ilk since."

"Proved himself then," Tori said. "Have you had reason to interact with him?"

"Here and there. He didn't drop dime on his own beating. But he's been willing to talk on the sly from time to time on some other things. He seems to be... observant."

"A deal here and there?"

Sills nodded. "He never names anyone directly, mind you. He more has suggestions on when and where to look at or for something. He's a networker, an angle player. It's gotten him an extra privilege or two, an accommodation here and there."

Tori grinned. "As I reviewed the case that landed him here, I got the impression that he was one of these guys who can suss out how things work and then find a way to slip in and benefit from it."

"I find that an accurate assessment."

"I'm thinking that if he has anything helpful, he'd be a willing dealer."

"If you're talking earlier release, I'd think for sure," Sills said and then stopped, retrieving his keys. "Here's our room. What's your play here? Do you think he really knows anything about your case?"

"Not sure," Tori replied. "But his name came up, albeit indirectly. He operated in a world we're looking to plug into. Like you said, maybe he can suggest *where* to look."

The interview room was a narrow and rectangular cinder block room painted a flat gray. Inside was a simple metal table and four padded chairs. Chew was sitting facing them, attired in his light-blue button-up prison shirt and navy-blue pants and bright-white tennis shoes. Braddock introduced Tori and himself after they'd taken seats at the table. "If you help us with something, maybe we could help you," Braddock said reasonably. "Win, win."

Chew shrugged in agreement. "What are you looking for help with?"

"The murders of two young kids," Tori replied, opening a folder, and placing photos of Reed and Ally on the table. The picture of Ally was particularly jarring, her neck sliced open, her dead eyes staring back at Chew.

"Whoa!" Chew blurted. "I never was involved in anything like this. Ever. I didn't kill nobody."

"As far as we know," Braddock charged.

"No. Nothing like this," Chew insisted. "No, no, no. Look, I got caught with my hand in the cookie jar on some stolen shit, but never anything like this. I'm no killer. No, sir. No, ma'am."

"A real humanitarian, then, huh? That's good to know."

"What happened to them? I mean I see they were... killed," Chew said, looking from Tori to Braddock. "And what's this have to do with me?"

"They were killed because they saw two men trying to steal a wakesurfing boat in the middle of the night."

"We're hoping you might be able to help us with that," Tori added. She and Braddock laid out the basics of the murder and boat thefts. "High-end boats. As you know, these new wakesurf boats go for $125 to $150,000 if not more, fully loaded, which these all were," Braddock said. "The two murders were in Shepard County. All these boats here were stolen in Shepard County. Someone is moving the stolen boats. We're looking for the who. You operated in that world. What can you tell us?"

"Shepard County? All of them?" Chew asked, examining the photographs.

"At least this year, yes."

"Here's what we're talking about." Tori stood up and laid out photos on the table of each of the boats and cabins. She observed Chew as he scanned the photos.

Huh.

Maybe it was the quick tilt of his head or perhaps the slightest almost imperceptible raising of his eyebrows that she caught.

Recognition.

Chew knew something, and his recognition was more than just a direction to steer them.

She slyly slid her eyes to Braddock, who met hers. He was slowly stroking his chin with the long fingers of his right hand, also closely observing. She knew that look too. He saw it as well. It had her thinking of what had been missing from the investigation of Chew and the stolen boat he'd sold and the other two found in his barn.

One thing about working with Braddock, they could read and play off one another without so much as a word. She raised her left eyebrow as if to say: *what do you think?*

Almost imperceptibly, Braddock nodded. *Take the shot.*

First, she had to lay some foundation.

"Tell us about the boat you sold to Ted McFadden," Tori said. "That's the one that got you caught right? The surf boat."

"It was a nice boat. Twenty-three-foot Malibu, black and white exterior with a dark-gray and black interior. It was a sharp one once I got done with it."

"What did you do to it?" Braddock said.

"Repainted it. Did some work on the interior, new flooring and then had the computer reprogrammed for the touch start. And put on a new Hull Identification Number, a plate over the one engraved in the transom." He made it sound so simple.

"How much did all that disguising of the boat cost you?"

Chew sat back, thought for a moment. "You know, probably six, maybe seven grand all in."

"Did you do all the work yourself?"

"Sure did, out in that barn that I'm sure that file tells you all about."

"Even the computer?"

Chew nodded.

"How do you do that?" Braddock asked, interested.

"Well, there's a few steps to it," Chew said as he sat forward and spent a few minutes explaining to Braddock how he reprogrammed the boat's computer to allow for a reset of the passcode for the touch screen start.

"And how old was the boat at the time?"

"Two years old as I recall."

"And you sold it for..." Braddock flipped through a couple of pages. "I know I saw it here."

"$78,500," Chew offered.

"And how did you get connected to McFadden?"

"He was referred to me by an acquaintance who told me he was looking for a boat. I just so happened to have such a boat. Simple as that."

"So, you had the boat when McFadden came calling?"

"Yes, sir."

"Then, Wade, that all begs the question," Tori started, sitting on the edge of the table, leaning in, "where did you get the boat from to begin with?"

Chew's eyes widened. "I... I... I... you know, I just don't recall."

Tori grinned evilly down at him. "Really, Wade. You just sat here and vividly remembered every single detail of how you remodeled that boat down to the colors and patterns, reset the computer, sold it to McFadden and the sale price. You remember every last bit of all that, but you don't remember where the boat came from?" She leaned in close, letting him get the slightest whiff of her perfume, and whispered, "Me thinks you're lying, Wade Chew."

She held his eyes for a moment until he looked down and away, afraid of her gaze. She turned to Braddock.

"Tori and I found it interesting that that important little nugget of information was nowhere to be found in the file," Braddock added. "Perhaps it was someone you wanted to protect. A good friend, family perhaps."

Chew squirmed in his seat.

"The investigators back then asked about it but they didn't press you on it," Braddock said. "They were more interested in the other more valuable items you'd moved back in the day and the people you moved them with. Us? We're interested in those boats."

"Wade," Tori said, leaning in. "The theft of that boat is not dissimilar to ours. Expensive boat from a more modest cabin. In your case four years ago, the boat was still on its trailer when it was stolen. Chopped off the deadbolt on the trailer latch and away they went. And I saw you, we both did, looking at those photos."

"You know something about this, Wade," Braddock asserted.

"I just see boats."

Tori laughed. "You see and know *waaaaaay* more than that. And now, because you didn't fess up then, people have died. Those two kids' deaths? You have responsibility now."

"You know, you could and should help yourself here," Braddock said. "We have some leeway on this one. We could make that supervised release come a whole lot sooner."

Chew scoffed. "You don't have that kind of juice."

Tori and Braddock shared a quick look.

"He doesn't?" Tori said, standing up, folding her arms, mock shocked. She looked to Braddock. "You don't?"

"I don't?" Braddock turned back to Chew. "Does the name Kyle Mannion mean anything to you?"

"Sure. Mannion Companies. That guy owns half of Shepard County. Hell, half the state at this point."

Braddock held up the photo of Ally and stuck it in Chew's face. "Well, dumbass, this is his *daughter*! I knew her. We both did. A beautiful, sweet, innocent girl mercilessly killed when she and her boyfriend accidentally stumbled onto these two men in the act of stealing a boat, a goddamned boat. Men *you* know."

"I don't know who these guys are."

"Mr. Mannion has a lot of friends, a lot of important friends. People who could go to bat for you on his request," Braddock continued, leaning into Chew. "If you help us out, we could get you out of here a lot sooner. Hell, I could get you out of here in the next week if the information proves good."

Chew shook his head. "I can't give you what I don't have."

The way he was shaking his head, squirming in his chair, avoiding eye contact with them, he was lying. Was he protecting someone or was he afraid of someone? Tori decided to pursue the fear angle. "You know. The flip side of all this can be true," she said, stepping back, folding her arms, and leaning against the wall.

"What's that?"

"Supervised release can be denied. Prison terms extended." She started looking around the room. "All kinds of bad things can happen... in a place like this."

"I mean it's a prison," Braddock added. "Go figure."

"That sounds an awful lot like a threat."

"Just an explanation of your reality, because she's right, you know something and you're not sharing."

"I got nothing more to say," Chew said, sitting back, folding his arms. "I'm done here. *Guard!*"

"I'm surprised," Sills said five minutes later as the three of them walked down the hallway. "At least based on what I know of him."

"Keep an eye on him," Braddock suggested. "He's protecting someone or he's afraid of someone."

"Or both could be true," Tori added.

Before Braddock had even backed out of the parking spot, Tori had Chew's and the investigation file open again.

"What are you hunting for?"

"If he's protecting someone, we have to figure out who because that person knows our killers."

TEN

"ARE YOU CLAIRVOYANT?"

The prison was an hour in the rearview mirror, although they weren't yet out of the Twin Cities. It was Friday night. Traffic from the cities up north to the cabins was bumper to bumper on Interstate 94, moving along slowly. The multitude of road construction projects didn't help either. They were still just crawling along as they reached the town of Monticello. "I'm starving. Let's stop off for a bite. By the time we get back on the highway, maybe the traffic will have loosened up," Braddock suggested.

"Not like I'm finding anything anyway."

The Monti Diner was busy enough on a Friday night, but they were quickly seated in a booth.

"I'd love a beer," Braddock muttered. "God, I'd love a beer."

"Me too. We're still working."

"Killjoy."

The server stopped and they both ordered sodas and dinner. Tori raised her eyebrows when Braddock ordered a salad. "Really?"

"It's still the steak salad, but, as you often say, we get into these cases and start eating like crap and these days, it goes right to my waist."

"Still seem pretty trim to me," Tori replied with a sly smile, before her lips slowly closed around her straw, her eyes looking up at him.

"Hmm. Perhaps you'd like to confirm that assessment later."

Tori smiled. "If you'll open a bottle of wine and rub my back, I could find myself... slipping into the mood."

Braddock smiled as the waitress returned with their meals, his salad, and her Buffalo Chicken Wrap. They shared in each other's plates, eating, relaxing a bit.

"Okay, so what do we know from today?" Braddock finally said, taking a drink of his Diet Coke. "Chew knows something."

"I'm certain of it."

"But he's not sharing. Why?"

"Well, you basically offered to get him out of prison four years early and he took a pass. That suggests to me he is unlikely to ever share. It's worth it to him to do the time."

Braddock nodded. "So who would have that kind of loyalty—"

"Or fear."

"Or fear, for?"

"Loyalty would be the obvious, good friends, or family. Fear would be for the guys that killed Ally and Reed."

"Do we really think Chew knew who they were?"

Tori pondered the question for a moment, chomping on an ice cube. "Chew sees something that strikes him. Maybe it's the boats and the method. Take our murderers and the boats they were stealing. Now, these guys could be stealing the boats and just selling them outright, or—"

"There is a middleman like Chew in the mix."

Tori's eyes lit up. "And what do you want to bet, that guy was in the mix before. Hence Chew's recognition. Hence the reason he won't give up who he got the boat from. Who is that?"

"Let's find out," Braddock said and he waved down the server and paid the bill. By the time they got on the highway the traffic had thinned with the setting sun.

Tori had the file for the Chew investigation open again and confirmed what she'd thought in the restaurant. The Itasca County Investigation, despite all the names and property recovered and testimony that Chew provided about all the stolen property he'd moved through his auto repair shop and barn and who he sold the property to, there was nothing after Chew. "Chew provided a lot of names it seemed, but really, all he did was just confirm what they already knew. He helped solidify other cases but he didn't give them anyone they didn't already have. And what would he have had to give that he didn't want to?" She took out her phone.

"Who are you calling?"

"Reese."

"It's Friday night," Braddock protested.

Tori just smiled back at him and had the phone on speaker.

"Tori?" Reese answered warily.

"Where are you?"

"Uhh... Well, I'm on a... date."

"You are?"

"Don't sound so surprised," Reese fired back though he was laughing.

"Is she sitting right there?"

"No. I'm at the bar getting us drinks."

"Is it a first date?"

"Yes."

"Is it going good?"

"It's early yet, but yeah, it seems to be."

"Are you thinking you want a second date then?"

"What do you need, Tori?"

"Braddock and I are driving back from the state prison, and we just had an inspiration and I thought if you were still at the

office or close by you could check something for us but you're
not. It can wait."

"Call Steak or Nolan," Reese said. "They're both still
there."

"They are?"

"Steak's been digging into something all day long. Nolan
said she'd stay late to help him. She wanted the overtime."

"Steak? All day?" Braddock said.

"You motivated him," Tori said as she called Steak, who
answered on the first ring. She didn't let him even say hello.
"Are you still at the office?"

"Uh... yeah."

"Is Nolan with you?"

"I'm right here," Nolan replied over speaker. "What's up?"

"Wade Chew. Everything we can find on his background."
She gave them a rundown of their day and their theory. "I'm
particularly interested in his family history and if there is
anyone else with a record, or who has drawn the interest of the
law."

* * *

Druk slowly drove by the house. It was dark inside, no lights on.
"What time did we say we were meeting him?"

"Ten thirty," Heath said, fiddling with his stocking cap.

"What time do you figure he leaves then?"

"From here? I'd guess ten past ten or so if he was going to be
right on time. Make it ten to be safe."

"That doesn't leave him much time to get home and out
again." Druk kept driving and drove around the block to find
another house set back in dense woods, the lights out, no vehicles in the driveway. He pulled into the driveway, backed out
and then parked along the side of the road just past the driveway. The driveway for a house on the opposite side of the road

was another ten feet ahead. If anyone drove by they might think
the truck could be parked for either house.

"I can't see his house anymore," Heath said.

"Didn't think we would be able to through the woods. We'll
have to hoof it and wait."

* * *

Now that was interesting.

"Hmm," Tori murmured.

"What?" Braddock asked.

Tori looked up from the Chew file. It was dark out now, just
taillights visible ahead. "Where are we?"

"A few miles south of Manchester Bay. You murmured.
What is it?"

"Joyner's Dock Install and Repair."

"What about them?"

"Isn't that who you use for your dock?"

"Yes. So?"

"Four of the six boat owners used them too."

"Not a shock. They have a big chunk of the market. Them
and Ewald's."

"Are they the only two."

"They're easily the biggest players I'd say."

Tori slumped in disappointment when her phone screen lit
up. Steak was calling. She answered on speakerphone and
immediately mentioned what she'd noticed for dock repair and
install providers.

"Are you clairvoyant?"

"Uh... you tell me."

"First, Chew. We did his family history. He's never been
married, no children, but has two sisters who provided him with
four nieces and one nephew, Dennis Kellin. Kellin worked for
him at his auto repair and used car dealership. He was selling

cars for him back then. Now fast forward three years. He moved to Pequot Lakes from Grand Rapids. He took a job at Ewald's last year. And this year—"

"Joyner's."

"Correct," Nolan said. "I picked up the service records from both places today. He did the dock install at four of our houses this year and the other two, he took the docks out of the lake in late September. I checked with both boat owners and those boats were on their trailers, sitting in their driveways still when the crew came to remove the docks. And there's one more thing."

"What?"

"Julie Taylor. Remember her? Ally Mannion's friend whose parents owned the cabin. She told me about a man she'd seen maybe a month or more before. He was putting tools in the back of the van parked behind the Wallaces' cabin. He gave her a long look and then she saw him again a week later at a bar in Deerwood. Same guy. He was described as dark haired, bearded, a little awkward. He tried to small talk her for a bit. It was awkward enough that she got away from him, but that was it."

She was leading somewhere. "It was Kellin?"

"I think so," Nolan said. "I just talked to Julie Taylor and sent her a DMV photo. She thought it looked like him. We're getting a feeling here. Kellin suddenly checks a lot of boxes."

Tori looked to Braddock. "We have to talk to him."

"And right now," he replied. "We need an address."

Steak recited the address and Tori punched it in as they drove past what would normally be their exit.

"We're on our way up there right now," Braddock reported.

"Then so are we."

* * *

Druk reached the edge of the dense tree line, Heath to his right, the house maybe forty feet ahead of them, set back on the heavily treed lot, a smallish backyard perhaps fifty feet deep cut out and grassed.

They stayed back ten feet into the woods, observing the house. Druk checked his watch. It was 9:35 p.m. He was cutting it close.

"You think he just went right to the bar?"

"That's possible. He said he was going to his softball game right from work. The game was at quarter to eight, but who knows if it started on time. After working all day and a game, I figure he'll stop here first. If not, we meet him at the bar."

A flash of light appeared to their right. It was a set of headlights illuminating the road in front of the one-story rambler-style house. A moment later a pickup truck turned into the driveway and roared up it before parking in front of the garage. They saw him get out, keys in hand, and unlock the side door into the house. Inside, lights came on and through the gap in the curtains they saw him in the kitchen. He opened the refrigerator door and took out a bottle of beer, twisted off the cap and then walked out of view. The next thing they saw was a light come on and then a few seconds later, another. On one of the windows, a shade was pulled down, except for a few inches crack at the bottom. The window was lifted up. A body walked into the room, looked to open a door and then they heard it.

"The shower?" Heath whispered.

Druk nodded and observed as the body opened the shower door and stepped inside. He'd had one idea but now another one was forming in his mind.

* * *

"Watch? What time is it?" It was 10:09 p.m.

Gotta hustle.

He slipped on his wristwatch and set the clasp, then quickly pulled on his shorts, T-shirt, and a light hoodie. Grabbing his half-drunk beer he made for the kitchen, his sandals right by the back door.

The kitchen light was off.

That's odd, I know I turned it on.

He sensed the movement to the right and flinched.

Too late.

In a blur, a rope was around his neck, a knee in his back.

He dropped his beer and instinctively he reached for the rope as he felt the cords dig into the skin of his neck, crushing his windpipe.

Then another man charged from the kitchen with a knife.

With his hands fighting the rope, he leaned back and kicked the attacker with both legs, catching him in the chest, feeling the blade of the knife cut into the skin of his right leg.

The force of the kick pushed him and the man with the rope around his neck back into the wall.

* * *

The impact of the kick to Druk's chest hurled him back and over a chair, the knife flying out of his hand. He looked up to see Kellin and Heath crash into the wall. Heath had the rope around Kellin's neck, but Kellin was a strong, wiry guy and was fighting, trying to croak out a scream.

Druk searched around on the floor for the knife.

"Ahrg!" Heath groaned trying to control Kellin as they wrestled, crashing into the walls, knocking over a table. "Get the fucking knife."

On all fours, Druk frantically searched for it and saw it under a sitting chair. He dove for it, grabbing it.

Crash!

Spinning around he saw Heath and Kellin crashing into and shattering the glass of a grandfather clock.

Oh shit!

Heath lost his footing. Kellin pushed him backwards over the couch and onto the coffee table, crushing it, the glass shattering, Kellin landing on top.

Heath lost the rope with his right hand.

"Help—"

Heath wrapped his right arm around Kellin's neck and clasped his left-hand over his mouth just as Druk plunged the knife into Kellin's abdomen.

Kellin convulsed as Druk kept driving the knife in, twisting it, his eyes fixed with Heath's until after another minute they both felt Kellin's body finally go limp.

Druk retracted the knife. Heath pushed Kellin off him and rolled to his right, breathing heavy. "Fuck."

"Dammit," Druk muttered before leaning over and grabbing Kellin's forehead to steady him and slicing his throat. "Have to be sure."

"He's dead," Heath said, breathing hard, sitting on the floor, resting back on his hands. "Put up a big fight though."

"We need to get the fuck out of here," Druk said, quickly wiping the knife on Kellin's T-shirt. "That made some noise."

Druk led Heath out the back door and they made for the backyard. As they ducked into the tree line he caught a flash of bright light to their right.

* * *

Braddock turned left off the H-4, across the frontage road that ran parallel to the H-4 providing access to businesses, over a set of now unused railroad tracks into a residential neighborhood, and then turning left again driving south two blocks, Steak now pulling up right behind. Their only option ahead was a right turn.

"The road then dead ends, doesn't it?"

"Yes," Tori directed. "Kellin's house is the second house, up on the right a bit."

The second house was well ahead on the right. "Big, wooded lots."

"Some people like their space, their privacy."

They approached the one-story house, the windows darkened, but a newish black pickup truck was parked in the driveway. Braddock pulled up behind the truck. As he got out, he turned around to see Steak and Nolan disembarking from Steak's Department Explorer.

"Psst. Will!" Tori whispered and nodded toward the house. "The back door. Does that look right to you?"

Braddock turned. Tori had pulled out her gun. He checked the back door. Two doors were open, the exterior screen door and interior storm door. Something was up.

He turned and held up his left hand and Steak and Nolan both froze and noticed Tori approaching the back door with her gun out.

Tori moved to the back step and to the left of the door and carefully peeked around the corner. A grandfather clock was lying sideways on the floor, the glass shattered. She saw a beer bottle lying on its side and a chair tipped upside down. She looked to Braddock who had his flashlight out and aimed the beam inside, his hands crossed, and moved in quickly. "Police!"

They were both inside ten feet when they saw a man lying in the middle of the living room floor, the shattered glass and crushed legs of the coffee table lying underneath him.

Tori rushed to the body and recognized immediately it was Dennis Kellin. He was lying in a pool of blood, stabbed multiple times, his throat slit. "His body is still warm. Very warm."

Braddock kneeled by a beer bottle and the wet spot on the carpet. "The beer is ice cold."

"This just happened," Tori said, standing up. "I mean *just* happened."

Steak was peering inside, scanning with his flashlight. "Geez." He started calling it in. "Dispatch—"

"What was that?" Nolan said before running off to the backyard.

"What is it?" Braddock called as he rushed out after her.

Tori was right behind them.

Nolan was walking the back tree line, scanning with her flashlight. "I heard something."

"I hear it too," Steak said, moving to the back right corner, zeroing in with his flashlight. "I think I... saw someone."

Thump!

"That was a door slam."

Steak and Nolan ran into the woods.

Tori started after them.

"No. With me!" Braddock ran for the Tahoe, the radio to his mouth. "Steak, talk to me."

* * *

Steak weaved his way through the woods, hurdling the underbrush. Nolan was to his left, their flashlight beams bouncing off the trees and leaves.

"Steak, talk to me!" Braddock's voice called over the radio.

Vroom!

That was a truck engine roaring to life as they emerged into the backyard of another house. "Will, an engine started. A vehicle is pulling away."

"To the east! To the east!" Nolan exclaimed.

The two of them ran around the east side of the house, down the driveway to the road and looked to the right.

"Will. I see taillights east," Steak reported. "It looks like a pickup truck."

The truck turned left.

"Red maybe!" Nolan yelled.

* * *

Braddock zoomed down the street.

"Red pickup truck, Will! Red, maybe burgundy but that kind of tint," came Steak's voice.

"Did you get a make or model?" Tori asked, having taken the radio while Braddock drove.

"Negative. Pickup truck is all we got a glimpse of."

Braddock turned hard left, his backend fishtailing and then flipped on his police lights. "I don't see anything!"

"The H-4," Tori said. "They're going for the H-4."

Braddock turned right and accelerated, crossing the frontage road, and jolting over a hump before turning hard right onto the H-4 and pressing south.

"You see anything?"

"No. Not yet," Tori replied, sitting forward in her seat. Braddock roaring south on the highway. "Where are the—" She glimpsed a flash of light to the right and looked out the passenger window. There was a red pickup truck in the distance, on the frontage road, angling away from them. "The frontage road. They might be on the frontage road."

"Steak, where are you?"

"Just got into the Explorer."

"They're on the frontage road that runs parallel to south-bound H-4."

"They're turning west. West!" Tori exclaimed. "They're heading west!"

* * *

"They're on the H-4. Coming up on the left!" Heath exclaimed.

Druk snuck a peek over his left shoulder and saw the flashing police lights. "We're good. They're out there."

"Not necessarily. They're not alone. They've called it in by now."

He looked ahead. There were two options, veer left and stay on the frontage road or take it to the right and out into the countryside. He veered right and pushed the gas pedal to the floor and drove out into the darkness of the dense forests west of Pequot Lakes.

"We should get off this road," Heath suggested, looking back. "This one stays straight for a few miles yet."

Druk slowed and took a left onto a narrow county road that he knew wound its way south.

* * *

"Steak, anything?"

"We got nothing, Will. I'm four miles west of Pequot Lakes and I have nothing ahead of me. They could have turned off any number of places."

"Heck, we don't even know if that was them," Tori muttered. "What do we put out? Red pickup truck? Only thousands of those in this county."

Braddock pounded the steering wheel. "Dammit."

ELEVEN

"A CLEANER CONSCIENCE."

Tori sat on the driveway, her knees up and her back against the driver's side passenger door of the Tahoe, a half-drunk bottle of soda dangling in the fingers of her right hand. Braddock was to her left, standing against the Tahoe, drinking a gas station coffee. Together, they surveyed the beehive of activity in and around Kellin's house.

The medical examiner and forensic team were onsite as well as what seemed to be half of the county's sheriff's department. Steak, Nolan and now Eggleston were out knocking on neighbor's doors. Thus far nobody had seen anything though one neighbor down the street said he was sitting out on his back deck, smoking a cigar and drinking a beer when he heard a crash. He said it sounded like breaking glass, but he didn't really think anything of it until he heard the sirens blaring a couple of minutes later. Braddock suspected that was either the sound of the glass coffee table shattering or the grandfather clock crashing to the floor during what was an obvious struggle.

Boe arrived on scene, took a quick peek inside the house before returning to them. "And this guy was who?" she asked Braddock.

"Dennis Kellin. He worked dock installation, repair and removal for Ewald's and Joyner's. They were the two companies that had the dock work for the six houses. We figure he worked the docks at the cabins where the boats were stolen from, and no doubt hundreds of others."

"He worked for Ewald's last season," Tori added, looking up. "The first two boats were from cabins he serviced while working for them last fall. He moved to Joyner's this season. Same job and the next four boats were stolen from cabins where he put in the docks and lifts."

"He was the scout. We figure he used the job as cover to identify the boats," Braddock continued. "He does the installation. Maybe he talks to the owners inside the cabin, or outside. While he's doing all that, he'd evaluate for boats and cabins that fit the profile."

Boe nodded along. "Then he what? Hires out the burglary or was he one of the killers of Ally and Reed?"

"Don't know yet," Braddock replied with a sigh before finishing the rest of his gas station coffee and crushing the Styrofoam cup. "We just got onto his name tonight on our way back from the state prison. We were coming up here to question him and then we find... this. Shit, fifteen minutes earlier he may still be alive and giving us answers. Four or five minutes earlier we'd have gotten here in the middle of it all."

"Who got to him first?" Boe surmised. "His uncle? Seems the most obvious choice."

"I just don't think that makes sense," Tori replied.

"Why not?"

"If he was willing to do this to him, he'd have given him up to us today to get out of prison four years early," Tori said as Braddock pulled her up. "He'd have given him up four years ago to reduce his sentence. He confirmed lots of names back then but there was not one utterance of Dennis Kellin. Not. A. One.

And back then he never said where he got the stolen boats from."

"He got them from Kellin," Boe replied now, seeing it. "He was protecting him."

"I'd have thought that after our little visit today, Chew may have tried to warn him," Braddock said. "And maybe he was trying to but didn't have time. Perhaps now that his nephew is dead, maybe Chew will be more talkative, especially if he knows who may have killed his nephew."

"*If* he was involved back then?" Boe questioned.

"He was," Tori said. "Otherwise, why protect him? Otherwise, why is he lying in there dead. It looks like he was strangled, stabbed, and then had his throat cut. A trifecta of bad ways to go."

"It begs another question, however," Braddock said. "If his uncle didn't set him up, how did whoever killed him tonight know it needed doing?"

"The answer lies with Chew."

"Back so soon?" Chew asked lightly when Tori and Braddock entered the interrogation room. This time there was a lawyer present. "You two look tired."

The wiseass bit was poorly timed, though he wasn't wrong. They had grabbed a couple of hours of sleep before making the speed run back down to Stillwater. The last day had left them exhausted and in owly moods. Thus, it was without preamble that Braddock placed photos of a dead Dennis Kellin in front of Chew.

Was he a friend or foe yet? It was time to suss him out.

"A little of your handiwork, Wade?" Tori charged.

She observed as the expression washed across Chew's face. It was one first of shock and then his eyes closed in sadness. He had not killed his nephew. Their sense he'd been protecting him was the right one.

"Oh, Denny." Chew sighed and closed his eyes. "When?"

"Last night," Braddock replied. "About five minutes before we arrived at his house in Pequot Lakes. We were on our way there from here."

"He was your source for the boats four years ago, wasn't he?" Tori said.

"Now hold on a second here—" the lawyer interjected. "If my client has information, what does he get in return?"

"A cleaner conscience," said Tori.

"The deal was better yesterday, but I'm still willing to put in a word," Braddock said. "If you got something, let's hear it."

"Not until I know what it's worth to my client," the lawyer retorted.

"I had valuable information yesterday and I didn't offer it," Chew said to his lawyer.

"Wade—"

Chew held his hand up to his lawyer and looked to Tori. "Yesterday, I had a name."

"Now you don't?" Tori said.

Chew shook his head. "No."

"What do you know?"

"Denny brought those boats to me. I asked him where he got them, and he told me he knew two guys who could steal just about anything."

"Two guys?"

"Yes."

"No names though?"

"Denny never said, and I didn't press him on it. In this line of work, the less you know, sometimes the better although God, right now I wish I knew. I would tell you."

Tori nodded. "Yesterday, I thought you recognized something in the photos we showed you. It looked familiar to you."

Chew nodded. "It looked like what Denny and these two guys were doing up in Grand Rapids. The kinds of cabins and boats. The going in on the prowl. That was what these two guys did. Denny didn't know shit about breaking and entering. He was the facilitator. Denny knew how to move the boats and make some good money, and everyone made out okay."

"Did Denny ever say these guys were violent?"

Chew grimaced and nodded. "I should have warned him after you came here yesterday. I should have called him. I thought about it, but I figured if I called him from here, the call would be monitored, and I'd just be setting him up. I figured you'd have an eye on me once you left. I was thinking on a way to get word out and now, here you are."

"They were violent?"

"Denny said these guys were... heavy. He said we could never jack them around on the money. 'You don't fuck with them, Uncle Wade' was what he said, and I knew what the tone of how he said it meant. God, I should have... done something."

"How did Denny know them?"

"I don't really know."

"Were they in Grand Rapids?"

Chew sat back and thought for a moment. "I think they were in the area. It wasn't like they were from out of town."

"Ever lay eyes on them?"

"No."

"Were they fishermen?" Braddock inquired.

Chew looked at him quizzically. "I... have no idea. I don't think Denny ever said. Why?"

"Just some evidence we have suggests they're fishermen."

"Them and two million more around here."

They had ridden quietly, and Tori had dozed off for a spell after they left the prison. She'd stirred awake to see the farm fields flowing by and knew they were somewhere just south of Manchester Bay. She stretched. "How long was I out?"

"An hour, maybe a hair more," Braddock replied from behind his sunglasses. "I noticed you were napping when we went through St. Cloud."

"Sorry." She rubbed her eyes and shook her head awake. "Kind of selfish of me to sleep when you can't."

Braddock scoffed. "No worries."

She stretched her arms and gestured ahead on the right. "What do we have there?" Two massive yellow Caterpillar earth movers were creating a wide path into a grove of dense trees. As they came closer, she could see several dump trucks and a large temporary sign. "Greyler Lake Meadows?"

"A new housing development," Braddock said. "Greyler Creek winds through there and feeds Greyler Lake, which doesn't have much on it but in a few years, apparently will."

"If memory serves, isn't that all kind of slews and ponds and stuff out there?"

"Yeah, I think so. My guess is they'll reshape all that, drain some, create others. They're building a golf course and then houses and townhouses around it. A planned community."

"Do we really need another golf course around here?" All the major resorts around the Northern Pine Lake Chain had multiple championship golf courses.

"Sure, why not," Braddock said with a sly smile. He'd taken up golf recently. "It'll be more of a course for the locals. It won't be attached to the resorts. My guess is the rates will be a bit more reasonable."

"Man, it amazes me how this area keeps expanding."

"Mannion Companies and the university," Braddock said. "They both just keep growing."

"Sure do," Tori said. "The university alone, the profile just keeps growing and expanding. I heard talk of adding a medical or law school."

"I'd prefer medical. Too many lawyers in the world."

"Amen to that," Tori said, lightly running her left hand down Braddock's arm. "What did you do while I napped?"

"I spent some time thinking."

"About?"

"Kellin identified the targets. These two guys would go in and steal it. Kellin would fence it and they all made out like bandits."

"Except now, these two don't have Kellin."

Braddock snorted a laugh. "They'll find someone else, or as Chew said his nephew said, these two could steal anything. Guys like that always have something else cooking, and other people they can access. They don't just go away."

"So where does that leave us?"

"Two things. First, you've been proven right. These two didn't just start now. They have a history and Kellin told his uncle they were heavy. That means Kellin knew they'd maybe killed before or at least were prone to some violence. That gives us a little more to work with."

"You said two things."

"The second is sleep. I need some. So do you. And Quinn gets home tonight. And—"

"Tracy and Sam arrive tomorrow. We were supposed to take the week off you know." She had been looking forward to her best friend's visit for weeks and had planned not to be working.

"You are," Braddock said.

"But what about the case?"

"The case is my responsibility. It's Boe's, Steak's and the rest of the team's responsibility. And if we get a break, you can jump back in. Your best friend is going to be here for a week. You're going to enjoy it. And so am I. I'm looking forward to it. You're benched."

"Okay." Tori smiled. "We go home and grab a nap. But on Kellin?"

"While you snoozed, I called Steak. He and the crew have been working on him all day. They've been at the crime scene at his house and digging into more of his history."

"Have they found anything yet?"

"Not yet, but it might be a few days before we have a fuller picture on him. So far what Steak has is he lived in Pequot Lakes for the last year after moving down from Grand Rapids. Up there is where most of his history is."

"No employment in Grand Rapids?" Tori said.

"He'd been in used car sales but his tie to his uncle made it hard to get a new gig. He went unemployed much of the last few years until he went to work at Ewald's and then moved to Joyner's. It's dock installation. The pay isn't great. So the companies take the guys they can get."

She scoffed a laugh. "I don't imagine the work was great, but it was a paycheck."

"Probably not a good one, which was why he was doing what he was doing," Braddock concluded. "Reese and Eggleston are running down his employment with both companies, co-workers, the usual, see what pops."

"I may be off for the week but that's the stuff I want to see while I'm out. Anything on Kellin. Every day, I want to see what they come up with."

"Every day?"

"Every day."

TWELVE

"THAT WAS COMICAL HYPERBOLE."

It was a warm and crowded Wednesday afternoon along Lake Drive. The Fourth of July had been yesterday but with it being a holiday week, the public beach was packed, the food trucks were still going strong and everyone along the shopping district was having holiday week sales. For Tori and Tracy, shopping was in order. They'd worked the north side of the street and were now sitting on a bench overlooking the beach, eating corn dogs from the Wheeled Dog food truck.

"So, is Manchester Bay what you expected?" Tori asked Tracy. They each had a full shopping bag.

"Yes and no," Tracy Sheets replied. "It's a little bigger than I imagined."

Tori laughed. "You actually thought I was living in the Yukon Territory, didn't you?" she said, calling back to a conversation they'd had in Chicago.

"That was comical hyperbole," Tracy said with a dismissive wave. She took a bite of her corn dog. "No, what I figured was that you were living in vacation land. Like the Catskills. But this is more than a quaint little vacation town. It's scenic and serene, and fun, the lakes and sunsets are stunningly beautiful, but the town itself looks like it's on its way to being a small city. And what a setting for one," she said, waving her arm around. "The lake, this main street, the university in the trees up the hill over there. And your home? It's just comfortable. It suits you and Braddock and who you both are. And that lake view? I could wake up to that every day."

Tracy had in fact been up every morning, sitting on the deck or out on the Adirondack chairs at the end of the dock with a cup of coffee, enjoying the peace and serenity of the water. "In New York, you just can't find that. I mean I can walk a few blocks over and look at the East River but... it's still the East River."

"In the middle of winter, you might think differently," Tori said. "When it's minus ten degrees. Winds howling and it takes five layers of clothes to keep the cold out and you have to walk around like the Michelin Man."

"Winter gets cold in New York too. That I can handle. Summer in the city is getting taxing, Tor. It's been sweltering in Brooklyn and the worst is yet to come. Sam and I need something like this to get away too." She sipped her soda. "That bay out there, it's on your lake, right?"

"Yes. We were in it last night when we took the boat for dinner at Mannions. You can kind of see the restaurant from here. If you look out in the distance you can see the long white stairs leading down to the boat docks."

"Ah, I see it. Your chain of lakes is beautiful. And some of the homes on it are stunning, that Scottish one?"

"Oh, now that one is my favorite," Tori said. "There is nothing else like it on the lake or any lake around here. I'd love to get in there for a look-see sometime."

"And you have all these little shops and boutiques and we drove by that corporate campus for—"

"The Mannion Companies," Tori said. "Same owners as the restaurant last night."

"Ahh." Tracy turned somber. "The funeral you and Braddock have on Friday. Their daughter."

"Yes."

They had discussed the Ally Mannion investigation in general terms.

"I assume that's the folder you've been reviewing in the mornings. The calls with... Steak? That's gotta be a nickname, right?"

"Yes. Steak is Jake Williams. He works for Braddock and is one of my oldest friends. I grew up with him."

"Anything new?"

"A thing or two that I want to dig into—next week." Tori's eyes brightened. "Hey, Vee! Over here." She waved. "Over here!"

"Who's that?"

"A good friend."

Vee waved back and came walking over, Dan with her.

"Hey," Tori said, standing up, giving Dan a warm hug. "Danno, it's been like forever."

"Tori, good to see you."

"Oh, my manners," Tori said, turning to Tracy. "This is a very good friend of mine from New York City, Tracy Sheets. Trace, this is Vee and Dan Akton, lifelong friends of mine."

"Vee?" Tracy said, shaking her hand. "There's a story there, right. I just learned the one behind Steak."

Vee smiled. "It's a long one. Vee is for Veronica, but I've always been called Vee by my friends and family since I was a little girl. Some might say I still am."

"I don't think you're short," Tori said.

"That's because you are too," Vee replied. "Tori said you're here from New York City?"

"Yes. My husband and I, a little vacation at Tori and Braddock's *massive* lake compound."

Tori rolled her eyes. "Massive. Right."

"What? It's beautiful," Tracy complimented. "Anyway, Tori and I worked together for years with the FBI. I'm still there. She couldn't hack it and moved back here to paradise."

"Yeah, yeah," Tori said. "When are you leaving again?"

"Oh, I'm staying *all* summer," Tracy retorted with a smile.

"What are you two up to?" Tori asked Vee.

"Oh, just taking a walk to eat our lunch," Vee replied, holding up her brown paper bag. "We were hoping to find an open bench."

"Here, you can have ours," Tori said. "We're done, right?"

"Yes," Tracy said, tossing their dirty napkins into the nearby trash can.

"We're going to go do a little more shopping. Are you working at the store today?"

Vee nodded.

"Well, we'll stop by in a bit," Tori said and then to Tracy. "She works at my absolute favorite store along here."

"Excellent."

* * *

Dan watched as Tori and her friend Tracy walked off, chit-chatting and laughing with one another, carrying their shopping bags, off to procure more.

"Compound, huh?" Dan said.

"Yeah, her and everyone else I guess."

"Who is Tori married to? I didn't see a ring on her finger."

"I don't think she is. She lives with a man. His name is Braddock, I assume that's his last name but I'm not sure. I guess he works for the sheriff's department, a detective. She works for the sheriff's department too, at least sometimes."

Dan nodded. "When I saw her, just for a second, I thought I was looking at—"

"Jessie?"

"Yeah, but then realized obviously I wasn't. I know they were identical twins but man, she looks just like her now."

"She does," Vee said. "She has developed what I think would have been Jessie's love of fashion. Tori doesn't shop the budget racks, let me tell you. And she's in good shape. I'm starting to get just a little soft around the middle but not her. I was helping her with a dress and there wasn't an ounce of fat on her anywhere." She took her sandwich out of the bag. "Have you looked at the donation site for Sarah lately."

"No. Why?"

"It was at $2,200 about a week ago. Tori made a donation, and all of a sudden others came flowing in. I think she must have sent a message to our whole graduating class. I recognized a lot of names on the donation list."

Dan grimaced. "God, I hate the thought of them all knowing about us like that."

"So do I, but the fund is up to just over $21,000 and it doesn't seem to be stopping. Sarah's uninsured bills are over $48,000. Ruth Ann has a cousin who works at the hospital. She told me if we offered the hospital half, they'd probably call it good. That's the amount the hospital usually gets from the insurance company after all the discounts get factored in if someone has health insurance. If this keeps up another week, we might get there."

"Huh. Who knew?"

"Yeah. It's amazing the money around here now," Vee said with a tinge of envy. "I mean the people who come into the store, mostly out-of-towners, but some locals too, that drop $400, $500, $600 like it's nothing. Nothing, Dan. And then they're onto the next store. Where does it all come from?"

"Lots of wealthy people on the lakes these days," Dan said. "I've driven around. There must be twenty massive teardown and rebuilds on Northern Pine at the moment." He took a bite of his lunch.

"And us? Well, we're... completely fucked."

Vee was revved up again. It was a good time to press her.

"I met Druk for coffee this morning. He and Heath want an answer." He knew what he wanted to do.

She closed her eyes. They wanted her to do something far more difficult and riskier than she once did for them. Vee opened her eyes and looked at Dan. "I'm in."

THIRTEEN

"NO RISK, NO REWARD, RIGHT?"

The funeral for Ally Mannion was on an overcast, muggy Friday morning, nearly two weeks after her murder. Thousands had seemingly made their way through the funeral home the night before and then packed the church in Manchester Bay earlier in the morning, and then the procession to the cemetery which clogged the northbound lanes of the H-4 for a half-hour.

"I'm getting really tired of going to funerals for college kids," Tori grumbled as she got into the passenger seat of her Audi. She let out a long slow sigh. They had gone to one back in March for two of the three victims of a drive-by shooting they were investigating. One of the kids was a student at Holmstrand High School, and the other a student at Central Minnesota State, who had brought along his girlfriend as well. They were cousins, just getting together for dinner, greeting one another on the front steps when they were shot and killed. Braddock and Tori were investigating the case and felt something of a professional obligation to observe the funeral. That had led to an unexpected break in the case.

Braddock leaned back against the driver's seat; his eyes

closed. "It's just so senseless," he murmured. "Over a goddamned boat."

They had been invited, or requested, to attend a private post-funeral gathering at the Mannion residence. They slowly walked hand-in-hand up the long driveway to the house. Eddie greeted them, along with his fiancée, Kaylee.

"Thank you both for coming."

"Of course," Tori said as she moved in to hug him. They had been close childhood friends, and in the same friend group through high school. She imagined he'd given and taken a lot of hugs in the last two weeks, but she felt it when she gave him one, the way he held on to it. This one meant just a little more.

Eddie shook hands with Will. "Thank you both. Please, go inside, both of you, make up a plate, there's so much food."

Kyle Mannion was a restaurant competitor, yet there wasn't a restaurant in town that hadn't sent multiple trays of food to the house. On the center kitchen island and along the length of the long dining room table, there was tray after tray of food.

"My word," Tori had murmured at the spread. "You could feed a thousand people with all this."

As warm and comfortable as Kyle and Brianna had made the house, it still was a large and expansive home reflective of their wealth. Braddock had once made the sly joke at a Mannion party that he spent the night looking for the gift shop. And it was packed with friends and family and many of the local community leaders, the mayor, business owners and executives, county commissioners, that Tori and Braddock would just as soon avoid. The ones that Boe had been fighting off for the better part of two weeks. Tori saw them all circling Boe and Braddock as they both perused the dessert trays and poured coffees.

Her initial instinct was to stick her nose in but then she was tapped on the shoulder. "Come on," Eddie said, tipping his head the opposite way, leading her out of the house and down to the lake, walking out to the end of the dock and sitting on the bench, peering out to the water.

The sun was high in the sky and there was a light south-westerly breeze that brought small waves into the shore. She slid on her sunglasses and sat back on the bench. Eddie handed her a bottle of water.

"I thought I'd rescue you before you got sucked into the wolf pack descending on Boe and Will."

"I appreciate it," Tori replied. "But I'm not off the hook, am I?"

"Ah, you know me so well."

"We know each other. You play the hero first with the lady, and then you get what you want."

"You make me sound so shallow."

"I know you're not, at least as it pertains to me. What do you want to know?"

"Just the truth about where the investigation stands. Boe has the political speak down to a science and Will plays things close to the vest, whereas you never pull your punches. Not in all the years I've known you."

"At least I'm consistent."

"If I hear it from you, I'll trust it," Eddie said. "Give me the Camel Unfiltered status of your investigation. It's been two weeks. Are you going to find my niece's killer?"

Tori exhaled a long breath. "There is a reason Boe is dancing and Braddock is reticent. At the moment, we're... kind of dead in the water."

Eddie's eyebrows shot up. "Dead... dead... in the water? What, what... about this man killed a week ago, Dennis Kellin. He was involved right?"

"Yes, but not in the murder, in the moving of stolen boats. We've taken his background down to the studs and we're not finding anything that tells us who these other two guys are, at least yet. He's the only contact we've made to those two but it's dead ending right now. But I haven't given up on that. Come Monday, I'm going to do my own digging on Kellin."

"Is there anything else you're pursuing?"

"We have a couple of other angles." She explained her theory that they may have killed before. "I just feel like that is a possibility. And another person related to Kellin told us that Kellin told him these two guys could steal anything."

"That's something."

"It is," Tori agreed. "And we are pursuing it, but, Eddie, right now, we're stuck in the mud. It doesn't feel like anything is imminent."

"I see," Eddie said after a minute, leaning forward, head down. "You make it sound kind of hopeless."

Tori snorted a weary laugh. "It kind of does when I hear myself talk about it." She looked Eddie in the eye. "Know this, we're not giving up. Braddock and I are not giving up."

"What comes next?"

"What every cop needs when they hit an investigative wall."

"What's that?"

"A break."

* * *

Vee stared at the ceiling, the comforter up to her neck. Dan was to her right, lying on his back, sleeping soundly. She glanced to the left and reached for her phone. It was 2:45 a.m.

The small egress window was open above her, the air of the night cool on her skin. The wind was whipping through the trees, and she thought she'd heard some rumbling in the distance, a storm rolling in. Duluth had been like this that night, windy, a chance for a storm. It was a night she didn't often let herself think of or remember but she let it in now, knowing that she was going to have to get her mind right if they were going to do this.

She flipped her pillow over and fluffed it a bit before gently resting her head on it. Closing her eyes, she breathed slowly, feeling the tenseness drain from her body as she relaxed into the softness of the mattress, her head still and comfortable on the fresh cool of the pillow. Slowly, she let her mind drift back to the fullness of that night fourteen years ago...

She had seen the big water of the lake many times over the years, even once making a trip to see the historic lighthouse at Split Rock with her mom. Yet, no matter the number of times she took in the ocean-like view over the years, the deep melodic baritone of Gordon Lightfoot had never entered her mind, until that night. Maybe it was the lights from the freighter ship she could see far in the distance, slowly steaming south toward the harbor, its deep rumbling ship's horn announcing its presence. Whatever it was, the sorrowful lyrics from "The Wreck of the Edmund Fitzgerald", the sad ballad about the massive freighter that sank in 1975, reverberated in her head, particularly the words: *Gitche Gumee. Gitche Gumee* was the Ojibwe name for Lake Superior.

The van windows were down, filling the inside with crisp cool air and the rhythmic roar of the ocean-like waves crashing against the massive rocks and firm sands of the shoreline thirty feet below. In the far distance the aerial lift bridge for Duluth Harbor was brightly alight.

The digital dashboard clock read 11:32 p.m. They were parked at the very end of a narrow gravel access road, entry to which was hidden behind a swing-arm gate two-hundred yards behind them. The thick canopy of trees swaying overhead gave them cover.

Druk sat in the driver's seat, his black gloved right hand

resting on the steering wheel, his black leather jacket open. Heath rested in the passenger seat, a black stocking cap on his head. She was behind them with Dan, all dressed in head to toe black.

"It's gusty out there, Vee," Dan remarked as the trees swayed with the heavy breeze.

"Always windy, and cool, down here on the shore," Heath noted casually. "It's July. It can be ninety everywhere in the state and it'll be sixty-three down here on the lake. Superior water is cold, like the Pacific."

"Actually, cool and windy are not the worst conditions for us," Druk remarked. "Nor is the rain that's coming in about four hours. It'll wash everything away."

"That's easy for you to say," Vee replied as she re-checked the contents of the duffel bag lying on the floor between her and her husband. "You're not going to be forty feet up in the air without a net below."

The four of them sat quietly, although all of them for the next ninety minutes continually looked to the northeast as houselights slowly extinguished.

"Amazing how many night owls there are on a Tuesday," Vee mused.

A half hour later, Druk took a long look in both directions. "It's dark north and south. We're a go."

Vee, along with Dan and Heath, slipped out of the van. They weaved down the bluff to the shoreline and picked their way northeast along the sand and rocks, using the light of the nearly full moon to work their way along the bottom of the bluff until they reached the steps and climbed their way back up, Heath leading. When he was close to the top, Heath stopped and scanned the back of the house straight ahead and then the one fifty yards to the left through a row of mature trees. All was quiet and he let his eyes drift to the right and the eight-foot-high wrought-iron fence with brick columns. "Come on."

They fast walked to the fence and the corner brick column. Vee easily scaled the wrought iron and brick column, flipping herself over and sticking the landing as if she was dismounting the uneven bars like the gymnast she once was. Dan followed, using the fence and column, throwing his legs over and jumping down to the ground. Heath tossed over their duffel bag which Dan caught and then muscled his six-foot-two, sturdy two-hundred-pound frame over the fence. While they were all wearing gloves, Heath quickly wiped the areas of the wrought iron they'd touched.

The three-story twenty thousand square foot mansion was fifty yards ahead, visible through the mixture of mature trees framing the wide six-acre property. In the daylight, the view from the mansion out over the lake and into Duluth a few miles south, was no doubt spectacular. At night, the immense redbrick and sandstone structure was heavily obscured behind the mammoth one-hundred-year-old trees.

Sprinkled amongst the trees were vast gardens with gravel paths that they weaved their way through to reach the expansive four-season porch that wrapped around the southeast corner of the mansion. Heath pulled out a small pair of climbing shoes that Vee pulled onto her feet, replacing her tennis shoes.

"Ready?" Heath asked.

"Yes," Vee said and stuck her right foot into Heath's interlocked fingers.

He hoisted her one-hundred-pound body up to the corner of the top of the porch. She gripped the roof and Heath pushed his hands all the way up and she raised herself onto it. Ten seconds later, Dan joined her and then Heath and they all hustled to the base of the fireplace stack.

Vee peered forty feet straight up to the small octagon window to the right of the fireplace stack. It was one thing to practice and visualize it. It was another to see it in person.

How in the hell was she going to do this?

She zipped up the top of her skintight body suit and then pulled her climbing gloves tight. Every five feet of the stack, there was a decorative horizontal row of bricks that extended out an inch. There were also two vertical rows of bricks that extended out. They would have to suffice as her footholds. This was going to be all about the strength of her fingers and toes.

"Ready, babe?"

"This isn't exactly the practice rock wall at Gander Mountain, is it?"

Dan smirked as a large gust swayed the trees. "Piece of cake."

"Yeah," she whispered and kissed her husband, newlyweds all of four months. "No risk, no reward, right?"

"You've got this."

She placed her left foot two feet up, finding the small notch between the brick and mortar and then reached up with her right hand for the first horizontal row, gripping it with her gloved fingers. She took one last look up. "Give me a boost."

Dan gave her a lift and with her right leg she reached for the horizontal row, set her foot and lifted herself up. She methodically worked her way up the stack, using the vertical and horizontal rows and the grip of her climbing gloves and shoes to Spider-Man her way up, feeling the moisture of perspiration on her skin underneath her tight black spandex and gloves. She exhaled a slow breath as she reached the level of the window. With her toes gripping a row of decorative bricks and her fingers gripped on the row just above her eye level she slowly edged her way around the right corner of the chimney and then to the body of the house. The porthole-sized window was three feet to her right.

Now the tricky part.

It was only three feet. But it felt like it was a mile away.

There was a tall window just below the porthole window.

She carefully twisted her right leg from the narrow brick ledge and slowly reached her foot and toes to the top of the slightly wider sandstone frame around the tall window and got a good toe grip. She exhaled a breath through her nose and looked down through her legs, Dan peering nervously up at her.

There was a hinge on the right side of the porthole. The window would swing open—if she could get it open. Feeling stable on her feet she slowly released her right hand from the ledge, reached down and unzipped the top of her body suit and reached inside for the stiletto knife. She pulled it out, hit the button and the blade snapped open. It was long and paper thin.

Please fit.

There was an inside metal latch securing the window. She slid the blade into the gap between the window and frame, with little resistance. She slowly lifted the blade up until it stopped at the latch. She applied pressure, lifting the blade but the latch wouldn't move.

Awkwardly angled, and her toes hanging on the ledges, she couldn't put a lot of power into it without risking her balance. She slid the blade down then lifted with more force.

Clink.

She dropped the blade down and lifted again.

Clink.

She felt a little give in the latch. She took a breath and steadied herself, securing her grip with her left hand and both feet. She lowered the knife once more and this time lifted harder.

Clink.

The latch opened. The window popped out just hair. She pronated her right wrist and used the blade to pull and then swing the window open.

Thank God.

She tossed the knife inside, hearing it thud onto the carpet. With her right hand she reached in and got a solid hold on the inside of the window. Carefully she inched her right foot to the right and with her good grip of the window, in one motion her left leg and hand released from the stack ledge to the window ledge, and she reached inside with her left hand.

Next question: *Do I fit?*

Only one way to find out.

Her hands inside, she pulled her shoulders in and made herself as sleek as she could, ducking her head and with her arms pulled herself inside, wedging her way through the window before crumpling down hard onto the floor.

Phew!

She stood up, looked out the porthole window and waved to Dan below who waved back and then rushed away. Vee closed the window, replacing the latch. She went to the hallway and opened the door on the right into the wide closet. The next door was on her left. She opened it and looked down the shaft. Five minutes later, having descended, she opened the door into the kitchen just enough to stretch around the corner and tapped in the four-number code for the security system. The panel beeped. In the reflection from a mirror, she saw the light on the security panel turn from red to green. She stepped out fully and opened the back door, letting Dan and Heath inside.

Heath handed them each a duffel bag. "Let's go to work."

An hour later, Vee reset the alarm. The three of them slipped out the back door, three full duffel bags in hand, and ran around the house to the driveway and the waiting van, full of even more treasure.

FOURTEEN

"IT'S LIKE A DOOM LOOP."

Braddock, Quinn, and Sam Sheets loaded up the speedboat tied up to the end of the dock. There were fishing poles, a tackle box, bait, a fishing net, a bottle of bug spray and of course, a full cooler.

"My husband, the fisherman," Tracy Sheets mused with a chuckle, sitting on the soft cushions of the sectional deck couch, twirling the stem of her empty wine glass, the table fire flickering. "You have a really good life here, Tori," she said, her legs curled up underneath her, nearly three months pregnant, but not yet really showing.

Tori had a speaker set on the table, fiddling with her playlist. "I've got something for you."

"What?"

"Ants Marching" from Dave Matthews Band roared to life.

"God, I love this song," Tracy bellowed. "I haven't listened to this in so long."

Tori grinned. "The Garden."

"Tenth row on the floor. So close to the stage."

"Oh yeah," Tori said. "Dancing away on the floor like we

had not a care in the world, just cutting loose. I was delirious that night, as were you."

"Was it the booze or the music?"

"Both, I think."

"That has to be what ten, eleven years ago."

"At least. It's funny, I can't remember the last concert I went too. That's something I'd like to start doing again."

"Tickets are pricey these days," Tracy said. "Did you see what Taylor Swift is charging?"

"Oh yeah. I've heard Quinn's friends' parents talking all about it."

The two of them sang along with the song for a bit.

"Tori, this setting on the lake, this house, is really something, girl."

"It is a nice way to live," Tori agreed, holding Tracy's hand steady and pouring her a glass of white wine.

"And Braddock, he is one good dude."

"He is."

"And studly. How many times did you fuck him this week?"

"*Tracy!*" Tori blurted, her mouth agape. "Seriously?"

"It's the wine."

"You haven't even taken a sip yet."

Tracy took a drink and grinned. "So? How many times?"

Tori laughed in reply, still stunned. "I'm not going to answer that."

"At least twice that I heard," Tracy murmured.

"Heard? You heard?"

"Yeah, girl, you know, you are really kind of loud."

"Oh my God. I am not."

"My guess is Quinn is quite educated by now. All that panting and moaning and headboard thumping."

Tori threw her head back, laughing. "You have no filter."

"I call them like I see them, or in this case, hear them."

The two of them laughed out loud.

"It's going to be one of those nights, isn't it," Tori declared before downing her full glass and then filling it again. "Cheers to a good week."

"Awesome week girl," Tracy replied and then chortled a laugh as the boat pulled away. "If Sam's law partners could see him right now."

Tracy's husband Sam was the epitome of a white shoe New York City Wall Street lawyer. Yet there he was an hour ago dropping not so subtle hints he'd like to go out fishing one more time. He caught a couple of walleyes their first night out and was hooked, wanting to go out whenever they could. Braddock and Quinn didn't need much encouragement. "He'll be begging to come back, you know."

"Begging won't be necessary. Yours is a standing invite."

"Yeah?"

Tori smiled and nodded. "Hell, yeah. We've loved having you guys here. Braddock has really enjoyed it."

"That's why I said he's such a good dude. I hope Sam dragging him fishing and golfing hasn't been too much?"

"No, not at all," Tori said with a laugh. "I love how they hit it off. I know Braddock's had to work some, but he's enjoyed having someone to pal around with. It's taken his mind off things. And you being here has taken mine off things as well."

"Like your double homicide?"

"Until you showed up, I hadn't been able to get Ally Mannion's face, the way we found her body, any of it out of my mind."

"Some things just don't change," Tracy said, taking a small drink of wine. "I can tell this one really stings, and not just you, but Braddock too. That family being friends and all. It's written all over both of your faces."

"That and..." Tori took a long drink of wine and exhaled a long breath. "I've been debating all week whether to tell you this. I still haven't been able to figure out how I feel about it but it's been tormenting me. Waking me at night."

"What?"

"Maggie Duncan called me? Marta Dudek to you."

"What? She did?" Tracy replied, shocked, sitting up. "When?"

"A few weeks ago."

"No way."

"I kid you not."

"And you're just telling me about this now?"

Tori shrugged, taking a long drink of wine.

"Well, what did she have to say?"

"Plenty."

Tracy knew the tone. "Oh, she got to you, didn't she?"

"Oh yeah."

Tori recounted the phone call with the once Chicago Mob hitwoman that resurfaced several months ago after some old Chicago Mafia operators and adversaries had killed the son and nephew of her neighbor in Holmstrand. Tracy and Tori had a previous history with her, having long ago briefly participated in an investigation of the killing of an FBI agent in Cleveland as part of a Mob hit that killed two other Cleveland Mafia members. The FBI agent had been undercover at the time and was executed by Maggie Duncan, who then went by her given name of Marta Dudek. Marta was a mysterious Mob hitwoman whose identity was only known to her handler, Angelo DeEsposito, or so she thought.

The killing in Cleveland had been a set-up, not only of the undercover agent, but of Maggie and DeEsposito, who was executed in Chicago at the same time she was pulling the job in Cleveland. She avoided the hit on herself and got her revenge on those who called the shot two weeks later and then disappeared for twelve years, establishing a new identity and life in Minnesota. She became a hairdresser, met and then married Rob Duncan, and settled with his two children in Holmstrand, turning into an athleisure-wearing basketball mom. At least until her neighbor and best friend's son was murdered in a drive-by shooting orchestrated by two former Chicago mobsters who had relocated to northern Minnesota. A shooting that awakened in Maggie the need to seek revenge for her friend.

Braddock had brought Tori into the investigation. Tori had given Maggie her cell number when interviewing her after the shooting, as she had to many others who'd been possible witnesses. Maggie had called Tori with burner phones, at times guiding, at others, chiding. Tori, with the help of Tracy, had gone to Chicago and uncovered Maggie's true identity, but not before she managed to slip away.

And then three months later Maggie called, while Tori was sitting on the dock, enjoying a leisurely sunny Saturday afternoon.

"So did Maggie, or Marta, or whatever we're calling her now, just want to chat?"

"Well, we did talk."

"About?"

"She said she and I are alike, Tracy."

"Please. You're not. Not even remotely." Tracy peered at Tori. "Don't for a minute tell me you're buying that shit?"

"Aren't we alike? We both lost loved ones as teens to murder. I turned out one way, she turned out—"

"Another."

Tori nodded and exhaled a breath. "She had a point."

"No, she doesn't."

"Well, I thought she did."

"You let her get to you."

"A little. She made me—"

"Like her?"

"Empathize. I believe her when she says had she known the

hit in Cleveland involved an FBI special agent, she wouldn't have done it."

"That doesn't matter," Tracy replied flatly. "She needs to be got."

"I know," Tori replied, nodding. "I know, from a legal sense, it doesn't matter, she killed an agent, she has to go down for it. But it mattered... to me."

"Why?"

Tori shook her head and scoffed. "Her marriage. Her love for her stepchildren tells me she had some inherent decency. There was good in there."

"Pfft. She was a killer. Don't ever lose sight of that."

"I've killed people," Tori said. "I've taken lives. Not as many as her but certainly more than I care to count."

"Doing your job as a special agent or an investigator for the county doesn't make you a killer. You are not her."

"But—"

"Don't but me. You're not. Maggie, Marta, whoever she is, she *was* a killer."

"Honestly, Trace, I don't care about all the Mob guys she killed. I don't care about the guys she killed here. They chose their life. In some ways, and maybe I'm delusional about it, I'm not sure she fully chose hers."

"Tori!"

"I know, I know."

"She had a choice. She chose to become what she did."

"Yes," Tori said, nodding. "But I also know, *I know*, way deep down inside, what that kind of loss makes you want to do. I know the kind of rage and anger it builds inside of you. It consumes you. It's like poison."

Tracy took a sip of her wine. "In some people, it's poison, that I get. But in you, that loss made you the special agent you are. It was motivation. It drove you to find missing children and to give families the answers you never got. In Maggie it was poison. She became a killer. Thus, you are not her." She took another sip of wine. "But to your point, this week has helped me truly understand what it all did to you, in part, because I see how you are now. The before Braddock you, the before therapy you, was driven for sure, but damaged too. I started seeing it in Chicago, but only now do I truly understand the difference. That Tori that I once knew, we'll call her former Tori, could have never had what you have now with Braddock."

"No," Tori agreed. "I couldn't have."

"I love both versions of you, but this version of you is *waaaaaay* better, way healthier."

Tori nodded.

"So," Tracy poured just a small extra dollop of wine in her glass. "Maggie just called to chat? To bond? To needle? To what?"

"It was all a prelude to ask me to look in on her husband, Rob," Tori replied with a headshake and wry smile. "She was worried about him. She wanted me to make sure he moved on."

"Really?" Tracy snorted with a laugh.

"She loved him, Tracy, she did."

"He wasn't cover?"

"No. She was out of that game."

"Until she came back."

Tori nodded. "Yes, until she went back. But her love for him was genuine. It was real. And that need to make things right for a friend, for her neighbor, that too tells me it was real. That deep down, there was goodness in her despite all she'd done."

"Lots of these Mob hitters were 'good' family men, Tori. Loved their kids, their wives, were good providers. They were still remorseless killers," Tracy counseled. "That's Maggie too."

"I don't know with her," Tori said, her voice soft. "I don't know if I buy that with her. I just don't."

"I've said my piece," Tracy replied and took a small sip of wine. "Did you do what she asked?"

"Braddock and I went and saw him."

"And?"

"He seemed to be doing alright, all things considered. I mean, his second wife was a former Mob assassin. He was still in a daze about it, but I think, in time, he's going to be okay. He appreciated that we stopped by."

"Did you tell him why?"

"No," Tori replied, shaking her head. "No. She asked me not to. She wants him to forget her. She can't come back, and he can't ever go to her. We treated it as a welfare check."

"His passport will be forever flagged," Tracy noted.

"Exactly. She wants him to move on, find someone else and live a good life," Tori said. "He's a nice guy, Trace. I don't think he'll lack for female companionship if he wants it, in time."

"I assume you informed the Bureau?"

"I called Special Agent Bahn in Chicago. Maggie called me from Australia, I think. He said they'd reach out to authorities there and see if there was something that could be done but she's undoubtedly changed her look, got a clean passport, and probably has enough money that she'll be unfindable."

"I bet she calls you back again," Tracy said.

"I hope not," Tori replied. "It just reminds me of dead kids. I think of talking to her and I'm back to seeing those three kids senselessly murdered. Just like Ally Mannion. It's like a doom loop."

Tori and Tracy had talked about the current case a few times during the week, mostly after there were calls from Steak. Over the course of their conversations, Tori told Tracy everything that had happened and everything they knew or thought they knew. The investigation had slowed considerably. Their two thieves had disappeared into the ether, or so it seemed.

"Can I say something?" Tracy asked.

"When have you ever had to ask?"

Tracy snorted a laugh. "Have you thought about quitting?"

"Quitting?"

"Yes, truly quitting. Stop being a detective, an agent. No police work whatsoever. You've done your duty, Tori," Tracy pressed. "All the kids you've found."

"A lot of them dead."

"And a lot of them alive! Back with their families. Saved because of you."

"And you. And Geno. And—"

"It was you, girlfriend. We're very good agents, Geno and I. We do the job, connect the dots, make the case. You're different. You have all the investigative instincts. You probably got them from your father."

"Maybe."

"I bet it was you, between you and Jessie, who sat with your dad and talked work. Talked cases. Amirite?"

Tori nodded. "Yeah, Jessie would be on the phone with a boy, or whatever, and I'd sit with Big Jim and ask about his day. Jessie loved him as much as I did, but she never was one to sit and talk work with him. I was."

"I figured. Jessie drove you to become a special agent, but your dad was a part of it too."

Tori nodded, sipping her wine.

"That doesn't mean that's all you should do. The cases you've had, in the Bureau, back here, that all takes a toll. I know you're seeing a therapist, talking things through and you have Braddock who is a rock for you."

"He is."

"It doesn't have to be your only identity. With your mind, you could do anything."

"I feel like I owe it to—"

"You don't owe anybody a damn thing. You don't owe your sister, your father, anyone anything anymore. You never did to begin with. Whatever debts you thought you had? They've all been paid, with interest."

Tori laid her head back and closed her eyes.

"Look—" Tracy reached for Tori's hand "—you are family to me. I love you like a sister. You're as happy as I've ever seen you. I just want you to stay that way."

"I know," Tori replied. "I've tried to step away."

"But you get sucked back in?"

"In a way. I just can't—"

"Turn it off?"

"Yeah. And, Trace, I still get something from it. That satisfaction. I do get that."

"That runs out."

Tori nodded. "I know. Braddock and I have talked about that too. There is a shelf life for this kind of life and work. I come and go as I please with the county. I teach."

"And you must have plenty of money."

"I do. I don't have to work but at the same time, I can't not work. And, curse that it is, this is what I'm really good at. In a way, it is who I am. But—" she exhaled "—Braddock has twenty years in. He wants to go until Quinn graduates high school, so another five or six years."

"You figure his window is your window."

Tori nodded.

"Look at you make long-term plans."

"I know," Tori said with a headshake. "Hard to believe."

"Yet so wonderful to see," Tracy said, leaning over with her wine glass to clink Tori's.

"And," Tori said, her eyes a little moist, "I love you like a sister too. You've always been there."

"And I always will," Tracy replied with a bright smile. "Now, on your case."

"Cripes. After that discussion, now we're going to talk about the case?"

"I'm on a roll and I really have only one question."

"Shoot."

"Riddle me this, Batman. Do you think your two killers are still around?"

Tori glanced at her friend. "I'm sensing you do?"

"You first," Tracy pressed.

"I think so. I think they're from here and if there is one thing about Minnesotans, they tend to stay. They don't seem to leave. Or if they do, they often come back. My sense is our burglars slash killers have been here pretty much all along. They're natives. Now—" she looked to Tracy "—your tone says *you* think they're still here. Why?"

Special Agent Tracy Sheets may not have worked in the field much anymore, having slowly drifted to more desk work focused on electronic and cyber investigations, but she still possessed a keen investigative mind. "I'm reminded of *Jaws*."

"The movie?"

"Yes. These guys you've told me about remind me of great white sharks. They're territorial. They'll keep going while the feeding is good. But, if you get a shot at them, don't miss."

"Because if we do."

"They'll be gone."

* * *

Druk checked his watch, 1:40 a.m.

"It's time. You ready?"

Dan tightened the straps on Vee's body harness. She had a black stocking cap on her head that would pull down to a face mask. It matched the skintight black nylon bodysuit she was in, and black gloves. "Is it tight enough?"

"Only if you want to cut off all my circulation," she quipped nervously, terrified of what she was about to do.

"Too tight?" Dan asked worriedly, looking her in the eye.

"Tighter is better. I'm not going to have much room to

maneuver," Vee said, taking a last sip of water, her mouth dry. "We need this right?"

Dan nodded and kissed her. "Good luck."

Vee nodded. "Let's do this."

"Dan, take the wheel," Heath said as they switched spots.

Dan dropped the gear shift and drove two blocks to the alley and turned right, extinguished the headlights, and zoomed ahead, taking a left into the parking lot and centering the van into the narrow walkway between the two, two-story buildings. The walkway was just wide enough. The building on the right was their destination. Dan stopped just underneath an old fire escape ladder, the bottom of which was perched fifteen feet above ground.

Heath opened the van's rear door and Druk climbed on top of the van.

"Vee?"

She took a step back and Heath boosted her and Druk pulled her up on top of the van and then Heath climbed up and joined them. Druk hoisted Vee up to the second rung of the ladder. She got a grip on the rung and Druk boosted her a bit more to help her reach the third rung and she started climbing, followed by Druk with a duffel bag strapped around his shoulders and then Heath.

Dan backed the van away.

Once all three were on the roof, Heath used an electric screwdriver to remove a vent cover on the duct running from the building's heating ventilation and air conditioning system (HVAC) roof unit. The duct ran from the main HVAC unit, turned ninety degrees, and ran down tight to the side of the building to the right of the fire ladder and then back into the building between the first and second floors.

Druk took the black rope out of the duffel bag. He quickly looped it through the carabiner on Vee's harness, pulling on it several times to assure it was secure.

Vee pulled a headlamp on her head, running a strap under her chin, and then stuffed AirPods into her ears and tight goggles over her eyes. The first two stages she would be in a twenty-four-by-twenty-four-inch duct. She took a peek inside.

How the hell do I fit in there?

And that wasn't the worst of it. The last section, where she had to do the real work, was only eighteen-by-twenty-four when it turned into the building, running along the ceiling of the first floor. It was the same exposed duct work along the ceiling that she saw daily in Fashion by Julia.

Druk noticed the look on her face and offered a smile. "You'll make it. Just think small because you are, Vee."

She sighed. "*Riiiiight.*"

Druk and Heath picked her up, holding her horizontal as she clasped her hands as if she were going to dive into water and they guided her head first into the opening, feeling the aluminum rub on her ribs and hip as she contorted her body to the left through the opening.

So, this is what it's like in a tube of toothpaste.

When she was a child, in the winter she would dig tunnels in the massive snowbanks built by the snowplows at the end of their driveway. The older she got, the longer and more twisted the tunnels her and her friends would dig, twisting and turning as they made their way through from one side to the other. That's what this felt like and she put her mind there, but with one difference. She could already feel the sweat building.

"Vee, can you hear me?" Druk's voice called calmly in the AirPods.

"Yes."

"Are you okay in there?"

No, but she was doing this.

"Moving forward," she said.

Move methodically, not frantically.

Economy and synchronicity of movement was required.

She forged ahead, right elbow, push with left knee, left elbow, push with right knee and all along she could feel herself pulling the rope along beneath her. It took her a few minutes to reach the bend in the duct.

"I'm at the edge. I'm going to push over."

"We've got you."

She free fell a few feet before the rope caught, the harness straps digging into her body, arresting her fall. "Whoa," she grunted.

"Are you okay?"

"Yeah. The drop just startled me." She let out a breath, dangling in the duct. "Start lowering me."

Slowly she was lowered down the duct. She could hear the rope rubbing against the turn in the duct above her as they lowered her. The turn into the building was coming, five feet... three feet... one foot.

She reached with her fingers, stretching to grip the top of the duct at the turn. "Halt! I'm at the turn."

If she could have, the easiest thing would have been to make the turn on her back, as if she were performing a sit-up and then once inside the duct, flip over onto her stomach.

That wasn't an option. There wouldn't be enough room in the next duct for her to flip over and she had to be on her stomach. Her only option was to go in head first on her stomach. To do that would require her to arch her back at almost ninety degrees to make the turn.

For the last four days she had been stretching and contorting her body in ways she hadn't in twenty years, preparing for this very next maneuver. She had practiced with Dan at home, him holding her in the air by her ankles, lowering her slowly while with her hands she pulled herself under their bed on her stomach, arching her back, making a ninety-degree turn. She'd done it a few times, but that was in their bedroom, not a tight duct, and with Dan holding her and there was no risk she could get stuck.

Now she was staring at the actual ninety-degree turn into a very small duct.

How the hell do I make that?

She had no choice but to try. "Hold me steady. I have to rotate my body."

Dangling, using her hands, she turned herself one-hundred-eighty degrees. She eyed up the opening into the smaller duct. Vee exhaled a breath.

This would entail the hardest upward dog move ever.

This was going to hurt.

"I'm set. Lower me a few inches... Good."

She reached inside the duct and got her head inside, feeling the hardness of the duct on the back of her neck. "Lower me a few more."

Her body dropped and with her hands, slowly pulled herself inside, the duct turn rubbing hard against her upper back.

"A bit more," she grunted.

She reached ahead, the hard edge of the duct now hard against her middle back, digging deep into her spine, as if she could feel the rigid corner of the duct jamming into the gaps between each vertebra down her back.

Grunting, she said: "Slack! Just a few more inches."

She felt her legs drop but the turn was still at her mid-back. "A... little... more." The seam of the duct turn was still six or seven inches above her waistline.

This was the part that was really going to hurt.

"Okay... more..." she groaned.

Vee reached forward as far as she could and then pushed up, arching her back, her head banging and then rubbing hard against the top of the duct as she wedged forward, her low back searing from the vent corner digging into the small of her back.

"Ahrgggg!"

It was at her waistline.

She felt her back pass the corner, the seam rubbing tight on her buttocks, her kneecaps hitting the duct bottom. Pulling herself fully into the duct, she laid on her stomach, resting her head to the side, gasping. Her whole back was on fire, the pain radiating down her legs.

"Vee? Vee? Are you okay?"

"Yeah," she sighed. "I'm horizontal now. Just give me a minute."

She lay in the duct, the pain in her back easing—some.

"What's next?" she said.

"You should see a vent opening up on your left. Where you need to cut is another six feet after that on the right side. Right in the middle of the fourth duct section."

How Heath and Druk knew this was something they wouldn't disclose but she took it on faith that they did. She wriggled herself ahead and stopped where Heath told her to. With her right hand, she reached down to her mid-thigh pocket and pulled out the cordless rotary tool and transferred it to her left hand and then attached the small saw blade and pushed the power button.

Whirrrrrrr!

Rolling as much as she could onto her left side, she pulled her knees up as far as she could, wedging her body and pressing her back against the left side of the duct to give herself maximum leverage. Using both hands, she started the saw, pressing it against the duct.

Her heart sank. It was just skidding along the surface.

She pressed the saw as hard as she could. Come on. *Come on!*

It burst through.

She let out a breath. "I'm through."

Vee cut a one-foot by one-foot square in the duct wall and pulled the piece away.

Fresh air rushed inside.

I'll be damned.

A foot away were three black cables and one beige one running vertically along the cement wall.

"I see the cables and the beige wire," she reported. "Now what?"

FIFTEEN

"I LOOK FRUMPY AND FIFTY."

There are many stages to a true Minnesota Goodbye.

There was the start, where just after 6:oo a.m. Sam said to Tracy, "We should really think about getting going. We have to be to the airport by ten thirty." That led to the first exchange of thank yous, hugs, and handshakes in the kitchen.

Then there was the walk to the back door, everyone carrying a piece of luggage. That led to a fifteen-minute talk there before Sam checked his watch and led them all out to the driveway, where Braddock helped him load their luggage into the trunk of their rental car.

When Sam shut the trunk, Tracy said, "Well, we should really get going," before she and Tori began talking about the work she had to get back to after a week off. That opened the door for Sam and Braddock to break off into another fishing conversation, such that Braddock had his phone out showing him a map of the lakes chain, and some other spots they'd have to hit next time. He even led Sam around the front of the house so he could point out how they'd get to the spots from the dock. When they walked back to the ladies, it was Braddock who was extending an invite for them to come back next summer. That added another ten minutes of chit-chatting about when a good time for another visit was.

It was 6:50 a.m. by the time Tracy opened the passenger door and dropped her shoulder bag on the front seat and turned to Tori, wrapping her up in a second, big hug, squeezing her tight. "This was so great. I loved every minute of it."

"I'm so glad you guys came out," Tori replied, her eyes closed, holding the third last hug from her best friend. "I'll miss you."

"Right back at you," Tracy said, letting go. "Call me, often."

"Count on it. I'll be looking for updates on Pending Baby Sheets."

"And you better visit when the baby comes."

"Aunt Tori will be there." Then she leaned in and whispered in Tracy's ear, "I will spoil this baby rotten, but I'll really, *really*, spoil a baby girl."

"I'll see what I can do."

"I want to see the baby too," Braddock said as he shook Sam's hand. The two of them had become fast friends.

Then Sam extended the invitation to visit them in New York.

"Seems a native Long Islander and a one-time Manhattanite ought to come back and see the big city. It's always changing, and, we'd love to have you."

"I haven't been back in quite some time," Braddock replied. "I'd like that."

"Then let's do it," Tracy said. "Let me pop this little one out first and then we'll get something on the books."

The four of them talked for another ten minutes before saying goodbye for what seemed like the fifth time before Sam and Tracy got into their car at 7:10 a.m. and Sam pulled away, giving them all one last wave.

"I had fun with them," Braddock said as they walked back

to the house, his arm draped around Tori's shoulder, holding her close. "Sam's a good, good dude."

"He is," Tori said. "I remember telling Tracy when she first introduced him to me that he was a good one. Which is just what Tracy said about you."

"Tracy is a very wise lady," Braddock said.

"And she has good hearing too. She says you're really loud."

"Really loud?"

"When we're... you know, naked and stuff."

"*What!* I'm loud?"

"Yeah."

"No way. *Me?*" Braddock replied, shocked. "She says I'm loud? You're the director, always telling me to do this or that."

"Hey, I'm just telling you what she reported," Tori said.

"The bedroom window was open, wasn't it?"

"She said she could hear you, loud and clear, groaning and moaning and grunting and thrusting."

"I don't grunt and groan. And you're the one that—"

"Hey—" she put her fingers to his lips "—it's okay. It's okay for you to be completely overcome with passion for me. I get it. I'm completely irresistible."

"Oh, for crying out loud," he replied, shaking his head when his phone buzzed in his pocket. It was Boe. "Jeanette, what's up?... Wait, hold on, say again... Overnight? Was anyone hurt? Well, that's good. Okay. Yeah, we'll be there as soon as we can."

"What is it?"

"You're not going to believe this."

A half-hour later, Braddock pulled up to the curb just down from Lakes Jewelers. A patrol officer for the Manchester Bay Police Department was awaiting their arrival. Eggleston also pulled in behind them.

"What do we have?" Braddock asked the patrol officer.

"Burglary. Cleaned the place out pretty good. The owner is there at the front. She'll show you."

The owner, Kristin Cooley, stood just inside the front door, hands on her hips looking sadly upon the interior of her store. She looked up to see Braddock, Tori, and Eggs step inside. "They wiped me out," Cooley said.

"Who is they?" Braddock asked.

"I don't know," Cooley replied. "Isn't that your job to figure out?"

"Fair."

Tori had been inside the store a few times given it was next to Fashion by Julia. It was among the newer clothing and accessory shops that occupied the rehabbed two-story red and brown brick buildings that made up the old downtown shopping district of her youth.

Not that she had a ton of experience with this kind of theft, but typically with a jewelry store burglary, all the display cases would be smashed. Instead, she noticed all the sliding case doors opened and various items removed, although many were also left behind. It appeared the thieves were particular about what they were after.

"How did they get the cases opened?" Tori asked. Each sliding glass door had a lock.

"Keys," Cooley replied. "The ones sitting on the top of the case by the register." She waved for them to follow her to a back room. "That set of keys hangs in here on this hook over the workbench."

The hook wasn't what caught Tori's attention, however. It was the large safe, the massive door swung open. It had an old-school combination lock on it. The inside of it was cleaned out.

"What was in there?" Eggleston asked, notepad at the ready.

"All of our customers' pieces we were making or repairing. We had diamonds, both cut and uncut, four different coin collections we were helping value and other pieces that we always lock up at the end of the day. Plus, cash. We sold but also on occasion, bought pieces, so we had cash at the ready."

"Value?"

Cooley sighed. "It's going to be over a million dollars when it's all said and done, between what they took up front and out of the safe."

"Who has the combination to the safe?" Tori asked.

"My store manager Penny, and me. Penny is on vacation in California this week. She's been with me for years, at my old location and now here."

"Nobody else?"

"No. I came to open the store this morning. The alarm didn't go off. Then I checked the security app on my phone, and it was down. No video cameras. And we don't have any lights either. The power was cut."

"How?" Tori asked.

"Right up there," Braddock said, holding up his flashlight, the beam up between an exposed duct and the brick wall. "Wires cut up there. All of them."

"Internet, power, security and video system," Cooley said. "Took the whole operation down in one fell swoop."

"And I see how. It looks like there is a hole cut in the duct up there."

Cooley waved for them to follow her through a door into a storage room. A vent cover was off the duct.

"Someone climbed in through there?" Braddock said, his jaw agape. The opening wasn't much larger than a wall vent.

"More like out I suspect. Whoever it was, they were small, very small," Tori said. "A lot smaller than me." Tori was five foot five, athletic, but petite. But as she looked at the vent hole the person came out of and just the duct work itself, she knew that even if she could have gotten in there, it would have been an extremely tight squeeze. "How would someone have gotten in there to start with?"

Five minutes later they were all up on the roof and Braddock saw it immediately, the duct running from the HVAC housing across the roof and then down the side of the building before it turned back into the building. There was a vent screen lying on the roof. The removed screen was for a small opening into a duct running from the HVAC housing. "Does this system serve only your store, or the clothing store as well?"

"Both," Cooley replied.

Braddock pulled on rubber gloves and examined first the vent cover and then the duct opening. "They entered here."

Tori and Eggleston walked over to the ledge and looked over. "Whoever it was didn't do this themselves," she said. "That is at least a twenty-foot drop. The person had to be lowered with a rope."

"My gosh, that duct is pretty tight, and then narrows as it goes into the building," Eggleston said. "Even a really small person wouldn't have but what, a few inches all around them to move."

"And how would the person have made that turn in the duct?" Tori said, shaking her head. "I mean that's a ninety-degree turn in that confined space."

"Had to be someone very small and Gumby-like to make that turn."

"I'm guessing the forensics officer will find rope fibers when they remove this cover," Braddock noted, looking at the vent cover again.

"Downstairs too," Tori said, joining him.

"And Jennison is here, so she'll get to work on it," Eggleston said, seeing the forensics van on the street and Jennison pulling out her case.

"So, this is at least a two, maybe three-person job. Through the duct to cut all the cables. If all the security is down, then all the person who went through the duct would have to do is open the back door. They had all the time they needed." Tori looked to Cooley. "Any idea of when the system went down?"

"The video feed ended at 2:03 a.m. It goes blank then, so I presume that's when the cable and power was cut."

"And your insurance?"

"I've already placed a call but..." She shook her head. "I can only imagine the battle I've got coming."

"One last question," Braddock murmured. "How did these people get up here?" The top loops of the ladder handle were thirty feet to the left of the duct. He and Tori carefully walked the stretch of roof from the duct work to the ladder before peering down. "They'd need a ladder to get up to the ladder."

"Maybe not," Tori replied.

She led him back down to the alley and to the narrow alleyway between the building and the one to the west. It was just wide enough for a vehicle. It looked to be fifteen feet to the bottom of the ladder. "I always wonder the purpose of having a ladder that nobody can reach to climb," she muttered.

"They cut it off it would appear. You can see where they bricked over a window someone would have used to access it."

Tori looked up at the ladder and then into the alley and a van for a local electrical contractor parked down the alley. "You pull up in a vehicle under the bottom of the ladder, get on top of the vehicle roof and pull yourself up. With multiple people, someone could do the boosting."

Braddock nodded. "We need to see if anyone had a security camera that catches this alleyway."

He walked the alley behind the jewelry store while Tori took the front. None of the stores along Lake Drive had an exterior or interior camera that had a view of the alleyway.

Braddock joined her on the sidewalk. There was a similar alleyway on the opposite side of the street that led to an east-west alley that divided the block. "Lookey there," he gestured.

Over the back door of a building was a camera facing out. "That's the sandwich shop a block over."

The store manager took them to his office and pulled up the surveillance camera on his computer screen. "We're looking for anything up there," Braddock said, pointing to the upper right corner of the video feed. "That alleyway."

"That's really far in the distance," he said of the live feed, which focused on the parking area behind his building but in the distance, you could see into the alleyway to the west of the jewelry store. "You can't see much that far in daylight. That's what? A good block plus away. What time are you looking for?"

"Start at 1:15 a.m.," Braddock said.

The manager ran the video, fast-forwarding through. The footage of the back parking lot was clear. In the distance it was less so, grainier.

"There," Braddock said. "What is that?"

The manager ran the footage back and then froze it. In the far distance, grainy as the footage was, a vehicle stopped, headlights extinguished. There was enough backlight however to see the silhouettes of three people climbing on top of the vehicle.

"Delivery van I'd say, based on the shape of the nose. Light colored. Maybe even white."

There were two larger people and one smaller person. The two larger men boosted the smaller one up to the ladder. They soon followed.

The van backed away and then turned to go west down the alley.

"White van," Tori said.

"Yep. It's just like you thought," Braddock replied. "That's how they got up there."

He pulled out his cell phone. To the manager he said, "I'm going to have a forensics officer come and get a copy of this footage. We'll see if they can get something more out of this."

* * *

Beep! Beep! Beep!

"Damn," Vee moaned as she rolled to the nightstand and hit the button for the alarm. She shuffled out of bed and jumped in the shower, using body wash to clean up, rubbing it on her shoulders and then turning to rinse. "Ow."

What the heck was that?

She got out of the shower, dried, and went to the mirror, turned to the right and saw the scratch on her left shoulder blade, maybe three to four inches long. It was bigger than she would have suspected, and it stung. In the bedroom, she looked in the long mirror, getting a closer look.

"Where did you get that?" Dan said.

"Probably when I was going through the duct." She tried reaching her shoulder blade with the ointment she'd squirted onto her right hand.

Dan got out of bed. "Let me."

He gently applied the white cream to the scratch. Vee then handed him a bandage that he put on before he kissed her on the shoulder and wrapped her in a hug. "How are you doing?"

She sighed. "I'm tired. It's going to be a very long day." She put her hair up in a tight bun and dressed in light-blue capri pants and a pink tank top.

"I haven't seen your hair in a bun like that in ages." She'd worn her hair short in various pixie cuts for years but had started growing it out the last few months. "You should maybe wear a sweater," he suggested. "Otherwise, half of the bandage shows."

"It does, doesn't it." She went to the closet and pulled out a loose-fitting, light, ultra-thin white sweater and pulled it on. "How's that."

"It's a little big but it works," he said. "You look nice."

"I look frumpy and fifty."

"That might be the look you want today."

"So, I do look frumpy and—"

"No, you don't. It's conservative. It's not flashy or particularly noticeable. That's good. You want to be ignored, right?"

"Yes."

"Drink some coffee, get some energy. You don't want people wondering why you're tired."

She nodded. "Speaking of why I'm tired. Where are the envelopes?"

"In the upper drawer. We shouldn't keep them here, though. We need to think about hiding them somewhere else. We don't want your mom finding them and then the questions that would bring. I'll give that some thought."

Vee kissed him and he went back to bed.

The store normally opened at 9:00 a.m. but she was scheduled to start at 7:30. Ruth Ann offered her some extra time, readying new apparel for the racks, checking it in, attaching the sales tags, simple, mindless stuff and she had said she'd never say no when extra work was offered.

The first thing she did was pour a cup of black coffee. It wasn't but five minutes into arranging a set of dresses by size when she heard the shrieks and shouts.

"Oh my God! Oh my God! No! *No!*" from the rear parking lot.

Even knowing they were coming, she still flinched at the outburst.

Ruth Ann had hustled next door and she'd followed a bit behind. The owner rushed out of the back of her store, her cell phone to her ear, calling 9 1 1.

"Kristin?"

"I've been robbed, Ruth Ann," she moaned. "My safe, the glass display cases, everything. My store is trashed."

"Oh, no, Kristin."

Vee quick walked around the building perimeter to look in

the store's front windows to see that all the display cases were half empty and the case keys were right where she left them, at the computer monitor where customers checked out. She walked around to the back again, sneaking a peek up at the duct, shuddering at the thought of being back in there again.

A half-hour later, she stood in the front display window, observing the police activity on Lake Drive, two patrol units in front of the store and then a black Tahoe arrived. That's when she saw Tori drop out of the passenger seat. She walked up with a tall athletic-looking man with wavy black swept back hair with light flecks of gray in it, wearing a sharp black suit with blue button-down dress shirt open at the collar, his sheriff's department badge on his belt.

"I see Tori is here," Ruth Ann noted, folding her arms. "And Will Braddock, the chief detective for the county." She leaned in to whisper, "You might have heard, I suppose, but he and Tori are a thing."

"I had heard something to that effect," Vee replied. She could see it too, how they moved with comfort in and around one another. "What's his story? Is he from around here?"

"No. He's a New Yorker."

"New York? How did he end up here?"

"Do you remember a girl named Meghan Hayes?"

"Uh, yeah."

"She went off to New York City, to Parsons, a design school," Ruth Ann said. "I dreamed of going there once. In any event, when Meghan was at Parsons, she met Will Braddock. He's from New York, though you wouldn't know it when you talk to him now."

"The accent has faded?"

"Pretty much. In any event, Meghan was a fashion designer and was starting to gain some notice. He was a detective with the NYPD. They were married, had a child and then Meghan got brain cancer."

"I see. So did they move back here?"

"Not then. She died in New York and that left him a single father. I asked Tori why he'd moved here *after* Meghan died. The timing seemed odd. She said he was struggling with her death and with raising his son on his own without any family to help him. Roger and Mary Hayes, Meghan's parents, you know who they are, right?"

"I remember the names. He's a business guy, right?"

"Still is. Real estate. Anyway, Tori said Roger and Mary went to New York and convinced him to move back here. So, he did. Went to work as chief detective for the county. I read an article about him in the *Chronicle*. He was a detective and worked on counter terrorism with the NYPD. He's seen a thing or two. He's a serious guy."

"And Tori?"

"Well, she came back a couple of years ago and solved her sister's disappearance."

"I remember my mom sending me an article about that," Vee said.

"Will Braddock helped her with that."

"And apparently a little more," Vee said. "He's a handsome guy. And tall."

"Yeah," Ruth Ann replied. "They're good together."

"Does Tori work... for him?"

"I don't think Tori takes orders from anybody," Ruth Ann said, laughing. "As I understand it, she is kind of freelance. She teaches at the university, helps the sheriff's department on occasion, and," Ruth Ann added with a smile, "keeps the women's clothing stores in town in business."

"That, I've seen. I thought Tori investigated missing kids, homicides, things like that."

"When she was with the FBI. I think now it's whatever comes along. I think if there is a big case of any kind in the county, she seems to be involved. Million-dollar robbery next door would probably pique her interest."

"Huh," Vee said. The last thing she wanted was Tori poking around.

"You and Tori were good friends in high school," Ruth Ann said. "I didn't know that."

Vee nodded. "Long before that. We go back to elementary school. I knew her, and Jessie, well. They were really good friends. They were popular in school, especially Jessie. I know they were identical twin sisters, but Jessie was like the... pretty one and Tori—"

"No way she was the ugly duckling."

"No. Tori was quieter though. And she wasn't as fashion conscious either. Jess was dressed to the nines and Tori was more modest. It's how we told them apart."

"She's plenty fashion conscious now," Ruth Ann replied with a smile. "She's a great customer with a really good sense of what looks good on her."

"That was my point in a way. Tori looks so much like I think Jessie would have looked," Vee noted, leaning forward, watching Tori pull on rubber gloves and step inside the store. "When I saw her for the first time in eons a few weeks ago, I did a double take. I thought I was looking at Jessie, then realized—"

"It had to be Tori."

"Yeah."

The phone rang behind them and Ruth Ann stepped away to answer it. Vee glanced down the street, observing as Tori, all business in a sharp dark-navy pant suit, stepped into the jewelry store. Will Braddock sounded and looked like a serious guy, and he was clearly the boss, talking with people, gesturing about.

They would be coming after her.

* * *

Dan woke up again just after 11:00 a.m. He rolled out of bed and went to the top dresser drawer and reached underneath his balled-up socks for the envelopes. Vee told him she found the envelopes on the top shelf of the safe. They were filled with cash. Druk had handed her both envelopes, telling her, "I know you two could use it right now. Take it."

Vee took them.

They'd put the envelopes in the dresser when they'd gotten home. Vee slept for two hours and then went to work, in part to keep up appearances and in part to see what happened.

He locked the bedroom door and retrieved the envelopes. The cash was non-sequential and was not bound in any way. It was simply cash that the store kept on hand. He knew they not only sold, but on occasion, bought as well. He counted out the cash and between the two envelopes, it totaled just over $20,000.

He hadn't seen that much money in a long time.

It was a start.

The question was what to do with it. It wouldn't be safe to keep it at the house if the police showed up for some reason and putting it in the bank would raise red flags as well, not only from the police but the bill collectors that were hounding them.

It was a problem, but for once, he was dealing with a good problem. They had some money.

And more was to come. He was anxious to hear from Druk and what their cut would be for the rest.

SIXTEEN

"THEN YOU BEST KEEP YOUR WITS ABOUT YOU."

Tori and Braddock made their way to the government center by late morning, leaving Eggleston with Nolan at the scene. Braddock went off to check-in with Boe and bring her up to speed. Tori went into the investigations offices and found Steak at his desk.

"Lakes Jewelry, huh?" he said.

"Yeah, they came in through the air duct from the roof."

"No shit!" Steak said with a big smile. "Tell me more."

Tori gave him a rundown of what they found at the scene. "They rolled up in what looks like a van. Three people climbed up onto the roof, they used the old fire escape ladder and the van backed away. From there, one of them came in through the duct and cut the power, internet, video, all of it."

"That's some *Ocean's Eleven* shit there."

Tori snorted a laugh. "Yeah, I guess we're looking for The Amazing Yen. It had to be someone very small and agile to slither through that duct."

"A four-person crew then," Steak stated. "Three up to the roof and a wheel man."

"Looks that way," Tori replied and sat down into her cube,

putting her feet up on her desk. "The jewelry store is interesting and all but not really my jam, you know. What's up with the Ally Mannion case? And Dennis Kellin?"

Kellin was their one good lead. Since his death, the investigation had stalled in the sense there were no other witnesses and minimal forensic findings. In the past week, while she and Braddock spent most of their time entertaining Tracy and Sam, Steak had worked two angles. A background on Dennis Kellin, which he'd forwarded to Tori. The other was to see if they could get onto their two killers through other crimes they may have committed. That had been the heavier lift.

"I reviewed the summary on Kellin," Tori said. "Until this heist interrupted my morning, I was going to come in here and dig into that."

"And you're digging entails what exactly?"

"Going up to Grand Rapids and kicking over some rocks. Paper is paper. I want to talk to some people. He has a relative or two up there still. Neighbors. Employers. He was in this bar fight and got arrested. Are there witnesses to this bar fight that were friends of his? He had a drug charge once. What was that all about? What was his life really like up there? I want to do some knockin', walkin' and talkin'."

"I've been meaning to run up there myself," Steak said. "I've been digging on our two killers. I have an interesting one we should take a look at."

Tori sat up. "Give me the skinny."

"Four years ago, there was a home invasion up in Grand Rapids. A husband and wife, both doctors, were attacked by two large men in ski masks when they arrived home from a political fundraiser for the governor. It was a black-tie event, or at least as black tie and fancy as it gets up in these parts. Lots of dignitaries at the event, which was held at the home of one Kyle Mannion."

"There's an interesting tie-in," Tori said.

"I got that jolt initially too, but I think, in this case, it is just a coincidence," Steak replied.

"So, these folks drove down here from Grand Rapids?"

"Yeah. What's intriguing is that it all went down around the same time that Dennis Kellin was living up there and working with his uncle."

"Wade Chew again."

"And Chew said his nephew was working with a couple of guys that could steal anything. I'm thinking it's possible it's the two guys we're looking for. The men wore masks. They put a knife to the throat of his wife and made the man open the safe before smacking him around some. They cleaned that out and got away with jewels, art, and cash. And get this, the home-owner said he swore one of the intruder's boots smelled like fish."

"That's intriguing," Tori said, nodding.

"I thought it might be."

"It's time for a road trip."

"I figured you and Braddock would want to head up there."

"He's tied up with the jewelry store deal for the time being. It's you and me, my friend. Let's kill two birds with one stone. We'll go talk to these victims of the home invasion and talk to some of Kellin's old acquaintances. See what we find. Make a day of it tomorrow."

Tori's phone buzzed. It was Braddock.

"What's up? Uh-huh. You want me to what?"

They met Jennison at the jewelry store in the storage room. She had a borescope cable running into the duct and a small monitor in front of her. "I was examining the duct shaft, seeing if we could find anything in there. And I did."

With the hand control she moved the end of the cable right to left, slowly. "This is the turn where that duct comes from outside into the building. It's where it gets really tight. Whoever it was that came down that duct, rubbed against a seam on that turn." On the monitor, hanging down from the seam in the duct were a few wispy black fibers.

Tori leaned in behind Jennison. "It's not just fibers though, is it. What's that discoloration? It's right on that seam."

"I thought you might see that," Jennison said.

"Ann, is that blood?"

"Could be, which could maybe give us an identification," Jennison said. "So, fibers and blood." She turned to Tori. "I can't remotely fit in there and I don't have anyone else on staff who can. You're small, skinny, and you've collected evidence. It's just a burglary I know, but—"

"I'm your only option." Tori exhaled a breath, her lips flapping. "Am I going to get stuck in there? Am I even going to be able to breathe?" She felt the beat of her heart already increasing.

"You'll be fine," Braddock said with a big grin. "We'll put a harness on you. I'll pull you out if you start freaking out."

"I'm, you know, kind of claustrophobic," Tori said, panicked.

"Just kind of though," Braddock said with a mischievous grin.

"This isn't funny!" She stepped up on the ladder and peered inside the duct. "How far do I have to go?"

"Well..." Jennison started, "ten feet, maybe a... little... more."

Tori shook her head. "That's more than ten feet. What if I screw this up because I'm, as you said, freaking out?"

"Then you best keep your wits about you."

Tori stared daggers at him.

"I can talk you through it," Jennison said.

Braddock dropped the jokes and turned serious. "We need you here. You can do this."

Tori closed her eyes and whispered through gritted teeth: "Fine."

Jennison helped Tori into one of her forensics full-body coveralls. She was taller and bigger than Tori so it was a bit long and bulky, but it would work. Next was the headset with a headlamp, earpiece, microphone, and small video camera. Tori tugged on rubber gloves and then checked her tools and supplies. Braddock slipped a rope through a carabiner at her waist.

"In all seriousness, if it gets to be too much. I will haul you out. Just say the word."

Tori nodded. "This is so going to cost you."

He smiled. "I'm good for it."

She glanced up at the vent opening. "Let's get this over with."

A uniformed officer was called inside, and he and Braddock lifted Tori up. She went in head first, on her back. That was the only way she'd be able to do it. They had to wrench and contort and pull her out once to get her body angled into the opening so they could turn her. Once she was inside, she lay on her back, the top of the duct mere inches from her face. She closed her eyes and tried to calm her breathing.

"Are you okay in there?"

"What do you think?" she snapped.

She'd had an MRI once, her full body in the tight tube. They'd had to pull her out three times so she could get some air. Whether she was claustrophobic or not, she didn't like confined spaces. This was most definitely that. She opened her eyes and looked past her feet. On the right, she saw where the thief had cut through the duct. *How the heck did they maneuver in here to do that?*

She exhaled a long breath.

It's only ten, maybe fifteen feet.

She closed her eyes. Using the backs of the heels on her

shoes, she pushed back. She repeatedly raised her knees and pushed back with her heels, sliding on the smooth metallic surface of the duct. Feeling she'd gone about ten feet, she opened her eyes and tilted her head back and could see the turn, the duct turning up. Two more good pushes back and the bright light of her headlamp shined on the small threads caught in the seam.

With her left hand she took tweezers out of a chest pocket. With her right hand she pulled out a small yellow envelope. Leaning onto her left side as much as she could, she was able to reach up with her right hand and pull the threads from the seam. She carefully moved the envelope underneath the tweezers and dropped the threads inside.

She closed the yellow envelope and stuck it in her chest pocket, along with the tweezers.

Now for the harder part.

She pulled out another envelope and a small pocketknife and snapped it open. Her headlamp illuminated the brown smudge. It was small, much smaller than she'd thought when she viewed it on camera. There wasn't much to work with.

Don't screw this up.

With the tip of the knife blade, she slowly scraped away the smudge, both of which were mere inches from her face, beads of sweat forming on her forehead. Even with the light, it was hard to see if the flakes were dropping into the envelope. She brought its opening close and looked inside. She could see one small dark dot.

You're missing the envelope.

She twisted as much to her left as she could and pronated her left wrist hard to the right to get the envelope right under the knife tip and scraped again. This time she saw a flake drop in. She scraped again and saw one smaller flake drop inside. The smudge was gone now. Deliberately, she closed the envelope and sealed it, stuffed it into the chest pocket on the coverall and then twisted flat onto her back. She closed her eyes and took a couple of breaths. Her body was in a full sweat.

"Get me out of here!"

Braddock pulled the rope. She slid forward, holding her heels up. The feel of his big hands grabbing her ankles allowed for a sigh of relief. Thirty seconds later Braddock, Jennison and the uniformed officer had wedged her out of the vent opening and she could finally breathe again. They lowered her to the floor. Tori lay on her back for a minute, just breathing, sweaty, dirty. She was pale as a ghost.

"That doesn't look so tight in there," Braddock mused and then looked down with a grin.

Tori crinkled her nose at him and took out the two envelopes from her chest pocket and handed them to Jennison. "See what you can do with those. Fibers. Hopefully blood. I scraped all of it."

"I saw," Jennison said, looking into the envelope with the blood shards. "I couldn't have done it better myself."

"See," she said to Braddock. "That's how you say thank you." To Jennison: "How long to find out on the blood?"

Jennison grimaced. "There's a backlog so a couple of weeks, maybe a month, unless we get something to match it against."

* * *

Dan pulled to a stop in the woods. The dashboard clock said 7:25 p.m. The dirt path was to the left into the dense woods. He followed the path as it wound its way through and around the mature trees and thick underbrush, the black shingled roof of the familiar old two-story house coming into view on the left. He emerged behind the garage, walked across the gravel driveway and up to the porch. He knocked on the back door and, a moment later, Heath let him inside. Druk was sitting at the table, drinking a beer. Heath fetched two more and they sat down at the table.

"We settled at $385,000," Druk said plainly. "That's what my guy would pay. That's about forty cents on the dollar, which is pretty standard."

Dan grimaced just a bit, which Druk noticed.

"Disappointed?"

Dan sighed. "It's a lot of risk we took—that Vee took. A man can hope for more, can he not?"

"That he can," Druk replied and then handed Dan a small duffel bag. "My guy paid $100,000 cash up front, and your half is in the bag. The rest will be wired on Wednesday to the account number you gave me. Good thing you kept that all these years."

"Wish I'd have left some money in it. Creditors have no idea it exists." He opened the duffel bag and pulled out a brick of cash, thumbing the bills.

"Be careful with that cash. Don't put it in the bank or even a safe deposit box. I wouldn't even keep it where you're living. And when you want to check if the money is in your offshore account, don't use a computer in your house or at work. Don't use your cell phone. All that shit can be tracked."

Dan nodded. "I assume you got cash too. What did you do with yours?"

"We have a place," Heath said. "You should find one too."

"I will."

"Now, as for what's next. You and Vee need to be ready."

"Already?"

Druk nodded. "We're moving quick on this one. We have to."

Heath stood up and finished the rest of his beer. "Come with us. We'll give you a preview of coming attractions."

"Vee will like this one better," Druk said. "No duct work."

SEVENTEEN

"THE FUTURE HAS NOT YET BEEN LIVED."

Braddock rolled over when the alarm went off. He was going to allow himself another hour. Tori jumped on the exercise bike and did a half-hour live class to get herself going. She met Steak in town at the government center. They bought coffees and sandwiches and set out on the ninety-minute drive northeast to Grand Rapids.

"How's the house? The project all done?" Steak said, chomping on his sandwich.

"Yeah. You've seen it, right?"

"No," Steak replied. "I saw it under various phases of construction. I haven't actually seen the finished product."

"We'll have to do something about that," Tori said. "I've got Mickey, Corinne, all the girls asking about it too. We'll have to throw a party."

"I'm down for that," Steak noted. "You two have the house, now all you have to do is get hitched."

Tori sighed in exasperation.

"Oh, oh. Did I step in it again?"

"Why? Why is it everyone thinks we have to get married? Why?"

"I don't know, I just assumed—"

"Assumed what?" Tori retorted. "That because I haven't been married, I'm dying to. That somehow getting married makes my life whole. That I have to fulfill my womanly destiny. What's next? I have to have a baby before I hit forty? Hey, Tori, better get going and kick one out—"

"Look, I didn't mean to—"

"No. I know," Tori replied, shaking her head. "I had this same conversation with my friend Tracy last week. I've had it with her a few times. And with Mickey, and Lizzy and Corinne and all the girls. It's relentless."

"Sorry."

She wasn't done venting.

"Let me ask you a question. What would marriage get me that I don't already have?"

"I don't know."

"I have Braddock. I have Quinn. I love them both. We have an amazing home, decent jobs, income, and some measure of financial security. How does marriage change any of that?"

"I don't know," Steak replied. "Maybe it doesn't."

"I mean lots of people don't even marry anymore. They have kids, build lives, have careers, and don't get married."

"I know, I know."

"And man, I see some marriages and I don't think either person is happy, but they're stuck together, because of mortgages, kids, debts, all that. We both know couples who seem to be like that, right."

"Yes," Steak said. "I didn't mean to push or pry or pressure—"

"I just... I'm happy. I'm content. I'm good."

"And if that's enough," Steak said. "Then that's enough."

They rode in silence for a bit.

"And Braddock *was* married," Tori blurted. "Meghan was the love of his life. The mother of Quinn."

"Meaning?"

"Maybe I don't like being second. And do I truly know if he's... moved on from all of that. Her parents live a half-mile away. Her brother a mile away. There are pictures of her in the house."

"Does that bother you?"

"No," Tori replied. "Well, not much anyway. And I don't even want to use the term bother, because that's not it, either. It's just that... she's there, still, you know. There's a presence. And removing pictures doesn't remove the presence. It's just... there."

"And then there's Mary," Steak said. Mary was Meghan's mother. Tori hit it off with Meghan's father Roger right away. His acceptance was almost instant. Mary's was another story. There hadn't necessarily been friction, but certainly wariness, on both sides.

"Mary and I are fine. No," Tori said, halting for a moment, "that's not even fair to her. She and I are good. She accepts me now. We talk, we have a relationship and it's getting better over time."

"Respect."

"Yes. Both ways. I had to earn it with her and she with me. And that's making it all the better I think."

"And the family?"

"I feel welcome, Steak, I really do. But Meghan's presence is still there. The only family I have is that one and it was Meghan's family. That's part of Braddock's and Quinn's life that will never go away."

"Nor should it."

"That's right," Tori agreed. "I've found some space in all of that. And I'm happy with it. I don't want or need any more than that right now."

"Yeah?"

"Yeah."

"If you're good, I'm good."

She had lots of girlfriends to talk to these days, and they all liked to talk, but Steak was her best guy friend. Every woman needed one or two of them for a perspective from the other side. When she was with the Bureau, living in New York City, it was Geno Harlow. Here, it was Steak. They'd been close friends since childhood, he, Jessie, and her. There was a bond there and he looked after her like she was his little sister, even if they were the same age. And he was one that was never afraid to call her on things and had, frequently.

"You've been back two years now. And I don't want you to ever leave again."

Tori smiled and patted Steak on the arm. "I'm not going anywhere, my friend. I'd like to take some more trips, travel, see the world, but this is home again."

"Permanently you think?"

"Who knows. The future has not yet been lived."

"Funny." Steak sat quietly for a moment. "One thing though."

"What's that?"

"And this has nothing to do with marriage, okay?"

"Okay."

"People can have more than one love of their life. You don't need to take a back seat to anyone. Not to Meghan's memory, not to her family. She's gone, Tori. You're here. You might have come along second, but now, you're number one."

"I know," Tori said. "But, buddy, it's also the case that it's all earned in time."

"And you think you're still earning."

"I think you always are. Aren't you with your wife?"

Steak chuckled. "Yeah, I suppose I am. She sure tells me I am. I suppose if you don't want to keep earning it—"

"Then what's the point," Tori replied. "Isn't that what a meaningful relationship is? Earning it every day."

Steak snorted a laugh. "How'd you figure that out?"

"Just because I never had any sort of a relationship pre-Braddock doesn't mean I wasn't observing my friends and colleagues that did. Tracy was married. Geno was married. I was around people with healthy relationships, and I envied them for it."

"Yet, you never had one?"

"For a long time, I wasn't built for one."

"But now?"

"Let's just say I'm a work in progress. I've got some baggage of my own you know."

"Ha! Tori Hunter and self-awareness. Where was that when you were seventeen?" Steak quipped.

"Very funny, very droll," Tori replied. "But to your point, I'm kind of neurotic and self-absorbed. There's my view or the wrong view and I'm often reluctant to let others in."

"You just let me in."

"You're basically my brother."

Steak laughed.

"I'm a bit of a Rubik's Cube but Braddock puts up with me. I've got a lot of, for lack of a better term, emotional stuff that I'm still reconciling. He is patient with it. I can run hot. He calmly handles it. He talks me off the ledge, and, on occasion, calls me on my shit like when I ran off to New York last summer because we fought. He didn't put up with it. He said commit or that's it."

"And you committed."

"Yes," Tori replied. "So, tell me, Steak. How can I not want to earn it with someone who has and continues to put up with all that?"

"I don't think he'd call it putting up with," Steak said with a headshake.

"He likes a challenge."

"You are that."

"Thanks, pal."

"But there's more to it than that, and you know it. He's whipped on you pretty good."

"As he should be," Tori said with a smile. "But enough about my relationship life. I'm tired of talking about it with *everyone*. Let's you and I talk about what we're going to do today."

Dr. Eustis Fowler lived just south of Grand Rapids on the Wendigo Bay Arm of Pokegama Lake. The Fowler residence was a large two-story home set on a multi-acre stretch of the lake, the waters of which were visible through some scattered trees. Dr. Fowler, along with Detective Lon Lempe, greeted them in front of the three-car garage. Introductions were made. Fowler's wife Tonya, also a victim, was on a trip out of the country.

"You think the men who attacked Doctor Fowler four years ago were responsible for the murders you're investigating?" Lempe asked.

"Possibly," Tori replied. "There are some commonalities." She looked to Fowler. "You noted that one of the men's boots or shoes smelled like fish?"

"Oh, yes, I remember," Dr. Fowler said. "I know the smell. My nose was like two inches from the boot. It smelled of fish and lake water."

"I know you don't want to re-live it, Doc, but can you walk us through what happened?" Steak said.

Fowler walked them to his garage. "Tonya and I got home from a formal event down your way. It was very late. We got out of our cars and two large men with masks were right on us, coming in the garage door. They boxed us in. One had a gun up, the other a knife.

"Tonya started to scream. The man with the knife grabbed

her, put a hand over her mouth and had the knife at her throat. The other rushed me, putting the gun in my face."

"Did they say anything?"

"Just for me to get us into the house and shut off the security system. Once I did that, he ordered me to open my safe." Fowler led them inside to his home office. The safe was installed inside a built-in cabinet. "I put a new one in after the theft, although these days I keep a lot less here and more in my safe deposit boxes at the bank. I tapped in the combination and opened it. That's when the guy hit me from behind and my face was by his boot. He smacked my head again, put tape over my mouth and then a pillowcase over my head. They did the same to Tonya and put us both in the corner."

"When he knocked you to the floor, is that when you noticed the smell of fish?"

"Yeah," Fowler replied with a furrowed brow. "I'd kinda forgotten about that. Why does that interest you?"

"It maybe ties in with our case in a way," Tori replied. "How did they even know you had a safe?"

Fowler shrugged. "I don't know. Maybe they assumed. They picked a good night though. They got Tonya's diamond necklace, earrings, and a brooch. And other jewels from the safe here, some watches, coins I'd collected and cash. I was a baseball card collector, and they took those as well. Then with us all tied up, they went through the house and took more jewelry and some pieces of art, our silver. Cleaned us out but good."

"You said they picked a good night," Tori noted. "Why?"

"Because Tonya was wearing her diamond jewelry. We'd taken the pieces out of the safe deposit box that day."

"Interesting," Tori murmured. "Now, you had been down in Manchester Bay, right? At Kyle Mannion's?"

"Yes," Fowler replied and shook his head. "And it was Kyle's daughter who was... murdered. I'm getting the connection now."

Tori shook her head. "That's more coincidental we think. We do think that it's possible that the people who robbed you, were the people who killed Ally. I assume there was a big crowd at this event?"

"Yes," Fowler said. "There were a lot of regionally connected people there. Some press because the governor and a senator attended. Lots of political types so it was something of a known event, I guess."

"Was the guest list published anywhere publicly? In the paper? Or the Internet? Via e-mail?"

"Not that I was aware of," Fowler replied. "Certainly not in advance, unless they had access to it through the governor or perhaps Kyle, his company, or someone hired to work the event. It was catered."

"Would the catering company have access to the guest list?" Lempe asked.

"We could check," Tori said. "But if they did, no offense, Doctor Fowler, but how would anyone know *you* had all of this in your home?"

"I don't know."

"Yet they were lying here in wait for you."

"I think so. Neither of us noticed them when we pulled up," Fowler said. "The way our driveway curves toward the garage, we wouldn't have seen them hiding around the side, but they certainly would have seen the approach of our headlights. It was late, well after midnight when we got home."

"Was it just the two of them?"

"I only saw two men."

"Before you were blindfolded?"

"Yes."

"Did they say anything to you other than take us inside and to the safe?"

Fowler thought for a moment and then shook his head. "I can't really remember."

Lempe had his investigation file, flipping through pages and then nodded. "I think I asked you the same question, Doc, four years ago. My notes say you heard one man say something, like in a whisper: 'Yo, over there.' I think that's when they were taking the Cezanne off the wall."

"Cezanne?" Steak asked.

"He's a quite famous painter," Tori replied.

"Somewhere in the world, that painting is up on someone's wall," Fowler said.

Tori went back to the attack. "Doctor Fowler, this man you heard, he said: 'Yo, over there.'"

"I think so."

"You're certain?"

"Yes."

Tori let her eyes slide to Steak. These were their guys.

"Now in the police report we saw the reference to boots or shoes smelling like fish. Now that we have your mind back in that night, do you remember anything else? Anything they said, did, other smells?"

Fowler bit his lip for a moment. "You know, I do. I'm an otolaryngologist."

"Which is what?" Steak said.

"An ENT," Tori replied. "Ears, nose, and throat doctor." To Fowler: "I'm guessing you're sensitive to smell."

"Yes," Fowler replied. "Which is why I picked up on the foul minty smell when the man's head was near mine."

"Foul minty smell?" Tori asked, uncertain.

"Chewing tobacco," Steak replied. "Skoal Wintergreen I'm betting."

"Your brand?"

"I've been known to indulge." There was a round tin in his back pocket.

"You should stop," Fowler counseled.

"You sound like my dentist, and my wife."

"Well, they're both right," Fowler affirmed. "I've smelled that smell many a time examining patients. The man was a chewer, no doubt about it."

Tori and Steak exchanged another look. She and Braddock had found tobacco pouches across the bay from the Taylor and Wallace cabins, along with sunflower seeds. "Any other olfactory smells, Doc?" Tori said.

"No, not that I recall, just the fish and that," Fowler replied with a sly smile.

"How long were they in the house?"

"An hour maybe," Fowler said. "At least an hour after I opened the safe and they tied me up and put tape over my mouth. I could hear them moving through the house, going in and out of the garage. I think one of them must have gone to get a vehicle. The last I remember hearing them that night was when the garage door was closing and one of them went out the front door. Then it was quiet. Not a sound. The next morning, Friday, was our house cleaner's day. She found us and called the police."

"Were you insured?" Steak said.

Fowler nodded. "Most everything had been valued in the last couple of years prior to the burglary."

"Any problems with coverage?"

"We had to go through the investigation with the police and insurance company, so it took some time, but yes, most of the loss was covered. Detective Lempe here was quite helpful in that regard."

"No doubt they were robbed. Insurance company was a little skeptical at first, but we weren't so... it just took a little time."

"To be honest," Fowler said, "I'm just glad we survived it. Everything else was replaceable."

Ten minutes later Tori and Steak talked with Lempe as they walked down the driveway.

"What do you think?" Lempe asked.

"It's possible it's our guys," Tori replied. "Two-man crew, taste for violence, the smell of fish."

"Thankfully, the Fowlers survived," Steak noted. "I suspect they were wearing masks so they didn't see their faces."

"And you talked to Ole' Wade Chew about them?"

"You knew him?" Tori said.

"Oh, hell, I knew he was dirty for years but never made anything stick until the Feds got onto him."

"Chew said his nephew told him these two guys could and would steal anything," Tori replied. "They were stealing boats down in our county and maybe up here too. And now maybe a home invasion to steal jewels and cash as well. My question is how did they identify Fowler? He's a doctor, went to a swanky affair and Mrs. Fowler wore her fancy jewels. How did they know that they would be doing it on *that* night? How did they know she had those jewels? They were lying in wait at the absolute perfect time."

"Schedule?" Steak said.

Tori nodded.

They all turned around and walked back up the driveway. "Doctor Fowler. One more question," Steak called, seeing him in the garage. "Do you have a record of your schedule in the weeks before you were attacked?"

Steak explained what they were interested in. Fowler said he would retrieve his schedule and email it to Steak.

"I keep pretty much everything on my work calendar: work, events, vacations, oil changes, boat drop off, golf rounds, all that stuff, along with all my patient appointments."

As the three of them walked back down the driveway, Tori returned to Dennis Kellin and Wade Chew. "Kellin was murdered, we think by our guys. Kellin was from here until about a year ago. Do you know anything about him?"

Lempe nodded. "I knew Denny Kellin, not well, but I knew

him a bit. Let's go to my office and I'll dig up what we have for you."

A half-hour later, Lempe handed them a folder. "That's all we have. He was busted for marijuana possession a number of years ago. It was probably enough to deal but he got probation. Four years or so ago he was in a bar fight at The Port out of Pokegama Lake. Popular spot with the locals. A lot went on that night there. I investigated the aftermath of the brawl and I remember interviewing Kellin. He was a regular there."

He flipped through the investigative notes he had. "It actually started with Denny. He was not the aggressor, other than hitting on a woman. Her boyfriend, a fella named... let's see here, Shane Buckley, *that guy*."

"That guy?" Steak said.

"Buckley was a guy with a colorful history of his own. He took offense to Kellin putting the moves on his woman and started throwing haymakers at Kellin and anyone in his vicinity. A bar brawl ensued, multiple combatants and lots of shit got broken. Kellin spent the night in jail with several others and was bailed out in the morning."

Tori took the file. There were photos of Kellin. She held it up. "He took a beating it seems."

Lempe nodded. "Yeah, pretty bad black eye. Buckley got his shots in. It was far from his first fight."

"Was he arrested?"

"Yes," Lempe said. "He was a real dick. I was none too surprised he ended up dead a few months later."

"Dead?"

"Found dead in a parking lot up in Ely. He was a guy who had some enemies. That night at The Port was not the first time he'd tangled with the law. He was a shit disturber, quick fuse type who never shied from an altercation. He might have been a militia guy, there is a little of that out in the woods around here."

"A little crazy then," Steak said.

"More than a little. He finally went too far and someone took him out. As I recall, he was basically beaten to death, with fists and feet, and then his throat was slit."

"Ooh," Steak grimaced.

"Not a great way to go."

"They ever find who killed him?"

"No," Lempe replied. "Unsolved as far as I know. As for Kellin. He did a night in jail and that was it. But like I said, he was a regular out there. If you want to know more about him, you could go out to The Port. Lots of long-time employees. They might know more."

They got to The Port just after what constituted the lunch rush, though the boat slips down on the lake were mostly full, folks sitting on the patio or at the outside bar having cocktails on a sultry summer day. They decided to go inside.

As they reached the host stand, a mid-thirties woman approached. "Would you like a table?"

Steak and Tori shared a look. They hadn't eaten. "Sure," Steak said. "And we're looking for some information on a once regular customer from some years ago."

The hostess said she would find the manager. While she did, they were sat at a high-top table overlooking the patio and further, the waters of Pokegama Lake. Beneath them were tables with umbrellas and an outdoor bar that had a tiki-like look to it that seemed to specialize in blended summer drinks like pina coladas and strawberry daiquiris. To the side were two sand volleyball courts, one of which was occupied by six swim-suit-clad college-aged kids who'd likely arrived by one of the boats tied up in the line of slips along the wide dock. They both took a quick look at the menu. The Port was known for its pizza, and they quickly settled on the Mexican.

"You like your lettuce," Steak mused. "Even on a pizza."

"You should like lettuce a little more, maybe."

"Ouch," Steak replied with a chuckle. He talked often of working out more. To this point it was mostly talk, though Braddock had managed to get him into some pickup basketball last winter.

"Are there still a lot of resorts on the lake?" Tori asked Steak as she sipped her water.

"I don't think as many as there used to be. Not the little six-eight cabin ones anyway. The big resorts are still hanging in there."

"Have you fished this lake?"

"Many a time." Steak didn't want to be tied down to one lake. He liked hauling his fishing boat or pontoon to different lakes. "I brought Braddock up here a few times pre-you, just for something new. That was back when he was learning to fish. Now, he doesn't need any help."

"Do you remember sneaking up here when we were in high school?" Tori asked with a mischievous smile.

"Oh." Steak laughed, throwing his head back. "I sure do."

"They didn't check IDs too carefully. And Big Jim wasn't the sheriff up here."

"It was The Quarry or sneak up here," he replied, grinning. "Those were the days when we could get away with some stuff, you know."

Tori smiled and nodded. "Lots of shenanigans back then." Jessie was the one with the idea to come up here and get away from the watchful eyes of their father and his deputies, who knew and were under unofficial orders to keep out a watchful eye for the Hunter girls.

"These days we're the fun police," Steak said. "Now I get

the same looks and eye rolls from kids I probably used to give your dad's guys."

"Cycle of life, my friend."

Two women approached the table. Betsy Davis was the manager and Stephanie Lake, a bartender. Tori explained why they were there.

"We both knew Denny," Betsy said, smiling. "It's so sad what happened to him."

"Had you seen him recently?"

"No," Betsy said and looked to Stephanie. "You?"

"I'd heard he moved away," Stephanie said. "It's months since I've seen him."

"What was he like?" Tori started.

"Nice enough," Stephanie replied. "Denny was around here all the time, liked to flirt with us servers, and really any other woman about. He was a volume hit'er on 'er."

"He *thought* he was a ladies' man," Betsy said with a small smile, "except, he really wasn't."

"He took his shots?" Tori asked.

"Oh yeah. He'd throw it out there all the time. Occasionally he got a bite," Betsy said.

"Occasionally?"

"Let's just say he was a better troller of fish than women."

"He try it with you two?"

Stephanie scoffed. "Only all the time. He'd lean in, closing time near and say: 'It's late, Steph. Two people like us shouldn't be alone on a night like tonight.' Then he'd flick his eyebrows."

"Oh God," Tori said, laughing.

"He was harmless that way," Betsy said. "He was also the guy that would walk you to your car to make sure you were safe. You could trust him in that sense. Not a bad guy at all. Just not one I ever had any interest in."

"We have a police report here," Steak said. "About a bar fight he was in. A big brawl."

They both threw their heads back in laughter. "*That* was wild, that night," Betsy said. "It was like one of those fights you see in the movies. Total *Road House* stuff."

"And Denny was right in the middle of it," Steph added. "He was the spark that lit the flame."

"How so?"

"We'd had our fishing tournament that day."

"The Three-Man Open?" Steak asked.

"Yes," Betsy said.

"I've competed in that. It's massive." He turned to Tori. "The Three-Man means a three-man fishing team—"

"I gathered," Tori said. "No need to mansplain."

"Oh, I like you," Steph said to Tori.

"Give it time," Steak retorted.

Betsy laughed. "And as the event sponsor, it's a massive day and night here. That night, it was late, and it was still standing room only. The fire marshal would not have approved of how packed it was." Betsy turned to Steph. "You saw it start."

"Denny was on the winning team, and he made sure everyone knew. He was right at the bar, having a good ole time and was putting the Denny swerve on a woman, a tall brunette with wild curly hair. She was clearly with another guy, who got pissed at Denny's relentlessness that night and finally gave him a hard shove back into the bar and then landed a punch, hit Denny square in the jaw. Denny threw one back and then all hell broke loose."

"The brawl was on," Betsy said. "Beer glasses are flying around, tables getting broken, people screaming. It was total chaos."

"The police were in here pretty quick, though," Steph noted. "They put all the 'warriors' in cuffs and hauled them off to the jail. I remember Denny, his face all bloody, was one they walked out, along with many others. Then the clean-up started."

"And Kellin won it? This fishing tournament?" Tori said.

"Yes."

"He would have had teammates. Who were they?"

Betsy looked to Steph. "Do you remember?"

Steph shook her head, "No." She turned around and walked to a wall on the other side of the bar and took a photo out of a long line of pictures and returned. "This was the team," she handed the picture to Tori.

Steak looked over her shoulder. Kellin was in the middle, holding a massively sized check for $10,000. One man stood to his left, another to his right, both bigger guys. Their names were typed on a white strip on the bottom: "Dennis Kellin, Ledyard Heath and Lenny Druk."

"Do you know either of those two guys?" Tori asked.

Betsy shook her head and looked at Steph, who shook hers.

"They're not familiar to me," Steph said. "You?"

"No," Betsy said.

"This place is busy most of the time," Steph continued. "There are lots of really regular regulars and then some not so regular types. I'm a Grand Rapids lifer but those guys don't ring a bell. They were clearly here that day though. That picture was against the wall right over there."

"Were they in the bar fight?"

"I have no idea."

"That brawl started," Betsy said, "and it was duck and cover time."

Steak called Lempe about Ledyard Heath and Lenny Druk. Lempe called back while they drove south from Grand Rapids.

"Those two were not in the group arrested that night. Perhaps they were involved but didn't do anything to throw more gas on that fire, but their names are not anywhere in the investigative report or witness accounts."

Tori had the faraway stare for much of the ninety-minute ride back to Manchester Bay.

"What are you thinking?" Steak asked after driving in silence.

"Do you buy it was a coincidence that this Buckley dude ends up dead a few months later?"

"The timing is... curious, though Lempe said he likely had a lengthy list of enemies."

"True, but it was just months after this fight that he met his maker."

"Beaten to death."

"His throat cut."

Steak shrugged. "You think it was the two guys we're after?"

"I don't know. The timing makes one wonder."

"Fine, but does that put us any closer to knowing who these two guys were that robbed the Fowlers and if they're the same people who killed Kellin, or Ally Mannion and Reed Schafer?"

"We could ask this Heath and Druk," Tori said. "Maybe we should have while we were there."

Steak called Reese to look them up. The call came back twenty minutes later. "They live in Garrison these days," Reese reported. "Druk has owned a home there for years. Heath lists his address there as well with the DMV."

"Hey," Tori said to Reese. "How did that date go?"

"Good. She did see me talking on the phone to you. I told her all about you and Braddock. Your exploits are legendary apparently. She knew who you were."

"Wise move. That got you a second date I bet."

"I'd prefer to think it was my charm and good looks that accomplished that."

"I'm sure that was a small factor as well."

Reese dropped off the line.

"We should go see these two guys," Tori suggested. "Close the loop."

"Sure," Steak said, checking his watch. "But tomorrow. The day is getting long and I'm a little worn out."

"A lot going on all the sudden."

"We have a regular crime wave with two crews operating in our waters, or so it would seem. The boats and murders and then the jewelry store hit."

"The jewelry store," Tori said with a wry smile. "Something like that is never funny but..."

"It sounds kind of cool, doesn't it?" Steak said. "Dropping someone down an air conditioning duct to cut the power. I'd rather be working that. That one will be fun."

It was after 6:00 p.m. when they reached Manchester Bay and the government center.

"That's a long day," Steak said. "I'm clocking out. You?"

Tori checked her watch. "I need to go see about a dress."

EIGHTEEN

"BURGLARIES, ROBBERIES, WHITE COLLAR CRIME IS NOT WHAT DROVE ME TO THE FBI."

As Tori approached Fashion by Julia, she saw the yellow crime scene tape strung along the front of Lakes Jewelry juddering in the light breeze of the evening, a day after the burglary. The jewelry store was still closed, though the lights were on inside. A Bureau of Criminal Apprehension truck parked on the street. Ann Jennison stepped outside.

"Hi, Ann. Still working this one?"

"Hey, Tori," Jennison greeted, surprised. "What brings you by?"

"A dress I have on order next door. I bought it a few weeks ago but it needed altering." She took a peek inside the jewelry store. "Besides my little foray into the duct, have you found anything?"

Jennison grimaced as she took off her rubber gloves. "Not really. There are fingerprints all over the store, the safe, work areas that we'll have to sift through. We found no prints around either the vent opening on the roof, where they cut the duct open to cut the wires, or inside that storage room. We have rope fibers, and they used some sort of small saw to cut through the duct so we have shavings, but I don't think either will get us anywhere. They tell us a little about the how, but not the who. The only possibility we have on the who are those fibers and blood. That's all TBD."

"And the showroom?"

"Plenty of fingerprints on the cases and the keys, but again—"

"They of course wore gloves. You wouldn't be so brilliant as to pull the whole come through duct routine and then leave fingerprints behind," Tori said with a nod. "Anything from the security system?"

"Nada," Jennison replied before taking a drink of water. "Internet, power and then the video and wiring were all cut. Took down the whole system in five seconds once they cut that hole in the duct. I'm sure there was convenience in having all that wiring together, but it was a security vulnerability as well."

"And someone knew of that vulnerability," Tori replied.

"Sheryl Eggleston has her work cut out for her."

"If I know her, there is one question she's already asking. How did these guys know to cut through the duct at that spot? And how did they know that if they did, that they could take down the whole system?"

"Inside job?"

"Of some kind," Tori said. "Maybe someone who installed those systems. Perhaps a former employee. It could be a vendor who noticed it and realized what could be done. Or the building contractor and any subcontractors. These buildings were refurbished in the past few years. Lots of workers in and out. And, of course, she'll have to investigate the owner."

"I fail to see how she benefits from all this."

"The only way I see it working for her is if insurance covers everything and then she gets paid on the stolen property, but I can't really see that all being worth it. She looked absolutely devastated when I was here yesterday. Years of business and customer goodwill lost in an instant with everything stolen out of the safe. A lot of personal pieces were stolen along with all the new stuff. Hard to get that customer trust back once it's gone."

Jennison leaned back against her SUV. "Still, Tori, this was no smash and grab job. They went to great lengths so that they could get inside and have time. I've heard of stuff like this before, but I've never seen it. Repelling down a duct? Really."

Tori chuckled. "You know Steak and I were talking about this." She related their *Ocean's Eleven* comparison. "Ann, I can tell you, the person to get through that duct had to be small. I just had inches within which to work to tweeze those fibers and scrape that blood. Whoever did it, had to be small, much smaller than me."

"A child?"

"It would have had to have been one hell of a brave one that could go down that duct in the dark and then use a saw and cut at the very right spot."

"Adult then," Jennison said. "A very small or thin one. The other thing is when I look at that duct work, the turn at the bottom back into the building is really tight. That required flexibility because I don't think even someone as small as we're thinking could do a full body rotation in there. If they were going to cut that duct, they had to come in on their stomach to get any sort of leverage in there. So, to make that turn head first, they were arching the heck out of their back."

"You do yoga, right?"

"Yeah. Don't you?"

"Yes. That's one heck of an upward-facing dog you're doing in that confined space to make the turn," Tori said. "You're having to arch the back to make basically a ninety degree turn in a twenty-four by eighteen duct. The duct has a slight bend in it but still, you'd have to be Ms. Superflex to do it. Someone like Vee there." She waved to Vee, who was working in the front display window for Fashion by Julia. Vee waved back.

"Why her?"

"In high school she was a gymnast, a good one."

"Ah, she's a friend of yours then?"

"Yeah. We graduated together," Tori replied, observing Vee finishing dressing a mannequin. "Someone like that, college aged, young, or maybe a young, small, thin yoga instructor who could twist themselves into an absolute pretzel. I mean I'm in pretty decent shape for my age..."

"Oh yeah, you're so old."

"My point is, though, I'm thirty-nine now. I do yoga a couple times a week but there is absolutely zero chance I could do that turn, not without permanently trashing my lumbar and maybe even thoracic spine. You'd need someone who was young and flexible."

"I see your point," Jennison said. "I'll keep that in mind, mention it in my report or to Eggs. That it would require flexibility, and for the suspect to either be super thin or super small. I'll cite you as my expert source given your experience in the duct."

"Then it's unassailable," Tori said with a laugh. "Are you calling it a day soon?"

"Yes. I was just getting ready when you got here."

"Then don't let me stop you." Tori opened the door and stepped inside Fashion by Julia and caught Vee's attention.

"What brings... you in? Oh wait—" Vee's eyes brightened "—your dress?"

Tori pulled a receipt out of her small clutch wallet. "Exactly."

"Let me grab it for you." A minute later Vee came back with the blue dress, pulling up the plastic covering. "I'm sure you want to try it on again to be sure we got the hem right."

"Yes, I probably should," Tori said. "Could you grab me a pair of three-inch heels if you would? Size five."

"Sure thing." Vee retrieved a pair of black pumps. "These should do for now."

Tori stepped into the changing room, kicked off her work shoes and quickly changed into the dress. She stepped out of the changing room and went right to the mirror. "What do you think?" Tori stood in front of the mirror in the flowery blue summer dress, turning to check out a profile look.

"You have a nice sense of what looks good on you," Vee observed, standing behind her and then kneeling to check the hem. "And the hem looks right to me."

"I think so," Tori replied as she slipped out of the shoes. Vee leaned down to pick them up, her sweater slipping off her shoulders. "Vee, what happened to your shoulder?"

"Oh," Vee said, standing up quickly and pulling the sweater up. "I... uh... cut myself, or really kind of got scratched."

"How?" Tori asked as they walked to the checkout area.

"Oh, I was trimming some bushes in my mom's backyard. I was bent over and then stood up and a thorn got me but good. I was wearing a spaghetti strap top. Not the brightest move."

"Hi, Tori," Ruth Ann said, approaching the checkout counter. "Your dress. We're good?"

"Very."

"Tori, is there anything else tonight?" Vee asked.

"No, just the dress, and," Tori said, "how about going for a drink? My treat for helping me with the dress."

"Tori, that's my job, plus I have more work to do. I'm not off for another hour."

"Oh, just go," Ruth Ann said. "It's slow. We've got this covered, Vee. Go ahead."

"You're sure?"

"Yes," Ruth Ann said with a dismissive wave. "Go. You two catch-up."

"Okay," Vee said and turned to Tori. "Where are we going?"

"The Bourbon Room," Tori said. "It's just down the street."

The dinner rush had long since passed and only a few of the tables still had diners. Tori and Vee grabbed stools at the bar. The bartender strolled over. "What can I get you two?"

"What are you drinking, Vee?"

"Uh…" She looked at the drink menu. "What do you drink here?"

"When I'm with Braddock, usually a Whisky Old-Fashioned but I've had a few too many of those lately. I'm in the mood for something more… summery."

"I could go for a mojito." Vee looked over to the bartender. "Can you make me one?"

"Sure can."

"Make it two," Tori said, and looked to Vee. "Are you hungry? I'm starving. It's been a long day. The flatbread pizzas are great here."

"I could go for a bite."

Tori placed the order and their mojitos quickly arrived. "Cheers," Tori said. "To old friends catching up."

Vee returned the toast and took a sip of her drink. "I saw you yesterday," she said. "Going into the jewelry store. After the robbery."

"Technically, it's a burglary since nobody was hurt, thankfully. Braddock got the call, and he dragged me along for a look."

Vee picked up on the tone. "What? Jewelry store robberies or burglaries don't interest you?"

"Burglaries, robberies, white collar crime is not what drove me to the FBI," Tori said, taking a sip of her drink.

"That, I imagine, was Jessie."

Tori nodded.

"Sorry, I shouldn't have—"

"No," Tori said, clasping Vee's left hand, "it's okay. I've

made peace with all that, at least mostly. I still think of Jessie everyday but now in a mostly good way. I can think of all the good times and smile about them. And there were lots of those, weren't there?"

"Yes," Vee said, nodding. "I do have to tell you, the first night you came in the store, I thought you were Jessie. I thought I was looking at her."

Tori smiled widely. "Well, we were identical twins after all, but we didn't dress alike or wear our hair alike. Jess was the model, I was the geek."

"I don't think it was quite like that. But Jess was the... louder of the two of you." Vee twirled her glass before taking a sip. "My mom sent me some articles, about all that with Jeff Warner. One of our own doing that to her. I couldn't believe it."

Tori nodded. "He played us all. I came back to confront all that, to solve it once and for all and then leave. I never expected to stay."

Vee smiled. "I also saw the reason why you stayed yesterday. He's a catch, Tori. Very handsome and very tall."

"Braddock," Tori replied with a smile. "Yeah, he is, and, he is."

"You always just call him Braddock?"

Tori nodded, smiling. "Yeah, I did that from the start, and it just kind of stuck. His name is Will. I don't use it very much, although I'm not sure why. I really like that name too but to me, he's Braddock. A good old Irish boy from Long Island."

"Did you know him when you lived in New York?"

"No. I met him here. Go figure."

"Ruth Ann said you're living together."

Tori nodded. "For about a year now. A new thing for me, that's for sure."

"Never married?"

"No," Tori said with a whimsical smile.

"Who says you have to be."

"That's right," Tori said. "To be honest, Vee, he's the first real true relationship I've ever had. I said I've made peace with what happened to Jessie. It took twenty years, solving the case, Braddock, and therapy to get me there."

"Hey, I'm not judging. I've only ever had one relationship," Vee said. "I just so happened to start dating my husband when we were freshmen in high school."

Tori chuckled. "And you and Dan are still together. That's a testament to the two of you."

"It's something," Vee said.

"The last year has been tough I imagine."

Vee nodded.

"How did you end up in Florida to begin with?"

"Dan and I finally got married, didn't yet have Sarah and wanted a change in lifestyle. Neither of us had ever left Minnesota."

"Some place with no winters."

"Exactly. I mean, do you like being back in them?"

"I never really left them. Boston and New York City, among other places on the east coast, have fairly brutal winters too. But, to your point, I did think I would clutch up at the cold, but I really haven't, at least yet."

"I'm pretty sure I will," Vee said as she sipped her drink and mocked a shiver.

"So, you moved to Florida."

"Fort Myers Beach. We were both working regular jobs when we saw this closed restaurant along the beach. We wanted to be our own bosses, so we cobbled together what we had, got a loan, bought it, and fixed it up over time. We had our own restaurant and then later a gift shop right on the Gulf," she said. "It was... great," she said wistfully. "It was hard work, but God, I loved it. We were successful, had a few dollars in the bank. Sarah was happy. Life was good."

"And then Hurricane Ian?"

"First it was Hurricane Irma a few years before that took us out the first time."

"The first time? This happened *twice*?"

Vee explained how the storm surge from Hurricane Irma wiped them out five years ago, and what their supposed insurance did and ultimately didn't cover in the way of flood damage. "We had a decision to make. Tap everything we had to rebuild or salvage what we could and just walk away."

"You didn't walk away."

"We probably should have, but we didn't. We wanted our life back, just the way it was. We figured what was the likelihood of another one-hundred-year hurricane hitting the area."

"It took five years."

"We had just gotten things on track again when Ian hit," Vee said. "Took out the business and this time, our house too under ten feet of storm surge."

"Oh, I'm so sorry."

"Yeah," Vee replied, shaking her head, taking a long sip of her drink. "We lost it all. We couldn't even find an apartment to rent. So—" she shook her head wearily "—we had to move back."

"Oh, Vee. All that hard work. I'm so sorry."

"And then we get back here and—"

"The accident," Tori said, having looked up the details of it. "I have a twelve-year-old boy at home. I can only imagine how tough that's been."

"She has casts on both legs, stuck in the house, unable to be a kid. She's healing though." Vee took a quick sip of her drink. "I meant to say thanks, by the way. I saw where you made a donation on the Help a Friend site. It seemed to trigger more donations. Thank you. Truly."

"You're welcome. I was glad to help a little, as are all our friends and former classmates. I told them you were working at the store. Most of them didn't even know you were back. Some of them might stop in and say hello."

"Yeah, I haven't really wanted to connect with anyone given our situation. I know that sounds kind of bad."

"No, actually, I understand that. When I came back to investigate Jessie's case, I didn't want to see anyone either, but they didn't give me a choice. They showed up at my hotel and dragged me out to the bar the minute they found out I was here. Turned out, it was great to see everyone."

Their pizza arrived and they each took a piece.

"Will Sarah be healed up by the time school starts, do you think?" Tori said.

"Gosh, I sure hope so. She'd only had about a month to get to know some kids before the accident. That took her out of school pretty much the rest of the year. She doesn't have much for friends here, so—"

"Nobody has been coming around to say hi. Nobody there to sit and watch a movie with her."

Vee nodded. "And there aren't many kids her age in my mom's neighborhood, so she's a little lonely so, hopefully, once school starts, and she can be there, things will get a little better."

"And she's going into seventh grade?"

"Yes."

"Do you know if she ever met Quinn Braddock? He's going to be a seventh grader too."

"I... don't know. I could ask her. That's Braddock's son?"

"Yes. Quinn is a great kid."

"I'm sure you help with that."

"I can take very little credit. He was a really good kid when I got here. He's a total wiseacre. I've probably helped him with that, much to his father's chagrin."

"I'm sure," Vee said with a chuckle.

"I'll ask him if he ever got to meet Sarah," Tori said. "If not, I'll make sure he does. Quinn knows everyone in the grade."

"Ahh, he's one of the popular kids, huh?"

Tori nodded. "He's a good kid, athlete, cute, lots of friends, big personality, tall like his father. He can get her introduced to the other kids and if he's doing it, it might help a little bit."

"Oh, I don't want to put him in a position—"

"Don't worry about that. Quinn is a more the merrier type. Friends and more friends. They're over at the house all the time. He'll be glad to introduce her around."

"That would be..." Vee's eyes watered just a little. "That would be so nice for her. She's really... lonely, Tori. It's been so hard for her."

Tori reached for Vee's hand. "Hey, when Sarah gets her school schedule, let me know. You can text me." Tori wrote out her cell number. "Text or call me. We'll compare the kids' schedules and go from there."

"Thanks."

"I know she's had a tough go, so consider it done." Their drinks were empty. "Tell you what. We're having one more. It's just so good to see you."

Braddock and Quinn were sitting at the kitchen table, digging into a massive pizza when she got home.

"Is that...?" she started.

"The Meat Machine," Quinn said with a big grin. "Size extra-large. The best!"

"Man, that's all I need," she replied with a chuckle, setting the dress over a chair. Sausage, pepperoni, Canadian bacon, double cheese, peppers, and everything else. Even those two with their voracious appetites could never eat it all in one sitting. "Your father will spend the whole night burping."

Tori grabbed the bottle of antacid tablets and set it down in front of Braddock. "You'll be needing those." She opened a cold beer and sat down with them.

"Where were you?" Braddock asked.

"I picked up my dress and then my friend Vee and I went out for drinks at The Bourbon Room." She turned to Quinn. "Did you ever meet a girl at school named Sarah Akton? She would have been a new student, toward the end of the year."

Quinn thought for a moment. "I don't think so. Should I have?"

"She was only at school about a month and then was in a car accident and got hurt pretty bad."

His eyes lit up. "Oh, I remember her. I remember a new girl and then some kids talking about the car accident. Broke both her legs."

"That's her. Sarah's mom is an old high school friend named Vee."

"Vee?"

"Veronica is her full name. They had just moved back here from Florida and then there was the accident. And her mom and dad have had some financial issues. That's why they had to move back. So there's that and she's been laid up in bed all summer. No friends. Nobody to talk to."

Quinn's eyes flashed horror. "You're not going to make me go over there..."

"No," Tori said, holding up her hand. "But you could do me a real solid when school starts and introduce yourself and introduce her to some kids around school? Help her meet some people. Include her in some things. Invite her over when you do one of those movie nights in your new game room over the garage. I can't begin to tell you what that would mean to her mom."

"You got this, right?" Braddock said to his son.

Quinn nodded. "Sure. I can do that. That's easy. Maybe when I get my school schedule, you can ask her mom what classes she has. If we have a few together, we'll probably be sitting close. You know, Akton, Braddock, teachers always sit us alphabetical."

"Thanks, kiddo."

Vee and Dan stared at the stacks of cash on the mattress. Just a hair over $70,000.

"And the rest?" Vee said.

"It will be wired tomorrow," Dan replied quietly. "You were having drinks with Tori? Really?"

"I didn't have much of a choice. She offered and Ruth Ann told me to take off early. I couldn't really say no."

"You probably didn't want to, either."

"You know, I had a good time. Tori couldn't have been nicer but—"

"But what?"

"She's also doing really well, personally and financially, and she's not shy about that either. It just flows out of her. The stylish clothes, the handsome boyfriend with the house on the lake, the brand new fully loaded Audi she's driving. She's got it all going on." Vee sighed. "A year ago, I was her. Tonight, I was accepting her... charity," Vee said bitterly but then smiled. "And all the while, I'm thinking here I am, part of the crew who robbed the jewelry store next door."

"And she had no clue?"

"No." She looked at the money stacked on the bed. "What do we do with all this money?"

"We shouldn't keep it here. I could keep a couple grand for just in case." Dan relayed what Druk told him. "We have to hide the rest of it."

Vee thought for a moment. "How about at your brother's place? He's out in the woods. And—" her eyes lit up "—he has those empty blue plastic buckets in his garage. Put the cash in there in the duffel bag and bury it in the ground on his property until we figure out something better."

"I'll do it in the morning. Now, the other job."

"When?"

"They have it all planned out. Our part is pretty easy actually."

"When?"

"Thursday."

NINETEEN

"WOULD YOU SETTLE FOR INTERESTING?"

The smell filtered into her nostrils, drifting up, and it was warm. Her eyes flitted open to see Braddock holding a cup of coffee just under her nose.

"Hey, sleepyhead. Look at you all curled up like a kitty."

Tori was in fact coiled up in a little ball under a blanket on the love seat in her office. Stretching and yawning she noticed the brightness of the sun filtering in through the blinds. Braddock's hair was wet. He'd showered and worked out. It was 7:00 a.m.

"Why are you sleeping in here?" he said, handing her the coffee cup. "Was I snoring?"

"You were tossing and turning a bit. I think the pizza was hitting you."

"Sorry."

"No biggee." He was doing a little of that, but it wasn't necessarily what made her seek out the love seat. She took a careful sip of coffee. "I came down here and read for a bit before falling asleep," she said, gesturing to a novel on her old trunk doubling as a coffee table.

Braddock picked up the book and read the cover synopsis

on the back, "A lawyer must defend her husband who is accused of killing his mistress. Sounds salacious." He looked to her. "How is it?"

"Preposterous and unrealistic for any number of reasons but also kind of mindlessly entertaining. The author has a flair for the dramatic."

"Hmm," he said, taking a drink of his coffee. "Why couldn't you sleep though? That's two nights in a row. Monday you were restless, then last night. What's up with that?"

Tori sat up. "I don't know. Sometimes you just can't sleep. The mind gets whirring."

"About?"

"Oh, nothing in... particular."

"That's a lie. You don't think about anything without a purpose." He stared her down. "Ally Mannion?"

Her murder, the vision of it, had interrupted her sleep more than once. "Yeah, that and when I tried not to think of that, Maggie Duncan pops into my mind."

"Still?"

Tori nodded.

"Her saying that the two of you were a lot alike, that's still bugging you?"

"That, and she killed a special agent but wouldn't have if she'd known and I find myself ambivalent about it."

"Or so you think."

"She wouldn't have," Tori insisted. "But like Tracy said, it doesn't matter. She did it and she needs to get got, yet I'm not lying awake at night figuring out how to find her. In fact, I don't even want to try."

"And that bothers you?"

"*Yes!* I should be trying to find her, but I'm not. Why? I can't reconcile that, Braddock. It bugs me to no end. I don't know why, but it does. I can't shake it. I will, in time, but—"

"I know," Braddock said, nodding. "I can compartmentalize things like that, you can't."

"Hey!"

"It's not a criticism," he replied calmly. "You're just wired that way. You... internalize things like that and you think about them, grind on them, keep them inside until they all come bursting out. I've watched you do it for two years. I wish you wouldn't, but it's kind of who you are."

"Now hang on—"

"It's a weakness."

She wanted to fire back but... she knew he was right. "I know," she sighed.

"Yet also a strength. It's part of what makes you good at what you do. It's part of what attracts me to you, you know. That drive, the fire, a little bit of the conflict. It makes you... challenging."

"Oh." She laughed wearily. "The neurosis is just super-hot."

"It has its tricky moments." He took a drink of coffee and leaned forward. "You can talk to me about it, you know. Wake me up if you need to. It's no good to hold it all in and keep it to yourself."

"I know. I know."

"When you're ready." He stood up, then leaned down and kissed her on the head. "Are you coming in today?"

"Yes." She shook her head loose.

"Did you and Steak learn anything yesterday on Kellin?"

"Uh, yeah, maybe. There are a couple of names we picked up. They might know something about his time up in Grand Rapids. They live in Garrison. We should go talk to them."

"When you get in, we'll go over there."

"Is Eggleston anywhere on the jewelry store robbery?"

"Not yet. Right now, she's digging on all the employees. The owner is getting together everything on the store's construction. The general contractor is providing his employee lists for the job, as are the subs. It's a sifting process right now."

"Because it was an inside job."

"They knew what to cut and more importantly where," Braddock replied. "Someone knew something."

"Are any employees of the store really small?"

"You're thinking about the duct?"

"Yeah."

"No," Braddock said. "Nobody that small. Nobody even as small and as slight as you and you were an extremely tight fit in there. I was wondering if *that* was keeping you awake. You know, a nightmare or two."

"Oddly, that hasn't really bugged me, though I'm not dying to try that again anytime soon."

"Whoever it was, it would have taken someone able to withstand that feeling of confinement because that's what they would have had all the way in."

"Some people like a challenge."

"True, or someone wants or needs something bad enough, they'll go to any lengths."

Tori nodded. "Okay, I'll get my butt going. I'll probably go for a quick run first, sweat out the toxins," she said, standing up on her tiptoes to kiss him softly and then let her cheek brush his. He smelled good, all fresh and clean from his shower, having shaved, his skin smooth.

"You cut a very handsome look there, Braddock."

* * *

"Hey, sweetie, how are you feeling today?" Vee said to her daughter, bringing her in some lunch and setting it on a tray and then placing it in front of her. The small flat-screen television in the corner was on Nickelodeon, an episode of *Friends* starting. Vee thought it perhaps not quite age appropriate, but at the same time, Sarah had suffered enough. She could watch whatever she wanted.

Vee sat down on the bed next to Sarah, while she ate her lunch and they watched the episode together, laughing out loud several times as Monica and Rachel got ready for prom.

"Ross's mustache. My God," Sarah said. "And the perm. Geez. Did people actually have... those."

"Yes, they did."

"Did Dad?"

"No. I wouldn't have allowed it. Now, as for prom dresses like that..."

The episode ended and Sarah wiggled her toes.

"I just want these off."

"I know, honey. You're getting very close."

Sarah wanted to be able to walk into school and seventh grade in the fall. They had another orthopedic appointment next week.

"Mom?"

"Yeah, honey."

"Can you help me with a wash tonight?"

Vee kissed her daughter on top of her head. "You bet. I might have some good news."

"What?"

"Did you ever meet a boy at school named Quinn Braddock?"

Sarah's eyes lit up. "I never really met him, but he was in a couple of my classes. He plays hockey, I know that. All he ever wore to school were jerseys and hoodies for hockey."

"Is he cute?"

Sarah shrugged.

That was a yes.

"Well, an old friend of mine is his dad's girlfriend. They live together. And she told me that she would have Quinn introduce you to some kids around school when the school year starts."

"Mom!" Sarah screeched, instantly embarrassed.

"What? I guess he's kind of popular with all the other kids."

"Yeah." Her daughter nodded. "He seemed to be. Always had a lot of friends around him."

"Who better to make introductions then? Tori is an old friend of mine. She says Quinn has lots of friends, so he'd be someone good to know at school, that's all. You do want to make some friends, right?"

"Yes."

"Well, having a really popular boy show you around and introduce you to his friends, can't hurt."

Sarah nodded. "Okay. Thanks, Mom."

Dan stepped into the bedroom. "Hey, sweetie."

"Daddy. We just watched the funniest episode of *Friends*."

"Yeah? Which one?"

"The one with the prom video."

"You know I think I remember that one." To Vee he said, "Ready?"

"Yes. Dad and I are going out to run some errands. But how about on our way home we pick up some ice cream?"

Sarah's eyes lit up. "Cookie Dough? Or maybe Cotton Candy."

"If that's what you want."

"I want one of those."

"How about both?"

"Can we afford it?"

Vee closed her eyes for just a moment. "Yeah, honey. I've worked a little extra. We can splurge for some ice cream for you. Now, if you need anything while we're gone—"

"I know, just call for Grandma."

"Can we afford both?" Vee said as they drove. "God. Makes me *furious*."

"With Sarah?"

"No. With me. Us. This," she added, waving at their car. "Everything."

"She's not blind, Vee. She's twelve. Old enough to know that things have gone off the rails. She used to live in a nice neighborhood in Florida in a house with a pool and now she's living in a shoe box in northern Minnesota with her grandma, while her parents are driving a ten-year-old piece of shit car. What do you expect?"

"It's embarrassing, living like this."

"That bag at your feet is a start on changing that. And we don't have to tell a soul about it."

"No—" Vee nodded "—we don't, do we."

"And there's more coming. And more to be gotten. We're getting back what was taken from us."

They parked in the driveway for Dan's brother Ron's house.

"They're not here," Vee said, peeking in the windows.

"I was kind of hoping that would be the case," Dan said.

Dan's brother Ron owned thirty acres northwest of Manchester Bay. The land was mostly woods, though the property did abut a small lake at the very back. Ron had a dock and a small fishing boat there. What interested Dan was the path from the house out to the lake. He strode to the side door for the garage and punched a code into the keypad above the doorknob.

Click!

Inside the garage, Dan grabbed two shovels, handing one to Vee, a large knife and then a blue knee-high storage drum with a screw on top. The container once held food for his dog, a large and old black Lab.

"I didn't see or hear Bruiser," Vee said, thinking of the dog.

"My guess is Ron is off somewhere and has that old boy with him. Lydia is working so we should be good."

They took the shovels and followed the long winding path toward the small lake. Just short of reaching the clearing for the lake, there was a small path that branched off to the right to another clearing for a small gun range.

"I can't believe his neighbors don't object to this," Vee said.

Dan laughed. "Some may, but the others he invites over to join him don't. It's legal. He said he had the sheriff's department out to evaluate it and they said have at it. Ronnie's not a gun nut. He mostly shoots trap out here." Ron competed in sporting clays.

Along the edge of the wood line was a dead tree, hollowed out. Were it nearer to the house, Ron would have likely removed it. Out here, what difference did it make. Dan used it as a marker, and he and Vee started digging a hole to the right of it. Once they were satisfied with the hole's depth, Vee opened the duffel bag. She held up one brick. "Keep one?"

"Yes. We can have a little walking around money. Just don't flash too much."

"I just want to buy ice cream, both kinds," she replied drolly. Vee transferred the rest of the cash into the bucket. Dan screwed the top back on, and they filled the hole. Dan carved an x into a tree straight ahead. "Ninety-degree angle between the dead tree and that tree marks the spot."

They brushed some cover over the freshly dug dirt and then walked back to the garage. The whole endeavor took a half-hour.

Another half-hour later, they were sitting at the picnic bench under an umbrella outside a tap room in Holmstrand, each having a pint, quietly drinking, not really talking. After ten minutes of relative quiet, Dan murmured, "Heath and Druk want to meet tonight. Late."

"And?"

"You have to come this time. Final run through."

"I'm in," Vee said, holding up her glass. "Whatever it takes."

* * *

Tori walked in the front door of the government center, swiped off her sunglasses and saw Braddock walking toward her.

"Hey! Turn around," he gestured.

"Sure," Tori said, turning on her heels. "You want to go talk to those two guys in Garrison?"

"I do, and we will, but we've got something else to go look at first."

"We do?"

"Yeah, you know that new housing development south of town? The one we drove by a few weeks ago. Greyler Lake Meadows, golf course, new homes."

"Yeah. We saw all the earth movers moving earth and the dump trucks hauling it away. What about it?"

"They're draining a swamp."

"Scintillating. That interests us why?"

"There's a Humvee at the bottom."

"Again, so?"

"With a dead body in it, strapped into the driver's seat. How does that happen?"

Tori snorted a laugh. "And you thought my morbid sense of curiosity would be piqued."

"Well... yeah."

"You know me oh-so well."

Braddock smiled. "Come on. You know there has to be a good story behind it."

"If there's a dead guy, how is it good?"

"Would you settle for interesting?"

TWENTY

"LIFE IS NOT ACCOUNTING."

Braddock drove them south of town, in no real rush, his right hand draped casually over the wheel.

"So, how is it they know there is a Hummer at the bottom of the pond with a body in it?" Tori said. "And by the way, that's a phrase I never thought I'd utter."

"The construction crew was pumping out a big pond, transferring the water into another man-made one. Why? I don't know. I assume it's so they can build more houses or something. What I do know is that as they were pumping it out, the top of a vehicle became visible. One of the construction workers had a kayak strapped to the top of his SUV. He paddled out and was certain it was a Hummer. That was when the first call was made for assistance. Then, as the water level dropped, the kayaker saw a skeleton in the driver's seat of the Hummer. I got that call. I figured this might pique your interest, much like that trashy novel you were reading."

"Huh," Tori said. "You know, I haven't heard of people driving Hummers for a long time."

Braddock nodded. "You know, I thought the same thing. It's so... 2008 you know."

"Exactly. They were a thing for a few years and then people started caring about the environment."

Braddock scoffed. "The environment? Please. Gas prices went to $3.75 a gallon and those things got like eight miles to the gallon. That math doesn't work."

The large wood sign for Greyler Lake Meadows was up on their left, massive mounds of dirt piled behind. Just inside the entry were two model homes with grass and driveways, giving you a visual idea of what the houses in the development would be. They passed the two-story model homes on the right and followed the dirt path winding its way through groves of trees and around wetlands until they made a sharp turn to the right and the sheriff's department SUVs for two deputies with flashing lights and the small crowd of workers at the wetland came into view. Braddock parked, Steak and Eggleston pulling in behind him.

The water was a foot below the roof of the Hummer.

"You don't see that every day," Steak said with a wry smile. "God, I love my job sometimes."

"Don't be so giddy. It is a dead body, you know," Tori scolded lightly.

"Yeah, yeah, that's probably been dead a long time. Weren't you going over to Garrison to talk to those guys?"

"That's what I thought," Tori replied. "He got this call instead and thought it more exciting."

Braddock playfully rolled his eyes. "We're going there next."

The sheriff's department water rescue and recovery team arrived, boat in tow, followed by a large tow truck. They chit-chatted with the divers as they geared up and then prepared to launch their boat into the pond. Dr. Renfrow arrived on scene.

"This should be interesting," the medical examiner said.

"Another one with morbid curiosity syndrome," Braddock said.

"Job requirement," Renfrow replied with a grin.

"We don't even know if anything nefarious is afoot here," Tori observed.

"Yeah, right," Steak said. "Hummer at the bottom of a pond. Dead body in the driver's seat. *Totally* normal."

A forensic investigator from the BCA pulled in. "Glad I picked the phone up on this one."

"You guys," Tori sighed, shaking her head in feigned disgust.

"Oh yeah, like you're not *totally* curious now," Steak retorted. "Please. I know you."

Tori playfully pinched Steak hard on the back of his fleshy left tricep.

"Ow! Geez, Tori."

"You deserved it."

Steak rubbed the back of his arm. "Are you going to do that to all the richy rich types at the ball you're going to tomorrow night?"

Tori grimaced. She'd forgotten about the fundraiser for the cancer center at the hospital. She looked to Braddock. "Do we have—"

"To? Yes," he said. "Sheriff Boe will be there. All the mucky mucks, including Kyle and Eddie. Kyle called me this morning to make sure we were attending. He was very insistent."

"The Mannion Cancer Center," Steak said. "It's going to be a heck of thing to have."

"Actually," Braddock said before lowering his voice, "keep this one under your hat, but Kyle told me they're renaming it the Allison Mannion Cancer Center."

"We can't miss that then," Tori said. "And it's... formal?"

"Formalish," Braddock said. "Not black tie per se. We don't really do *that* here. My new black suit and tie though for me."

"I wonder what I have to wear?" Tori mused. "I might have to buy something," she teased.

"At this point, the shops in town come to you for inventory."

The divers launched their small rescue boat and puttered out thirty feet to the left of the top of the Hummer. One diver went over the side and went under the water briefly on the driver's side before making his way to the back of the SUV and then diving again, this time staying under for a couple of minutes before surfacing and climbing back into the boat.

"One body, seat belted into the driver's seat. It's skeletal at this point but looks fully intact," the diver reported.

"How about the vehicle itself?" Braddock asked. "Intact, damaged?"

"Intact. No noticeable visible damage to the exterior that I saw," the diver replied and turned to the tow truck operator. "It's settled in the muck a bit, I can't reach underneath it. But it's a Hummer. It has those heavy hooks embedded in the rear bumper. I think we can hook the cables up to that and haul it out."

While the divers and tow truck operator discussed logistics, Braddock looked to Tori. "A Hummer that is undamaged, driver seat belted in, what do you make of that?"

"I don't know what the terrain out here was before all this construction, but it seems unlikely he simply took a wrong turn and ended up at the bottom of the pond, don't you think?"

"I do. That leaves suicide or—"

"Something else," Tori finished. "Given how things are going lately. It's—"

"Probably something else."

"You still all excited now?"

It took a half-hour for the divers to hook up the cables. Secured, the tow truck driver slowly pulled the large Hummer out of the water and to the shoreline.

"No license plate," Tori observed as the yellow-colored vehicle emerged. "Odd. Unless it was new?"

Once the Hummer was clear of the water and on dry land,

Braddock carefully approached the driver's side and jotted down the VIN number and handed it to Eggleston. "Can you run that?"

"On it."

The body, a male, was seat belted in, skeletal in nature, little flesh remaining, the clothes on the body nothing but thin soaked rags.

Eggleston returned. "VIN number was registered to a Loren Randolf of Manchester Bay."

"Say again?" Steak said, snapping his head around. "Did you say Loren Randolf?"

"Loren Randolf?" Tori muttered and then recognition set in. "You mean Duffy? Is that Duffy Randolf?"

"I wonder."

Eggleston led them back to the Tahoe and the computer screen.

"I'll be damned. That's him," Steak said and then looked to the Hummer. "So that's what happened to him."

"Who is Loren or Duffy Randolf?" Braddock asked.

"He's a good ole boy Tori and I went to high school with," Steak explained. "He up and went missing fourteen, fifteen years ago. Nobody knew what happened to him or where he went. Here one day, gone the next. I was a newbie deputy at the time, not long out of college but if I remember right, his mom filed a missing person's report. She hadn't seen nor heard from him for a few days. He never turned up."

"Was he a friend?" Eggleston said.

"I would say loosely," Steak said. "His cell number wouldn't have been in my directory, but I was certainly friendly with him when I saw him."

"Everyone was when we were in high school," Tori added. "He was a year ahead of us, but he was Duffy. He was a guy who you'd go to if you needed something that you couldn't get... legally."

"Meaning beer?" Braddock said.

"And maybe other... substances, for those that were so inclined," Tori replied. "Any guy with the nickname Duffy is usually a good enough guy. Steak is right, he was good-natured yet a bit of a dumbass loudmouth if you ask me."

Steak nodded. "Exactly. Good guy. Put his foot in his mouth if you gave him enough time or beer. And man, he liked his beer. The more he drank the louder and more obnoxious he got."

"You found him by VIN?" Tori asked Eggleston.

"Yes. He was the only listed owner of the vehicle. Either the license plates were removed or—"

"The Hummer was new," Braddock said. "Hmpf."

For now, Braddock declared the Hummer a crime scene. It would be hoisted onto a trailer, wrapped, and transported to the BCA lab to be processed and have the body removed for autopsy.

"There's nothing left to do here," Braddock said. "The body has been in the water fourteen years. Let Renfrow identify him, the BCA process the vehicle and then we'll go from there." He looked to his watch, having let some of the day get away.

"I should go see his mom," Steak said.

"We don't know for sure it's him," Braddock replied.

"We don't?" Steak replied skeptically. "Come on. It's him. Word will get out soon enough on this. There's a news truck for the local station just over there. I'd rather she heard from me, a somewhat friendly face, than from the news. I'll tell her we might have found him. That we'll know for sure in a day or so."

Braddock nodded. "Go ahead." He turned to Tori. "You want to drive over to Garrison? Talk to these guys who fished with Kellin?"

. . .

"What's the story with these guys?" Braddock asked as they made the drive east to Garrison.

"Ledyard Heath and Lenny Druk. We got their names yesterday up in Grand Rapids." She relayed the details of the fishing and bar fight. "Druk owns the house and Heath lists his address as there, at least for the last three years."

Braddock drove south on Highway 169 past Garrison Boat Works another two miles. Lake Mille Lacs was to their left, relatively calm on this day, though the prevailing wind was usually from the west so calm along the western shores was not uncommon, until you got out aways into the water when the wind was no longer checked by the higher land and tall trees.

"It's up on the right," Tori said and the white two-story house with a front porch came into view.

Braddock slowed and turned into the driveway and motored up the gentle incline to the house, which was set back from the highway about one-hundred yards. "I bet the views of the lake from that porch are nice. So do you go to the front or the back?"

"I think the back, the way the driveway leads around that way."

There was a pickup truck parked in front of a detached two-car garage. To the left of the garage were two fishing boats, on their trailers. Braddock knocked on the back door.

Tori stood a few feet back. The house seemed quiet, though windows were opened a crack, curtain bottoms flitting with the wind. Braddock knocked again while Tori stepped back down to the driveway and scanned the grounds, but all seemed quiet.

"I don't think they're home," Braddock said, checking his watch. "You want to hang here for a bit or go into Garrison and give them another shot in an hour?"

"I could eat."

They went to The Goose and ate an early dinner. Ninety minutes later, they stopped at the house again, achieving the same result. Nobody was home.

"We're here. Let's sit and wait. It's pleasant out."

Braddock backed up his truck so that it sat under a shade tree near the garage and away from the house. A half-hour in, he asked, "Are these guys we need to be interested in?"

"They were friends of Kellin though interestingly, nobody at this bar that Kellin hung out at all the time seemed to recall them. They won this fishing contest on Pokegama Lake."

"The Three Man?"

"Yes."

"Huh. The pros show up for that one. When was this?"

"Four years ago." Tori showed Braddock the photo she'd taken of the picture the server at The Port had brought over. Kellin was front and center holding the check, Heath and Druk behind him, smiling.

"How tall was Kellin?"

"Six feet," Tori said.

"They're bigger guys it looks. You get a tinge of something?"

"I often get a tinge of something and then it's nothing."

"You know what I mean."

"Maybe I just want there to be something. I look at these two, they knew Kellin well enough to win the Three Man. They fish. Garrison isn't all that far from Grand Rapids. I'm at least curious. Or maybe I just want there to be something. We've come up empty for Kyle and Bree."

Braddock nodded. "That's the way it goes sometimes."

"I really don't want Volume Five of the Philosophy of Life from Will Braddock right now."

"Too bad. Why should Kyle be any different, Tor? Why does he deserve answers any more than anyone else, any other victim's family? Aren't the people we serve all the same?"

"Yes... and no."

"Spoken like the ex-Bureau agent you are."

"Whatever."

"Why? Why is this different?"

"Because, he's our friend? Because he—"

"Saved your life once," Braddock said.

"You and him."

Braddock nodded. "That was my job, though." He reached for her hand. "Though I was particularly motivated." He raised her hand and kissed it.

She smiled. "It wasn't his, though, yet he put it on the line for me."

"He wanted to save Eddie."

"Yes." Tori nodded. "He did want to prove his brother inno-cent, but he didn't hesitate to go with you, did he?"

"No. Not for a second."

Tori sighed. "I owe him, Braddock. I. Owe. Him."

Braddock grimaced. He understood it. He just worried about what would happen if they didn't find the killers. How it would weigh on her. "Life can't be about balancing ledgers. Life is not accounting. Debits and credits do not always equal, in fact, they often don't."

"But—"

"Life does not balance. You have to accept that on occasion. Just because he did for you, doesn't mean you'll be able to do for him."

"What are you? Mr. Miyagi now? If you say wax on, wax off, I am going to kill you."

Braddock smiled. "All you owe Kyle is your best. Do you think you've not given it?"

Tori pursed her lips for a moment. "I feel like a lot has happened that has distracted us. Kellin, though it may be related. The jewelry store. Now, Duffy Randolf's body surfacing in a Hummer H2 after fourteen years. What's the story behind that? There has to be one. And then, Tracy and Sam were here for a week."

"That's life."

"But—"

"I'm going to stop you right there. Do not feel guilty for one second that you took a week to spend with your best friend. What did I just say?"

She huffed a sigh.

"We've had a lot happen. It's stretched us a bit thin but that happens because—"

"Yeah, yeah, yeah, because life doesn't balance out," Tori replied, nodding. "I can still try for it."

"Hell yes," Braddock replied. "Every day. It's getting late." It was after 8:00 p.m. "We will get back here first thing tomorrow. We'll see what they have to say for themselves."

* * *

"So that's the plan?" Dan asked, looking to Vee, who had no expression at all.

"You up for it, Vee?" Druk asked.

"What's the take?" she asked flatly. "What do we walk out of there with?"

"Hard to say for sure, but every bit as much as the jewelry store, I would think. Once we move it. You're getting just under $200,000 out of that. We should each get that on this one as well. I expect we'll find cash and the house is full of treasure."

"And it has to be tomorrow?" Vee said. "No other choice?"

"If we want the biggest possible return on this, yes." Druk handed her a photo.

"I see," Vee said, evaluating the photo. "Then we do it." She looked to Dan. "We need the money. It's that simple."

"Okay, one other thing," Druk said. "And this is bad timing, but I have to tell you about it because it impacts all of us."

"What?"

"Duffy."

"Duffy? Duffy Randolf?" Vee replied. "What about him? Why bring that up now?"

"Because that motherfucker's body turned up today," Heath said and explained what had happened at the Greyler Lakes Estates development. "I never, ever, thought that would be found. I saw the construction out there, but that pond was so deep and so far in that I can't believe he and that stupid ass Hummer of his were found."

"But it was," Druk said evenly. "Now, he was in the water for fourteen years so what can they possibly find?"

"Nothing," Heath said.

"That said, just like when he went missing, now that he's resurfaced so to speak, the police might come around and ask some questions of the people who were Duffy's friends back in the day. We were all friends of his."

"And if they do?" Dan asked.

"We all need to know. If we're going to be garnering police attention, we need to be mindful of that."

Vee laid in bed.

Duffy Randolf.

Why now? Why of all times, now?

She stared at the ceiling tiles and thought of that night. It was supposed to be the night they all celebrated. Druk had their money from the Duluth job.

In Duluth, they'd all had a role to play.

Duffy had identified the job to begin with six months earlier.

Vee was the lock pick, the tool to get into the mansion the only way that was possible.

Heath had the touch to get into the safe.

Druk had the relationship with the fence.

Dan was the wheel man.

They all were going to be paid.

News reports pegged the loss due to the burglary at over

$2.5 million in art and jewelry along with just over $300,000 in cash. The cash was split evenly five ways when they got back to Manchester Bay. After they split the cash, Druk had warned them all, "Hide the money. Keep a low profile. Don't do anything flashy. The police *will* come around. Especially to Duffy, and maybe Dan."

The police had come, for Duffy. Duffy had worked on the crew that installed the security system for the house and then on a service team six months later that troubleshooted some problems the system was having with motion sensors in the kitchen. Duffy was brought in for questioning, once. While the police pressed him on his work on the security system, he had an airtight alibi for the night of the burglary. He was the only one of the five of them not in Duluth that night.

Dan had been concerned the police would come for him too as he had worked at the security company when the system was purchased, had serviced the initial account, though he'd changed jobs eight months after the purchase and four months before they pulled the job. But in the weeks after, the police hadn't darkened Dan's door.

Heath and Druk invited them all to have dinner in a booth at The Goose in Garrison, just down the road from Druk's house. Vee and Dan arrived to find Heath and Druk sitting in a horseshoe booth, drinking beers, cautious yet pleased.

"Have the police questioned you?" Druk asked Dan quietly.

"No," Dan replied. "We've been keeping an eye open. Nobody has called on us, nobody has been watching. I don't think I'm on any radar anywhere. And we haven't spent a nickel of money. We've hidden it."

"Perfect."

"But speaking of money, do you have it?" Vee asked.

Druk nodded with a sly grin, leaning over. "It's all set, Vee. I have more cash and the wire instructions back at the house. We'll have a nice little celebratory dinner here and then go back to the house, take care of the business. You did good. We could have never done it without you."

"Let's eat," Heath said.

"Where's Duffy?" Dan asked as he picked up the menu.

"He should be along any—" Druk started and then his eyes bulged as he looked out the window to the parking lot. "You've got to be kidding me."

"Are you fucking dry humping me?" Heath muttered as he peered out the window. "I knew he'd do something stupid. I just fucking knew it."

They all looked out the window to see Duffy parked in the first row, standing in front of a brand-new yellow Hummer H2. You couldn't miss the thing. It was as if it had a spotlight on it.

Heath smacked the seat, gritting his teeth. "That dumbass—"

"Let it go for now," Druk said calmly. "We'll deal with it later."

"Hey, guys!" Duffy greeted loudly with a wave, sporting a flashy new silver watch on his left wrist.

Duffy's decibel level increased with his beer intake while the rest of them drank at a more controlled pace, not wanting to draw notice.

Vee remembered letting her eyes shift from Heath to Druk to Duffy as the five of them ate burgers and fries. As the beers continued, she saw it in Heath and Druk, the narrowed eyes, the subdued reactions, simmering ire. She leaned to her husband, and whispered, "Dan."

He saw it too. "Ignore it, babe. Let them deal with it."

As The Goose began to empty on a quiet early September night, Duffy leaned in. "Do you have the rest of it?"

Druk exhaled a breath. "Yeah, let's go over to our place."

The five of them left and drove a couple of miles south on

Highway 169 before turning right into a gravel driveway that snaked back a few hundred yards to Druk's house. Everyone parked. The only sounds were the hum of Highway 169 and the crickets in the nearby wetlands.

"So how much did we get?" Duffy asked, eagerly rubbing his hands together.

"A new Hummer?" Druk growled in a low voice. "A new fucking Hummer? What did I say to you, dumbass? To everyone?"

"Would you relax. It's no big deal. I'm the one with the perfect alibi, remember?"

Dan grabbed Vee's hand and pulled her back a step or two, murmuring in her ear, "This isn't good."

Druk and Heath stepped toward Duffy.

On cue, Druk punched Duffy in the jaw, knocking him back off his feet, to the ground.

"What the fuck?" Duffy grimaced, spitting out blood as he pushed himself up. "What was that for?"

"For being the dumbest motherfucker ever," Druk growled.

"We all are laying low, all of us, except you, dipshit," Heath barked, grabbing Duffy by the shirt and pulling him up. "Nobody else felt the need to go blow a wad of cash on a Hummer. You ever think about the police, you moron?" He punched Duffy in the stomach, dropping him to the ground again.

Duffy struggled for his breath. "They interviewed me two weeks ago. It took an hour, if that. They haven't been back since. Alibi, remember? I was in fucking Staples."

"And you think that's it? That they won't come back? It wasn't a one-person job, you fuckwit. We stole a lot of shit. The media is still reporting on it. Police are investigating. The insurance company is investigating. The security company that *you work for* is investigating because their system failed."

"When did you buy that thing?" Druk asked.

"Today. Drove it off the lot down in the cities and came back up here."

"And I bet you paid cash.'"

"What of it?"

"You drive that to work you don't think it raises alarm bells. You pay cash for it? You don't think that sends up a red flag. Where does a clown, a low-level tech for a security company come up with the scratch for a new loaded Hummer, even on a trade-in?"

"Whatever," Duffy said. "I traded in a two-year-old loaded Dodge Ram for it and paid the difference in cash, yes." He massaged his jaw. "Fine, perhaps it's a bit much but would you fuckers just relax. I'm in the clear. We're all in the clear."

"No, I'm not going to fucking relax," Heath growled.

"D-D-Dan," Vee murmured when she saw Druk snap the knife open.

"No!" Dan blurted as Druk plunged his knife into Duffy's midsection. "Oh God. No!"

"Wha..." Duffy coughed, his eyes wide, looking to Dan and Vee for help.

They both froze.

Druk turned the knife, driving it up under the rib cage as Duffy's legs gave way and he collapsed down onto the driveway. Druk finished the job, jamming the knife up, Duffy's body trembling.

"Oh my God, oh my God," Vee bellowed frantically. "We... we... We have to get out of here."

"Hey, be cool," Heath said, holding his hand out to calm her. "Be cool, Vee."

"But, but—"

"He could have screwed it up for all of us. The minute he drove that thing to work, company HR would have called the police and they're on him like white on rice. And if he's dumb enough to do this, he wouldn't have held up to the scrutiny coming his way. We'd all go down. It was him or us."

Vee shook her head. "What stops you from coming after Dan and I? Dan worked there too. Duffy was our friend too. He was just seen with all of us at The Goose. People are going to ask questions."

"Did you two go out and buy a new truck and flash a bunch of cash?" Druk asked calmly.

"No," Dan said.

"That's right, you didn't. You're living in the same small apartment and driving the same used car and truck and working the same jobs. You've done nothing to raise any suspicion whatsoever. I don't want to go to prison. You don't want to go to prison. It's too risky to leave him out there. And, Vee, there's more for all of us because of his stupidity. We're all a little richer and a lot safer."

"So, what do we do now?" Dan said.

"Wait here," Druk said while Heath brought out a tarp and laid it on the ground next to Duffy. He rolled the dead body onto the tarp and then wrapped him up. Druk came back out of the house with a black nylon duffel bag and handed it to Dan. "Here's your cut. And, Vee, if we were going to kill you, we'd do it now before I gave you the money. Instead, I'm handing you guys $200,000 in cash, which adds in $50,000 from Duffy's cut." He handed her a slip of paper. "This is the bank account for the bank in the Caymans. The rest is all there. A little over another $250,000. Heath and I are going to keep the remainder of Duffy's cut because we're responsible for... that," he said, gesturing to the tarp. "That's on us. We'll dispose of the body."

Dan looked to the money in the duffel bag and then to Vee, who nodded. They had the money, suddenly a lot of money. They weren't about to argue with them. Druk wasn't wrong. Duffy could have screwed them all.

"Look, my advice, my... request, is that you give it a few

months and take a trip down to the Caymans, a vacation when the weather turns, and then do with that money what you will."

"But be discreet," Dan murmured, throwing the duffel bag over his shoulder.

Druk nodded. "Look, I don't worry about you two. You're both pretty smart and you both keep your mouth shut. However, all the same, it's probably best we all are not to be seen together. We go our separate ways, right now. At least for a good long while."

"We've got plans," Vee said. "We're going to move to Florida."

"Maybe we'll look you up some time," Druk said. "That's a good spot. Nobody will bother you down there. Easy to get to the Cayman Islands from there if need be."

Dan looked inside the duffel bag at the bricks of cash and then nodded. "Okay. What about the body?" he asked, gesturing to Duffy, now wrapped in a tarp.

"Heath and I will take care of that and the Hummer. Neither will be found."

And they hadn't, until now.

TWENTY-ONE

"READY, FIRE, AIM WAS THE STORY OF HIS LIFE."

Braddock was up and out of the house early. Quinn was heading out of town with friends from school over to Wisconsin for the weekend. Tori dropped him off at 7:30 a.m., returned home, went for a run and then spent some time arranging an outfit for the evening fundraiser. Braddock had laid out his black suit and tie ensemble. She had settled on a black cap sleeve cocktail dress, sterling-silver tennis necklace and black pumps. They would certainly match. She thought to herself she'd probably want a photo of the two of them looking so sharp. Fully dressed and ready to head into town, her phone buzzed. Braddock.

"What's up?"

"Meet me at the medical examiner's office."

"Why?"

"You said there was probably a story behind your old high school friend. Well, you're right. He was murdered."

"On my way," she replied as she started packing up her materials.

Twenty minutes later she found him waiting in the entryway for the medical examiner's office. "Murdered?"

"That's what Renfrow is saying."

"Well, in a way, that's not a huge surprise," Tori said. "Being found submerged in water, in your brand-new vehicle, strapped in and missing for fourteen years is suggestive of foul play of some kind, is it not?"

"I quite agree," Braddock said, leading her down to the medical examiner's office. "Like you said, there is a story behind it." He pushed the door open to find Renfrow awaiting their arrival. "What did you find?"

"I confirmed with dental records that this is Loren Randolf," Renfrow reported. "And he was murdered."

"We were just talking about that. Not a total surprise," Braddock replied.

"How, Doc?" Tori asked.

Renfrow walked them to a gurney and pulled back the blanket covering the corpse which was a skeleton. He gestured to the bottom of the rib cage and a deep slice on the edge of the bottom rib. "Here on the right side. The width of that slice is from a knife, a substantial knife, heavy knife. And he was stabbed with great force to leave that kind of mark." He opened a folder. "There were some strands of clothes still on the body. He was wearing a canvas shirt and a T-shirt underneath." He held up photos. "See the discoloration here? The darkness on both shirts?"

"Yeah," Braddock replied.

"I'm betting that's blood. I sent it to Ann Jennison to see if she can verify that. And there was a slice-like hole through both shirts. He was stabbed, from the front, right under the bottom of the rib cage. I'd surmise he bled out."

Braddock turned to Tori. "What do you think?"

"Let's go see what Jennison has found."

The Hummer was in the rear garage of the crime lab. Jennison met them and walked them back.

"Doc sent me the shirt," Jennison said. "I cut out some

swatches, and tested them and they came back positive for blood, so I think he's right, Randolf was stabbed. I just don't see the Hummer, however, as your primary crime scene. It's been fourteen years, but I think how he was found, buckled in, suggests he was killed elsewhere and then sent to the bottom of the pond, never to be found."

"Was the SUV in neutral?" Braddock said.

Jennison nodded. "Yes."

"Fingerprints can survive on metallic surfaces underwater, right?" Tori asked.

"And other surfaces. Such as the steering wheel, keys, dashboard, seat belt buckle, all of it. We tried printing it but got nothing off any of the surfaces."

"It was in the water fourteen years."

"Plus, think of this. If they transported him from the murder scene to that pond, someone drove the Hummer there. I'd guess they wore gloves when they did, or they wiped the damn thing down and probably both. Any other trace evidence disappeared in the water. It is why killers throw bodies in the river. The water washes everything away."

"The Hummer isn't going to tell us who killed him," Braddock said.

"He did something," Tori muttered. "Fourteen years ago someone stabbed him and murdered him. Why?"

Braddock and Tori went back to his office, and he pulled up the electronic investigation file on Loren "Duffy" Randolf. Tori looked over his shoulder as they read what was on screen.

Duffy Randolf went missing fourteen years ago in September. He failed to appear for work on Wednesday and Thursday for Northern States Security Systems, had not called in sick and was not answering his landline or cell phone, leading to a welfare check on him at his apartment on Friday morning.

At the same time, his mother called, saying he'd not been answering his phone for several days, which was unusual. The investigator's notes said he generally checked in with her daily, or if not that, every other day.

Detectives searched his apartment but found no signs of foul play. Although they did find, in a duffel bag in the back of his closet...

"$22,250 in cash," Tori said. "Even these days, how many people have that much loose cash hanging around their house?"

"Wealthy people," Braddock said.

"Exactly. Duffy wasn't that. He worked at Northern States Security Systems. He was an install and repair technician. Where did he get that kind of money? In cash?"

"Don't know," Braddock said and then scrolled down further. "Interesting."

"What?"

"It says here the police were looking for his truck. A red Dodge Ram."

"Not a Hummer H2?" Tori said. Further down there was a notation that he had in fact purchased the Hummer, when detectives were searching for the Ram and tracked it down to a dealership in the town of Rogers, a suburb northwest of Minneapolis. He'd purchased the Hummer three days before he was reported missing, having traded in the Ram.

"What was his bank activity?" Tori said.

Braddock scrolled down. "Hmm. He'd made two deposits in the two weeks before his disappearance. $9,500 each, both just below the $10,000 IRS reporting threshold. Those deposits then led to a cashier's check for $15,258 that allowed him to cover the difference between the trade-in value on his Dodge Ram and the Hummer. Is there a paper file?"

"I imagine there is. What are you looking for?"

"What was his wage?"

Braddock picked up his phone and called his assistant who

turned for the file room. In the meantime, he scrolled down further. "Ah, there is a paycheck notation here. Bi-monthly gross of $2,010.42, that equates to—"

"$48,250," Tori replied, using her phone calculator. "Not huge but not terrible for someone who was twenty-five years old fourteen years ago. But does the math on the Hummer H2 add up?"

Braddock switched screens and completed a quick search on retail prices for a Hummer H2 fourteen years ago. "$60k back then for your basic H2. Add in some bells and whistles and it was most certainly more." He paused. "You know, it is not wise to own a vehicle worth more than your salary."

"Suze Orman would have said: *Denied!*"

Braddock's assistant came into the office with a file. "There is an evidence box as well that I've recalled. They'll bring it up."

While Braddock continued with the electronic file, Tori opened the retrieved paper copy. There was a knock on the door. Steak.

"Duffy was murdered?"

"Yeah," Braddock replied. "Stabbed at the bottom of his rib cage according to Renfrow. I'm scanning the old investigative file now. It's a little, shall we say, musty."

As Tori flipped through the paper file, it was largely the same information that she'd seen in the electronic file, though there were more photos taken of Randolf's apartment. When she got to the back, however, there was a second folder in the paper file. It was a Bureau of Criminal Apprehension investigation, a state investigation of the Locher Mansion Burglary.

Steak looked over Braddock's shoulder and the two of them read from the file to each other, out loud. "They don't know what happened to him. He disappeared. They found the money, which was suspicious, but that's about it."

"Or is it?" Tori said. "You don't have all of it." She held up the BCA file. "There's more. A lot more. I think they had an idea of what happened." Tori walked over to the small meeting table in the corner of the office and started spreading the BCA file out. "In short, it looks like they think he was involved in a burglary of the Locher Mansion in Duluth." She looked up. "Have either of you heard of that?"

"The Locher Mansion was a big old-money mansion on Lake Superior in Duluth. Robbed in the middle of the night, right?" Steak recalled. "It was in the news for a week or two after. Unsolved as I recall."

"Maybe not," Tori said. They all took turns reading parts of the investigative file.

On a Tuesday night in July, fourteen years ago, the mansion was robbed. The Lochers, a fifth-generation family living in the house, were away on vacation in Italy at the time, though they were expected to return on a Wednesday night, late. However, early on Wednesday morning, around 1:20 a.m., the security code was entered into the keypad in the kitchen and the system was deactivated. The burglars proceeded to open the old safe behind a large portrait in the main floor study. They stole jewels, several coin collections and cash. From the master bedroom closet, most of Mrs. Locher's jewels and Mr. Locher's watch collection were stolen. In addition, several pieces of art were removed along with all their silver.

"The whole take was valued at a little over $2.5 million plus another $300,000 in cash," Braddock stated. "That's a big number, especially for Duluth."

"Agreed," Tori affirmed. "The focus of the investigation quickly moved to the security company, who was—"

"Northern States Security Systems," Braddock finished. "Based right here in Manchester Bay. Go figure."

"The system had been installed a year earlier. It covered the whole house and there were some hiccups after the installation. Service was called and adjustments were made to the system. On the service team was, one, Loren Randolf."

"Duffy," Steak said.

Tori traced the investigation notes with her finger. "The homeowners claimed that the BCA started looking into anyone with the security company and in particular anyone involved on the installation and service call."

"And Duffy? What did the police find on him?"

"He had an alibi for the night of the burglary. He was with three friends at a bar out in Staples until closing time, which then was one a.m. Staples is a good half-hour west of Manchester Bay. And Duluth is two hours east of Manchester Bay. No way he was there, at least for the burglary."

"Yet, he was murdered," Braddock said. "And he was found with a bunch of cash."

"Cash?" Steak asked. Braddock and Tori ran him through the duffel bag of money that was found, the suspicious bank deposits and the purchase of the H2. "Okay, that raises some questions."

"Buying a H2 escalates the suspicions," Braddock said. "When your income doesn't really support it."

"Duffy doing something kind of dumb would be right on brand for him though."

"Despite the alibi, as I read between the lines of these notes, I think the BCA investigator still thought someone from the security company was involved, and that included Duffy," Tori noted. "He was there when the adjustments were made. Mrs. Locher recalled finding the security code written on a notepad in the kitchen. It was her husband's writing. The code may have been needed for the install or whatever repairs they were making to the system. She didn't think anything of it at the time. It was six months later that the burglary took place. They never changed the code for the keypad. And then, two weeks after the investigators interviewed him, he went—"

"Missing," Braddock finished. "He *was* involved. Was he a guy with loose lips?"

"Oh, I wouldn't doubt it," Steak replied. "He was the type to let money burn a hole in his pocket, for sure, which probably explains the Hummer. Where was he last seen?"

Tori flipped a page. "It says he was last seen at The Goose."

"In Garrison?"

"I think so," Tori said. "He had a credit card transaction there. It was a Tuesday night."

Tori found surveillance photos from The Goose. One was taken of a booth in the distance. The second was an enlargement, a touch fuzzy from the pixelation. The camera was at an angle to the left of the booth. Tori picked out Duffy right away, sitting at a table with four others, three men and one woman. One of the men and the woman were talking to each other, sitting with their backs to the camera. There were two more men and then a gap to Duffy Randolf who was chatting with a woman standing at the edge of the booth. She had a round tray in her hand so was probably a server. She examined it and then passed it to Braddock and then Steak.

"He's sitting in a booth with some friends, having a good time," Steak said. "Beers, burger baskets, looks like normal stuff."

He handed the photo back to Tori. She was going to stuff it back in the folder but then took another closer look, especially at the two men sitting side by side at the table.

"Wait a second."

She pulled out her phone and tapped into her photos and sent it to her department e-mail.

"I'll be right back," she said and rushed to her computer, opened the e-mail, the photo and printed it. The photo was larger now and clear enough. "This can't be," she murmured, rushing down the hall. "You two have to see this."

She set the photo she'd just printed next to the one from The Goose. "Tell me the two men with Kellin in this photo aren't the same two guys sitting with Duffy."

Steak and Braddock both leaned down, looking closely.

"Well, that's interesting now, isn't it?" Braddock said, turning to them. "Kellin was stabbed. Randolf was stabbed. And we have a famous burglary here that your old friend was involved in."

"You talked to Duffy's mom, right?" Tori asked Steak.

"Yes. I stopped to tell her we might have found him yesterday. Evelyn isn't far from here."

Braddock looked to Tori. "Let's go see her."

* * *

"Steak, he stopped by yesterday to inform me," Evelyn Randolf said, letting Tori and Braddock into the house. "He'd been friendly with my son, and I seem to remember Duffy talking about you once or twice, Ms. Hunter."

"Probably more my sister, Jessie. She was the popular one in high school," Tori said easily, as Evelyn led them into the kitchen. She had coffee at the ready and poured cups for them.

"I'm so sorry about this news," Tori said solemnly. "I didn't know Duffy really well, but I liked him. He was always fun to be around. He liked to go to parties, drink some beers, make some noise."

"Oh, that he did, Tori," Evelyn said, smiling. "That he did. I had to pick him up at places I'd rather not have had to on occasion. He was a wild man." She took a slow drink of coffee. "That's why I'd figured... something bad happened to him. He didn't go on the run. If he had, he'd have sent me word, even if he was hiding from someone or something, he'd have contacted me."

"You knew he was gone."

Evelyn nodded. "I just didn't know where or how or why."

"I know from personal experience that this is difficult, finding answers some years later," Tori said softly.

Evelyn nodded. "I suppose you do. As for my son, well, Duffy and trouble were often in close proximity to one another."

"In that regard," Braddock started, "we have some questions to ask about what he might have been doing around the time he disappeared."

"Oh, I figured you might," Evelyn replied.

Braddock took out his notebook. "Ma'am, I'm sorry to say this, but your son was murdered."

Evelyn let out a startled breath. "H-H-How?"

"He was stabbed, Evelyn," Tori said softly. "At the bottom of his rib cage." She gestured to her own, to show where.

Evelyn closed her eyes and then shook her head. "Why?"

"That's what we're trying to figure out. We have an idea or two."

"Did you know your son had purchased a new Hummer H2 the day before he was last seen?" Braddock said.

"Uh, no." She looked to Steak. "You said he was found in that, and I wondered why. As I remember it, he had a pickup truck that was newer."

"Duffy worked for Northern States Security Systems at the time he disappeared, correct?" Braddock said.

"Yes. He was a service technician for them. Worked there for a few years. He seemed to like the place though he complained about his pay from time to time, which all people do I suppose."

"He worked on security system installations, correct?"

Evelyn nodded. "Why do you ask?"

"Do you remember fourteen years ago, the Locher Mansion burglary?"

"Uh, no. Should I?"

"It was a burglary of some notoriety in Duluth. It happened about six weeks before your son disappeared. The burglars had the security code to the security system and were able to get in the house, tap in the code and escape with jewels, money, and art valued at just over $2.5 million plus cash."

Evelyn's eyes bulged at the number. "And how does that involve Duffy?"

"He was on a NSSS crew that installed and then later serviced the system several months before the burglary. The police interrogated him a few weeks before he disappeared."

"They did?"

Braddock nodded.

"And?"

"Well, he had an alibi for the night of the burglary. He was out in Staples with friends at a bar."

"At a bar, with friends, an hour away on a Tuesday night with Wednesday being a workday. That sounds about right for my son," Evelyn retorted whimsically, and Tori could see where Duffy had gotten his lighthearted attitude from.

"Maybe so. However, even with his alibi, the investigators were still interested in him at the time he disappeared. He was at the mansion on a service call several months before the burglary. The security code had been written on a notepad on the kitchen counter."

Evelyn nodded along. "But how does—"

"That involve Duffy?" Tori asked. "Despite his alibi, the detectives in Duluth strongly suspected he was one of the people who could have given the security code to those who robbed the mansion. At the time they had four people under suspicion. They cleared the other three. Duffy went missing."

"Duffy," she muttered, looking away, shaking her head. "So... stupid."

"You're not surprised," Braddock said, observing her reaction. "Are you?"

"No."

"Like you said, he found his way into trouble on occasion."

Evelyn nodded. "He was... extremely gifted that way.

Ready, fire, aim was the story of his life. And you think he was murdered for this? By whom?"

"We're hoping you might help us with that. I have a photo for you to look at," Tori said, pulling it out of a folder. "This was taken at The Goose."

"In Garrison?"

Tori nodded. "He was reported missing by you and his employer two days later." She handed Evelyn the photo. "He is with four people in that booth. I'm curious, can you identify those two men?"

Evelyn slipped on her reading glasses and examined the photo, squinting at them. "Oh yes. Those two," she said darkly. "Heath and Druk."

"And who were they?"

"Trouble."

It was the way she said it that had Tori and Braddock sharing quick glances with one another.

"How so?" Braddock inquired.

"As I said, as Tori said, Duffy was a troublemaker, but good of heart. My son was a bonehead, but harmless, until he started hanging with those two. When he did that, things got darker. They were a little older, far more mature and I think manipulative. Duffy liked to fish and so did they. I think that's what they both did. They were fishing guides."

"Hmpf," Tori murmured and then led. "That doesn't seem so bad. Where was the trouble?"

"Late nights. And while Duffy had a regular job with the security company, it paid modestly. Remember, I said he complained about it. Yet he always had money to go out, to afford a townhouse, new clothes and buy his pickup truck fully loaded. And he'd bring me gifts."

"It didn't add up?" Braddock said.

"No. And then..." Her voice trailed off.

"Evelyn?" Tori asked.

"When was the Locher Mansion burglary again?"

"Fourteen years ago. July twenty-first. A Tuesday night. Duffy went missing six weeks later."

"Wait right here," Evelyn said. She walked into the back of her house. A minute later she came back with a small purple velvet pouch. "Duffy gave me this about six weeks before he went missing." She handed the pouch to Tori.

"What's inside?"

"A brooch. And I don't think it's one you buy at the local jewelers."

Braddock took out a rubber glove and handed it to Tori, who pulled it onto her right hand. She undid the bow and opened the pouch and poured its contents into her gloved hand. It was a brooch with a large blue sapphire surrounded by small diamonds. It was stunning.

"How does *my* son afford something like that?" Evelyn asked.

"Did you ever ask him?"

"Yes. And he just smiled."

"And you knew," Tori said with a nod.

Evelyn offered a whimsical smile. "Well, let's just say I knew it was something I'd never be able to wear in public."

Tori examined the brooch and then looked to Braddock. "The detectives in Duluth might be interested in looking at this."

"I imagine they might," he replied before picking up the photo again, gazing at Ledyard Heath and Lenny Druk.

Tori turned to Evelyn. "Tell me more about these men, Heath and Druk. Did you meet them?"

"Oh yes, several times. They were pleasant and polite enough when they'd come here. Druk was quiet. Heath? He was kind of gregarious. He'd come inside: Yo, Evelyn, how you doin?"

"Yo?" Tori said, shifting a side eye to Braddock and Steak.

"Yeah. Yo, Evelyn. Yo, this pie is great. Yo, Duffy, let's go man."

"Like a verbal tick?"

"Yeah. I suppose."

"He'd say it casual like. It just rolled off the tongue?"

Evelyn nodded.

Tori took out her phone. "I want you to listen to something. It's maybe going to be hard to listen to, but bear with me." She pulled up the audio file and pushed play.

"911, what's your emergency."

"Oh my God! Help me! Help! No! No! Stay Away!... Get her!"

Evelyn looked to Tori. "What's that from?"

"Something awful that happened recently. Now, I'm going to play an enhanced version of it for you."

"Help! Help!"

She stopped it. "Now the second part." Tori pushed play.

"Yo, get her."

Evelyn listened intently. Crooking her head as she listened. "Play it again."

Tori nodded and pushed the play icon again.

"Help me! Help! No! No! Stay Away!... Yo, get her."

"Evelyn?"

"It's him."

"Are you sure?"

"That's Heath's voice."

TWENTY-TWO

"A PICTURE IS EMERGING."

Braddock, Tori, followed by Steak and Eggleston, made a speed run to Garrison and then south to Druk's house. They had two deputies with them in support and another two in reserve a quarter mile down the road parked in a resort parking lot. Geared up, they pounded on the doors to the house, but nobody answered.

Tori and Braddock took a walk around, noting that the same few windows open yesterday remained open now.

"It doesn't look like they've been back," Braddock said.

"No, I don't think so," Tori replied, but then walked off the back porch to a small grassy patch near the driveway. She pulled on a rubber glove and picked up an item out of the grass. "I think these things are so gross." It was a discarded tobacco pouch.

Steak handed her a small evidence bag and she dropped it inside.

Braddock looked to the two fishing boats on trailers resting by the garage. "These guys fish. They're guides. Who do they work for?" Braddock said.

It took them fifteen minutes of phone calls to determine

they worked as fishing guides for Red Moody at Garrison Boat Works. They had visited Red a few weeks ago about his insights on boats. Who knew how close they'd actually been to it all.

They left Steak and Eggleston to watch Druk's house along with backup. "Call if they arrive," Braddock ordered. As they drove to Garrison Boat Works, Tori blew out a sigh, looking at the photos of Heath and Druk. "You know, I think I've seen Heath before."

Tori and Braddock arrived at Garrison Boat Works, and Red Moody and Eve greeted them. They went into Moody's office. "Are two of your guides working today?" Braddock asked. "Ledyard Heath and Lenny Druk."

"Heath and Druk? Neither of them are on the schedule today or for the next two days. They've been off much of the week. Why?"

"We have some questions."

"Questions from two people like you suggest I got myself a problem," Red said. "Do I?"

"Tell us about them," Tori said. "When I think back to our first visit, Heath stuck his head in the room, didn't he? Said he had a list of supplies."

"You know, I think he did, now that you mention it." He turned to Eve. "He's been with us what? Three years, maybe four. He and Druk."

"They're excellent guides," Eve said. "Quiet, not super talkative types, but they always put people on the fish. I was pleased to hire them. They're good."

"Where did you hire them from?"

"I hired them between seasons. They had been up at a resort on Pokegama near Grand Rapids, but they were from here and there are few people who know the lake better. Druk has lived on it most of his life, Heath too."

Tori nodded. "I've heard that said of them."

"Asking others about them?" Eve asked nervously.

"We're starting to."

"Why would that be?"

"Eve," Braddock started. "You know what Tori and I have been investigating these past several weeks."

Eve looked to her dad. "Maybe that's why they gave notice."

"Notice?" Tori asked, sharing a look with Braddock.

"Yeah, just on Monday. Two weeks," Red said. "I was peeved with them. It leaves me short on guides for the last busy months of the season. And as Eve said, they're money when it comes to finding the fish. They've been good for business. Repeat customers ask for them all the time. What do you think they did?"

"I can't say for sure—yet," Braddock said. "I can't even say for sure they're guilty of anything yet."

"Your tone betrays the neutrality of your words," Red said. "Do I need to be worried about my customers?"

"They gave notice. Accept it."

Red looked to Eve. "Pull them off the schedule."

"But don't tell them just yet," Tori said.

Red Moody said he would call if he heard from them.

Tori and Braddock went back to Manchester Bay and stopped at the BCA, dropping off the evidence bag with the tobacco pouch to Jennison. "ASAP."

"On it."

They went to the government center and brought Boe up to speed.

"Are they our killers?" she asked.

"A picture is emerging," Braddock said. "They're connected to Kellin, to Randolf, to burglary and robbery. They're fishing guides. Renfrow found fishing scales in the wounds for Ally Mannion. These guys would know boats. And if they were in on something like the Locher Mansion heist, picking the lock of some seasonal cabin would be child's play. If they stabbed and killed Kellin and Randolf, it's not hard to see how they would have done Ally and Reed Schafer. They'd have just been two more in a long line. And this Shane Buckley guy, his murder in Ely unsolved, his throat slashed. I wonder if his demise is as a result of these two as well."

"An awful lot of smoke there," Tori said.

Boe wasn't hedging. "They're killers. We have them covered?"

"Steak is on their house with heavy backup. We've got a deputy watching Garrison Boat Works. We'll work this from here."

"And I'll see you tonight, right?"

"Well, with all this going on—" Tori started.

"We'll be there," Braddock said.

After they left Boe's office, Tori started to object.

"We're going to that event," Braddock said. "That's part of the job too."

They went back to his office and Steak had forwarded them both an e-mail. It was Dr. Fowler's calendar, the six months leading up to the home invasion. Tori scanned through the entries. As Dr. Fowler had said, he truly kept everything on his work schedule. It had taken him twenty-four hours to redact or de-identify any patient information from the calendar.

"HIPAA always just getting in the way," Tori muttered of the medical privacy law.

"The dreaded PHI," Braddock said in agreement. "You ever run into HIPAA on an investigation?"

"Psychotherapy notes are always tough to access," Tori replied. "Had to get at those a few times. Lawyers and doctors would get in the way. Good thing about the Bureau, no shortage of attorneys to call upon. Heck, plenty of special agents had law degrees."

Fowler had everything on the calendar, his golf rounds, dinners with friends and family, and multiple vacations.

"I'm always amazed at how much vacation doctors get,"

Tori muttered to Braddock. "He sent me six months of his calendar and I'll be damned if he didn't have five weeks of vacation on it. Florida, Hawaii, Arizona, Bahamas, and London."

"I could have been a doctor," Braddock smirked. "You know, if it didn't include all those classes on biology and anatomy."

Tori laughed. "You have a good bedside manner." She stopped. "Huh. Would you look at that."

"What?"

"Fishing charter. Five weeks before the home invasion." Tori called Fowler and put him on speaker with Braddock. It took him a minute, but Fowler recalled the fishing trip.

"I was out on Pokegama with several ENT colleagues from the cities. They came up for a conference and then wanted to fish. I like to fish, but there was no guarantee I could guide everyone, so I hired it out. There were guides tied in with one of the resorts. I rented them for the morning. My God, we caught fish that day. They took us out in two boats and we both hit it. Stringers and stringers of walleyes. Everyone limited out."

"Do you remember the guides at all?"

"Oh gosh," Fowler replied. "They were big guys. They each had decked out fishing boats with all the monitors and gear. They were really good. Well worth the money."

"How about their names?"

Fowler took a moment. "I can't remember."

"Did you take any pictures?" Braddock asked. "You kill the fish like that, you usually take photos."

"Give me second," Fowler said. "Okay, I have several photos from that morning. I'll e-mail them to you."

It took a few minutes, but they came through to Braddock's computer. He slid through them.

"Right there," Tori said, pointing to a photo of one man with the fishing rod in his hand and the other taking a large walleye off the hook. "Doctor Fowler. Do you remember if one of the names of the guides was Ledyard Heath?"

"Uh... you know, Heath, that seems to ring a bell. The other fella in the other boat, had a kind of unique name he went by as well."

"Druk?"

"Yes!" Fowler replied. "Hold on. Were they the men that did this to us? Were they the ones to rob us? It wasn't long after that fishing excursion now that I think of it."

"We don't know," Tori said. "Can I send you something to listen to?"

"Certainly."

Braddock looked to Tori. "The 911 call?"

Tori nodded and sent the audio file to Fowler. It wasn't the full call. It was the section where they'd recorded the man's voice.

They could both hear Fowler listening to the audio recording on the other end. He listened to the clip twice. "Give me a moment. I'm going to put on some headphones." A minute later, Fowler was back. "The voice is... familiar. What is this from?"

"A 911 call."

"The woman's voice? Did she?"

"Yes."

"Oh my. What I put the headphones on for is I heard something very faint before he says: 'Get her.' I heard a—"

"Yo?"

"Yes."

"You said you remembered that from the home invasion?" Tori said.

"Yes," Fowler said. "I can hear it with my headphones. The Yo. Sent a shiver right down my spine."

"You think it's the same voice?" Braddock asked.

"Can I say for certain? Boy, I don't know but like I said, I heard it and it... registered."

They spoke for a few more minutes. After Fowler rung off, Braddock looked to Tori. "They're our guys. They have to be."

"Now, we just have to find them."

"And we will," he said, looking at his watch. "We have to boogie. And before you object, I have my phone," Braddock said. "If anything changes, we can leave that fundraiser. The case isn't going anywhere. We have people on it and they're plenty capable, are they not?"

"They are."

"We need to go to this shindig."

"God, I hate these kinds of things," Tori grimaced.

"*Please*," Braddock mocked. "You die for occasions where you get to wear a fancy dress, designer shoes and sparkly jewelry. Unless, of course, you only buy that stuff just to fill the closet."

"Well... no."

"I didn't think so. These guys will turn up. When they do, our people will put them in bracelets for us and then we're going to have a whole lot of questions." He stuck his hand out for her. "Come on. Let's go."

"What if something goes down tonight and I'm in a dress?"

"Wear a pantsuit then. You have some very flattering ones."

"I do?" Tori asked, eyebrows raised.

Braddock smiled. "Yes, my darlin', you do."

"Okay, I'll let you take me," she said as she packed up the file.

"You're bringing that home?"

"Maybe it'll help me sleep."

"Knowing you, I doubt that."

TWENTY-THREE

"I DON'T DO PLACATING."

Braddock turned into the long drive for the Northern Pine Lodge, the historic vast resort on the north end of Northern Pine Lake. The expansive main lodge was perched on a hill that provided for a majestic south to southwest view of the lake. Any high-end Manchester Bay event generally was held in the grand ballroom that opened to a broad patio that allowed guests to take in the picturesque view of the finely manicured grounds, long sandy beach, and the blue waters of the lake.

"That's a chamber of commerce photo if ever there was one," Tori observed. "What a gorgeous night."

"You'd never know we're supposed to get thunderstorms later," Braddock said as he parked.

"Good evening," the parking attendant greeted.

"Evening to you," Braddock said as he unfolded out of Tori's Q5 and handed him the keys and then buttoned his suit coat. "Do me a favor. I'm with the sheriff's department." He handed the attendant a $20 bill. "Don't bury it. There is a chance we might have to leave in a hurry."

"Yes, sir."

He came around, opened the passenger door, and offered

his hand to help Tori as she arose out of the passenger seat. Rather than a dress, she'd made a last-minute audible to a black sleeveless jumpsuit. Consistent with Braddock's parking request, it was a just in case selection. As they walked inside, he leaned down and whispered in her ear, "I like that jumpsuit better than any dress. You look quite sassy."

It fit a bit of her mood.

They stopped at the check-in table. Tori handed over their donation check. She'd insisted on writing it out of her account. When pressed the other day as to why, she'd told Braddock: "You built me my dream closet."

He'd laughed. "That was for us."

"You've given me a home, and I'm not talking just the house," she'd insisted. "Let me make a real contribution to it. I'll be proud, really proud, to have our names, yours, mine and Quinn's, together on a brick for a children's cancer center."

"Me too."

They angled toward the bar. "Are we drinking tonight?" she asked. A glass of white wine looked so good right about now.

Braddock crinkled his nose. "I tend not to at these. There are a fair number of people here who don't like me for this reason or that. I'll play it safe. You can, though. I'm driving."

"We're a team," she replied. "And stuff is going on, so, just in case."

"Be ready."

To the bartender, Tori said, "Two club sodas, tall glasses, with limes." To Braddock she said: "We'll look social at least."

While initially they didn't think this was really their scene, they quickly realized there were a lot of friends in the room. The hospital, and the fundraising committee, had cast a wide net for donations. It seemed like half of the hockey association was in attendance. And Roger and Mary were also there, sending them a warm wave from across the room. They mixed and mingled through the crowd, saying hello to friends and family alike.

As they mingled, they noticed the looks and then whispers.

A lot had happened over the last month, little of it good. The vibe of it all said: *Why haven't you done something about it? When are you going to arrest someone?*

An hour into the affair, Boe guided them to a corner to chat. "How many looks are you guys getting?" she asked with suspicious eyes that continued to dart around the room.

"Do you want to count the obvious ones, or do we include the more subtle lookaways as well?" Tori said under her breath.

"Nobody has physically run away from us yet," Braddock replied sarcastically.

"Funny," Boe retorted. "We're on a heck of a run here. I can only imagine when word on this Hummer H2 you pulled out of the pond goes fully public, probably tomorrow. People are already asking questions and then we'll have that too. I don't have a lot of answers. Have these two guys you're looking for showed up yet?"

"Not yet, but when they do, Steak and Eggs will call. Hence, club soda," Braddock said, holding up his glass.

"When they do, are you bringing them in?"

"We'll see. That was our original thought but the more Tori and I talked about it, we might want to watch for a bit first and see what they're up to."

"The physical evidence needs to catch up to our suspicions," Tori added.

"Man, I remember the Locher Mansion case," Boe said with a headshake. "Now, solving that would be cool. How about the jewelry store? Any progress on that? Naturally, other business owners are suddenly worried they're next. I've had a few of them make that little point tonight."

"Not so far," Braddock replied.

"That had to be an inside job," Tori theorized. "Someone

who knew the systems the owner had in place and where they were vulnerable. To go down through that duct and cut at the right place. That required inside knowledge."

"To that end, Eggleston is digging through former employees, people involved in the remodel of the buildings a few years ago to see if anything pops."

"Doesn't sound promising," Boe said.

"It's only been a few days," Braddock replied defensively.

"I'm not being critical," Boe said to Braddock under her breath. "I know we're doing all we can but... I'm just telling you people are asking questions."

"Jeanette, they always are. If I listened to all the complaints people had, I'd never get anything done."

"I know, which is why you don't. That's my job," Boe said and then offered an evil grin. "But shit flows downhill, my friend."

"Fair nuff, Sheriff."

At eight-thirty, an emcee stepped to the podium and introduced dignitaries from the hospital and the community, finishing with Kyle Mannion, who nodded to the crowd and stepped forward to the podium. He thanked everyone for coming and for their contributions to help build the cancer center at the hospital, for which he was funding a significant percentage of the construction.

"This has been an important project for Brianna and I for several years as we've thought we need something like this here." He talked about how two of his employees' children had cancer and had to travel down to the Twin Cities for the treatment they needed. "I thought," Kyle continued, "we're Manchester Bay, we can have that here. Those families that inspired this project are with us tonight." He spent a few minutes introducing them and talking about their story.

Then he got to the end of his remarks. Kyle offered a pause and audible sigh, and the room went silent, sensing what he was going to talk about next.

"As you know this past month has been a trying..." His lip quivered for a moment while he steadied himself. Brianna hooked her arm through his. Kyle nodded and continued. "It's been a trying time for our family. We have been truly touched by the support we've received from all of you. It's why we call this community home and always will. Our daughter Allison was a young and vivacious girl, full of life, who as some of you in this room know, liked to babysit and not just for the money, although let's be honest, the money was nice."

The room laughed.

"She loved kids. To... um... have had her taken away from us..." He halted for a moment. "It has helped us understand even more what a parent whose child has cancer is experiencing and fearing. That fear that their child will be taken from them. I've felt it." He closed his eyes. "It is my hope that this cancer center will prevent that from ever becoming a reality for any family in our community, at least due to cancer. So—" he looked out at the audience, his eyes moist, taking a long pause, composing himself "—I hope you'll indulge Brianna and me a bit here, but we've made a last-minute change to the name of the cancer center. It will not be the Mannion Children's Cancer Center, but instead will be named the Allison K. Mannion Children's Cancer Center."

The room roared in applause.

Kyle offered a small nod to the crowd. "Thank you very much. And thank you for your generosity to this project."

The applause continued for a long minute as many approached the stage to embrace Kyle and Brianna.

"Wow," Tori said, wiping away a tear.

"Yeah," Braddock said in barely a whisper. "I don't know how he just did that. No way I could."

"Me neither."

They took a moment to compose themselves and then slowly began moving about the room again, chatting with people they knew. Then Tori spotted her good high school friend, Lizzy White, and her husband, Tom, standing with another couple and strolled speedily over to them.

"Lizzy, you look *gorgeous!*" Tori said.

"Right back at you," Lizzy said, hugging Tori. Braddock shook Tom's hand.

"Tori, Will," Lizzy said, "I want to introduce you to good friends of ours, Thor and Ella Johansson. They actually don't live too far from you. Their place is out on Paradise Point. Thor and Ella, this is my lifelong friend Tori Hunter, and Will Braddock."

"A pleasure," Thor Johansson greeted warmly. "Your reputations do proceed."

"I'm not sure *that's* a good thing," Braddock said, which elicited a laugh from everyone. "Did you say Paradise Point?" He looked knowingly to Tori, and said, "You wouldn't happen to have the house out on the point? The one you have to go over the little bridge to get to?"

"That's us."

"I'm sure you hear this all the time, but I *love* your house," Tori said, smiling brightly. And she did. She wasn't overly impressed by all the money that had moved onto the lake in the last twenty years. She thought there was a bit of design and exterior sameness to the expansive homes that had replaced the more modest and rustic cabins and cottages of her youth. However, the Johanssons' house, that one impressed her. She made Braddock putter slowly by it whenever they were in the boat, taking it all in, imagining how nice it would be to have that house on that point with that view. And it was unique. The Scottish Lodge like structure, a mix of gray stone and dark wood, was uniquely built in something of a rectangular horseshoe on a densely treed squared point jutting out into the water, the lake visible out three sides of the two-story home. "Your home is just spectacular. And your spot on the lake, you just can't do any better than that."

"That's so kind of you to say," Ella replied, smiling.

"You should see the art collection inside," Lizzy said in a half whisper. "It is really something. The collection of paintings is remarkable."

"Lizzy," Ella said with a mock dismissive wave. "She overstates things."

"No, I don't," Lizzy insisted. "Tori, it's a really neat little private art gallery." And Lizzy would know. She was an art history professor at the university and curated the campus's museum of art. That, and she painted as a side hustle, lake and landscapes mostly, and sold the paintings in a local art gallery. Tori had bought one. It hung in their new bedroom. "Ella and Thor have such wonderfully understated taste. And, of course, they've been very generous to the university."

"I've been through the museum on campus with Lizzy. I'd love to see yours sometime," Tori said, wanting to see the house in general, not just the gallery.

"Tori and Will are on the lake," Lizzy added.

"You are?" Ella replied. "Where, may I ask?"

"South of you about four miles," Braddock said. "Down in the bay on the southwest side, not too far from town."

"They just added a beautiful addition," Lizzy said.

"I know that one," Thor said. "You expanded out to the back over the garage, right?"

"Yes," Braddock said.

"I've driven by several times in the last few months. It looks terrific, how you blended it in with your existing home. I know your contractor. You're happy with it?"

"Very much so."

"I know Tori is," Lizzy said. "I've seen photos of the finished product. The walk-in closet. Girl, I would kill for that."

"Oh really? Tell me about it?" Ella said, taking a drink of her wine. "I've had some thoughts in mind for ours."

"Oh, it's no big thing," Tori said, blushing. "Really."

"It isn't?" Braddock needled. "Are you kidding? That would be Tori's art gallery. It's like a clothing museum in there."

Ella looked at Tori with raised eyebrows.

"Okay, okay," Tori said and took out her phone and showed pictures of the closet. "The designer used every nook and cranny of the space. I could spend hours in there."

"What do you mean *could*?" Braddock jested.

"Stop it," Tori replied, playfully batting him on the arm.

Everyone laughed.

"I'd love to see it, in person," Ella said. "I've had some changes to our master closet in mind. I don't think I did a good job on it the first time."

"Oh, here we go," Thor said with an impish eye roll.

"Tell you what, Tori," Ella said, "you show me yours and I'll show you mine. And then after we'll go to lunch, you, Lizzy, and me."

"Let's do it," Tori said, having taken an instant liking to Ella who was warm and engaging, even with several thousands of dollars of diamonds around her neck, dangling on her ears and wrapped around her wrists. Thor was gregarious and liked fishing, and he and Braddock immediately started talking about the current conditions on the lake. It turned out Thor had been an investment banker now retired. He and Ella moved onto the lake and built their house ten years ago, moving up from Minneapolis.

They spent several minutes speaking when out the corner of her eye, Tori caught Kyle Mannion. Their eyes met and he tilted his head for her to follow. She casually leaned to Braddock. "Kyle wants to talk."

"He does, huh?"

"I'll go," Tori said. "You mingle. If we both duck out—"

"Gotcha."

"If I don't come back in fifteen minutes, do come rescue me though."

Tori followed Kyle, who was carrying two drink glasses and a bottle of whiskey down a long hallway, the noise of the grand hall drifting away. He took a right turn into a small meeting room, flipping on the lights. She turned inside.

"Evening," Kyle greeted, pouring himself a drink. He offered her one.

"Not tonight."

"Are you on duty?"

"Not officially. Unofficially, we've got an iron or two in the fire."

Kyle nodded. "I thought we could talk for a minute."

"I'd meant to get over to you, but—"

"I saw you talking to the Johanssons. Really nice folks, by the way." He took a sip of his whiskey and then looked to her as if to say: Well?

"I didn't know if you'd want to talk about that, especially tonight."

"I didn't either but then I gave that speech and..." His voice drifted away. He closed his eyes. "Is there anything new."

"Maybe," Tori said. "We might have something."

"Might?" He snorted his disapproval. "What does might mean? Is that to placate me or is it legit?"

"I don't do placating."

"Hmpf. So, something? Tell me about it."

"Kyle—"

"I could just pull rank and drag Jeanette Boe in here. Tell me something."

"I'm at a fundraiser wearing a black jumpsuit, drinking club soda when I ought to be in a formal dress, four-inch heels and drinking my third glass of wine. What does that tell you?"

"Sorry, I was—"

"An apology is unnecessary, Kyle."

"No." He stopped her, shaking his head. "I'm out of line. *You* do know what this is like."

"Which is why I took zero offense. Do you know how many times I asked my father and all his investigators what they knew about Jessie? They never knew anything or had any answers. You think I didn't get angry with them? I'd yell and scream at them, at my father, at Cal, repeatedly, as if the volume of my voice and the nastiness of my words would somehow produce the answers I wanted. They couldn't give me what they didn't have. I realized that years later but at the time, my anger was such—"

"I'm not... angry with you, Tori."

"I wouldn't blame you if you were." She stepped to Kyle and took his drink glass from him, taking a small sip of bourbon and then handing it back to him. "I've been frustrated too. Are you sleeping?"

"Not much. Are you? You look... weary."

"Not well lately, to be honest."

"How about Braddock?"

She scoffed a laugh. "You know, he seems to be able to shut it off better. When he's at home, he's at home, he checks out of work, leaves it at the office mostly. I should too but... sometimes, God, I just can't do it."

"Well, it hasn't been quiet around here. A few other things have come up too. This jewelry store thing. And this Hummer being pulled out of the pond and the dead body found inside."

"You know about that?"

Kyle looked at her as if to say: Really?

"It's not fully public yet but I suppose you're you."

"The builder is a good friend of mine. I saw him last night

and he told me about it. He said you and Braddock were all out there."

"Irony is the body found in the driver's seat was an old high school friend of Steak and I," Tori said. "He went missing fourteen years ago. That's a homicide now, too. And, it may actually have something to do with the 'maybe' I mentioned earlier."

Kyle's eyes flickered at that.

"Kyle, Ally's death was random. She was in the wrong place at the wrong time. However, we think her killers have been active for a long time in different places. Professional thieves, willing to kill."

"And have you identified them?"

She paused. "That's the maybe."

She'd said enough. If she stayed any longer, she was going to start in on the whiskey. She glanced at the clock on the wall. "You know, people will start talking if we don't get back to the party. And you know Bree will be looking for you. Come on," she said, hooking her arm through his.

"You'll tell me if this 'might' really does turn into something," he said as they walked back to the fundraiser.

"You know I will." She stopped and looked him in the eye. "And if it doesn't, I'll be the one to tell you that too."

When they came back into the grand hall, Kyle found Brianna who wanted him to come say hello to someone. Braddock approached. "How did that go?"

"About how you'd expect, and I said more than I probably should have. It's ten thirty. Can we go?"

"I think we've done our civic and friendship duty."

She slipped her arm through Braddock's hooked one, and they slowly strolled out of the room. "Anything from Steak?"

"Only that the house is still dark. No sign of them yet."

As they walked out the front door to the valet parking stand, they saw two familiar faces, the Johanssons.

"Ah, Tori," Ella Johansson greeted. "Now I meant it about that lunch. I very much want to get that on the calendar."

"I'd really enjoy that." Tori wasn't a social climber. If she was, there would have been opportunities within the FBI to work her way up, make her way to Washington. Those options had been made available to her and she never pursued them. That said, she still found her way to upscale events on occasion where she met people who had climbed the social and financial ladder. And while many of those people took on an air of superiority, which Tori disdained, there were some who remained grounded despite the success they had attained. She always found those people interesting to talk to. In Ella, maybe it was the way she spoke, the touch of sophistication in her voice, her manner, how she carried herself, but for some reason, she reminded Tori of the more wealthy, yet grounded people she met from time to time in New York City. She wouldn't mind a little of that back in her life.

"Now, you've known Lizzy since childhood?"

"I have," Tori said, smiling. "I met Lizzy Cowger, now White, the very first day of sixth grade at Manchester Bay Middle School. In art class, now that I think of it."

"Oh, that's funny."

"Lizzy was very talented, even then." Tori leaned in. "I don't have a creative art bone in my body. Neither did my twin sister. Lizzy helped us both with our homework in that subject."

"That just meant you had an eye for talent at any early age, Tori," Ella said.

Their vehicles arrived and in the far distance out to the south over the lake, they saw just the briefest flash of lightning.

"Storm's coming," Braddock murmured.

TWENTY-FOUR

"WE'RE COOKED IF WE DON'T."

Dan had backed the van in between two other white vans that belonged to the resort. For the past two hours, they had a view of the three parking valets who were loitering around the bottom of the grand steps leading into the main lodge for the Northern Pine Resort. The lodge was all alight for the event.

"I used to come here as a kid all the time," Dan said, sitting back in the driver's seat. "We'd ride our bikes up the path along the east side of the lake from Manchester Bay. We'd swim, relax on the beach, buy ice cream at the concession stand and look at all the city girls up here on vacation, staying in all the rental cabins."

"Did you?" Vee said with a hint of annoyance.

"We did. At least, you know, before I met you."

"Yeah, right." She turned her attention back to the lodge, raising the binoculars to her eyes.

"They're coming down the steps."

Dan raised his binoculars and observed as the couple walked to the bottom of the steps and the man pulled his parking ticket from his breast pocket and handed it to the valet.

"Would you look at that necklace. And the bracelet on her wrist. It's practically glowing, even from here."

"Don't talk about it that way," she whispered angrily. "Like you're Druk or Heath. Just... don't."

"But?"

"Just... just shut up."

The jewelry store was one thing. This was going to be another. To her, this was more dangerous than being in that duct. One look into the back of the van told her that.

"It'll be okay. We do this one and we're done. We're out. And we get out of the hole. Just focus on that."

"It's all I've been focused on," Vee said and then closed her eyes for a moment. Her hands were almost shaking. She wasn't the least bothered by the taking. They would be taking from people who would have plenty left over. It was the method that worried her.

Breathe.

She let go of a long exhale. Dan was right, just get through it and they would be where they wanted to be. She refocused on the couple. Their view of the valet area was obstructed by the narrow tower like trunks of the Norway pines, hundreds of which dotted the property. "Oh, oh."

"What?"

"Look who they're talking to."

Dan focused his gaze. "Is that?"

"Yeah. Tori. And the tall guy is Will Braddock, her boyfriend. He's the chief detective for the sheriff's department."

"He is a pretty tall guy."

"Everyone is tall next to us." She focused on Tori, who was chatting with the woman. "They look friendly."

A Mercedes Benz sedan pulled up, followed by an Audi SUV. The valets got out and handed over the keys, collecting their respective tips.

Dan started the van. The two of them watched as the

Mercedes and Audi took the wide looping driveway away from the lodge, passing them on the left. Dan turned the headlights and pulled out. The Mercedes and Audi both signaled left turns from the resort onto County Road 44, the two-lane road that made a long loop around the south, west and north of the lake.

Dan put the burner phone on speaker and set it in the center console.

"Where are they?" Druk whispered.

"They're south on 44 now, five miles away," Dan reported quietly as they followed. The Audi was following the Mercedes closely, traveling in the same direction. He got a sudden sinking feeling and glanced at Vee, his voice low. "They were talking like old friends at the valet parking stand. Tori is following them closely. Are they going with them? Back to the house?"

"What is that?" Druk said.

"There might be a complication."

"What?"

Dan quickly explained. Tori was who they knew, but she wasn't driving, it was the man she was with, Will Braddock. But they were following tightly along County 44.

"Are they friends with them, Vee?" Druk asked.

"I have no way of knowing. We were close friends with Tori in high school, but not necessarily now. I don't know anything about her social life, who her friends are outside of our old high school group, or who Will Braddock's friends are, any of that."

"If they follow them home, though—"

"Then we have to abort," Vee said. "You don't want to get into a mess with them."

"We'll see," Druk replied.

"No! We won't," Vee barked. "Not with those two you're not."

They followed, a quarter mile behind, while the two vehicles made their way around the northwest corner of the lake.

"The turn is up here in a mile," Dan said. "Then we'll know."

The two of them held their breath. The Mercedes slowed to make its turn. The Audi veered out to the right and passed them on the right shoulder.

"They're coming your way—alone. Thirty seconds."

Druk pulled his mask down and stood with his back to the wall of the garage, the narrow bridge to the point sixty feet to his right, just around the corner. Heath stood to his left. Druk had a gun stuffed at the small of his back. They both had their utility knives in their hands, opened.

"They're coming your way—alone," Dan reported. "Thirty seconds."

Druk exhaled a breath. "Here we go."

Heath stood silently to his left.

The glow of the headlights filtered through the woods and then they heard the tires ruttering over the thick wood planks of the bridge. The garage door hummed open, and the light triggered by the opener filtered out the three rectangular windows high on the back garage wall. Then the brighter light of the car's headlights blazed out.

Druk turned around the corner, rushed along the side of the garage, Heath on his hip. Peering around the corner, Druk saw the back half of the Mercedes pulling into the center stall.

"Let's go!"

Druk went for the driver's side and Heath turned for the passenger side, the woman out of the car, seeing him come around the corner.

"What! No! No! *Thor!*"

Heath hit her on the side of the head, knocking her to the garage floor, then put the knife to her throat. "Shut up, bitch!"

"El!" Thor yelled.

Druk hit Thor on the left side of the head, just above the temple with the butt of the knife handle, dropping him immediately to the ground. He put the knife to the man's throat. "Not a word. Not a fucking word!"

"Ohh," the man groaned.

"Just shut the fuck up!" Druk hissed, stuffing his knife in its sheath on his hip. He quickly ripped a strip of gray duct tape and placed it over the man's mouth.

Heath did the same thing on the other side, slamming tape over the woman's mouth. He slapped her across the face. "Yo, just do what I fucking tell you."

Ella Johansson, her eyes wide, nodded frantically.

"On your feet."

Druk picked the man up, still disoriented from the blow to the head. His legs were initially wobbly, but he steadied.

"We're not here for you. You're going to unlock the door, shut off the security system and then take us to the safe. Understand."

Thor nodded.

Druk took the keys out of the man's suit pant pocket and dragged him to the door, while Heath did the same with the woman. She looked at her husband, terrified.

The man opened the door, stepped inside, and turned off the security alarm.

Inside the house, Druk reached for the burner phone. "Come. Now." To Thor, he pulled his gun and put it to the back of his head. "The safe. Right now!"

* * *

Dan drove past two houses that were angled to the northeast, one with a light on in the back before he hit the narrow stretch of paved road and then drove over the wood planked bridge and to the wide squared driveway in front of the three-car garage to the right. He pulled in and backed up to the open middle garage stall.

Heath opened the doors to the back of the van. "Dan, Vee, inside."

Dan pulled down his mask and jumped from the back of the van.

* * *

Braddock opened the back door and immediately went to the refrigerator, grabbing bottles of water for them, then loosening his tie and tossing off his suit jacket.

"Is that leftover pizza still in there?" Tori asked, kicking off her heels and setting her blazer and flats on the dining room table. "We did all that talking and mingling, we missed out on most of the hors d'oeuvres."

Braddock took the pizza box out of the fridge and set it on the center island.

She retrieved the Loren Randolf file from her office. She opened it and then grabbed a piece of pizza. "Still nothing from Steak?"

"No. I actually sent him and Eggs home. I have deputies in plain clothes watching, at least as best they can. The way the house is situated on the property and along the highway makes it a bit difficult."

"Hmm," Tori said, pulling out the picture from The Goose. "Evelyn said these two were trouble. And she recognized the voice. So did Doctor Fowler."

"Yeah," Braddock said, standing to her side, looking down at the photo, and then leaning and kissing her on the neck. "You smell good."

"Down boy," Tori said, and took another bite of pizza. "Ella and Thor Johansson seemed nice."

"They did. That was quite the jeweled ensemble she was wearing."

"No kidding," Tori said, taking a bite of pizza. "It was gaudy, but tasteful. She could have had security walking with her."

"That pizza looks good," Braddock said, taking a piece for himself. He took the photo from Tori and examined it. "This is the last photo of Duffy. He didn't show for work the next day, right?"

Tori nodded.

"The other two at the table with them. It would be nice to know what they thought on the night," Braddock said. "We never asked Evelyn about them, did we?"

Tori shook her head, taking another bite of pizza. "Can't really tell who they are. The woman has her hair up in tight little bun. The man's hair is loose, down almost to his shoulders. Their backs to the camera."

The police radio on the counter crackled and Braddock leaned over to listen, turning up the volume.

"What is it?" Tori said.

"Ah, it's just a noise disturbance of some sort a few miles north. A deputy is responding."

* * *

With the gun to his head, Thor Johansson walked them through the main level to an office with floor-to-ceiling windows overlooking the lake. The man gestured to a built-in cabinet to the right of his desk, knelt to the lower cabinet and opened the cabinet doors to reveal the safe.

"Open it," Druk ordered.

The man tapped in the four-digit code. The safe beeped and he depressed the handle and opened it.

Druk grabbed the man by the back of his suitcoat and

dragged him across the floor and pushed him to his stomach and quickly crossed his wrists and duct taped them and then did the same with his ankles.

Heath burst into the office. "Yo?"

"It's open," Druk whispered.

Heath rushed to the safe with a large duffel bag. He emptied the safe's contents.

"The wife's jewels?"

"I've got them," Heath said. He held up two stacks of cash before stuffing them into the duffel bag, and then retrieved more. He took out a box and opened it. It was another diamond necklace, worth thousands no doubt. There was another box. "I've got all this too."

"Take the wife upstairs. Clean it out up there."

Dan and Vee stuck their heads inside. "What do you want us to do?" Vee said.

"Go with him to get the jewels." To Dan he said: "Then get down and start on the paintings. Be quick about it."

Heath dragged the woman up the stairs. Vee and Dan followed into the master bedroom and to the closet. Heath took out pillowcases and handed them out. "Get her shit. Don't be picky. Take it all. Check everything."

Vee and Dan went into the large closet and began opening drawers and boxes, dumping the contents inside. The woman had expensive taste and a lot of jewelry.

"Oh my God," Dan murmured as he dumped tray after tray of jewelry in the bag. "There is a lot here."

Heath grabbed the woman, knife to her throat and pulled away the tape. "His stuff! He must have something!"

"In the dresser. Over there. Top two drawers."

"Check them all."

Vee and Dan hustled to the dresser. She looked back to see Heath holding the woman, a knife to her throat.

"Dan? I'm worried about him."

Dan reached for her hand. "It'll be okay. He just needs her scared."

"Well, it's working. On me!"

"Steady." Dan glanced to his right and saw another shorter dresser. He opened the top drawer and found watches. He held one up before tossing it and the rest into his bag.

"Didn't tell me about that drawer, did you, bitch?" Heath said, repeatedly punching and kicking the woman in annoyance. "Is that everything!" Heath growled, slapping her again. "Is it!"

The woman nodded, groaning in pain, barely conscious.

"It better be."

He looked at Vee. "Take the bags to the van and keep watch." To Dan he said, "The paintings. Get started. Double quick."

Vee grabbed the pillowcases and rushed down the stairs, through the house and kitchen and into the garage and then jumped up into the back of the van, placing the pillowcases inside a larger soft black duffel bag. She looked back to see Druk arrive. He threw in another large duffel bag, and she heard things clink. "Stay here." He hustled back into the house.

She checked her watch. They'd been in the house five minutes, maybe a few more. Peering out the front of the van, she didn't see any movement about. The only noise was a dog barking in the distance.

Faster. Faster.

There was rustling again in the back. This time it was Dan. He had a large, framed painting. She helped him set it down and then grabbed one of the blankets to cover it and started assembling bungee cords to strap that and others that were coming.

"Go," she said worriedly. "We have to get out of here."

Dan rushed back inside the house, and she turned to look out the front window of the van. She could see house lights through the woods distantly. And she'd seen a set of headlights out along the road that led to the bridge. People were still up and awake.

It wasn't late enough.

When they'd done the job in Duluth years ago, or even the jewelry store, it was the middle of the night. This was too early, and it was Thursday. A night that people tended to get the early start on a summer weekend.

* * *

"You made the call, sir?" Deputy Collins asked the man standing on the front steps of his home.

"Yes, ma'am. I stepped out here to turn off the hose, I had the sprinkler going. Just after I turned off the water, I swear I heard someone scream, down there to the east. There are only two other houses and then the big Johansson place out on the point."

Collins looked to the east, down the road. "And what exactly did you hear?"

"I couldn't make out what it was. It was short, but it didn't sound right. I don't think the folks at the next two places have come up for the weekend yet. I think it was Johansson's place out over the bridge. They have the big Scottish-looking place out on the point."

"I know the one," Collins said. "Thank you for calling it in."

Collins jumped back into her Explorer and slowly pulled ahead.

* * *

Vee crept back up to the driver's seat and saw the headlights slowly approaching, stopping close to the bridge entrance. It was an SUV, and she glimpsed what looked to be a police light bar on top. And then the spotlight turned on and started sweeping the area, brushing the front of the van.

Not good.

She slipped out the back of the van as Dan came into the garage carrying another painting. "Put that down," she whispered. "We've got trouble."

"What is it?"

"Police."

"Oh, no."

"Keep an eye on the bridge." She ran into the house and to the library. "We have company. I think police."

"What?"

"Headlights out on the other side of the bridge. Just holding position."

Druk looked to the man and hit him on the back of the head, sending him to the floor. He hit him again and then one more time. The man lay motionless. He ran to the stairs and called upstairs to Heath. "We've got company."

* * *

"Hmm," Collins murmured to herself as she approached the bridge. She could see the van straight ahead, backed up to the open door of the middle of the three garage stalls. The rear doors were open.

"Dispatch. This is Collins. I'm requesting immediate backup. Paradise Point Road. Possible 10-82 in progress."

"Copy."

She reached for the driver's side door spotlight, flicked it on and focused it on the van. *Odd.*

The police radio burped. "Two units on route."

* * *

Braddock leaned with both hands on the counter, looking down at the photo from The Goose. "We were in The Goose yesterday. We sat in a booth just like that, didn't we?"

"We did. So?"

"The backs of those booths aren't very high, are they?"

"No, now that you mention it, I don't think so," Tori said, looking down at the photo again. "Why?"

"The man and woman with their backs to the camera, aren't very big or tall that's for sure."

The radio burped again.

"Dispatch. This is Collins. I'm requesting backup. Paradise Point Road. Possible 10-82 in progress."

"10-82?" Tori said, looking up from the folder. "Burglary?"

"Yes."

"Heath and Druk are in the wind."

"And Paradise Point? You know who lives there?"

"The Johanssons."

"All those jewels she was wearing," Tori said anxiously. "The art in the house? Dr. Fowler was attacked after he and his wife attended an event like tonight. You don't suppose?"

"We better go find out," Braddock said, grabbing his keys. "Our gear is in the Tahoe."

"I need different shoes."

* * *

When they came into the garage, they could see the spotlight slowly sweeping the driveway area and the front of the van.

"Have they approached?" Druk asked Dan.

"No. I think it's just one officer, but they're suspicious. They're standing outside, searching with that spotlight."

Heath looked at Druk. "More will be on the way."

Druk pulled the gun from his back and slid past the car parked in the first stall and snuck a peek out the garage window. In the distance he saw the headlights and then the spotlight focused on the front of the van. They were sitting ducks in here. The deputy knew something wasn't right. Druk glanced to Heath. "We gotta make a move."

Heath reached inside the van and unhooked the bungee cord holding up his AR-15. He whispered to Vee. "Get in the van. Scream like I'm attacking you."

"Vee?" Dan said questioningly. "We do this?"

"We don't have a choice now, do we?" she said. "We're cooked if we don't." She got into the back of the van and crawled toward the driver's seat.

Druk snuck toward the middle garage door while Dan held his position. Heath eased out of the van.

* * *

That van is damn peculiar, Collins thought, popping the snap on her holster.

"No! No! Stop... You're hurting him! Stop! STOP! STOP!"

She pulled her gun. "Dispatch, Collins. I need that backup! I need it now. *Now!*"

Collins pulled her gun and rushed forward, crouching, holding the flashlight in her left hand and her gun in the right, hewing to the right side of the bridge.

* * *

Braddock backed out of the driveway, jerking the wheel hard and accelerating and turning left for the county road. A sheriff's unit with lights and sirens raced by, rushing north on County 44. A few seconds later Braddock turned right and picked up speed, the sheriff's unit, and another up ahead with flashing lights and sirens.

* * *

Heath peered around the edge of the garage door. The deputy came over the bridge, crouched but they'd pulled their gun. By the way the officer moved, he could tell it was a woman. She reached the end of the bridge.

"Now!"

Vee hit the high beams.

* * *

The light was blinding. "Dispa—" but she sensed movement to her right. She saw a man, and the gun. She fired.

"*Crack!*"

* * *

Bap! Bap! Bap! Bap! Bap! Bap!
Pop! Pop! Pop! Pop! Pop!

The officer collapsed, falling face first, the gun dropping from her hand.

"Let's go! Let's go!" Druk yelled, jumping inside, followed by Dan and then Heath. He jumped behind the wheel, started the van and raced ahead past the downed officer.

* * *

"Those were gunshots!" Tori exclaimed, her eyes wide in worry. "Go! Go! Go!"

"What do you think I'm doing?"

"Do it faster. *Faster!*"

* * *

Druk drove around the parked patrol unit and zoomed ahead and turned right onto County 44, accelerating. In his rearview mirror he saw police lights.

"They're coming already!" Druk yelled, checking the side mirror. "They're coming on us."

"Haul ass!"

"I am. I am. This thing doesn't have their engine," he said, his foot all the way to the floor, two hands on the wheel, the engine roaring.

Get off the main road, get into the woods, was his instant thought. Use the terrain. It was their only chance.

"Hang on! Hard left coming. Grab something."

* * *

The first set of police lights ahead of them disappeared around the curve to the right. The second unit was about to do the same as Braddock was closing on them.

The radio crackled. "Dispatch, Frewer. I have a white panel van, just exited Paradise Point Road, heading north on 77. I'm maintaining pursuit."

"White panel van! White panel van!" Tori exclaimed. "Does that tie to the—"

"Jewelry store?" Braddock questioned. "It might."

"We're not looking for two crews, just one. If they did Locher Mansion, stole the boats, worked with Chew, killed Kellin, why not the jewelry store too."

They came round the corner to see Frewer in the far distance. The second patrol unit turned hard right onto Paradise Point Road.

"Continue the chase or go to Collins?" Tori said.

"Chase, we gotta chase," Braddock replied, burying the

accelerator, reaching for the radio. "This is Braddock. Hunter and I have joined the pursuit."

The radio burped again. "The van has turned left onto Elmhurst Road," Frewer's voice called.

Tori looked at the dashboard map. "Will, he's going to try and lose us in the woods." She pointed to the road on the map. "That's Elmwood. That's a long winder of a gravel road, it branches off... everywhere."

"In that case, my money's on Frewer. Nobody knows those roads better."

The other patrol unit radioed. "Officer down! Need paramedics and ambulance. Paradise Point!"

"Shit!" Braddock growled as he turned hard left to catch up to Frewer. "Hang on," he said as he hit the first curve to the right.

* * *

Druk drove as fast as he dared on the tight road as it wound its way through the woods and around small lakes and ponds, his end sliding as he took each turn more and more aggressively. The deputy was behind them. They weren't losing him.

"He's closing on us."

* * *

Braddock came around the left curve and the road straightened. Frewer's flashing lights were well ahead. But now they could see it.

Tori updated dispatch on their location. They had turned off Elmwood and were now on Sycamore Ridge Road. More units were on the way, but they were being led into a maze of gravel roads in the deep woods.

"Help is miles away," she said, looking to the map. "I'm not sure where to direct them. Look at this map. And if this keeps going, we'll come up on the Cass County line."

"We need Cass County in on this," Braddock said. "Dispatch, Braddock..."

* * *

"There's another set of police lights back there," Druk yelled, having made a few turns. "We need to get them off us. I can't outrun them."

Heath checked the magazine for the assault rifle and then jammed it back in. He looked out the back window, the deputy edging closer. The second set of lights was closing as well. There wasn't much time. "Let him get closer."

"Closer?"

"Yes," Heath answered. "Dan, get over here."

Dan shuffled to the back door.

"You're going to pop that right door open and then get back. Vee, grab his belt. When he opens, pull him back. Understand?"

They both nodded and Dan reached for the handle and nodded to Heath.

Heath set himself. "You have to keep it steady."

"Got you," Druk said as he eased back just a hair, letting the patrol unit close on them.

* * *

"Are they... slowing," Tori said as they were maybe five hundred feet behind Frewer now. "Or are we gaining."

The back door of the van flew open.

"No! No!" Braddock yelled. "Get your head down!"

* * *

"Now!" Druk screamed.

"Do it!" Heath said.

Dan pushed the door open and Vee yanked him back, pulling him on top of her.

Heath fired.

Bap! Bap! Bap! Bap! Bap! Bap! Bap! Bap!

* * *

"Frewer, look out! Look out!" Braddock yelled.

"Shots fired! Shots fired!" Tori exclaimed into the radio.

Frewer's unit began to swerve.

"He's losing it! He's losing it!" Tori shouted.

Ping! Ping! Ping!

"Whoa! Down!" Braddock yelled as the shots pinged off the front of the Tahoe.

* * *

Heath hit the patrol unit with an unrelenting barrage, peppering the hood, windshield, grill.

Bap! Bap! Bap! Bap! Bap! Bap!

He hit a tire. The patrol unit started swerving and fishtailing.

"Whoa!" Dan yelled.

The Explorer flipped in the air and then over and over.

Heath kept firing, aiming further in the distance at the pursuing vehicle.

Bap! Bap! Bap! Bap! Bap!... Click!

He pulled back.

"Go! Go! Go!" Heath yelled, ejecting the magazine, and jamming in a new one.

Druk floored it again.

* * *

"Sweet Jesus," Braddock blurted.

Frewer's unit flipped over and over to the right, careening off the road and down the embankment.

"Stop! *Stop!*" Tori exclaimed.

Braddock skidded to a stop, the back end of the Tahoe swerving on the gravel, his headlights shining directly on Frewer's collapsed unit. He was out in an instant.

"We need fire rescue and an ambulance!" Tori called. "The panel van is still northwest on Sycamore Ridge Road. We've broken off pursuit. White panel van. We don't have a make or model, but white, two windows on the back, none on the side. It'll be muddy from the gravel road." She dropped the radio and got out.

Frewer's unit was an upside-down mangled mess. One of his arms dangled out through the shattered glass of the driver's side door window. Braddock called to him. "Frewer! Frewer!" He slid down to the driver's side window and reached inside.

Tori skidded to a stop. There was smoke and now a flame flickering from the undercarriage. She ran back to the back of the Tahoe and got the fire extinguisher. She rushed over and hit the flames and smoke with it.

"I think he's alive," Braddock said. "We have to get him out."

Tori dropped the extinguisher and peered inside. Frewer was upside down, unconscious but still restrained by the seat belt.

Braddock tried opening the driver's side door. It was no good, too smashed. "I think we can pull him out if we get him unbuckled."

"Will," Tori said, the fire extinguisher emptied. "This thing is still smoldering."

Braddock stood up quick and evaluated it. "Yeah. We don't

have much time." He laid down on the ground and looked inside. "If I try for the seat belt release from here his body falls on my arm."

Tori rushed around to the other side, the SUV listing on the side hill. It wasn't steady, teetering, but the passenger side glass was also shattered. She could fit.

Here goes nothing.

"Be careful, huh," Braddock warned as she climbed in through the window and reached for the seat belt release with the tip of her finger. The seat belt released and Frewer's body dropped to the roof of the cab, and she felt the SUV start rocking and pulled herself fully inside as the Explorer slid down the side hill several feet before coming to rest again.

"You okay!" Braddock called, leaning in.

"Yeah," Tori said as she grabbed Frewer's right arm and used it to turn his torso enough that Braddock could grab hold of both Frewer's wrists. "Pull. Now!"

Braddock pulled Frewer's body out the window and dragged it up the side hill. Tori crawled over and then rolled onto her back to push herself out as the SUV started to rock again.

"Braddock!"

The Explorer started sliding.

He grabbed her wrists. "Gotcha." He pulled her out as the SUV slid down the hill, the undercarriage on fire now. The Explorer crashed into two trees and burst into flames.

They each grabbed one of Frewer's arms and pulled him up the side slope to the edge of the road.

In the distance behind them were approaching flashing police lights.

Braddock checked Frewer for a pulse while Tori examined the wound in his left shoulder. He moaned. Another deputy arrived with the ambulance right behind. The paramedics were out in an instant. One rushed over while the other got out the stretcher.

Tori and Braddock backed away and let the paramedic assess Frewer.

"He's alive?" the deputy asked.

"Beat to hell, but yeah," Braddock said. "Anything on the van?"

"No. We got units coming."

Braddock rushed back to his Tahoe and got inside, looking at the area road map. Sycamore Ridge Road ended at a paved road in Cass County several miles ahead.

"How far is that?" he asked, pointing.

"Seven, eight miles maybe?" Tori said, looking from the measure scale to the map route. She checked her watch and calculated how long it took to get Frewer out. "They might not have reached it yet."

"Dispatch. Is there a Cass County unit at the end of Sycamore Ridge Road?"

As they waited for a response, Braddock ran his finger along the map. "You were right. This thing branches off all over the place."

Tori took the radio and called the deputy watching Druk's house. "Have they returned for the night?"

"No. House is still dark," the deputy replied.

Dispatch called. "Detective Braddock. Cass County has a unit parked at the end of Sycamore Ridge."

"Copy," Braddock replied and looked to Tori. "What do you think? Is it them?"

"Put the BOLO out there," Tori said. "Put the names out."

"Dispatch, we need a BOLO on Ledyard Heath and Leonard 'Lenny' Druk." Braddock finished with the details. To the deputy: "You have the scene."

"Where are you going?"

"Hunting."

TWENTY-FIVE

"YOU HAVE TO HAVE A SPOT."

"Did we just kill a cop!" Vee yelled once they were away from the chase. "Two cops! And you know they called in this van."

"Calm down, Vee!" Druk said flatly, his eyes darting between the road ahead and the rearview mirror.

"But this van—"

"We stole it two years ago. It has Wisconsin license plates. Even if they call the plates in, they mean nothing. They lead nowhere."

"What do we do now, though?" Dan said more evenly. "Every cop, deputy, trooper out there is looking for a white panel van."

"We drive," Druk said plainly.

"Drop us off. Take us to our car and drop us off," Vee said. "We didn't meet you far from here."

"Exactly, you didn't. But we can't drive this van there. Not now. Just hold tight. We have to get to a place."

"Where?"

"You don't think we store the shit we steal at my house, do you?" Druk replied and then slowed to ease into a right turn.

Ten minutes later, Druk was driving down a narrow road

through what seemed like another tunnel of a road through dense woods.

"Do you have any idea where we are?" Vee whispered to Dan.

He shook his head. "I did during the chase," he whispered. "Now? No clue. I don't know if we're going north, south, east, or west I'm so turned around."

There was another turn, this one leading down a winding road through a tunnel of dense trees that led back to a small clearing and in the distance, what looked to be a garage.

"If they were going to kill us, this is where they'd do it," Vee whispered in his ear. "Middle of nowhere. Nobody would hear a thing. Dump us like Duffy."

"Hey, don't worry, you two," Heath said, noticing them whispering to one another. "You're going to be fine."

"Are we?" Vee asked.

"If we wanted you dead, we'd have already done it. I'd have shot you ten minutes ago after we evaded the police. You both kept your mouth shut with Duffy. We trust you will now, especially since you both are every bit as guilty of everything we are tonight. I can't imagine you want to leave your daughter an orphan, do you?"

Dan looked at Vee, who shook her head.

"Then we understand each other," Druk said as they approached a garage with a dual cab red Chevy pickup truck parked to the left of it. Heath, Dan, and Vee filed out the back of the van and into the cool night air, the wind wiping in the trees above. In the distance, there was bright flashing in the sky, lightning and then there was a rumbling of deep thunder.

"A storm is coming," Druk said. "That could be good for us if we hustle."

Dan took in the surroundings. "What is this out here?"

"Storage," Heath said as the garage door opened. Druk backed the van up to the garage. In the middle of the garage was a seating area, three mismatched old couches arranged like a horseshoe around a long throw rug. A wide and long wood coffee table sat in the middle.

"Nice garage," Vee muttered.

"It's not just a garage, it's a hunting shack," Dan said. "A nice one," he added, scanning the interior with old but comfortable furniture, two queen-sized beds along the far wall along with a two bunk beds, a small functional kitchen with stove, refrigerator and sink and a small bathroom that had a shower, or he assumed so given the orange shower curtain he could see. You could hunt and then relax and easily make a weekend of it.

"Dan, help me with the table," Druk said. The two of them picked the table up and moved it. Heath started rolling up the rug. Underneath was a metal door in the floor.

Heath went to a small desk positioned near the door to the bathroom, opened the middle drawer, and pulled out a small key ring. He selected a key and unlocked the door. He pulled the door up and open, took a few careful steps down a steep ladder before flipping on a light. Underneath the cement slab for the garage was a storage space. Dan and Vee looked down inside to see shelves, racks, and a locked cabinet. They both turned to Druk.

"You have to have a spot," he said.

"But isn't it in your—"

"Name?" Druk finished. "It's in someone's name, but neither of ours." He reached into the back of the van and took out the duffel bag that had cash inside. He set it onto the coffee table. "You know what I love about rich people? Cash on hand. Why, I'll never know. Banks are far safer."

"Yeah, we've never robbed a bank," Heath said with a snicker. "Wouldn't even dare try."

"It's ego," Vee said. "Rich people like to display evidence of their wealth. It validates them. That's why they wear gaudy jewelry, build their palaces, and have stacks of cash. All show and projection."

Druk and Heath looked back at her.

"I saw it all the time in Florida. I see it here now too. People flexing their wealth. With the shit we've been through the last year, I don't have a problem taking some of it."

Druk evaluated the stacks, some of which were hundreds, then fifties, and twenties. He set them out, then divided them in two. "Yours are on the left, ours on the right." Vee, who had been counting along, started feverishly scooping their stacks into another duffel bag. She thought it was somewhere between $90,000 and $100,000.

"Let's unload the van and get the heck out of here," Druk ordered. "Then we'll get you two dropped off."

Vee watched as Dan, Heath and Druk moved the four paintings that were in the back of the van down the narrow steps to the storage area underneath the floor slab for the garage. Each painting was wrapped in a blanket.

Dan scanned the storage room. There were some other art and silver pieces stored on the shelves. And there was the cabinet. Druk put the jewels and their cash inside. He caught a glimpse. There were more jewels and at least two what looked to be shoeboxes inside.

"You couldn't sell all this other stuff?" he asked Druk.

"Not yet. But we will. In time."

These two had been busy, and for quite awhile.

They climbed out. Heath closed and locked the door and then rolled the carpet back over it but left the furniture off to the sides. Druk backed the van inside the garage. Heath put the keys back in the desk.

"We'll dispose of it after things quiet down in a few days."

The four of them piled into Druk's Chevy Silverado pickup truck.

Druk turned around. "Alright, you two, lay down on the seats."

"What? Why?" Dan said.

"You saw more than you should. I trust you two."

"But only to a point," Vee said.

"Yeah," Druk said. "Lay down. Relax. We're almost done."

Dan and Vee spooned on the back-bench seat, though Dan tried to get a sense of what direction they were going. It was difficult. The only thing he recalled seeing was an odd small yellow flag under a streetlamp. Otherwise, it was all darkness, except for the lightning flashes, which were getting closer and closer while Druk made turn after turn.

Vee turned her head to him and whispered, "It feels like we're going in circles."

"Yes and no," he replied. His own internal compass left him with the general sense they were traveling east, northeast.

"You two can sit up now," Heath said.

Dan checked his watch. They had been driving for fifteen minutes. They passed a road sign that said they were approaching County Road 92. At the corner, he saw a street post sign for Tompson Road.

Druk turned right, and drove east, cruising along easily, passed only by one vehicle before they turned left and drove around to the backside of Long Necks, an out of the way bar on the north side of Lake Lucinda several miles northwest of Pequot Lakes. The bar was long closed for the night, the only vehicle in the back of the parking lot, sitting under a low hanging branch of a withering pine tree was a dinged up ten-year-old white Mazda.

Vee grabbed the duffel bag with the cash, and they climbed out.

"I'll reach out to you when I hear from my man," Druk said, his window down. "I'll get you your instructions and our account will be square."

"Okay."

"Keep your heads down. Live your normal lives. It'll all blow over, just like this storm that's coming."

Heath and Druk raced away, turning right back onto the road.

"Isn't a left faster for them?" Dan said, watching the pickup turn.

"Who cares," Vee said. "Let's just get home."

TWENTY-SIX

"WE END THIS, RIGHT NOW."

"It's almost three a.m.," Tori observed as they cruised down yet another tight gravel road, deputies patrolling a broad area in the hunt for the panel van. There was a rough road grid that units from Shepard and Cass County were working, but it was the middle of the night, and they didn't have air support. The hope was that with enough units flooding the broad area, the van wouldn't sneak through, someone would see them and then they could converge. The sky flashed brightly in lightning. Tori had the weather radar up on her phone. A heavy band of thunderstorms was rapidly approaching. "We're about to get seriously walloped."

"We've been searching what? Three hours?"

"'Bout that," Tori replied. "I'm thinking they got out. By the time we had enough people and resources in the area, they could have slipped out and are long gone."

"We haven't enough resources as it is. We only have so much to deploy to begin with. Yet," Braddock paused, "they haven't shown up at home. They could be hunkering down out here, waiting for us to loosen the dragnet, so to speak."

Braddock's phone buzzed. It was Steak. This was a call they'd been waiting for.

"Will, Tori. Collins…" He sighed. "She didn't make it!"

"Oh," Tori gasped, putting her hand to her mouth. "Oh my God."

Braddock simply sighed. "Tell me."

"They lost her twice in the ambulance on the way to the hospital and somehow got her back. They were rushing her up to surgery, she was on the damn table, but… the damage was so extensive. She was shot nine times, man. The vest took three of them, but six got through, took her lower abdomen all apart."

"Frewer?"

"In surgery. He made it to the hospital alive. Docs are working on him."

"The Johanssons?"

"Thor Johansson is in a coma."

"And the doctors are saying what? Will he survive?"

"I don't know. It's early but they're tight-lipped and grim on him."

"And Ella?" Tori said.

"Alive, but unconscious. She was beaten severely, just like her husband. The docs seem a little less dour there. They have adult children in the cities. They're on their way up here. Will, Boe wants to know what your story is."

"It's been three hours and nothing so far. We've got units cruising the paved roads and we're working a grid along the gravel ones, but there is nary a vehicle out."

"It's the middle of the night," Steak said. "And a thunderstorm is literally on top of you guys."

"Any warnings we need to be aware of? The last thing I need is to drive into some tornado."

"No, nothing that severe, but it's going to rain hard for sure. It's already started here, coming down in sheets." He paused for a moment. "Do you think they got through?"

"More than likely."

"They haven't made it home. We're tight on that and I mean tight. I ran over and rechecked it myself ninety minutes ago. They show, they're going down. A Tactical Response Team is in position. The house is still dark. Heath's black Dodge Ram is there but not the red Chevy registered to Druk. Every cop, deputy, trooper out there has that truck, and any white van out there is getting pulled over, no matter the make or model," Steak said. "They'll show up."

"Unless they wise up and go on the run," Tori said. "If these guys have been as busy as we think they've been, they'd be ready to run at a moment's notice if we got onto them. After tonight, how can they not question that? How can they assume they're safe? Didn't Red Moody say they'd given notice?"

"He did at that," Braddock replied.

"They could already be on the run."

* * *

"Go east and get to the H-4?" Heath asked as they were about to pull out of the parking lot. "Might beat the storm that way," he added, looking up to the lightning show. The rain was starting, big spread out drops, a sign of heavier showers to come.

"I feel like we're more likely to run into state patrol, sheriff's deputies along there. I want to make a wide drive west, through the storm and swing down to Motley. We get there and we can drive back to Garrison on 210 where there should be less patrolling."

Heath nodded. "You're the boss."

"There is one other option, though."

"What's that?"

Druk let out a sigh as they drove ahead. "We call it a day right now. We go back to the garage, we scoop up the jewels from the safe and go right to the jeweler in San Francisco. Our other passports are there. We have a change of clothes or two and we get the hell out of here."

"And your house?"

"It'll still be there. The boats are covered. I can get someone to take care of them for us, close up the house."

"Seems quick to pull this trigger."

"Is it? We have all this tonight. Even worse, Duffy's body turned up. The police are going to show up and ask us questions, just like last time. Who knows what else they ask about? Dan and Vee are out there."

"You want to deal with them?"

Druk shook his head. "No. I saw the looks on their faces tonight. They wanted the money, they needed the money. I don't think they cared about the rest, but the police might darken their door too." He took a moment. "We're pushing our luck, man. We've been pushing our luck since those two kids, and I've been the one pushing it. We need to get the heck out of here and not come back for a good long time."

"Leave the country?"

"That's why I mentioned the passports. Are you still in contact with that guy down south of Tijuana?"

"Raul in Ensenada?"

"Yeah."

"Talked to him a few months ago. We could lay low there for a bit and make some plans," Heath said. "Easy to get on a boat there you know." The rain's intensity suddenly increased, pelting the windshield.

"That's what I was thinking," Druk replied as he put the windshield wipers on full. "We empty out the storage, drive to San Francisco and see the jeweler with what we got tonight. Deal with him direct."

"Cut your fence out?"

"I'll send him a little something. Then we go south."

"Are you cutting Vee and Dan out of the deal?"

"No. Do that and they might talk. We'll get them their piece of this... in time. Once we see how things all shake down with our man in San Fran. The money will be wired. I don't have to hand Dan the instructions. I say we bail, get on the road, and I'll call Dan in a day or two and let him know what's happening."

"You're the planner. I roll with you."

"I think that's what we should do."

"Then let's go," Heath replied as he gazed ahead through the downpour and saw a set of headlights appear at the edge of the road. "What's that up there?"

A black SUV turned right, driving east, coming at them.

* * *

The rain was pounding the Tahoe, the windshield wipers struggling to keep up. Braddock approached the end of another gravel road, a paved road ahead.

"Where are we even?" Tori said, looking at the GPS map. "I'm a little lost. And I can't make out much in the rain."

"Northwest of Pequot Lakes. This is County 92. East gets us to the H-4. We can do another surveillance loop from there."

"Copy that."

Braddock turned right, the headlights of a pickup truck approaching. They both observed the truck as it zoomed by.

"That was a red pickup truck," Tori said, looking back. "I think a Chevy. It had the gold emblem on the tailgate."

"You're sure?"

"Yes."

"Could be anyone."

"Out at three in the morning in a thunderstorm?"

Braddock made a quick U-turn. "Only one way to find out."

* * *

"They turned around," Heath said, looking back.

"They know who we are?"

"How?"

"I don't know."

Druk slowly depressed the accelerator, speeding up into the deluge. He took his gun and handed it to Heath. "I reloaded it. It has a full magazine."

* * *

"He's sped up," Tori noted.

"He has," Braddock said, matching the pickup truck's speed, but he didn't turn on his police lights. He wanted to get close to see the license plate first.

"Minnesota plate," Tori said, squinting, trying to see through the rain.

He pulled in close enough they could make out the plate.

"That's Druk's truck! They switched vehicles out here somewhere."

"Dispatch, this is Braddock on County 92 to west, a few miles west of the Long Neck. We have a sighting of a red pickup truck belonging to Leonard Druk. Requesting immediate backup."

The pickup truck accelerated, rapidly.

"There he goes!"

Braddock flipped on his lights. "Dispatch, we're now in pursuit."

* * *

"Haul ass," Heath said as he climbed over the front seat into the back of the cab and slid open the back window. He had two guns, Glock 17s. Each magazine had seventeen rounds. He had another magazine in his back pocket.

* * *

Tori checked her gun and chambered a round. She stuffed another magazine in the pocket for her vest. She looked behind and didn't see any backup coming, at least yet. The road ahead was also clear, as much as they could see in the rain, which was side swiping them now, the wind having kicked up.

"Not good conditions for this," Braddock said, both hands gripping tightly to the wheel, his posture upright, tense.

The radio crackled with chatter, units turning to come their way.

Braddock had dropped back some. "I don't need another firefight with these guys, especially if they still have that assault rifle. And I can't see in this... shit."

* * *

"They're not coming up on us," Heath called. "He should be."

"They're playing for time and waiting for backup," Druk replied as they came around a bend in the road, feeling his back end hydroplane on the road, swerving. Once straightened, he saw the green street sign on the right and jerked the wheel, turning right onto a dirt road. "I know this road. Hopefully he doesn't."

* * *

Braddock turned right.

Tori took over the radio. "Dispatch. The chase is now on... Shell Lake Road." She looked to Braddock. "They're trying the same thing over again," she said, the road winding its way through the woods.

"Get us one on one."

"I don't care. Do you?"

"No! They killed Collins. They killed Ally. We end this, *right now!*"

* * *

Heath slid the rear window open and fired just above the headlights.

Crack! Crack! Crack!

* * *

They both ducked as the bullets pelted the hood.

Braddock peeked over the dash, the pickup a hundred feet ahead. He looked at the GPS on the dash. In a quarter mile there was a left hairpin turn and then a bridge over a stream.

"Enough of this shit."

He hit the gas hard, accelerating rapidly, closing the gap.

"Brace yourself!"

* * *

"Here he comes!" Heath yelled, firing.

Crack! Crack! Crack!

* * *

The shots hit the windshield and then Braddock rammed the back end of the pickup truck, pushing it ahead.

The bend was coming up.

Braddock rammed his back again, the pickup truck now fishtailing. He kept on the pickup's bumper, pushing the truck.

"He's losing control," Tori yelled, peeking over the dash-board. "Back... back off."

"Not yet."

* * *

Heath was knocked into the back of the front seat from the collision, the gun still in his hand. The truck was swerving on the wet road, throwing him around the back seat. The SUV pushing them, jolting him.

Druk was trying to correct the swerve, but he was out of control, the bridge coming up, the right bridge abutment ablaze with the glow of his headlights.

He was going to hit it.

* * *

The back end of the truck swerved to the left as they hit the right turn. The driver tried to correct.

"He's not going to make the turn!" Tori exclaimed. "Back off! Back off!"

Braddock pushed the rear bumper again.

"*Braddock!*"

He pulled back, jamming the brakes.

The pickup truck hit the wood bridge abutment at an angle, riding up it and then vaulting over the side of the bridge, the taillights disappearing over the other side.

Braddock skidded wildly, careening off the guardrail and stopping on the bridge. "Dispatch, we're on Shell Lake Road. The red Chevy is in the stream. It's in the stream. We need backup. Where is it?"

"On route."

"*Faster!*"

Tori opened her door, immediately hit in the face with driving rain.

"Careful," Braddock warned as he did the same.

Braddock had his flashlight in his left hand, his gun in his right and they both cautiously approached the bridge rail, the rain already soaking through their clothes.

* * *

Heath was wedged between the back seat and back of the front seat. "Druk? Druk?"

"Yeah," he moaned.

"We have to get out! We have to get out!"

"Yeah, yeah," he replied, coming to, reaching for his gun, a beam of light coming from high, scanning the back of the truck. "Is it just the two of them?"

Heath looked up just over the back of the truck. "I think so."

* * *

The pickup truck was nose first into the rustling waters of the stream; the rear axle caught up on a downed tree along the bank. The engine was revving, still in gear, the front left tire spinning, water and mud spraying.

"Can you see them?" Braddock said.

Tori stepped to her right, keeping the side of the bridge between her and the truck. "There's movement inside. The rear passenger window is going down."

* * *

Heath reached for his door handle on the passenger side. Druk did the same.

"Power down the window. I'll use your door to cover you," Druk said.

The window powered down.

"Now!"

Heath pushed the door open.

Druk jumped out, firing at the flashlight beam.

Boom! Boom! Boom!

* * *

"Get down!" Braddock yelled, pushing Tori down, landing on top of her as the bullets ricocheted off the thick wood ties of the bridge. They both heard rustling and splashing. Braddock peered over the edge of the bridge with the flashlight and scanned the area of the truck.

"They're running!"

One of the men turned around and fired.

Boom! Boom! Boom!

Braddock popped back up and fired.

Crack! Crack! Crack! Crack!

He hit one of them in the shoulder, sending him down along the right edge of the stream.

"Cover me." Tori jumped up and started shuffling down the hill.

"Tori! No. Hold on. Hold on!"

She descended the steep bank.

"Shit! One of these days—" He scanned the riverbank with his flashlight but couldn't see anyone. They were on the move again.

Braddock looked back to see two sets of flashing police lights fast approaching. He turned back to the stream and now he couldn't see Tori in the torrent of the rain either.

* * *

Druk face-planted into the mud and water, hit in the back of his left shoulder. "Ahrg. Dammit!" he groaned, pushing up in the soft mud with his right arm.

Heath hooked him under the right arm. "Come on! Come on!" He got Druk onto his feet and they started fast walking and then jogging along the right side of the now raging stream that had cut a deep and narrow crevice with steep vertical sides.

"We need to get up and out of here," Heath said. "Get in the woods."

* * *

Tori slid the last twenty feet down the embankment to the right of the truck. She looked back up and Braddock was waving down the road and she heard the sirens and then saw the blue and red police lights filtering through the rain and trees. She spun around and looked ahead.

There was a lightning flash. She saw Heath and Druk, scrambling together along the side of the bank, one man helping the other.

She pushed ahead, careful to keep right and avoid the rushing waters of the stream.

* * *

"Can you see her?" Braddock yelled as he made it to the bottom of the bank, nearly falling into the water.

"No!" a deputy replied.

Two more were right behind him.

"Get a spotlight out here!" Braddock yelled as he worked his way ahead.

* * *

Heath dragged Druk along the bank. If they could get across the water to the other side, he saw a narrow path leading up into the woods.

He glanced back and saw flashing police lights, and

someone was following, they were small, darting along the stream's edge.

"We have a tail," Heath said. "They're gaining."

Druk pushed himself up and spun around as lightning lit up the sky and thunder boomed.

* * *

Tori hewed to the edge, moving from tree to tree, checking back. She looked back and others were coming down the bank.

She glanced left around the tree. The next one twenty feet ahead. She burst out into the open, crouched, jogging, her gun up.

Lightning filled the sky and lit the stream. She saw one of them spin around.

Crack! Crack! Crack!

The bullets rustled through the trees above her. She dropped to her right knee and fired.

Bap! Bap! Bap! Bap! Bap! Bap!

* * *

"Ahhhh," Druk shrieked, the bullet ripping through the back of his left thigh.

"Ah shit! Ah shit!" Heath screamed, hit in the back of his left shoulder.

Druk tried to push himself up. "I... can't," Druk groaned. "I can't get up."

Bap!

"Uhh..." The shot hit Druk in the center of his chest. He fell lifelessly back into the stream, his body instantly swept away by the rushing waters.

Heath turned and saw the body bobbing in and out of the trees, still coming.

He ran ahead, seeing large rocks spread across the stream, the water flowing around them. That was the way across.

Another flash of lightning filled the sky as he jumped for the first rock.

* * *

"Will!" the deputy yelled as the body came flowing down the stream, a man on his back, a beard, his arms spread out, riding along the current.

"Get that body!" Braddock yelled.

Lightning filled the sky. He caught a glimpse of Tori, far ahead darting from tree to tree in pursuit. There was another burst. Further in the distance a man was trying to cross the water.

"Tori!" Braddock called as thunder rumbled, the waters rushing.

* * *

In the flash of lightning, she saw Heath jumping across the rocks, thirty yards away.

Bap! Bap! Bap!

He just kept going.

* * *

He jumped from the last rock, landing in the water, falling to his knees. "Ahhh," he groaned as he pushed up with his right arm, the pain searing through his entire torso from the wound in his left shoulder. "Ah, dammit!"

He looked back and saw the cop coming. It was a woman.

* * *

Tori saw him stand up. He spun around.

Crack! Crack! Crack! Crack! Crack!

She dove to her right behind a tree and into the mud.

The shots stopped.

He's out. Unless he had another magazine. In the darkness and rain, she caught glimpses of him climbing a path on the far side.

Tori pushed herself up and saw the same rocks and nimbly jumped across them, taking a big leap from the last one, landing on her feet in the water just short of shore, but quickly high stepping out before the current took her.

She rushed to the embankment and then halted for a moment, peering up the trail and not seeing anything. Looking back, everyone was still a long way off. She eyed the steep path, strewn with rocks, a washout of the embankment. *I can make it up that.*

* * *

Braddock saw Tori skip across the rocks. She wasn't going to give up the chase, not now.

"Cripes," he muttered, sprinting ahead in the mud.

* * *

Heath reached the top of the embankment, the pain coursing thought his upper left side, his gun magazine empty. He wasn't going to be able to outrun her. He needed to stop her and make those following stop at her.

He took refuge behind a wide tree and pulled the knife from the sheath on his belt. As he glanced around it to the right, he saw something bobbing, a head, working its way up the slope. It was the woman. She reached the top and stopped, her gun up, her back to him.

The knife in his right hand, he secured his grip.

* * *

Tori reached the top and stopped, just short, peering over the edge, scanning the woods, starting on her right, panning with the gun, not seeing nor sensing any movement. She took two more steps up, now on flat ground. Scanning.

Crunch!

She pivoted left and fired.

Bap!

"Ahhh, you bitch!" She caught him in the left shoulder, but he steamrolled over her, the two of them rolling on the ground, the gun knocked from her hand. They rolled over a second time, and she caught the glint of the steel of the knife in his right hand.

They careened into a downed tree.

He landed against her, crushing her into the trunk. Heath pushed himself back and raised his right arm, the knife coming down.

Tori quickly pulled her legs up and kicked him in the chest with both feet, pushing him back, standing him up.

Boom! Boom! Boom! Boom! Boom!

Heath seized up. "Uh... Uh... Uh..." He slowly collapsed sideways before falling to his back.

She looked to her left.

Braddock.

He climbed up the rest of the embankment and walked slowly to Heath, who was immobile, gasping for air. He stood five feet away, looking down at him, his feet set.

Boom!

He shot Heath between the eyes.

"There will be no trial," he murmured.

Tori leaned back against the log, breathing heavily, her body battered. "Sorry, I know I should have—"

"Waited?" Braddock said, kneeling to her. "Yeah, you should have."

"I just... took off."

He nodded. "My only regret is you got to them first."

* * *

Tori's body and clothes were caked in mud, her black jumpsuit ruined, her hair, in a clunky ponytail, chunked up with mud chards, her arms scratched, blood streaks on her forehead. Braddock was little different, his dress shoes trashed, his suit caked in the same mud, his face streaked with dirt, hobbling as he walked. They both desperately wanted to get out of their clothes and to get clean. There was one stop to make before they made it home.

It was just before 7:00 a.m. on Friday morning when Braddock pulled to a stop in Kyle Mannion's driveway. Tori and Braddock filed out, filthy and exhausted, and started walking to the house when the front door opened. Kyle and Brianna came out on the wide grand front stoop.

"We got them," Tori said without preamble. "The men who killed Ally and Reed are dead."

"At both of your hands?"

"Yes."

Kyle nodded. "Good."

TWENTY-SEVEN

"BEST KEEP UP APPEARANCES."

Dan put the duffel bag of money in the trunk of the car and thumped it shut when a bright burst of lightning made it seem like daylight. It was immediately followed by a sonic boom of thunder that made him flinch.

"It's going to storm, big time," Dan said as he took a left turn and made for the H-4. The posted speed on the road was fifty miles per hour and he set the cruise control, the two of them quiet, eyes alert, scanning. A mile short of the H-4, they saw flashing blue and red lights coming at them.

"Oh, oh," Vee murmured.

They shared a brief look as the sheriff's department SUV roared right by them, lights flashing, siren blaring, in a hurry going west.

As they reached the H-4 turn another SUV with siren and flashing lights came from the north, turning right and racing west. Dan turned right and drove south on the H-4 when they saw yet another set of flashing lights come from the south on the highway. Vee looked back and saw that unit also turned left on County 92. "Do you think?"

"I don't know, honey. They're driving Druk's pickup truck, not that van."

"What if they know about Heath and Druk though?"

"How would they?" Dan replied. "It could be something else."

"It's not."

"No," he agreed. "It's not. If they're onto them, they might be on us."

"What do we do?"

Dan thought for a moment. "One thing we can't do is be found with all this money."

They were just south of Pequot Lakes when the rains hit. Five minutes later he made a right turn off the H-4 and made his way to his brother's house and parked just inside his long driveway, well back from the house, his headlights off. They waited for the heavy rain to pass, which took another good twenty minutes. A Minnesota thunderstorm packed a real punch, but they often moved through quickly. The thunderstorm having moved east, there was still light rain, heavy wind and gusts on the backside. Another wave could come, there was lightning to the west still. All of it provided good sound cover.

"Come on," Dan said.

They crept up the right side of the driveway to the detached garage.

"Dan?" Vee whispered. "What about the dog?"

"He's old. He doesn't hear and he'll be sleeping with them on the other side of the house."

The shovel Dan used previously was still propped up on the side of the garage. He still had a flashlight he used for the robbery and found the path back into the woods and the makeshift gun range. At the marked tree, Vee held the flashlight and duffel bag while Dan started digging around the blue bucket, pulling away the foot or so of dirt. He screwed the top off and there was still plenty of room. They quickly dumped the money inside the bucket and then covered it again.

"How much you figure that is now?" Dan said as he quickly re-filled the hole.

"$200,000, maybe $220,000 give or take," Vee replied. "Maybe a bit more." That was in addition to the money now in the numbered account. Dan had gone to the library that morning, jumped on the internet on the public computer, and checked. The payment from the jewelry store job was there just as Druk had promised.

A half-hour later, Dan pulled into the driveway. They had assiduously looked behind for the remainder of the drive home but had not detected anyone following them. However, if the police were lying in wait for them, this would be when they would pounce. They waited, almost expectantly, but nobody came. Warily, they got out of the car and peered around, but the street was quiet. As they walked to the house, they took a long look along the streets in front and to the side of the house, which sat on a corner. The streets glistened from the night's rain, the moisture in the air thick, leaves and small stray branches littering the neighbor's yards. It had been a fierce storm, but there was not enough damage that anyone would have felt the need to be up at 4:00 a.m. on a Friday morning.

They slipped inside the house, tiptoeing their way down the steps and to the bedroom. "I have to work at ten," Vee moaned.

"Best keep up appearances."

"I know."

The two of them stripped out of their clothes and slipped into bed, lying in the quiet, a small fan humming in the corner.

"You know," Vee said. "If it was those two the police were after, and they're caught."

"I know," Dan said. "I know. I also know this, after tonight."

"What's that?"

"They won't go willingly. They shot one cop, maybe two,

might have killed them both. That's life in prison. We know they've killed others. I don't think they'll let themselves be arrested. I think they'd fight it out to the death before they'd let themselves be caged."

"Fine by me," Vee said coldly. "However, there is a problem with that."

"What's that?"

"We won't ever get our cut for the jewels, the art, any of it. I want my money for doing this."

Dan let out a breath. "Me too." He let out a long breath. "Let's see what tomorrow brings."

"You two were sure out late last night," Mona said as Vee yawned, sipping her second cup of coffee, checking her watch. It was 9:30 a.m. She just had to make it through the shift and then she could come home and crash. "Where were you?"

"Just... out, Mom," Vee said. "We did a little drinking is all. Just like we did Sunday night."

"I see," Mona replied, the tone disapproving.

"Mom, just don't start. Please."

Dan sat wearily in a kitchen chair by the window, keeping a watchful eye out to the driveway and the stretch of the street he could see, which included the three-way intersection at the corner. Sarah was up and with them. She was the most chipper of the group.

"We had a few beers, no big thing and then waited out the storm," Dan said, before standing up and stretching, walking into the living room with his coffee cup, taking a quick drink of the coffee as he peered through a slit in the curtains.

"What time do you work?" Mona asked her daughter.

"Ten, so," Vee checked her watch. "In a half-hour. I work until six. Long day ahead." She looked to Dan. "Drive me in?"

They both kissed Sarah on the head. They stepped out of

the house and they each made a subtle scan of their block. People were up and about, working in their yards or walking their dogs, but it all looked normal.

Once in the car, Dan made a point of checking the rearview mirror frequently as he made his way to Lake Drive.

"Anything?" Vee asked.

"Nobody followed as best I can tell," Dan said lightly. "So far, so good."

"Just don't get too comfortable," Vee replied flatly. "I have a feeling we're going to have to look over our shoulders for the rest of our lives."

TWENTY-EIGHT

"WHERE DID THE VAN GO?"

Tori's eyes flitted open. She looked at the clock on the nightstand, and it was 2:30 p.m. She heard rustling down in the kitchen.

Her head and body ached. As was to be expected when a two-hundred forty-pound man lands on top of you and rolls you into the fallen trunk of a massive tree. She slowly pulled the comforter off and stepped gingerly to the floor. Her back and neck were not happy. She should have iced but all she'd wanted to do when she got home was shower, wash the mud and blood off and get in bed. She dressed in gym shorts and a loose T-shirt and careful with each step, deliberately made her way down to the kitchen.

"You're awake," Braddock said, holding a plate with a sandwich and a large slice of fresh watermelon on it. "Are you hungry?"

Tori smiled. "Starving." She leaned up and kissed him. "Will you please make me one of those?"

"Sure thing, Annie Oakley."

"Ha," she scoffed as she sat down on a stool for the center island. "Very funny."

"Last night, very true," he said as he too gingerly shuffled about the kitchen, putting together another sandwich.

"Last night we were lucky," she said, shaking her head, leading into an apology for her recklessness. "Not sure what I was thinking, going off on my own like that."

"I don't think either of us were thinking too clearly at that point. The adrenaline was going. They killed Collins. They gunned down Frewer. Did what they did to the Johanssons. Ally and Reed. They had to go down for that. So, they did. I have no regrets. We did what had to be done. The end."

She thought he'd be mad at her, or at least mildly irritated. She'd expected a bit of a scolding at some point, and thought it may be a bit warranted, but nothing could be further from the truth. "You sound almost... proud."

"I am. We got them. We both did. I'll never lose a wink of sleep over it."

"Even the last part," she said, alluding to when he executed Heath.

"That was justice."

They got home just after 7:00 a.m., showered the mud off their bodies and out of their hair and collapsed into bed. He'd only been up fifteen more minutes than she had. He set a sandwich down in front of her, along with a can of soda water and four aspirins.

"Four?"

"You look so sore," he replied, kissing her on the top of her head. "I've never seen you move so slow."

"I am sore. I am so, so, sore. I've never felt old before. I feel old today."

"Yeah, we're not twenty-five anymore, running around the woods like that."

She noticed he was limping, dragging his left leg.

He noticed that she noticed. "I sprained my ankle somewhere along the way. Woke up and she was barking at me but good."

They were lucky all they were complaining about was bruises and sprains.

Braddock suggested they eat outside. It was a pleasant day, a pleasing southerly breeze, a partly cloudy sky, the lake air refreshing. They ate quietly, tired, yet satisfied.

There was a knock on the back door. They turned to see Steak and Sheriff Boe standing there. Braddock waved them through.

"I'm glad to see you two alive," Steak said when he came out on the deck. "From what I'm hearing—"

"Yeah, yeah," Braddock said, offering a dismissive wave. "To be honest, we don't want to relive it. How is Frewer?"

"Conscious. Recovering," Steak said. "Thankful to the two of you for getting him out."

"We'll go see him later, or maybe, tomorrow."

"How are the Johanssons?" Tori said.

"No change. Thor is in a coma. He's in a bad way. Ella remains unconscious. Their children are with them. Hope and prayer time there."

Tori checked her phone and Lizzy had been texting her. She would have to give her a call.

"The press has wind of it all now," Boe said. "The names of Ledyard Heath and Leonard Druk will go public shortly. We're pinning all last night and Ally Mannion and Reed Schafer's murders on them."

Tori looked up. "I think there's at least one, if not two events missing there. Lakes Jewelers and Locher Mansion."

"The white panel van," Braddock added. "It was just like the one used for the jewelry store. We're thinking that was them too."

"Interesting you mention the van and the jewelry store." Steak had a laptop with him. "I have the bodycam footage here for Collins, as well as Frewer's dashcam." Tori moved her chair next to Braddock and Steak put the laptop in front of them.

"First, Collins. I've shortened it to the relevant footage. You two haven't been to the Johanssons' house yet so I'll give you the basics. Collins is at the west side of the wood bridge over that little creek, her headlights and the spotlight focused on the white van in the distance."

He pushed play.

"Now, she makes the call for backup and then Dispatch says units are on route."

"So why the hell didn't she hold?" Tori said.

"Just watch."

Collins is at the bridge, flashlight in her hand. Holding position.

"*No! No! Stop... You're hurting him! Stop! STOP!*"

"Now Collins makes the call," Steak noted.

"*Dispatch, Collins. I need that backup! Now!*"

Collins started across the short bridge, her weapon drawn, her flashlight beam leading the way. When she reached the end of the bridge, the van's high beam headlights came on. Collins pivoted right.

"And they opened up on her," Steak muttered.

"Oh my!" Tori blurted.

Collins hadn't stood a chance.

"Those bastards," Braddock murmured.

"One of those was an assault rifle," Steak said through gritted teeth. "As I'm sure you discovered shortly thereafter."

"Hold on a second. I want to replay that segment again," Tori said. "Was that a woman's voice that drew Collins? Play that back again."

Steak nodded and replayed the video.

"That's a woman's voice in the distance," Tori said. "No doubt. And the nose of that van is like the one from Lakes Jewelers."

"I agree on both counts," Steak said. The van raced by Collins bodycam and out of view. Steak leaned down. "Now Frewer."

They all watched as the chase unfolded.

"Frewer got close enough a few times that I was able to get the plates. Wisconsin. But don't get excited, they were stolen two years ago. I'm betting the van was too."

Frewer came around a bend and the back door of the van flew open.

The shots came fast and furious, hitting the grill, hood, the windshield and then Frewer himself, his Explorer swerving and rolling over repeatedly before the feed cut out.

"Tori and I were back of Frewer for most of this," Braddock noted. "Rattling through all those woods."

"Good thing you were," Boe said.

"But..." He reached over and ran the tape back to the point where the van door flew open.

"That's the assault rifle again," Tori said.

"Yeah, but the way the door flies open, and he starts firing at Frewer," Braddock said. "It's not just the two of them, Heath and Druk, in that van. Someone is driving, someone opened that door and someone else fired. They had help. And if they did the jewelry store, we know they had at least two others."

"Now we know why Collins did what she did."

"A woman's voice drew her across the bridge," Tori said. "Was that Ella Johansson?"

"I don't think so," Steak replied. "We found Ella unconscious upstairs in the master bedroom, her mouth duct taped."

"They had a woman with them," Tori said. "That's who went down that duct. A woman. A small woman." She turned to Braddock and sighed. "We're not done here. There's two more to get."

"You two need rest," Boe said.

"Yeah, but—"

"I'm ordering you to stand down—for a day at least. Get some rest. You both look... wrung out. Neither of you are to leave this house today. Just lay low and stay out of sight. Understood?"

Tori nodded. She was tired, and sore, and didn't really have the energy.

"One thing, though," Braddock said, sitting back in his chair and then looking to Tori. "We caught up to them in that pickup truck. Where did the van go?"

"And everything they stole," Tori said. "Do their two partners have it?"

"That or they hid it somewhere. Two guys like this who have been active in this game, probably far beyond what we know of, would have a place where they store things until they're ready to move them. It's off the grid. I assume we found nothing at Druk's house?"

"It was breached to make sure they weren't hiding inside," Steak said. "Otherwise, not a lot has happened there. They're dead. Nobody is rushing to look their place over."

"We'll need to give it a look."

"Yes, you will, *tomorrow*," Boe insisted. "As for the van, they got rid of it, didn't they?"

"Possibly. It was three hours give or take between the original chase and when Tori and I found them again. Still, we didn't recover any of the stolen property and I don't buy that they'd have left that with anyone else," Braddock said. "This was their operation. This is what they do. They would have had control." He shook his head. "I think it's possible that it's all out there somewhere still waiting to be found."

"By us?"

"Or by the other two who were involved."

* * *

Vee handed the customer her receipt and bag. "Thanks for stopping in."

The afternoon had been a rapid blur of customers through the store, which had distracted her from her other thoughts. Now, it was nearly 5:00 p.m. she looked out to the sales floor and there was but one customer remaining, and she was being assisted.

An hour left in her shift. She yawned.

"You look beat. Take a break for a few minutes," Ruth Ann said. "It's going to be quiet now."

With the sales floor empty, she slowly took the steps up to the second floor and the kitchen area and the television was on. She grabbed a Diet Coke and sat down, slipping off her heels. Her arches ached, as did her lower back.

She looked up to the television and saw a breaking news chyron and the sheriff standing in front of a small bank of microphones. *Where's the remote?* She found it and turned up the volume.

"You say that the men responsible for the home invasion and the death of officer Collins are dead?"

"Yes. They were killed in a confrontation with officers of the Shepard County Sheriff's Department northwest of town out on Shell Lake Road. Two men are dead. They've been identified as Ledyard Heath and Leonard Druk. They were residents of Garrison. Those two men were responsible for the death of Deputy Collins while engaging in a home invasion last evening."

Her phone started buzzing in her back pocket. It was Dan.

"Are you watching TV?" she asked.

"Yes."

She glanced around the room, making sure she was alone. "You were right. They weren't taken alive."

"Which is good news for us. Get home. We have things to discuss."

Two hours later, she arrived home to find Dan working the grill on the back deck. Sarah was out there, sitting with Mona. Brats and hot dogs were on the grill. It was a pleasant evening, a bit cool for this time of summer. She retrieved a seltzer from the refrigerator and joined them while Dan cooked. After dinner, they sat with Sarah and watched a movie. Sarah spent as much time talking about getting her casts off her legs in a few days as she did about the movie itself.

By ten, Vee was fading, lying against Dan with her eyes closed when the movie finished. They put Sarah to bed and then made their way down to their bedroom and changed into their sleeping clothes.

They talked about where they'd gotten in the last week. "We have money that we don't have to tell a single soul about," Dan said. "It's enough for a fresh start."

"When?"

"We have to give it some time and we act poor, like the couple that is broke and in bankruptcy. We give it a year and finish the bankruptcy process. We let Sarah get healthy and back on her educational track and then we can think about going somewhere else if that's what we want to do."

Vee nodded, lying back against the pillow. When they left Minnesota thirteen years ago, she never wanted to come back. They had hardly visited the state since they had left, preferring to fly her mother down or host Dan's brother rather than come back. The thought of spending a full winter in Minnesota filled her with dread.

"What about our cut for last night?" Vee said. "We go through all that. We're exposed to what we're exposed to, and we don't get the rest? We just get that cash?"

"I was thinking on that myself."

"You know," Vee said. "If we could find that garage, wherever it was, we could get it all. I'm betting we could double what we've gotten?"

"Maybe triple," Dan said. "I saw inside that cabinet. There was plenty in there."

"We'd end up with more than we got out of Duluth."

Dan went to the dresser and grabbed his laptop off the top. He brought it back to the bed. "After you went to work this morning, I spent some time looking at the area where it might be."

"Might be?"

"I'm just guessing. When Heath told us we could sit up, we were on Tompson Road coming to County 92." He pointed to that point on the map. Three miles to the east on 92 was the Long Neck. "Now, when we were sitting in the back of that van, I had no idea where we were, but I wasn't dialed into where we were going other than getting away. And while we were lying in the back seat of the pickup truck, I couldn't see much of anything either, a few things, a flag, a streetlamp here and there, but my sense was that we were driving kind of east northeast and coming out at County 92 and Tompson says I'm right." With his finger, he circled a wide area to the southwest of County 92 and Tompson Road. "It's somewhere out there."

"That's not very specific," Vee said, studying the map, pulling it onto her lap. "That's a lot of area where it could be."

"Yeah, but I figure I have the time," Dan replied. "I pack a lunch, take the car, my mountain bike and go driving around. But if I can find it, I know where the keys are, we could still get our payday."

"Let's find it. Whatever it takes," Vee replied. "You knew that guy down in Fort Myers. He came to our restaurant every so often. The big guy from Philly. What was his name?"

"Big Al DiMao."

"He seemed connected. I bet he'd know a person or two who could help us."

"I was thinking the exact same thing. And, I still have his number."

TWENTY-NINE

"IT'S A PROCESS OF ELIMINATION."

They slept in late on Saturday, at least for them, lying in bed well past 9:00 a.m., not really moving until the phone rang. It was Ann Jennison.

"For what it's worth, Tori, the tobacco pouch is a match to those you found on the other side of the bay from the Wallaces' cabin. You two were right, Heath and Druk observed that cabin from across that small bay."

After the call, they both gingerly rolled out of bed.

"Sometimes the second day is the worst," Braddock said, his back stiff, hobbling on his ankle. Tori had him sit down on a chair in the kitchen. She examined his swollen ankle that he had spent much of yesterday icing.

As he lifted his leg onto her lap, he asked her: "How are you feeling?"

"Like I got run over by a truck."

"You kind of did," Braddock said. "Ow," he yelped when she pressed against the outside of the left ankle.

She looked up. "Pretty tender there, buddy. Maybe you should have this looked at. It's probably a sprain but you should make sure there isn't ligament damage."

He nodded. "Maybe Monday. I have an ankle brace I use when I play basketball. I can wear that for the time being. We got Heath and Druk but there's two more people out there. One of them lured Collins. I want them. As long as we don't have to chase *them* down, I'll be fine."

"Okay then," Tori said. "Where do you want to start?"

"With Druk and Heath."

Their first stop was the medical examiner's office. They didn't want to see the bodies. They were interested in their personal effects.

"Anything from the cell phones?" Braddock asked.

"Not really," Jennison said. "They didn't have the phones on them. They were at the house. I checked the call history for each. The calls were pretty much to each other, and to Garrison Boat Works and some other random ones. No calls to Kellin for example. No calls to Ewald's or Joyner's. I think they kept all that off the grid."

"Not a surprise. They probably did a lot face to face."

Both men had money clips with multiple credit cards, a driver's license, fishing license and cash, each a couple of hundred dollars. There were two sets of keys.

One was found in the truck ignition and was assumed to have been Druk's. There was the key fob for the truck and a short set of keys, one of which looked to be for the house, two others that looked like business keys and two smaller ones that looked to be for padlocks. "The small keys I'm betting are for the boat trailers," Braddock said.

On Druk's hip, when he was retrieved from the stream, was a fishing knife. It had an orange plastic handle. The blade was serrated and had a cut hook on it. "Probably not the knife that killed Ally or Reed," Tori said. "But I bet it's just like it."

Braddock nodded and began to dig through Heath's personal effects. His knife had been retrieved from where Braddock had shot him. It was a knife similar to Druk's. He held it up for Tori to see. "Not a shock. These two were attached at the hip."

Heath too had a set of keys, though his ring was fuller. "House," Tori said, working through them. "Business, just like Druk," she said, holding up two gold ones. There was the truck key fob, several small keys that looked to be for trailers, two keys that she was certain were for a boat and one more. "This is a P.O. box key."

"Well, he lived at Druk's house. Maybe he had a P.O. box for his mail."

Tori took a photo of it, and in particular the serial numbers for someone to track down.

"You want to bet the knife would match that tomographic image of the knife blade that Renfrow took on Reed Schafer's murder wounds?"

"No bet. I doubt it was those very specific knives, but these guys strike me as the type to have something they find useful and then keep using it. Much like their thefts. Keep doing it as long as nobody is onto them."

"We got onto them."

"Not fast enough."

Their next stop was Druk's house. There they found Steak and Eggleston waiting for them.

"You two are supposed to be off today," Braddock said.

"Yeah, well, if you two are working, we're working," Steak said.

"For Collins," Eggs added. "And if we need Reese and Nolan, they'll come too."

Braddock cut the police seal over the back door and they entered the house.

The two men were bachelors and it showed, the house a male mess. The biggest culprit was fishing gear. There were fishing poles, tackle boxes, lures, clothing, electronic fish finders and other related gear strewn in different areas. The fishing guide work was no cover. They appeared to be fanatics. And they also appeared to have been hunters as well. There was a locked gun case in a side room. Inside the gun case were four twelve-gauge shotguns, as well as boxes of various kinds of shells.

Steak evaluated the case contents. "The green box is good for pheasants. The others are steel shot which is good for ducks and geese. These guys were bird hunters."

"Where do you hunt birds?" Tori said.

"You get a license and hunt public land. You could get permission to hunt on someone's private land. Others have their own private hunting land. You know, just like my brother and I and our deer hunting land."

Tori found the narrow steps to the second floor and walked up, Eggleston right behind her. Each of them took a bedroom. As with the main level, they would not be considered neat freaks.

"I wonder if either of these guys ever had a woman around," Tori muttered, noting the less than sanitary condition of the bathroom, not to mention the fatigued nature of the sheets on each of their beds.

She sat down at the desk in one of the rooms. It belonged to Heath.

"Is there anything we're looking for in particular?" Eggs asked.

"One thing we haven't found is that van. Where is it?"

"The bottom of a body of water probably."

"Fine. But what about everything they stole? Where is all that?"

"Ahh. Do they have other property?"

"Exactly."

"I'll take the other room," Steak said, sticking his head in the doorway.

Tori and Eggleston started working through the desk drawers. Heath did not keep organized files. For example, for his taxes all years were put into one brown expandable. This would have offended Braddock no end. Braddock had his taxes organized by year, in green folders for income, red folders for property taxes, every utility and credit card bill organized within a file, his banking records quickly retrievable. He'd taken pains to show Tori where his will and trust was in case something happened to him. She had been inspired by his organization and had followed suit with all her records though Braddock joked it was nothing but credit card bills. As she sifted through the file drawer for Heath, documents and records were mixed together, just jammed in without any thought to order.

"What a mess."

"Find anything?" Eggleston asked.

Tori shrugged. "How would I even know?"

"Heath didn't own anything," Braddock observed, having come up the steps. "It's like he was Gilligan and Druk was the Skipper, the brains of the operation."

They spent a couple of hours going through the documents.

"Nothing is really jumping out, is it?" Eggleston said.

"One thing is curious," Braddock said, leaning against the doorway. "The money."

"All the money they made?" Tori said. "Where is it? It's not in the banks Heath uses." She held up a stack of paper. "These are his bank records. His highest balance I've seen is just over $13,000. Not poor, but if they were as active as we think they were, where is all that money?"

"I didn't see anything for Druk either," Steak noted. "Similar type bank balances."

"Offshore?" Eggs said.

"Perhaps," Braddock said. "Still, did we see any records for that?"

"None that I see," Tori said. "But there would be records. Somewhere you would think."

"Maybe on the laptop on Druk's desk. The BCA will have to hack in and see if they can find anything on that."

"Hmm," Tori said and took out her phone. "I wonder."

"What?"

"That P.O. box key I found. What if—"

"That's where the records go?" Braddock said.

"I'll check it out tomorrow," Steak said as Tori sent him a copy of the photo. "I'll figure out what post office it belongs to."

"Anything else downstairs?" Tori asked.

Braddock chuckled. "They were committed to the craft. They liked to fiddle with their fishing gear. And, to your point earlier on the knife, I found a whole box of them out in the garage along with a whole lot more fishing gear. These guys had it all. It's like a Cabela's around here."

"Maybe *that's* where all the money went."

* * *

"Can you believe the news on that home invasion?" Ruth Ann said when she came up to Vee after she'd checked out a customer. Summer Sundays were usually slow, so it was just the two of them for the afternoon.

"It was kind of crazy from the sounds of it."

"And the police officers who were shot and that couple, beaten in their home," Ruth Ann said, her hand covering her throat. "The paper said they were in comas. I know those folks."

"You do?"

"Well her, anyway. Ella Johansson. A very nice lady. She comes in here every so often."

"It's all so... terrible," Vee said. "I guess you never know what's coming, do you? Life is all good one minute, and it goes to hell the next. I know a thing or two about that."

Ruth Ann nodded. "I suppose you do."

"Do you mind if I go up and grab a soda?"

"No. Go right ahead."

Vee made her way up the steps to the small lunchroom and took one of her Diet Cokes out of the refrigerator. Then she called Dan.

* * *

"Any luck?" Vee asked.

"Not so far," Dan replied as he took a long drink of water, sitting in the driver's seat of the car, the door open, his bike shoes off. For years in Florida, he had been part of a cycling group that rode two days a week. He'd had all the gear and attire. He'd sold two of his bikes but had kept his mountain bike, and clothes, such that he looked the part with the helmet, wrap-around sunglasses, and biking shorts.

He'd been up at the crack of dawn and had been at it for six hours. On a map, he'd bracketed a broad area, perhaps a hundred square miles southwest of the junction of County 92 and Tompson Road. Within his rectangular zone, he had made a grid. Alternately driving the car and riding his mountain bike, he was methodically working his way through the grid, crossing off areas as he completed his search.

"Nothing?"

"I had one possibility that looked good." It had been a gravel road and a right turn off the road. It had been promising the way the driveway wound its way back into the woods but when it led to a structure, it was an old double wide. He had found some hunting land, just not the right parcel.

"It's a process of elimination. It's out here somewhere."

"Maybe."

* * *

Red Moody was at the counter when the two of them walked inside. He nodded for them to follow him to his office, where he closed the door.

"I saw the news," Red said, wiping his brow with a red hanky. "Thor Johansson? He was on one of my charters a month ago."

"We think that's one of the ways they identified their marks," Braddock explained. "I suspect one of them overheard Thor talking about art, or jewels, or just his success, his home on the lake, and it piqued their interest. They probably did a little research and reconnaissance and figured he was worth robbing."

"My God," Red said, closing his eyes. "I employed them, but I never suspected something like this. Will, you have to believe me."

"I do, Red," Braddock replied. "They did the same thing to another couple up in Grand Rapids who'd used them as guides through a resort up there. They did this kind of thing for years and nobody knew until now."

Red Moody sat down behind his desk, shaking his head.

"Were these guys hunters?"

"Uh... yeah," Moody said. "I seem to recall them talking about grouse hunting a time or two. It's why they weren't available as guides much past mid-September. It was time to go shoot things."

"Do you know where they hunted?"

"I don't. I know they talked about their hunting land, but I never hunted with them."

"Any idea where that land is?"

"No," Moody said. "Other than I think it wasn't too far away."

"Why do you say that?"

"I just remember them both coming in one Saturday afternoon to pick up their paystubs and they were in camo. They said they'd been out hunting all morning and when I asked where, they just said their land. I just assumed it mustn't be too far away."

* * *

Dan pushed through the back door of the house, just after 7:00 p.m. Vee was sitting with Mona at the kitchen table.

"Where have you been all day?" Mona asked.

"Bike riding. I used to ride all the time in Florida. Thought I'd start again."

"But all day?"

"Sometimes," Dan lied. "It was good to just get out," he said. "I'm going to go out again tomorrow for a while, I think. We'll see how I feel in the morning."

"I thought you were job hunting?"

"I am, Mona," Dan replied, testily. "I have been. And I will continue to be until I find something."

He walked over and kissed Vee on the cheek and Sarah on her head. "I'm going to take a shower."

Vee was waiting for him in the bedroom when he'd finished his shower. "So?"

He pulled out his map. He'd covered about a third of the area he'd bracketed. "I had another one right here that I thought could be it." He pointed to a road on the map. "But the road led back to a regular house in the woods with a detached garage. There was a car there, so I turned around quick and biked out of there. Lots of those out there. People with places back deep in the woods. A few of them were kind of scary, you know. Dog kennels. People who look like they have an arsenal somewhere close by."

"Geez. Be careful."

Dan nodded and let out a sigh. "I feel kind of foolish just driving and riding around with no real idea of where we were. Wherever this garage was could be well off this grid."

"You won't feel so foolish, if you find it," she said as she sat down behind him and lightly rubbed his shoulders. "It's worth the effort."

* * *

Quinn returned from his friend's cabin at dinner time and Braddock grilled burgers and corn on the cob on the grill. They all talked around the dinner table for an hour, the two adults steering the conversation away from work whenever they could. Quinn had heard about the chase. Neither of them was keen to discuss the details with him and avoided it.

"They won't be hurting anyone else is all I'll say," Braddock said. "And that's the last I want to say about it."

"Okay, Dad." Quinn was tired from his weekend of fun. He went to bed early.

Tori and Braddock retired to their comfortable master bedroom and turned on the television.

"Anything interesting on a Sunday night?" Braddock asked when he came out of the closet, in a T-shirt and gym shorts. He gingerly climbed onto the bed, careful of his ankle.

"Just *The Shawshank Redemption* for the ten thousandth time," Tori said.

"What point?"

"Andy is about to go into the pipe to crawl to freedom."

"Hmpf," Braddock said, throwing his arm around her, letting her fall into him. "Get busy living or get busy dying."

"So, what's next?"

"I was thinking of driving over to Duluth. I spoke with a detective there named Saunders. Told him about the brooch. I say we get up early and return it. And, if that job is part of our thing, I want to give it a look."

"And make Boe look good."

"She's had our backs all the way. We ought to have hers."

"I agree."

Braddock's phone buzzed on the nightstand. It was Boe. "Hey. Yes. Okay. That's a good thing. Yes." He hung up.

"What is it?"

"Ella Johansson is conscious. She's going to make it."

THIRTY

"DID THEY SEEM LIKE THEY WERE A COUPLE?"

They were up with the Monday morning sun and Mary was over to look after Quinn and get him to his activities. Ella Johansson was awake again although weak. While they wanted to speak with her as soon as possible, she wasn't ready yet. "It might be a day or two," Boe had said.

Duluth was a two-hour drive.

Tori read aloud from the Locher Mansion file they had, particularly on the details of the burglary. It turned out that the burglary was far more complicated than just having the security code. There was a real art to the heist. The safe combination was defeated. Money, jewels, art were all stolen.

"It must have taken them a good hour, if not more, to get all that out of there," Tori said. "Here's my question. The security system was shut off in the kitchen, yet neither the kitchen door nor the door from the garage, where the other keypad is located, were opened before the code was entered. How does that happen?"

"Was there a control pad anywhere else?"

"Just the master bedroom," Tori replied, flipping up a page.

"On the second floor. And there were motion sensors on that level as well."

"The system was turned off from which control pad?"

"The kitchen."

"Hmpf."

"Hmpf, what?" Tori said, turning to Braddock who had a sly grin on his face. "You know something?"

"I have an idea."

"Which is?"

"For once, I'm going to make you wait to see what the answer is."

"That's not fair. Give me a hint at least."

"Okay, a little hint."

* * *

Their first stop was the Duluth Police and Detective Saunders. Braddock handed him the brooch. "Oh yeah," he said right away and opened a file with photos. He held the brooch next to a photo. "There she is," he said. "I'll be eff'n damned. This is the first piece ever recovered. And you got this from the mother of Loren Randolf you say?"

"Yes, a few days ago," Braddock said. "We've had a bit going on the last few days since we retrieved it, or we'd have been here sooner."

"That you have. I'm very sorry about your deputy. A bunch of us will be driving over for her funeral in a few days," Saunders said. "Now, you've done for me. What can I do for you?"

"Take us for a look at the Locher Mansion," Braddock said. "We have a theory or two to test."

Saunders made some quick calls and a half-hour later, the three of them arrived at the massive three-story mansion. The Locher family was old Duluth money, the family fortune first earned in logging and then later in the railroads. The current

Lochers were sixth generation. The brooch had been in the family for three of those generations. Helen and Thomas Locher invited them all inside. Saunders handed the brooch to Helen.

"Oh my God!" Helen Locher exclaimed. "Eileen's brooch." Eileen was Thomas Locher's grandmother. The brooch had been handed down as an heirloom. "Where did you find it?"

Braddock explained their investigation and how it was recovered.

"So this man was one that robbed us?" Thomas asked.

"He was not here that night, but he was clearly involved," Braddock said. "He worked on the crew that installed and repaired your security system."

"Detective Braddock thought he might have some insight on the burglary?" Saunders said. "How they actually did it."

"We were curious as to how the security system was shut off, that somebody didn't first come in through a door," Tori said.

"That flummoxed us as well," Saunders agreed.

"There were motion sensors, though, correct?" Braddock inquired.

"Yes. On the first two floors and all the way up the stairway to the third floor," Saunders answered. "There were control panels by the garage door, the rear kitchen door and in the master bedroom on the second floor. It was the kitchen control panel that was deactivated. There was space allowed for someone to come in from the garage, turn off the alarm and it wouldn't set off the motion detectors. That wasn't the case for the kitchen back door."

"That's true," Thomas Locher said. "Our kids set them off a few times. That led to calls from the security company and using the password with the security company, so the police weren't called."

"Or so we thought," Saunders noted. "We thought maybe

there was a dead zone, or they had some way of blocking the motion detector so they wouldn't set off the alarm."

Tori nodded. "And it was the first two floors that had motion detectors, correct?"

"Yes," Saunders said.

"But *not* the third floor."

"No, although all the windows were wired up there."

"All of them?" Braddock asked.

Saunders and the Lochers led them upstairs to the third floor and to the south wing and a small sitting room that had a love seat and two chairs arranged in front of a small brick fireplace. There were small porthole windows to the right and left of the fireplace.

"There?" Tori said, looking over to Braddock, who nodded.

Tori examined the window to the left of the fireplace. It had a window latch hook but no lock. The portal window itself was small, existing to allow in some southern light but it did open, out, secured by a hook latch.

"You think someone came in through there?" Thomas Locher asked in disbelief. "No way."

"Those two windows were the only two that weren't wired," Braddock said, examining the left window over Tori's shoulder.

"But the window is so small."

"So am I, kind of," Tori said and flipped the latch and pushed the window open. "Would you mind if we tried something?"

"Be our guest," Thomas said. "This I want to see."

Braddock and Saunders held her legs as Tori maneuvered her body, trying to wedge through the window, which she managed to do after a minute of effort and a few stops and starts to get her positioning right. She pushed through to her waist, to prove she could get through, before they pulled her back in.

"Okay, you can get through, although you'd have been three stories up hanging on to what exactly?" Saunders asked.

"It wouldn't have been Tori," Braddock replied. "It would have very likely been someone smaller, perhaps much smaller than her, if it was the same people who robbed the jewelry store in Manchester Bay, which we think it was. Let's say for just a minute that someone came in through that window. They're standing here and to get to the kitchen, they have to get past the motion detectors on the first two floors. How would they do that? You've told us the stairway was covered with sensors. Is there some way to get from here down to the kitchen without going through all that?"

Mr. Locher's eyes bulged wide. "You've got to be kidding me."

Braddock looked to Tori and smiled. To Mr. Locher he said, "Dumb waiter, right?"

Tori laughed. "Why didn't I think of that?"

"How did you know?" Mr. Locher said.

"This theft reminds me of a strange homicide I worked as a young detective with the NYPD. Someone used the dumb waiter to commit a murder, not a theft, but old houses, mansions like this still had those systems within the walls, even if they were no longer in use. I assume you're telling us there was one."

Locher nodded and led them out of the room to the hallway and a closet door on the right which he opened and led them inside to another narrow vertical door that opened to a narrow-squared shaft. "This goes down to the kitchen. The dumb waiter itself was taken out decades ago." Tori took a peek inside and looked down. This one she wasn't going to try.

Mr. Locher led them back down to the kitchen. The security panel was mounted on a wall right next to the door for the dumb waiter.

"I've always used that as a closet for our cleaning lady's supplies," Mrs. Locher said.

"But if you could get down here, and you had that code,

you could disarm the system. And nobody would be the wiser," Saunders said. "But how does one get down the shaft?"

"If someone climbed the chimney outside and got through that porthole window," Braddock said. "They could figure out how to get down that shaft. That's how they pulled it off."

Fifteen minutes later they stood in the driveway. "I saw something in the news about that jewelry store thing. You think it's the same people?" Saunders said.

"We can't prove it one hundred percent yet, but you can take it to the bank that Randolf, Heath and Druk were involved in this one."

Braddock's phone buzzed and he excused himself.

"Anyone else involved?" Saunders asked.

"Had to be," Tori replied. "Someone small enough to get through that porthole and down the dumb waiter. So at least one more person was in on the gig."

Saunders chuckled. "Well, this goes a long way toward solving this case."

"And we might be able to learn even more," Braddock said to Tori. "Ella is awake, and she wants to see you."

Braddock drove back west to Manchester Bay with flashing police lights, making it back in just under ninety minutes. Sheriff Boe, Steak, Eggleston and a doctor were waiting for them in the hallway as they jogged in.

"She wanted to talk to you, Tori," Boe said. "She insisted. Are you two friends?"

"Just acquaintances. We met at the fundraiser last Thursday. I really liked her. One of my good high school friends, Lizzy White, is close friends with her though."

"Well, you made an impression then."

"How is she, Doc?"

"Weak," the doctor said. "But getting better. I don't know how long she'll last so I'd make it as quick as you can in there."

Tori started walking with the doctor. "And how about her husband?"

"Still in a coma. No change in his condition yet."

The doctor led them into the hospital room. A woman in her mid-twenties was sitting next to Ella. She introduced herself as Claire, Ella's daughter.

"Tori," Ella croaked, reaching out with her right hand.

"Hi, Ella," Tori said, taking a seat, gently holding her hand. "I'm so happy to see you awake and on the mend."

"But Thor."

"I know. I know. I'm praying for him."

"You got the men who did this to us?"

Tori nodded and looked to Braddock. "We got two of them but, Ella, there was more than that, wasn't there?"

She nodded.

Tori took out photos of Heath and Druk. "These were the two men we—" she sighed "—took care of later that night. They're dead."

Ella looked at the photos for a minute. "They were wearing masks. But the two men who attacked us in the garage were big. They're big?"

Tori nodded. "How about the others. How many were there?"

"Two."

"So four people total?" Tori asked, looking to Braddock.

"Yes."

Tori looked to Ella. "Can you run me through what you remember. Take your time. Every little detail you can recall matters."

"We got home and pulled into the garage," Ella said in almost a whisper. "When we got out of the car, two men were on us. Came right in the open garage door and they had guns.

One of them hit me on the side of the head and knocked me down on the garage floor. And I know the other man hit Thor," Ella said, shakily. "He... he... he went down... hard."

"Did you yell out? Scream? Call for help?"

"Yes. I just reacted, you know?" Ella replied, her eyes moist again, her lip trembling.

"I know," Tori said, still holding her hand. "It's natural. Go on."

"The man put tape over my mouth, then slapped me across the face and put a knife against my throat."

"He wanted you compliant," Tori said softly. "What happened next?"

"They pushed us inside the house and to the library."

"Did you ever see a van?"

Ella shook her head. "I heard them call for it, but I never saw it."

"Did they call or use a name when they called for the van?"

"No, not that I recall."

"But you did see the others?"

"Yes. The other two were smaller, much smaller actually."

Tori nodded. "Were they both men?"

"No," Ella replied. "One was a woman. I heard a woman's voice."

"You're sure?" Tori asked.

"Oh yes. She was wearing a mask, but I heard her speak and she... moved like a woman. And she was small, very small but... kind of agile and quick. She buzzed around like a nervous squirrel."

"And where did you see her?"

"Upstairs, in the master bedroom. There was her, another smaller man and one of the big ones. I had to show them into the closet, where my and Thor's jewelry was."

Tori nodded. "So we have a woman. She was very small. Another man, who was smallish?"

"Yes."

"Was he taller than the woman?"

"Yes. Four or five inches maybe. Quick, athletic kind of."

"And this woman. She was, you said, agile and athletic too?"

"Yeah," Ella said. "She was moving from here to there. The other, small man was a bit calmer it seemed. He was there for a few minutes and then was called away. I never saw him again."

"You said she was small. Can you give me something more specific?"

Ella closed her eyes for a moment, as if she was going back to her master bedroom. "In our bedroom there is a sitting area, in front of the fireplace. There are two high-backed chairs. She was standing right behind one of them while I was lying on the floor. I could only see her head."

Tori looked around the room and saw a chair off in a corner. Braddock saw it too and carried it over.

"Ella, was the chair this tall or taller?"

"Taller."

Steak held his hand over the back of the chair. "Here?"

"Higher."

He raised his hand a bit more. "Here?"

Ella nodded. Tori went to the chair and stood behind it, squatting down so that her chin met Steak's hand.

"Like this?"

"Yes."

There was a doctor's office scale in the hallway. Braddock rolled it in and lowered the arm that measured height to Tori's head. "Four feet eleven inches, give or take."

"I'm five-five, Ella," Tori said. "Was this woman smaller than me?"

"Yes." She nodded. "Lithe and athletic like you, but much shorter."

"And the man, again, he was short too? You're sure?"

"Yes. He was. A good head shorter than the other man."

Braddock and Steak shared a look. Tori was dialing in on something.

Tori reached for her backpack, zipped it open and took out the photo from The Goose. Something Braddock had said a few days ago, about how small the man and woman seemed to be, was suddenly registering. You could only see their heads above the booth backs, which weren't that high to begin with.

She took a closer look at the two of them, the man and the woman. Their backs were to the camera, but the woman, her hair up in a tight bun, was turned just slightly right so that she could make out some of her profile. The hair up in a bun. Small, agile, athletic, buzzing around like a squirrel.

Tori closed her eyes.

Could it be? Please don't let it be.

"Ella," Tori said, looking up from the photo. "Did you see the small woman and small man interact with one another?"

"Yes."

Tori looked at the photo again and then to Ella. "Did they seem like they were a couple?"

Ella's eyes lit up, the most life they had shown. "Yeah, you know, now that you say that, I think so. They were in the bedroom together, the way they moved, interacted, spoke with one another and he touched her once, patted her on the arm. I think to calm her. I think they could have been, if not husband and wife, they were certainly close. He was comfortable in her personal space for sure."

Braddock knew where she was going. "That small couple that you can barely see the heads of in the back of the booth," he said. "Them."

She patted Ella on the hand. "You did good, Ella. Real good. You rest now." Tori stood up, put her hand over her mouth and rushed out of the room.

Braddock looked to Steak and Boe. "What the heck was that all about?"

In the hallway, they didn't see Tori. Braddock saw a nurse sitting at a counter. "Did you see a woman come out of that room?"

"Yes."

"Where did she go?"

"She rushed into that bathroom," the nurse replied.

Boe cracked the door. "Tori?"

The three of them heard her puking.

"Whoa, whoa, whoa," Braddock said as he stepped inside with Boe. He rushed to the stall, finding Tori on all fours, the toilet bowl filled with vomit. She flushed the toilet and sat back against the wall, her eyes closed, breathing heavily.

"What the heck is going on?"

Tori wiped her mouth with the back of her hand. "I know who the man and woman are."

THIRTY-ONE

"DESPERATE PEOPLE BECOME DANGEROUS PEOPLE."

"How did I not see this," Tori lamented, plopping herself down in a chair and taking a drink of water. "It's been staring me right in the face. I must have seen her, next door to the jewelry store, a half-dozen times in the last month. God, I think I'm going to be sick again."

"Vee and Dan? Are you sure?" Steak asked in disbelief. "Tori, they're our friends. With all their issues, you want to put this on them too?"

"It's their issues that make them prime candidates. Especially when you consider everything else. Tell me you don't see her in that photo. The profile of that woman. The hair up in a tight little gymnast's bun like she used to wear all the time in high school. That photo is what, five or six years after we all graduated? Tell me that doesn't look like Vee, and the little guy next to her, that's Dan. They dated since ninth grade for crying out loud. They were *always* together."

"I don't know, I just don't know," Steak replied, not wanting to believe it. "I mean that could be anyone."

"Vee and Dan were friends with Duffy, weren't they? She

grew up just down the street from him. Vee lives just down the street from Duffy's mom now if she's living at Mona's."

"True," Steak conceded. "Which could explain why she and Dan were at The Goose that night."

"The last night Duffy was ever seen," Tori asserted. "The night Heath and Druk killed him. He was stabbed."

"You don't know that for certain."

"Come on, buddy,' Braddock said. "Right there in that picture are the people who robbed the Locher Mansion."

Braddock explained what he and Tori had found in Duluth.

"Duffy Randolf pilfered the security code but for protection, when it all went down, he was in Staples two-hundred miles away. The rest of them pulled it off. Vee was the one who climbed the chimney and in through the small window and down the dumb waiter to turn off the security system. To do those things required someone of the right size, with agility and athleticism."

"Vee was a great gymnast," Tori added.

"She was."

"Heath and Druk, one of them was good with safes and opened it by touch," Braddock continued. "Dan Akton probably served as wheel man, and they took what they wanted from the house. Duffy was in on it. It explains all the cash he had. It explains how he could afford to pay cash on the Hummer H2. It explains the brooch."

"This picture is six weeks later, Steak," Tori said, holding it up. "The day he bought that Hummer H2. You can just see what went down knowing what we know now about Heath and Druk and what they were capable of. The police still strongly suspected Duffy's involvement."

"Heath and Druk knew that, or were worried about it," Braddock said. "They knew Duffy was a dumbass loudmouth."

"Even his mom knew it," Tori added.

"That Hummer was like a big red blinking light saying arrest me. Heath and Druk killed him before anyone noticed.

"And the four of them split the take."

Steak nodded. "I follow where you're going. I do. I see the logic but still—"

"And then there is Vee and Dan's financial issues. What better motive?" Tori said, sitting down at a computer. She pulled up the Help a Friend page. "They've been soliciting donations to help pay their daughter's medical bills. We've both donated."

"Because you sent out that text," Steak replied. "Tori, they're not the first people who've had that problem. I've made other like donations before. The cost of healthcare in this country is ridiculous."

"It is," Tori replied. "But they weren't insured. They didn't have health insurance."

"Well… that's just dumb."

"Or maybe it was a symptom of their larger financial problems. Vee told me that she and Dan were wiped out by Hurricane Ian last fall in Florida. Let's do some research. See just how bad it really is."

Tori, with Steak's help, spent the next several hours, a large pizza and a round of beers researching Vee and Dan's financial issues.

It was bad.

Dan and Vee were in a world of financial hurt.

They'd lost their business and home and had a several pages long list of bankruptcy creditors and little in the way of assets, most of which they'd already offered up other than the clothes on their backs.

"I will acknowledge their financial situation is dire," Steak said. "No wonder they're living in Mona's basement."

"You know what interests me?" Braddock said from behind his desk. "How your friends had the front money to open that restaurant and gift shop thirteen years ago in the first place. They put down three hundred thousand in collateral at a local bank for the loans to build their restaurant and gift shop. Where did they get three hundred G's?"

"Well, if you guys are right, Locher Mansion," Steak said. "I see the motive. But still, it's one thing to have motive, and with Heath and Druk, the means, another thing to do... all this, Tori. You're saying they were accomplices to shooting Collins. You're saying it was Vee who lured her in, to charge across the bridge."

"Yes. I am."

"You think she's capable of something like that?"

"Desperate people become dangerous people," Tori replied. "They'd done something once with Heath and Druk and got ahead quick without earning it. This was their ticket back to doing it again."

"And your only proof of that is a groggy Ella describing the small man and woman as a couple the way they moved together and a partial profile on this photo in a dark bar. Even if I buy what you and Braddock are saying, what proof do we have?"

Braddock looked to Tori. "Now, he has a point."

Tori sat back in her chair and thought for a moment before she offered up a smile.

"What? What are you thinking about?"

"A blue summer dress."

THIRTY-TWO

"I THOUGHT YOU WERE BOYCOTTING FRIENDS."

The sun was setting on his third day, the dirt from the gravel roads having coated his body. Dan felt filthy and tired as he took a drink of water, his mountain bike leaning against the car. He was parked in a small jut off the road, an open field to the west, dense trees behind him.

The last two days had been filled with many possibilities that turned into false alarms. He'd been down several long gravel roads and driveways, and he'd gotten lost more than once along the way on his bike, all the while trying to avoid drawing any notice as he did so. As he looked at his map, he figured it would take at least another two days just to complete the search of the area he'd marked. The words needle and haystack flitted about his mind as he reviewed the map and decided to call it a day. He picked up the bike and secured it to the rack strapped onto the back of the car.

He got into the car and decided he would drive home southeast, taking back roads, and relax a bit. The country rock music was ringing out his open car window, his arm draped casually over the side when he skidded to a hard stop.

The yellow flag. It was a yellow golf flag. The pin.

When he'd been lying with Vee on the back seat of the pickup truck, he'd adjusted himself just a minute or two after they'd started driving, to get himself more comfortable. His head had raised just enough to catch the oddest of sights out the window. Under a streetlamp he'd caught just the quickest glance at a small yellow flag on what looked to be the top of a narrow pole. What he'd seen was a golf flag marking the hole on a green.

There it was.

The streetlamp was on the corner.

The golf flag was centered in the middle of a small circular green, but he wasn't looking at a golf course per se. He pulled ahead, across the intersection and looked across the semi-open land. The landowner must have been a golf enthusiast. He looked to have built three golf holes on his own land, a sort of mini course. One of the holes ran along the road to the corner. He took a three-hundred-sixty-degree survey of the immediate area and then checked the map. This spot was much further to the south than he'd thought they'd been. It was well outside his map grid.

So much for your sense of direction.

He took out his cell phone and pulled up the satellite map. On the gravel road to his right he detected what looked to be a narrow driveway at the end of the gravel road ahead. It snaked back far into the woods, and then there was a clearing before the driveway curled to the right and back under another grouping of trees.

He drove to the end of the road and peered to his rearview mirror, which was clear. Turning right he followed the narrow driveway, two worn tracks with a wholly grass stripe down the middle. The familiar clearing emerged to his left, a pond, a small slice of water visible amongst the tallish cattails. The driveway eased to the right and there it was, up a slight rise, resting under the thick grove of oak trees, the garage. One thing he hadn't noticed the other night was the boat trailers stored to the left. They must have been blocked by the pickup truck parked there at the time.

The structure, he thought of it as a garage given the wide double door, even though the inside was furnished a bit more like a house with some furniture, a small kitchen, and functioning bathroom. It was a hunting shack.

He parked and walked around the perimeter of the garage, looking for anyone about but it was quiet, nothing but the gentle sounds of nature humming around the pond in the distance. He stood at the door to the right of the double garage door. There was a window to the right of the deadbolt. There was the slightest of gaps in the curtains covering the window. He knelt and squinted inside.

There it was.

The white van the police were no doubt still looking for.

He looked around again, surveying the terrain. Tempted as he was to break inside now, he didn't want to do it in the daylight and if they were to empty the whole storage unit, including the paintings, he would need something other than his car. And he didn't dare use the van. Found driving that and he would be done for.

He'd seen Heath leave the keys for the van inside it. Druk had put the keys for the door beneath the van in the drawer for the small desk by the bathroom door. Back in the car, he circled his location on the map, the sun now down in the sky behind the thick wall of trees way beyond the waters of the pond. He couldn't see another structure or living soul around.

An hour later, as planned, he picked up Vee from her shift at the store, still dressed in his biking gear, filthy from the day, a dirty grin on his face.

"I found it."

. . .

"What should we do?" Vee said after Dan had finished his shower, wrapped in a white towel, taking a satisfied drink of his beer.

"First, we rent a storage space. Temporarily. I'm thinking not some place around here. Maybe St. Cloud, Little Falls, maybe up to Walker. Someplace I'm unlikely to be recognized. Second, I'll rent us a van. A panel one like Heath and Druk used. We need that cargo room if we're going to empty that storage space."

"Assuming it's all still there."

"It is," Dan said. "Those two were caught not long after they dropped us off. We saw the police vehicles converging on the area. They didn't move it. I looked inside. The van is still there, right where they left it. The jewels are still there. Their cash is still there." He stepped to his wife. "And tomorrow night, we go get it. All of it."

Vee smiled and then stopped. "We were going to go to that gathering at the Steamboat Bay Taproom. Lizzy called me tonight to remind me. She invited us to come. Said lots of our old friends would be there. She was quite persistent."

"I thought you were boycotting friends. You didn't want to see any of them."

"I didn't," Vee said, as she undid her husband's towel, letting it fall to the floor. She leaned up and gave him a lingering kiss. "But now that we've got a fresh start, and so much more to come, maybe I wouldn't mind dressing up a little and seeing them."

"We should probably thank some of them. They have generously donated to that Help a Friend page."

"They all have the money. I may not have spent much time with them since I've been back, but I've certainly seen how many of them are living and they're living pretty well. And now, we're going to live like that again."

"Indeed, we are." Dan picked her up, carrying her over to

the bed, laying her down and then playfully pulling off her summer shorts, before leaning down to her neck, taking in the feel of her. It had been some time since they'd done this. It had been some time since they'd wanted to do it. "You know, it might not be the worst thing going to that tomorrow." He lifted her T-shirt up over her head. "Everyone will see us out on the town, having a few drinks with friends, everything normal as can be, people even whispering about our financial plight."

"Sympathetic even."

"And then after that—"

"We take the van out under the cover of darkness and empty that garage."

THIRTY-THREE

"I'M JUST PAYING IT FORWARD."

Dan opened the door for the Steamboat Bay Tap Room and Vee strolled inside dressed in a casual light-blue notched tank top, white capris, and three-inch wedges. Dan was in tan shorts, a linen beach shirt and docksiders, clothes they often fancied living in Florida when going out on the town for date night. As they glanced around, they saw a lot of familiar faces.

"Tori wasn't lying. There are lots of people here," Vee said.

"Danno!" Eddie Mannion greeted with a big wave, approaching, offering his hand. "Good to see you're here. And, Vee, look at you!"

"Hi, Eddie," Vee replied, giggling, as he picked her up, giving her a big bear hug, swinging her around.

Several others approached to say hello. Friends they hadn't seen in many years.

"Come on, welcome to our monthly soirée. I'll get you guys a drink?" Eddie offered, leading them to the bar. "Vee? What are you taking?"

"A seltzer if they have one."

"We have Steamboat Tap Seltzers, raspberry or lemon," the bartender said, holding up two cans.

"Raspberry," Vee said.

"Dan?"

"I'll take a blond pilsner."

"Hook him up," Eddie said. "My tab. And I'll take another club soda."

"Club soda?" Dan asked.

Eddie nodded. "Sober. Two years. And it's been good, let me tell you." He waved a woman over. "This is my fiancée, Kaylee. These are my old friends, Vee and Dan. They recently moved back from Florida."

"How do you do," Vee said to her. "How long have you two been together?"

"About two years," Kaylee replied. "We met in—"

"Rehab," Eddie finished. "That's why it's all been good."

"I love your ring," Vee said, taking it in her hand for a closer look. "It's stunning."

"Thank you."

"Vee! Vee! Vee!" Lizzy called out, rushing up. "So happy you could make it."

"Hi, Liz. Thanks for the call."

"It's so good to see you!" Lizzy said, hugging her.

She and Dan made their way around the room, saying hello to their old classmates, some of whom were part of their friend group, others they knew only in passing. Lizzy caught up to her again. "How are things?" Lizzy asked. "How's your daughter?"

"Some good news," Vee said. "Today she got her casts off her legs."

"Oh, that's good. How was the walking?"

"Slow. But it's a start. She'll walk into school in a month and that's what she was hoping for." They migrated to the bar area. Lizzy turned around. "Tori!"

"Hey, Lizzy." Tori waved and walked over with Braddock in tow. He was even taller than she realized, especially in a pair of summer shorts and long sleeve Henley and sandals. His legs went forever.

"Hi, Vee. Glad you made it," Tori greeted and then introduced Braddock.

"Tori!" Dan greeted. "How are you?"

"I'm well, Danno. Nice to see ya." She gave him a quick hug.

The bartender approached. "Can I get anyone another drink?"

"Another seltzer would be good," Vee said, holding up her empty can.

"Good. I can take that one for you."

Tori and Braddock ordered tap beers. Braddock introduced himself to Dan and they chatted a bit. The bartender returned with their drink orders. Vee reached for her wallet, but Tori stopped her. "Not tonight. Tonight, we've got this." Tori handed the bartender her credit card.

"You don't have to do that," Vee said. "You bought for me the other night."

"Are you kidding," Tori said in a whisper. "Vee, when I came back, nobody let me buy a drink for a year. I'm just paying it forward."

They all chatted for a bit before Braddock moved about the room, greeting people as if they were his old friends.

"He knows everyone?" Vee asked Tori, astonished.

"Braddock?" Tori asked and then laughed. "Meeting people is not something he struggles with. When I got back here two years ago, I hardly had to introduce him to anybody. He already knew them all. I'd been gone for nearly twenty years, hadn't been back once. I was the one they didn't know."

"They knew you."

"They did and they didn't. I'd been gone a long time. I'd changed in a lot of ways. I was a different person. Everyone had to get to know me again and figure out who I was, who I really was. Was I someone they wanted to be friends with again. I'm grateful they all did."

"This is home now?"

"It is. For you?"

"We'll see."

"Well, you're here now. Cheers." She held up her beer and she clinked Vee's seltzer can. "Let's mingle about, shall we?"

The crowd remained full for another two hours, starting to thin around 10:30 p.m. Vee finished her third and last seltzer and left it on the bar. "One more?" the bartender asked as she cleared away the can.

"No, it's getting late." She walked over to Dan who was talking with Steak and his wife. "We should go, honey," Vee said.

"Okay," Dan said and shook hands with Steak. As they walked out, Dan remarked: "That was kind of fun."

"Yeah, it was."

Dan had parked the panel van out behind the shopping mall along the H-4. They jumped into the van and Dan took his time, taking the meandering path to the garage, maintaining a keen eye on his rearview mirror, which remained clear the entire drive through the countryside, quiet on a humid summer Tuesday night. He made the right turn and they drove through the tunnel of trees along the winding driveway until they came to the clearing and then the garage up on the right. Dan parked well away from the garage. "I need room to get the other van out."

"Just be careful what you touch," Vee warned.

Dan smiled. "I brought gloves. And a pair for you as well."

Vee pulled on the gloves.

His first step was to go the side door and with his hand wrapped fully in a thick towel, punched out the small windowpane to the right of the deadbolt. He managed it in one punch, and then reached inside with his gloved right hand and rolled the deadbolt over and pushed inside, turning on the interior lights. There was a door opener pad on the wall, and he tapped that. The garage door opened.

He got inside the van and pulled it out of the garage, parked it, and then backed their van up to the opening. Inside, Vee rolled back the rug to reveal the door to the storage area. Dan retrieved the keys from the small desk, unlocked the door, and opened it. He took two steps down and flipped a light switch.

"Bingo," he murmured, looking back to Vee, who followed him down the steps and underneath the garage.

Dan immediately went to the cabinet at the other end, cycling through the keys on the ring until he was able to open it. Inside were the two duffel bags. One had all the jewelry inside.

Vee took out the diamond necklace and held it up. "My God. It's gorgeous." She slipped it on. "What do you think?"

"As good as it looks on you, I want the money it'll fetch instead."

Vee nodded and took it off. "Me too. Although it is stunning."

Dan riffled through the other duffel bag, making a rough count of the money, a combination of hundreds, fifties, and twenties. "I'd say this is ninety grand, give or take." He took down a shoebox sitting on a shelf and looked inside. "Bingo."

"What?"

He held up more bricks of cash. They were all bundles of $100 bills. "This has to easily be another hundred grand."

"Oh my God!" Vee squealed.

"Add it to what we have and we're pushing four hundred thousand dollars. That's a lot of cash. We'll have to figure out what to do with it."

"It's a good problem to have. That blue bucket is getting full," Vee said giddily, holding up the bag with jewels.

"We might need to bury two of those things out there."

"I see a trip to Florida in our future to meet our old friend."

Dan nodded and then looked at the paintings and other art pieces and silver on the shelves. "I'm not yet sure what to do with all this."

"We can figure something out. Maybe our Florida friend would have a suggestion. I read somewhere that the Mob in Europe likes to traffic in art. It was on a Netflix documentary I saw."

She climbed the narrow set of steps and stopped. She looked back to Dan in horror, finding his eyes wide in shock as well.

Leaning against the right side of the garage opening, his arms folded, staring back at them was Steak.

Will Braddock was standing to the left, his right hand resting on the grip of his gun on his hip. His face expressionless. Ready, as if he hoped one of them pulled a gun.

Sitting on the bumper of the delivery van, handcuffs dangling on the index finger of her left hand, was Tori.

"Vee and Dan, I'm sad to say, but these are for you."

THIRTY-FOUR

"A + B = C."

Two days later, Vee watched as her lawyer opened his briefcase. He was young, a public defender who couldn't have been out of law school long. That said, he seemed on the ball, knew people around the government center, the jail, and the judges.

Dan's lawyer was of similar age and experience, although she was from a small local law firm for which criminal work was one of their practice areas. His brother had stepped up for him and paid for a retainer. Based on her own mother's anger with her when visiting yesterday, Mona wasn't going to hire her a lawyer. Mona was retired, living on a small retirement nest egg and monthly Social Security. There wasn't much discretionary income available and now she was likely going to be responsible for Sarah. Vee was on her own on this one.

The lawyer sat down. "You'll likely appear before the judge later today. And they'll charge you."

"And what will the charges be?"

"The assistant county attorney has not said. It may be why the detectives with the sheriff's department want to talk to you now. As I explained the other day, they have you and your husband right now for possession of stolen property. I'm going to ask you again, is there anything else I should know about that? Other than what you told me about what you knew of that garage and why you were there?"

"No," Vee said, shaking her head. "Where do you see this going?"

"Not sure. But like I said, the police want to talk to you now. It's a chance for you to explain yourself. They have you with possession of the stolen property. You broke into that garage to steal it. There is no getting around that. Now, it helps that you have no prior criminal record. Neither does your husband. If this is simply you and your husband thinking this Heath and Druk had something worth selling, and you two needed the money, and thought you could get an easy payday, that's a story that is understandable anyway. It may garner some sympathy, but I don't see you avoiding at least some time on this."

"What's 'some' time?"

"If this is all there is, a few years, with early release and probation. A police officer was killed during the theft of jewels and cash found in your possession. That'll matter, especially if you know anything about that. Do you?"

"No."

"Because if you do, it would be better if I knew that now. It would be better to get ahead of it."

"No, we just figured there might be something out there given what we kind of knew about them. Any chance they'll cut a deal along the lines you mentioned?"

"Possibly. Hunter and Braddock, they're friends of yours, right?"

"Tori and I grew up together. Played soccer together. Ran in a similar friend group. We *are* friends."

"That might help. If you could get her to sympathize with you, she might put in a good word for you that could help with a deal."

"Would we be able to do that today?"

"If two sides want to, they can make a deal at any time. What are you getting at?"

"Dan and I talked. I'll confess to what we did. We broke into that garage. We did have the stolen property in our possession. As you say, there is no denying it."

"Throwing yourselves on the mercy of the court so to speak," the lawyer said. "If you want this over fast, it's the best way to go. The county attorney might go for something on that."

Vee nodded. What had her a little on edge was how the police knew about the garage to begin with. The only thing she could think of was that they had identified the garage through either Heath or Druk and were waiting around to see if anyone showed up. They had set a trap. She and Dan had walked right into it.

There was a knock on the door. Tori stepped inside, along with Braddock. They took seats on the opposite side of the table. Tori exhaled a breath. "What the hell are we doing here, Vee? What is the matter with you, and Dan?"

Vee looked to her lawyer, who nodded. "It was a mistake. A huge, huge, mistake."

"A mistake how? I mean you and Dan seemed to have a pretty good idea what was out there, Vee."

"We didn't know what would be there, but we assumed something would be."

"You assumed?"

"Yes."

Tori frowned. "And you assumed this why?"

"We've known Heath and Druk a long time. All the way back to high school. They were friends of ours, visited us in Florida a time or two, but we also... knew about them."

"Knew what?"

Vee snorted a laugh. "We knew from time to time they stole stuff. A lot of stuff. They as much as admitted it in the past. They visited us in Florida once and talked around what they'd been up to. Druk talked about a man he knew who helped him move things."

"A fence?"

"I guess. We assumed that with the home invasion and their being killed after that police chase, that they stole something, or had been stealing things. We saw it on the news. Dan had been out to their hunting garage a few times. We know they got into the shoot-out with you out that way based on the news. The news also said the stolen items had not been recovered. We figured they might have stored them at the hunting garage."

"You could have told us that," Tori said. "I'm sure the Johanssons would have paid a reward for that kind of information. They're very wealthy. People like the Johanssons could have been a great help to you and Dan, you know, given the dire nature of your financial situation."

Vee sat back and folded her arms. "Don't talk about that like you know something about it."

"What? Life giving you a bad break?" Tori replied. "I don't know a thing or two about that? Really?"

"Well—"

"For the life of me, that's why I can't figure what you and Dan were doing out there."

Vee looked down, taking a moment. She let her eyes well up a bit. "It's embarrassing, Tori. You know why. You know we've had our... financial issues."

"I'm sure it's been tough," Tori replied sympathetically. "For both of you."

"Heath and Druk were dead. We thought we could take whatever they stole and sell it. It was... stupid. We have all these bills, and then Sarah, and her unpaid medical bills, and all that. We were wiped out by the hurricane. We lost our business, and our house. We're in bankruptcy."

"I understand the mindset."

"We shouldn't have done it." She shook her head. "But we did. I'm sorry for that. We both are."

"You know, my deputy was killed when Heath and Druk stole that jewelry, art, and money from the Johanssons. Another colleague is in the hospital. Thor Johansson is only now, a week later, showing signs of coming out of a coma. Ella Johansson is still in the hospital. You were willing to look beyond all that just to get some money?" Braddock said. "That's blood money."

"I know," Vee said. "It was wrong. I still can't believe that they did that to those people. I knew they were thieves, but I never thought they'd do those... unspeakable things."

Braddock nodded, clasping his hands. "So, it was just a mistake by you and your husband."

"And I know we have to pay a penalty. I was just hoping we could... work something out for the stolen property possession. You know, so we can look after our daughter."

* * *

Tori stood up and started pacing slowly behind Braddock, taking a moment. "That's not the whole story." She looked at Vee. "You're not telling us everything."

"I swear, Tori. I am."

Tori sighed. "No. You're not."

"Where were you this past Thursday night?" Braddock asked. "10:00 p.m. until, say, 3:00 a.m.? If it'll help jog your memory, it was the night of the home invasion."

Vee took a breath and looked to her lawyer, who nodded. "Dan and I were out drinking with each other. We parked in the woods, out west of town. We've been doing that a fair amount lately. Just going out, getting away from life for awhile."

"Just you and your husband?"

"Yes."

"Where?"

"On Thursday, we parked at the end of a dirt road west of town at a pond. I can show you the spot on a map."

"And what is it you were doing out there?"

"Drinking mostly. Trying to forget about our lives for a bit. How everything went all to shit back in Florida. How we're nearly forty and flat broke. Heck, at this point, we'd take broke."

"I see," Braddock replied as Tori leaned back against the wall behind him, her hands in her pantsuit pockets.

"What other nights have you done that of late?" Braddock asked neutrally.

"Oh, quite a few. A week ago, Sunday. It was either Tuesday or Wednesday the week before. Dan would pick me up from work and we'd go out for a few hours. We don't have a lot of money these days. It was cheap light beer or seltzers, sit in the car, listen to the radio."

"Fool around a little?"

"You know, maybe a little. We don't have a lot of privacy at my mom's place as you can well imagine, although to be honest we haven't been in the mood for a lot of that as of late. Hard to be... in the mood when we're dealing with—"

"The hurricane, and the financial problems and what happened to your daughter," Tori said, looking to the floor, shaking her head. "Vee, it's time to quit the pity party."

"I beg your pardon."

"You're lying."

"About what?"

"All of it." Tori shook her head. She no longer looked at Vee as a friend. She was an unrepentant criminal. "Every word you've uttered since we came through that door has been a complete fabrication." She knocked on the one-way window.

A moment later, Nolan stepped into the interrogation room with a laptop and a box, handing them to Braddock.

"You think this is just about your little breaking and

entering maneuver and possessing stolen property?" Tori asserted. "That that is all you're going to be charged with?"

"Hold on now," the lawyer said.

"Sit back and watch, Counselor. We're going to give you a preview of coming attractions." Braddock opened the laptop and turned it so they could all see. "This is a week ago, in the wee hours of Monday morning."

Tori kept her eyes on Vee.

Braddock pushed play on the video, which caught the white van in the distance stopping so that three people could jump up on top of the van and then climb the old fire escape ladder to the roof of the building housing Lakes Jewelry. He pushed play a second time and then stopped it. "You'll see one small person who has to be boosted up to that ladder rung. Now, that is a big guy boosting that person up."

Tori had been watching Vee, observing her reaction. Her face remained neutral though her eyes had given the slightest hint of recognition. Her body gradually tensed as the video played, her fingers slowly clenching, her hands becoming tightened balls in lap. A small boil was starting.

It was time to stir.

"That person is you, Vee," Tori said. "The other two are Heath and Druk. Dan is driving the van."

"Four-person team," Braddock noted. "It took that to pull this off."

The lawyer scoffed. "This video is from what? A block away? And they're all dressed in black with masks. You can't identify any of them."

"No?" Braddock said with a wry smile. "Oh, I think we can and will."

"The two big guys certainly weren't going down the duct to get into the building," Tori said. "It was the small person. And to get from the roof, through the duct down the side of the building and then to make the turn back in? I mean that took someone not only small, but incredibly flexible. Someone who could arch their back to an amazing degree. Someone like a gymnast. Even if she is thirty-nine years old."

"That's where the desperation comes in," Braddock added. "Someone motivated by all their financial troubles. The hurricane, the bankruptcy, their daughter's injuries."

Vee looked to Tori and then to Braddock. "I was with Dan that night."

"Ha!" Tori said, walking around the table, stopping, and leaning on the table in front of Vee. "You're not nearly as clever as you think you are."

"We figured you would say that," Braddock said. "And, of course, you and Dan, being married and all, can't be forced to testify against one another because of marital privilege. I'm sure he's giving Steak the same line of BS right now."

"Still, Vee," Tori paused and leaned on the table, "you're lying."

Vee folded her arms and wouldn't look at her now, though she had the lawyer's full attention.

"Tori was in that duct," Braddock said. "It's tight in there, isn't it?"

"Yes. For someone to make that turn from the side and back into the building, they'd have to be a lot smaller and flexible than me and I'm not all that big to begin with."

"There's lots of short, small people in this world, Special Agent Hunter," the lawyer stated. "And I'm sure plenty with criminal records. I'm sure plenty around here with criminal records."

"Heath and Druk didn't have criminal records," Tori retorted. "And they were up to all kinds of bad shit."

Braddock reached inside the box and took out a folder. He opened it and handed Tori a plastic bag.

"The reason I was in that duct was to retrieve these." She tossed the small plastic evidence bag on the table. "Black nylon fibers. They were caught in a seam in the duct." Tori walked behind Vee.

"So?" the lawyer said.

"There were small blood streaks on that seam along with the fibers," Tori said as she lightly touched Vee's upper left back, making her flinch. "That scratch. I bet it's still there. The one you had the bandage on. Remember? I saw it. That night I came into the store and picked up my new blue dress. The night I took you out for drinks. It was a night after the burglary at the jewelry store. You told me you scratched it on a bush in your mom's backyard. Yet another fib in the long line of fibs you've told."

"Keep your hands away," the lawyer warned. "You want to see something you'll need a warrant."

"I don't need to see shit, counselor. I have all I need."

Braddock pulled three evidence bags out of the box. Each bag had an empty seltzer can in it. "Recognize these? You were thirsty on Tuesday night." He turned to the laptop and hit another video clip. "You, Tori, and Lizzy chit-chatting. Tori's buying another round. The bartender takes your seltzer can right from your hand and replaced it with a full one."

"I can see a chain of custody issue there," the lawyer.

"Oh, if only the bartender wasn't a lead forensics officer with the BCA," Tori snickered. "Rest assured, we were quite diligent with chain of custody. And the DNA on the saliva from those seltzer cans matched the DNA from the blood we found in the duct." She stepped forward and sat on the side of the table. "You were in that duct. You cut the power, internet, surveillance, and you, along with Heath, Druk and your husband, burglarized the jewelry store. Walked out of there with in the neighborhood of a million dollars. Split four ways. What did you get, forty cents on the dollar through Heath and Druk's fence? As you said earlier, they had one."

Tori glanced over to the lawyer, who was on the edge of his

seat, warily looking at his client. This was all news to him. Vee hadn't told him everything, not remotely close. The key was to keep going before he intervened. "We have you for possession of stolen property from the Johanssons and we've got you for the jewelry store. Then there are Johanssons themselves."

"You were there," Braddock said.

"No," Vee replied, shaking her head. "We weren't there."

"Ella Johansson is alive. She said there were four people present. Two big goons, which we know to be Heath and Druk. And a smaller man and a tiny woman she thought under five-feet tall. She said the woman buzzed around like a nervous squirrel."

"Kind of describes a gymnast," Tori noted. "Or a certain soccer player I once knew who was like a voracious gnat on defenders."

"That's not evidence of their presence," the lawyer said.

"You really think we're not going to prove that?" Braddock said. He turned to Vee. "This is how we found that garage to begin with." He held up another evidence bag. "It's a P.O. box key that Heath had on his key ring. Property tax statements as well as account statements from a bank in the Cayman Islands, were delivered there." He held up copies of both. "Now we know where the money they were paid was going. I bet you and your husband have one of those too."

Tori watched as Vee closed her eyes for a moment at that nugget of information.

"Now, we knew two more were involved in the Johannsons' home invasion. So, we set up on that garage to see if anyone else would show up. And you did. And your husband did, *twice*."

"As we expected."

"He rented a van and a storage space. How would he know what kind of van he was going to need—"

"If he didn't already know what was in there," Tori asserted.

"So, Counselor, your client and her husband were found

with the van that was used in the burglary of Lakes Jewelry and then the Johanssons' home invasion," Braddock argued. "They had in their possession the stolen items."

"A + B = C. A jury will buy that," Tori added. To Vee, she said, "You knew those items were in that garage because you were there. You stole them."

"I wasn't there," Vee asserted.

"You need to get ahead of this, Vee," Tori said. "You need to let me help you somehow."

"You want to help me? It sure doesn't sound like it."

"Why did you do this?"

"Don't answer that."

"I..."

"I recommend you not say anything," the lawyer counseled.

"You were there at the Johanssons'. What happened?"

"I..."

"*What happened!*" Tori yelled.

"Don't—"

"I never thought they'd kill anyone," Vee blurted. "I didn't sign up for that."

Tori stood up and stepped back, taking a breath. She shook her head. "Even after all this, you're still lying. If you told me your name was Veronica at this point, I'm not sure I'd believe it."

Braddock hit another video on the laptop.

Collins was standing at the bridge, waiting for backup.

"*No! No! Stop... You're hurting him! Stop! STOP! STOP!*"

"Dispatch, Collins. I need that backup! *Now!*" Collins started across the bridge. Braddock let it run until Heath and Druk unloaded on her.

Vee closed her eyes, not watching the video.

"That's your voice, Vee," Tori said quietly. "That officer was twenty-four-years-old. How could you?"

"I..."

"Don't. Don't say anything." The lawyer turned to Braddock. "I need a minute with my client."

Tori leaned in, close to Vee. "You knew that calling her across the bridge was setting her up for a certain death. *You knew!*"

"I didn't think it would ever get to this. I didn't think they could do something like that."

The lawyer pleaded. "I need a—"

Braddock slammed a photo on the table. It was of the assault rifle. "This was in the van. What the hell did you think it was for? They had that and other guns. We know. We fought them."

"We chased those two down a few hours later. We're the ones that killed them," Tori said coldly. "He and I. But you, Vee. It was *you* who led Renee Collins to her death."

"They had a gun on me, and I had no choice, Tori," Vee pleaded. "It was the cop or me. I had no choice..."

"Just stop!" Tori demanded. "Stop!"

"I didn't have one!"

Tori scoffed. "You had a choice. You had a choice all along not to do any of this. You knew exactly what you were getting into with Heath and Druk. *Exactly!*"

Braddock flipped another photo on the table. It was the photo from The Goose from fourteen years ago. "The Locher Mansion," he said, sitting back in his chair. "Fourteen years ago you did it just like the jewelry store. You climbed up the chimney stack, slipped in through a window nobody else could get through, lowered yourself down the dumb waiter shaft and put in the security code. Open sesame."

"And then you watched those two gorillas kill Duffy six weeks later," Tori said, staring Vee down. "He was stabbed to death. Just like those two stabbed Ally Mannion and Reed Shafer to death. Like so many others they killed. Those two weren't just thieves, they were murderers, and you knew it. The hell you didn't have a choice. You had a job. Friends willing to help and pitch in. Did you ever think to come to me for help?" She looked to Braddock, shaking her head. "We're good friends with Kyle Mannion. We could have gotten you both hired there. You'd have gotten on your feet—legitimately. But no, you and Dan chose the easy way out. And now, that choice is getting you charged with burglary, armed robbery and murder, Vee. You're going to prison for the murder of a police officer."

Vee stared back at Tori, no longer with tears in her eyes, but with seething rage.

The lawyer piped up. "I'm going to need some time with my client."

"Take all you want," Braddock said. "We're done here."

THIRTY-FIVE

"SOME PEOPLE ARE DRAWN TO THE DARKNESS, AND SOME ARE DRAWN TO THE LIGHT."

Tori sat with Quinn out on the patio couch, the table fire burning, a glass of white wine in her hand. They talked about his hockey, his friends, possible girlfriends, the upcoming school year, and her promise to take him school shopping in the next few weeks. Last year she spoiled him. He was no doubt hoping for a repeat. Eventually, they got around to talking about her day.

"Dad is inside talking with the county attorney," Quinn said. "It seemed pretty intense."

"Our day was intense," Tori replied, taking a drink of her wine. "I saw a friend, a mom, throw away her life with her daughter." She shook her head. "I still can't believe it. I still don't understand it. It's like I didn't even know her by the time we were done today."

"Is that the girl you wanted me to introduce around school?"

"Yes. She's going to have a rough go of it I have a feeling. Both her parents are going away to prison for a long time."

"That's not her fault."

"No," Tori said. "None of it is."

"What was her name again?"

"Sarah Akton."

"I suppose with what you and Dad had to do with her parents, she won't be too fond of me."

"That's not your fault either. People will talk about her, about her parents, she'll be an outcast unless—"

"Unless what?"

"You guys don't let that happen. Don't let people pick on her, Quinn. Maybe your cousin Peter could stand in, introduce her around school. You and he would be doing a good deed, making sure someone innocent doesn't get picked on. Don't let her be bullied."

"We can do that," Quinn said.

"Thank you."

They sat for a while longer before Quinn stood up. "I'm heading in."

Tori nodded and sat up. "Come here. Tonight, I could really use a hug."

Quinn smiled and went over to her. She wrapped him up, squeezing him tight, kissing him on the cheek, whispering, "I love you, kiddo."

"I love you too."

Quinn went inside and she sat back down on the couch, pulling a light blanket over her legs, and took another sip of her wine. The gas fire flickered in the glass rocks down the center of the table while she just sat, light rock music playing on the portable speaker. It was some minutes later, darkness having set in, when the sliding door opened, and Braddock finally came out, a beer in his right hand, her open bottle of wine in his left.

"What's the verdict?"

Braddock exhaled. "The Aktons realized they were in a big world of hurt. Steak and Eggleston worked Dan over pretty good too, though he didn't crack to the degree his wife did. They'll make a full confession on Locher Mansion, the jewelry store and the Johanssons. They'll turn over every nickel they did get. I guess they've buried some of it somewhere. In return, they'll each get twenty years. State medium security prisons."

"What do you think?"

"I'd like to lock them up and throw away the key forever. Twenty years is a long time, yet it feels light. You?"

"I don't know anymore," Tori said, as Braddock sat down, and she leaned into him. "I think about Vee, and I think about Maggie Duncan. Why do I feel so different about them? Maggie killed an FBI agent, by mistake, but also killed over twenty other Mob guys. She *was* a stone-cold killer. And yet, I give her something of a pass. Or at least, I'm not trying to find her. Vee was not a killer, yet I want her to go away and never come back."

Braddock offered a light laugh. "Maggie played you a bit. You both lost people you loved at young ages, and she has you wondering could you have ended up like her."

"People thought I was devastated when Jessie disappeared. That I was crushed."

"Weren't you?"

"Yeah, but I was also filled with so much rage. And then when my father died. I was that much angrier at the world. I carried it for twenty years. Same thing with Maggie when her father was murdered, the rage and anger. I end up an FBI agent, she ends up a contract killer. Was I just lucky?"

"Maybe a little," Braddock said. "Some people are drawn to the darkness, and some are drawn to the light. You are the latter. Maggie was more of the former."

"And Vee?"

"Was *weak*," Braddock said dismissively. "Life kicked her in the teeth and her reaction was to kick someone else for it. Fate, chance, a hurricane swept it all away. She and Dan didn't want to do the work to get it back. Hell, they didn't do the work to get it in the first place, not the honest work. That's weakness and dishonesty." He took a drink of his beer, pulling her a little tighter. "You know, maybe in the end, how you feel about Maggie, and Vee, comes down to that, honesty."

"The truth?"

He nodded. "I've been telling you to let that Maggie call go and you need to."

"I know."

"But part of the reason you can't shake it is that she was honest with you, Tor. She admitted she killed the FBI special agent. It was a mistake. She says she wouldn't have done had she known he was an agent. You've chosen to believe that."

"You think I'm wrong to do that?"

"To believe her? No. Because I think there is truth in that. Your ambivalence about catching her? I'm not so sure about that but then again, I'm not about to suggest you go on a worldwide manhunt to find her either. Leaving that to others, I'm good with. And for the record, I wouldn't want to be the one putting that lass in a corner. She's dangerous.

"Maggie was honest though. Vee was not. She lied to you almost from the moment you first saw her weeks ago. You saw an old friend, someone you wanted to and did help, and was willing to help more and all she did was lie to you."

"Criminals lie all the time."

"They do, but Vee was a friend when you went into the interrogation room today. You wanted her to tell the truth, to come fully clean. Honestly, I think had she done so, despite what she had done, you'd have still tried to help her in some way."

Tori nodded.

"She lied to you. She tried to play you and your friendship. She played on your sympathy. That's why you didn't see it right away. You knew her as one person when in reality, she was someone else completely. It was interesting to watch the metamorphosis of your view of her change in real time today. When she wouldn't stop lying, you started prosecuting the case against her. She was no longer your friend. Vee was a criminal, and you took her down. You did what you had to do. We both did. This probably won't help because I know and love you, but you shouldn't lose any sleep over it. Vee made her bed. Let her in lie in it. Don't give her another thought because she's just not worth it." Braddock reached for the bottle of wine and poured her another glass. "Did you call Lizzy and Eddie and thank them for their command performances at the bar, getting Dan and Vee there and then plying Vee with drinks," Braddock said.

"I did."

"How were they?"

"Disappointed in Vee and Dan. If it's any comfort, they said much the same that you just did. It's on Vee and Dan. They said I did right. I'm good with that."

"You should be."

Tori sipped her wine. "And Thor Johansson looks like he's going to make it. Thank the Lord."

They sat comfortably, the darkness full, the trees above them rustling in the breeze which was just enough to keep the bugs away.

"When Tracy was here, she said she'd never seen me so happy."

Braddock kissed her. "You are happy, aren't you? You seem happy."

"I am. As settled as I've ever been," she said, rolling so that her arm was wrapped across his chest. "I want to stay that way. When Tracy was here, we had a long talk about... life, about Ally's murder, about Maggie. She asked me if I ever considered quitting."

Braddock lay still, lightly scratching her back. "Did she?"

"She said there is a shelf life for this kind of work."

"On that point, I think she's right," Braddock said. "Have you reached that point?"

"I need a break," Tori said. "From stuff like this. From Ally

Mannion, Maggie, Vee, those three kids who were killed last winter."

"Permanently?"

"Probably not permanently, but you've been bringing me in on a lot of stuff and I love working with you, and Steak, and everyone, you know that, but... I'm not sleeping. And when I do, my mind races and the dreams have not been good ones. There's not a dark cloud over me but I kind of feel like one could be forming if I don't stop for awhile. I can just feel... slippage."

"Do you need some time with Professor Lane?" She was Tori's colleague at the university and also a psychologist who had treated Tori since she'd moved back to Manchester Bay. "You've seen her less it seems. Maybe a little more time is in order."

"I texted her earlier and we're going to talk tomorrow."

"That's good."

"I just want to forget about all this stuff for a while. You know, it's almost August."

Braddock nodded. "Summer will be over before we know it."

"It will." She leaned up and kissed him. "I love the home you've given me. I want to spend the rest of summer enjoying it with you and Quinn. I want to have our friends over and share all that we've done to the place. I want to have a party. I want to put the last several months behind us."

"Let's do it. A big blow out. Friends, family, everyone."

"Yes," Tori said. "And there's one other thing I want to do."

"What?"

"I'd like to sneak away for a few days, a long weekend, just you and I."

"What do you have in mind?"

"Denver, or just outside of Denver."

"Huh," Braddock replied, surprised. "Not what I was thinking you might say. What's there?"

"Red Rocks."

"Ahh, a concert. Who are we going to go see?"

"Dave Matthews Band."

Braddock grinned. "That's a major part of my college soundtrack."

"Mine too. They have a concert there in a month on a Saturday night. I searched for tickets on the secondary market, and we can get them, really good ones. I want to take you. I want to go stay at a nice resort, get pampered at the spa for a few days, maybe make a little noise, and go see a great band and just lose myself in the music."

"Book it."

A LETTER FROM ROGER

As always, I truly appreciate that you've chosen to spend some of your hard-earned free time reading *Their Lost Souls*. I hope you enjoyed it. If you did, I'd like to keep you up to date with all my latest releases, just sign up at the following link. Your email address will never be shared, and you can unsubscribe at any time.

www.bookouture.com/roger-stelljes

For me, the excitement of writing a series revolving around a couple of lead characters in Tori and Braddock and all their quirky friends is that I get to create this world of Manchester Bay and all the characters in it. Every book, I am provided the opportunity to think about my characters and what they'll look like after I peel back the next layer of the onion. This is ever more gratifying because I'm using as my story locale northern Minnesota and the lakes area that I've loved and spent time in all my life. I wake up every day thinking about this world I've created and what is next for Tori, Braddock, Steak and all the rest of the gang. I truly hope you enjoy reading their adventures every bit as much as I do creating them.

One of the best parts of being an author is seeing the reaction from readers, both those who have read all my books and those new to the scene. My goal every time I write is to give you, the reader, what I have always looked for in a book myself. An exciting story that draws you in, puts you on edge, makes you think, on occasion pulls at the heartstrings, and always, *always*, makes you want to read just one more page, one more chapter, because you just couldn't put it down. That is my litmus test for a good book. It is my credo as a writer. I endeavor to deliver it to you, the reader, every time.

If you enjoyed the story, I would greatly appreciate it if you could leave a short review. Receiving feedback from readers like you is important to me in developing and writing my stories but is also vital in helping to persuade others to pick up one of my books for the first time.

If you enjoyed *Their Lost Souls*, and it's your first time with Tori, Braddock, and their friends, they can also be found in *Silenced Girls*, *The Winter Girls*, *The Hidden Girl*, *Missing Angel* and *The Snow Graves* and in more stories to come.

Thank you,

Roger

www.RogerStelljes.com

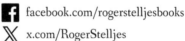 facebook.com/rogerstelljesbooks

 x.com/RogerStelljes

instagram.com/rogerstelljes

PUBLISHING TEAM

Turning a manuscript into a book requires the efforts of many people. The publishing team at Bookouture would like to acknowledge everyone who contributed to this publication.

Audio
Alba Proko
Sinead O'Connor
Melissa Tran

Commercial
Lauren Morrissette
Jil Thielen
Imogen Allport

Data and analysis
Mark Alder
Mohamed Bussuri

Design
Ghost

Editorial
Ellen Gleeson
Nadia Michael